Edge Your Bets

Edge Your Bets

Kiaran O'Brien

Published by Dawnie Publishing
Fulham
SW6 7DB

EDGE YOUR BETS

ISBN 978-0-9930394-0-9

Book formatted by www.bookformatting.co.uk.

Review by Kim Sanzone

Edge Your Bets
Kiaran O'Brien

"'Edge Your Bets' contains all the right ingredients to make it a truly absorbing read, a literary feast for lovers of our noble sport as well as those just showing a passing interest in the game.

Kiaran's colourful characters come to life and by the end of the book I felt I knew them all intimately. The story contains great factual details for the novice greyhound enthusiast but packs enough content for even the most ardent true crime fan, the rollercoaster plot and clever twists make it the most 'unputdownable' book I've read in a very long time – in fact it will have you on the 'Edge' of your seat – can't wait for the sequel!"

About The Author

Educated in Bristol, Kiaran never completed his 'A' levels and moved to the West of Ireland where he lived for three years.

A move to the Isle of Man followed and a progressive career within the International Life Insurance industry saw him travel to many continents and encounter many cultures. His first love however was always greyhound racing and having settled back in the UK he bought his first racer in 1995 and has been heavily involved since, being part-owner of the 2004 Champion Hurdle and Irish Grand National winner Joe Bananas. He has worked in Racing Offices at Catford, Oxford, Sheffield and lastly Henlow, where he was Racing Manager.

Now living in London with his wife Dawn, Kiaran currently works full time for the betting exchange Betfair as an on-course Horse Racing representative.

'Edge Your Bets' is based on his own experiences and knowledge of the industry; the sport itself and those people who run the show. As an avid Crime fiction reader, he is yet to find a similar read and is hoping this book will fill the void in the market and be a literary feast for all those Greyhound and Horse Racing enthusiasts out there.

CHAPTER ONE

Where did it all go wrong?

The long drive back from Wolverhampton on a damp, foggy Friday evening always seems to trigger the same question. Normally I reach junction 11 of the M40 before the brain automatically goes into reminiscent mode but I was still on the M42. It was a long way home from here.

It had been a winning evening betting in-running with Jacks Asleep swooping late in the handicap finale, turning a small profit after expenses into nice tidy sum. It didn't make my mood any better.

But how had it come to this?

Two years ago to the day I had been happily overseeing a run of the mill Greyhound meeting at Stony Stratford as Racing Manager. It was a job I was good at, it was a job I enjoyed but most importantly of all it was all that I knew. At 10:45pm that evening my career in Greyhound Racing was over and to this day I have still not been able to come to terms with it.

When General Manager Paul Colley called me into his office after the final race that Wednesday I thought it was for our normal five minute run through of the evenings events. It was the same every Wednesday with my report on whether there had been any injuries, gambles or any issues out of the ordinary.

Not this Wednesday.

Colley, a plump man from Nottingham going on 60, was seated as he always was when I entered his office "take a seat Joe" he indicated with a wave of his right hand.

So I did, and the next five minutes are the same five minutes that have turned over in my head for the last two years, causing numerous mood swings and sleepless nights.

"Had a good evening Joe, any problems?" Colley asked.

"All went ok Paul. Track ran a bit slow early on because of the rain before racing but in the main ran normal with no injuries which is good news; especially at this time of year. Ann Hibble went for a bit of a touch in the penultimate race but her bitch had to lead and was always going to struggle with Nearly New Sir on her inside."

One of the skills of being a Racing Manager was being able to put six greyhounds of similar ability in a race that had an equal chance of victory without the risk of injury. Most racing managers are able to memorise the running style of every greyhound they grade, whether a dog is fast away, slow away, where it runs on the track and whether it was an improver or had reached its level.

And then it came.

"Joe, there is no easy way to say this but I am going to have to let you go."

"Pardon, can you repeat that?"

"I have received a letter with some photographs that seem to question your integrity and with the pending sale coming up Head Office don't want the bad publicity. I've had them on the phone all bloody day calling for blood and they have given me instructions to….." he paused "….to sack you."

I was gobsmacked and speechless, for thirty seconds I was in a daze and struggled with what to say, it was just as well I was sitting. Then it all came out.

"What photographs, what letter, from whom, when?"

Colley sat in silence as if he hadn't heard me.

"Paul, what photographs, what letter, what does it say?"

By now I was back on my feet, pacing around the room. I could feel the heat in my cheeks and the tears in my eyes start to well up. This wasn't happening.

There was still nothing from Colley; he wouldn't look at me. He looked instead to his left and down, a sure sign he wasn't telling me everything. His gaze had not altered. I caught a glimpse of a large brown envelope, the padded type with bubble wrap on the inside.

He looked nervous and embarrassed but at this point I had no sympathy for him.

I caught him off guard. I quickly dashed around the desk and I soon had the envelope in my hands, it was A4 in size with on the front in big capital letters FAO PAUL COLLEY, GENERAL MANAGER.

I will always remember the red ink it was written in.

I pulled the contents from the envelope slowly, there were six photographs. I ignored Colley's protests as I studied each print slowly. I knew exactly where they had been taken, I knew exactly who was in them and I knew exactly what it looked like.

I also knew I had just been stitched up.

Colley had raised his large frame from his chair.

"Give me back the envelope Joe" I could just about decipher as my head began to spin. I was struggling to take it all in.

"Where is the letter Paul?" I demanded.

"What?"

"You heard me. You said there was a letter that accompanied the photographs. I want to read it, where is it? Give it to me."

He paused but didn't argue, he knew I wasn't going anywhere without it. He walked slowly back to his desk, opened up his bottom right hand draw and pulled out the letter. It was typed, three paragraphs long and unsigned.

I read it twice.

Dear Mr Colley

I attach for your perusal six photographs of your Racing Manager Mr Joe Jackson. The first four show Mr Jackson in a compromising position with Mrs Orla Quinn (wife of one of your contracted trainers Richard Quinn) and in the fifth and sixth Mr Jackson receiving a cash payment from Mr Ken Kelly (kennel hand of Mr Quinn).

Unless appropriate action is taken I will be left with no alternative but to bring these photographs to the attention of the authorities and the Racing Press.

Copies have been sent to your Head Office.

I gathered my thoughts and was tempted to say 'I could explain' but decided Paul was in no mood to listen or had any intention of going against a Head Office directive. He never had done and didn't have the backbone to do so now.

"You can't just sack me Paul on the basis of that, it isn't legal. I have rights. These photographs prove nothing apart from the fact I was having it off with Orla Quinn which you knew about anyway and it ended six weeks ago. Quinn never received any preferential treatment and you know that too and ………."

Colley brought his fist down heavily on his desk forcing his half-drunk coffee cup to take off into orbit and spill its contents into his now seated lap.

Reason had gone from his tone and it was his cheeks that were now turning a darker shade of pink.

"Enough is enough Joe, my hands are tied, Andy will take over the office duties with effect from tomorrow and Mike from HR will call you first thing in the morning."

And that was that, in those five minutes I had gone from Joe Jackson Racing Manager to Joe Jackson unemployed.

The next two months were hell on earth. Try explaining to your wife of five years you have lost your job because of an affair you were having that she knew nothing about. Within a week I had moved out.

The meeting with Mike from Head Office was like talking to a brick wall. In his eyes the photographs were damning and whilst the relationship with Orla could be explained it could be deemed gross misconduct and a sackable offence on its own, but the photographs with Ken Kelly just about pushed them over the edge.

Kelly had been interviewed and convinced his interviewer that the payments had been going on for months and he had no idea who would have taken the photographs. Maybe it was someone from the tabloids he had said. I knew that was total rubbish but in Mike's words it was my word against Kelly's and the photographs got the casting vote.

Two years on I was still angry, some would say bitter; I had a pay-off from the company rather than a long drawn out legal battle.

My wife had filed for divorce after the revelation of the affair and I was now scraping a living as in-running betting exchange punter at Wolverhampton and Kempton with a couple of days a month working as a commentator for SIS in their Milton Keynes office.

I hadn't spoken to Paul Colley since or been near the dog track. I had no intention of doing so either.

I left the M40 at junction 9 and headed for home.

The old Mondeo, with one dodgy headlight and squeaky brakes made its way as if on auto pilot through the twisting roads of Bicester to Buckingham and then to Wolverton in Milton Keynes.

Home, if you could call it that, was a one bedroom rented ground floor flat that was so cold the windows would freeze on the inside during the winter. It contained all I needed, a bed, a television, a bathroom and a decent broadband service. I was single and I was used to it.

The answer phone flashed in the corner, there were three messages. I really must remember to take my mobile off silent when I've finished working.

I pressed the message button.

"Joe it's Ella. Why don't you ever answer your bloody mobile? What is the point of having a mobile if you don't answer it? You are so frustrating. Can you call me back first thing in the morning to confirm you are still collecting the kids from Mummy and Daddy's on Sunday as me and Steve are off to Paris for a couple of days? Bye bye."

Ella is my soon to be ex-wife who was born with a silver spoon in her mouth but to her credit had worked her socks off to qualify as a vet, and she was a bloody good one. We had met when she stood in at Stony Stratford for six months as maternity cover just after she had qualified. We got on great, dated for about a year after her stint at Stony Stratford had finished and were married within 18 months much to the disgust of her over bearing mother who thought her only daughter was sure to marry an Oxbridge type rather than a man with three GCSE's from a Comprehensive School.

The affair had hit her hard and within six-months she had

moved herself and our children Jenny and Stephanie to Perthshire where she was now a partner in a veterinary clinic. I rarely saw my children and missed them greatly. I would call her back in the morning.

The second message was from Kris Lawson asking if I could pick up one of his shifts at Satellite Information Services (SIS) on Monday as he had a dentist appointment after losing a tooth playing five-a-side. I texted him straight away, hoped he felt better soon and thanked him for the shift which I would happily pick up.

The third message was a huge surprise.

"Hi Joe, Phil Clarke here," his broad Bristolian accent came booming from the answer machine "I know I haven't been in touch frages (translates as for ages) but be really grateful if you could give me a quick tinkle. Tonight before 11pm or first thing tomorrow would be good. Ta for now."

I checked the clock on the wall. 10:48pm.

I pressed 5 and returned his call.

It only took two rings before "Hello Clarke residence, master of the house speaking" came back down the line.

"Hi Phil, you called?"

"Ah Joe me old mucker, how's you been, thanks for calling me back, give me two secs just want to get me specs and get me self-comfy like."

Phil Clarke was an ex-army something who had worked his way up from a foot soldier after leaving school to being part of the MOD's integrity department before early retirement 10 years ago. The last time we had spoken he was part of the Greyhound Racing Board (GRB) Integrity team.

Everyone liked Phil, but most importantly of all, I trusted him.

"Now then young man, I will cut to the chase as it is getting late and we all need our beauty sleep but I wondered if I could treat you to a spot of lunch on Tuesday? Please feel free to say no but I am paying."

"Why?" I replied.

"Why what?"

"Why, after 18 months of non-contact from anyone at the GRB, who right royally hung me out to dry, why would someone, especially someone like yourself, want to treat a person of such ill repute like myself, to lunch?" I could feel myself starting to smile.

Phil obviously took the humour in my response as agreement. "Meet you in the Harvester at Kidlington at 1p.m. on Tuesday. There will be a pint with your name on it. Oh and Joe, do me a favour, turn your bloody mobile on. Goodnight."

He rang off.

CHAPTER TWO

Four years earlier - Ireland

A large crowd had gathered outside the Church of the Sacred Heart in Oola, County Tipperary for the funeral of one of its elder stateswomen.

Agnes McGrath had reached the fine age of 88 and the whole village and surrounding villages had come out in force to welcome the hearse and convoy of black limousines which had now come to a stop outside the Parish Church. The traffic on the main road was being directed by the local Garda to keep things flowing.

The Parish Priest, with his altar boys on either side waving incense waited patiently on the top of three steps as the coffin was slid from the rear of the hearse and lifted slowly and carefully onto the shoulders of the four pallbearers.

One woman smartly dressed in a black overcoat and boots felt she should have been part of the arriving entourage. Instead she stood and watched proceedings from afar. She did not know those around her who had come out on mass nor did she divulge who she was. She just stood and listened to the idle chatter and watched intensely those who were now only feet from her.

In her view she did know that these mourners didn't know the real Agnes McGrath as well as she did.

"There's the son's" said a woman in the crowd as two gentleman in their late sixties exited the first of the limousines, "and that must be the daughter's" said another as two slight, grey-haired ladies, one with a walking stick, were helped out of the second car accompanied by their respective husbands.

"I thought she had five children?" said an elderly man to the right.

"She did" said another, "two boys and three girls. The eldest is a priest if I remember rightly and didn't the other son join the Christian brothers to teach in Latin America? I saw him a few years ago when he was last over. Nice man who enjoyed a game of golf."

"Sure didn't the eldest daughter marry that Morrison fella up in Cappamore, the big dairy farmer and the other stayed close by I believe?" said another.

The coffin had made the short journey to the front of the church. The chief mourners filled the front two pews on either side of the aisle with the villagers cramming themselves into whatever seat they could find as the Priest began the service.

The congregation sang 'The Lord is my Shepherd' in full voice. The organist did her best but she was missing the odd note here and there, not that anyone cared much.

The service complete, the coffin was carried slowly back down the aisle by the pallbearers; they were guided down the three steps before the coffin was placed in the awaiting hearse for onward transit to the cemetery some miles away in Cashel where most of the locals were buried.

It was the eldest brother who spotted her.

"Sally-Ann, I so hoped you had got the message. Come and join us, we are just going over to Cashel for the burial now and then back to the house" he said.

"Thank you but no. Judging by the expressions on the faces behind you I think it safe to say you hadn't told them I was coming."

He shook his head and looked over his shoulder to his sisters and brother who were waiting patiently for him to return to the cars. There weren't many tears between them she thought.

"I will this afternoon I promise. Where are you staying and can you give me a number and I will call you later?" he asked.

She reached into her black purse and pulled out a business card that had the hotel details on it she had taken from reception so she could make her way back safely by taxi.

"I am in room 20 and will be there until tomorrow morning. I fly back out from Shannon at noon. Don't leave any messages as you know how rumours spread in a small place like this" she said with determination.

He placed a leather gloved hand onto her wrist and squeezed; "I will call you later sis, I promise" he said before turning briskly to re-join the others.

So all the children had made the funeral but she doubted her elder sisters, who she had not seen for thirty years had been 'sorry for her troubles.'

He called as promised that afternoon but kept the call brief as he was surrounded by other family members who he didn't want to hear the conversation. The pair arranged to meet in a bar in central Limerick that evening for a meal.

She was first to arrive and sat in the corner with a large glass of white wine to keep her company. She twice declined the food menu she was offered by a roving waitress but did confirm she would be eating later as she was waiting for a friend who was running a bit late.

He arrived full of apologies and looking tired.

"Sorry I am late" he said giving her a kiss on the cheek "been a very long day as you can imagine."

"So did you tell them you were meeting me?" straight to the point before he had even taken his jacket off.

"I did."

"And what did they say?" she asked making herself more comfortable.

"I'm afraid our sisters were far from happy you had attended the funeral and their instructions to me were that under no circumstances were you to be brought back to the house. I'm sorry. It is probably not a good time what with mother only being buried today. It is still raw for them."

"Jesus, the bloody hypocrisy of that woman, still ruling by fear even when she is six foot under the ground. Have they not got an ounce of compassion in their body to forgive me for a mistake I made 30 years ago?

That woman, our mother, ruined my life. She would be down the church every Saturday and Sunday with her split personality sucking up to the Priest and all who would listen whilst at home she was knocking back the gin and belting us around the house with an iron poker from the fire.

You never saw the worst of it I can tell you. You had gone off by then whilst the other three were as useful as a chocolate teapot. Is it surprising I eventually rebelled?" she said with anger in her voice.

He shrugged his shoulders, "I'm sorry, I should have been there for you."

Yes you should she thought.

"You can be there for me now Sean" she said grabbing both his hands, "I need to know what happened to my little boy. Our delightful mother made me give up the lad at two days old. I was only seventeen! She froze me out of the family, turned my own brothers and sisters against me. I wrote letter after letter to you all and none of you replied. I wasn't told of our father's death until two weeks after his funeral. I know the boy wasn't adopted through the proper channels as I have done all the checks. She must have told you or someone where he had gone and who he had gone to?

Sending me over to Auntie Bridget was horrible. I never left the house for five months after I arrived as I wasn't allowed to be seen in my condition. As soon as I was fit and well enough they kicked me out to fend for myself with twenty pounds in my pocket."

"She didn't tell me Sally-Ann but I will be going through her things over the next couple of days and I promise you should I find anything I will let you know but we need to stay in touch more regularly now. I have been a terrible brother to you and I am glad you sought me out after your husband died. I will do my best to make it up to you" he said sincerely.

The mention of her dead husband brought a tear to her eye.

"I never did tell Sid you know. He worked so hard as a bookmaker to give us a good home and a good living standard and I couldn't provide him with an heir in return. I will always have the guilt of keeping it from him.

He would ask about my youth and family and I would tell him I was an only child who had been adopted after my parents had died in a car accident. It was easier than telling him the truth. I had no family at my wedding; do you know how that looked? He deserved to know and for that reason alone I need to find my child" she said.

"Are you prepared for the upheaval and distress it may cause if you do find him? You have a good career now and a nice home. Is it not enough?" he asked more in hope.

"No it isn't and you know it isn't. I will find him and when I do I will take my time to integrate myself into his life and be the mother I was never allowed to be. It can be done. I need to do this. Yes I have a good solid career but what use is money if I am not happy?"

The waitress arrived for a third time and took their food order.

CHAPTER THREE

The journey from Wolverton to Kidlington would take no more than an hour but I left myself an extra 20 minutes in case of any delays on the A34.

The cold snap was hitting the country hard and there was a slight dusting of snow as I headed towards Buckingham. The days' horse race meetings had been called off because of frozen tracks and even the all-weather meeting at Lingfield had become a casualty after heavy unexpected snowfall overnight meant the surrounding roads were treacherous and in places impassable.

Just outside of Bicester my mobile rang. The number was withheld.

"Hi Joe, glad you brought your mobile, slight change of plan. Lunch is now at the Harvester in Wheatley, will see you shortly," said Phil and hung up.

Fortunately there wasn't much of a detour as the Wheatley Harvester was at Junction 8 of the M40. I drove through Bicester and 25 minutes later pulled up outside the pub.

There was a pint waiting for me as promised.

Phil rose from his seat by the open fire and offered me his hand, which I accepted gladly. He looked pleased to see me and I him. I took the seat opposite him and sipped my pint. It was good.

Phil waited for me to remove my jacket and make myself comfortable before speaking.

"Sorry for the late change of plan mate but can't be too careful, and anyway they do a better steak here" trying to make light of it. "If you don't mind me saying so you look like shit and have lost a fair bit of weight."

"Thanks, I'm thinking of starting my own form of 'Weight Watchers' and calling it the 'Stitched Up' diet. No change to your eating habit required, just worry yourself silly about how you will pay your bills when you have lost your job" I replied.

"Andy Whelan has gone missing."

He leant back in his seat, pint in hand and watched for my reaction.

Andy Whelan had been my assistant when I was Racing Manager and had assumed the title the day I had been sacked. He was a capable grader but I never thought him Racing Manager material due to his inability to communicate with owners and trainers in his care. The role is akin to being a football referee. In a football match neither team will like the referee but you can't have a game without one. The same analogy could be said of a Racing Manager. For every six dogs that line up there can only be one winner, unless you get the occasional dead-heat.

So like a football referee a Racing Manager is not always the most popular man on the racetrack but you can't race without one.

The key to being a good one was always to take on board what is said to you; no matter how heated it is when you are collared unexpectedly by an owner or a trainer. I had learnt not to give an answer straight away without the necessary facts and figures close to hand. A polite reply of 'I will look into it and come back to you by the next meeting' defused many a likely heated debate in the kennelling area and racing office.

I had worked with a few Racing Managers in my early years that had tried this and never came back with answers. This just inflamed the situation. Andy was always going to fall into this category for me. He didn't have the patience for confrontation.

My response to Phil was a measured one.

"Really, when was this and why are you telling me this in a pub in Wheatley when you could have done this over the phone from the warmth of your office in Holborn?"

"Shall we eat first, I'm starving" he replied.

For a Tuesday afternoon the dining area was surprisingly busy, our waitress showed us to our table past a new Christmas tree that was currently in the process of being dressed for the forthcoming festive season. We were sat by the window overlooking the car park, far from any other table. Knowing Phil he would probably have asked for a quiet spot. He had a personality that normally got him what he wanted without causing much fuss.

So what did he want with me?

The waitress took our order; I chose a steak well done with all the trimmings and Jacket Potato, whilst Phil went for the Mixed Grill. We both chose the salad cart for starters and the waitress departed.

Having consumed the contents of our salad bowls in virtual silence I decided it was time to establish why I was actually here and why Phil had sought me out in person.

"Right Phil, spill the beans, you haven't traipsed all the way from London to Oxford to buy me lunch and comment on my diminishing waistline. What is this all about and why the late change of location?"

"One word, gambles. Lots and lots of gambles and they are really doing my head in and the big firms are getting hammered and getting on to me to get to the bottom of it and I am completely stumped, I've exhausted every avenue."

Wiping his perfectly trimmed moustache with his napkin he continued.

"Over the past four months there have been four well-orchestrated gambles at Stony Stratford taking out over £500,000 from the three big firm's coffers. The gambles have been on two different dogs with one trainer. We have had everyone in, from the cleaner up to the new track owner. The trainer is baffled and is swearing blind he knows nothing, Bookmakers Media Services (BMS) are threatening to withdraw the track's contract which would put them out of business and the high street bookies are considering restricting bets from the track. We have had the dogs drug tested after each race and come up blank. Three weeks ago we sent the drug testing flying squad down to the kennels unannounced and they tested every dog registered, even the retired kennel dogs.

The results came back Friday lunch time and every single one was clean. It has cost a bloody fortune."

A track like Stony Stratford would fold without a BMS contract and I could easily understand why the new owner would be desperate to protect it. In a nutshell the BMS contract meant the track was paid to stage racing that would be shown in all the betting shops throughout the UK and Ireland as well as many parts of the world. Each track would be paid a contracted amount for every race completed and the amount varied from track to track depending on the turnover in the betting shops. A track like Stony Stratford would be paid anything from £8,000 to £10,000 for every meeting staged on its service.

The loss of this income would make it virtually unviable for the track promoter to continue trading as the income from the other two meetings during the week wouldn't cover the overall running costs.

"So why are you telling me all this? I am not in the game anymore Phil. I haven't been to the track since the day I left and I take no notice of what is going on there. It was you remember who told me to stay away and it was the owners and GRB who insisted on me being excluded from the venue and any other track for two years. It is all there in the compromise agreement I signed, you helped draft the thing."

He looked me straight in the eye and said "Your two years were up as of last Friday."

He was right and before I could come back he hit me with a low blow.

"And you owe me."

He was right, I did owe him. Phil had been the only one in the industry who had fought my corner when I'd been sacked. He had gone on record with his superiors and stated that Ken Kelly was lying through his teeth. In his opinion and in his time dealing with me he found me to be 100% reliable and my integrity was unquestionable. He had offered to resign and had spent six months trying to get me in at other tracks without success.

Eventually it was Phil who had convinced a close friend at SIS to give me the chance to learn a new trade as a voice over a few times a month at their Milton Keynes studio. I suppose without his intervention and support I have no idea where I'd be now.

It was my turn to sit back in my seat as the waitress came to refresh our now empty glasses and clear our plates. Phil was right; they did do a good steak here.

"So what is your definition of gone missing and how long ago?"

"He was last seen at the track two weeks ago last Thursday afternoon; the day after the last gamble was landed. As you know he is single so we had no wife or girlfriend to contact and his personal file had no name to contact as a next to kin. He moved about three months ago to a flat in Towcester but no one at the track actually knew his address. We only found out by chance from the track vet who lives close by. We got the Police involved a fortnight ago and they did their usual enquiries of asking the neighbours and by all accounts he kept himself to himself and no one could shed any light on when they had seen him last."

Phil went on to describe how the Police followed their normal procedures of checking bank details. No transactions in the last fortnight. They checked his telephone records, home and mobile. No calls or texts in the last fortnight. They put his number plate into the Police National Computer (PNC)."

The drinks arrived and he took a large gulp before continuing.

"His car was found burnt out in a Travel Lodge at Holyhead last week."

I hadn't expected that.

"Don't worry Joe, nothing sinister. The car fire was an accident" he continued.

"So he has gone off to Ireland then, mystery solved" I replied.

"Maybe, but I do doubt it. The Police have been trying to contact Andy to tell him as the hotel is shitting themselves as the fire was on their property. It would appear that not only did Andy not tell the track he had moved but he hadn't told the DVLA or his Insurance Company either. The PNC check linked the fire and the MisPer and Milton Keynes Police and North Wales Police have been talking since and have kept me in the loop as I reported Andy missing."

"So why didn't he just take his car to Ireland?"

"The local Police were happy to think he had just hopped on a boat with cash in his pocket and would turn up eventually until……" he paused and leant forward in his seat.

"Until what?" I urged.

He looked around the room before continuing.

"When they read the North Wales Police report the hotel had reported the car had been parked up by someone who didn't fit the description I had given them! The hotel had CCTV installed only the day before the incident after some youngsters kept setting fire to the industrial bins in the back car park. The night the car was left the bin was set alight again and something exploded and went underneath it which set the car alight. The hotel checked the external CCTV coverage against the reception coverage and whoever parked the car didn't actually check-in. I have a friend in the Milton Keynes force that I reported Andy missing to and they called me Thursday to say they had seen the film and said the driver was definitely not Andy going by the description I had given."

Phil really did have a way of getting information he wanted and I didn't dare ask how.

"How are you certain it wasn't Andy?" I said thinking out loud.

"Because unless he has grown six inches and lost his distinctive limp he had after he had his ankle reset all those years ago then Andy was not driving the car."

Andy Whelan was forever telling us about his 'Kathy Bates' moment from the film *Misery* when the doctors had to break his right ankle so they could reset it as they believed it was the cause of his chronic back problem. I remembered him being on crutches for about three months which was a great excuse for him not coming up to the Stewards box which was situated up three flights of stairs in the roof of the grandstand.

The surgery had been successful in curing his back problem, but it left his right leg one inch shorter than the other, causing the limp. When he stood still he would have given the Leaning Tower of Pisa a run for its money.

"Could he have been a passenger in the car?" I asked.

"Nope. No one else was in the car."

"So who was the driver?"

"I have absolutely no idea. The film isn't that clear apparently and you never see their face. Of all the people who knew Andy, you knew him probably better than anyone else. He worked with you for 10 years. Did Andy come across as someone who would up sticks without telling anyone?" he asked with frustration.

I had known Andy for longer than 10 years, closer to twelve as he had been a kennel hand to one of the trainers when I became Racing Manager. But did I actually know him? He was a practical joker who said what he thought which more often than not caused offence but apart from that we never really inter-acted outside of work. He wouldn't however in my opinion just do a runner.

"Phil, I'm still not sure how you expect me to help. I am completely out of the loop with regards to greyhounds apart from those I commentate on at work. You seem to be taking this very much to heart. Surely the powers that be aren't putting that much pressure on you? Yes I know you want to get an answer but I can't imagine they would be too happy knowing you are talking to me."

He grimaced before saying "They don't know, hence the change of location and the separate mobile."

Well that gave me the answer to one of my questions.

"You have got to be kidding me!"

"I'm afraid not. You pissed off a lot of people when you were sacked and it cost them an awful lot more money than they had bargained for when you threatened legal proceedings over unfair dismissal. They had their legal team in for two weeks solid as you had their balls in a vice, squeezing slowly.

The straw that broke the camel's back was when I told them I had signed an affidavit with your solicitor stating I believed you and not Ken Kelly. The QC they had employed advised them to settle out of court and do it quickly. The legal bill if the rumour was to be believed was in excess of £15,000."

He had never told me any of this before but it would explain why I was paid six times the amount they had originally offered and I got the figure I had asked for. I really did owe Phil.

"I spoke to and saw Andy on the day of the last gamble" putting his now half empty glass back down on the table.

For the first time Phil looked angry.

"I told him I would not leave any stone unturned until I got to the bottom of it and if I found out he was anyway involved I would hang him out to dry. He told me he wasn't and he would continue to help with my enquiries."

"You didn't believe him?"

"No. He then sent me a text just before midnight to this phone" he said pulling a small black device from his inside pocket.

He unlocked it, played with a few buttons and showed me the text.

'Tings aren't always as they look at the start. Do nut boy has deep pockets and the solution will b in touching dist.'

That was it. I handed the mobile back to Phil none the wiser.

"What does it mean?"

Phil put the mobile back in his inside pocket and for the first time since we sat down smiled. He reached into his other inside pocket and brought out two envelopes.

"The one thing it means is that Andy knew something to give me this tit bit; I am more interested to know what else he could have told me. I think he did a runner before he was exposed and I need to find him and I need your help to do it and these might help," he said handing me the contents of the first envelope.

It consisted of four Stony Stratford track DVD's and a sheet of A4 paper and a typed list.

"On here are all the trial and race meetings videos from the last five months. I have listed the races where the big gambles were landed and the races where the same dogs have run and been beaten. Also listed on the trial disc are when the dogs had their initial trials."

Not all race tracks took recordings of their trial session's but we had decided to do it about four years ago as it meant we could review the trials without having to memorise what four dogs had done in a qualifying trial. It had worked for us and I was glad Andy had continued with it.

He then handed me the second smaller envelope.

"The Charity Greyhound Ball is on this Sunday and you are coming as my guest" he said as I held the ticket in my hand. "It is about time you got back into circulation and there are some people I want you to meet so no arguments."

He checked the bill the waitress had brought over, opened his wallet and left two crisp twenty pound notes on the tray; which she took away.

Rising to his feet and pulling on his overcoat he looked through the steamed up windows to see the light snow flurries had become quiet heavy.

"Take it easy going home, be no surprise if the roads haven't been gritted."

By now I was on my feet and with my own jacket in hand and scarf around my neck followed him out to his car. We shook hands and he gave me the number to the mobile I was to contact him on. I wasn't to contact him at the office. He said it would be off most of the time but I was to leave a message if I had any news.

Having cleared away the excess snow from his windscreen and rear window Phil took his seat in his silver Mercedes.

"Phil, there is one thing you haven't told me" I asked leaning in through the driver's window that had descended smoothly, "who is the trainer who has had all the gambles?"

Making himself comfortable he looked up at me and smiled before saying "Didn't I, how remiss of me?"

"No" I paused "you didn't?"

"Richard Quinn."

He drove off, leaving me rooted to the spot.

CHAPTER FOUR

The heavy unexpected snowfall that had hit the south on Monday evening had continued north over the next two days leaving the country as a complete white out. Temperatures had not been above freezing since Tuesday and motorists were being advised to remain indoors unless their journey was essential. Train lines were running with a limited service due to speed restrictions and frozen points and the emergency services were stretched all over the place.

You can't beat snow to get some extra work.

Being based close to the SIS studio in Milton Keynes enabled me to pick up four extra shifts as colleagues struggled to navigate themselves in and out of their homes to work.

To produce a comprehensive service for the Betting industry there would be eight voiceovers and commentators in the studio. There would be the two main SIS presenters who would be the main voices you would hear during the day in the betting shops. They would be commentating on the morning Greyhound Racing from around the UK and Ireland, gap fillers of Virtual Racing and Horse Racing from abroad, be it France, Germany, South Africa or South America would ensure a constant flow of betting opportunities were highlighted to shop punters.

There would be two others providing commentaries in Spanish for the Spain service and two English speakers for the Greek service.

Then there was my role in which I was to provide an online / telephone service for one of the big named firms. For some races I could be commentating to absolutely no one if they hadn't paid to listen in. I was glad of the work as I wouldn't be earning anything from the in-running punting whilst the racing was off.

With all the horse racing in the UK and Ireland a victim of the weather and with some of the greyhound racing meetings also off, I could look forward to a pretty quiet day of commentating on cartoon racing as we liked to call virtual horse and greyhound racing. It paid the bills.

I hadn't yet looked at the DVD's Phil had brought to our lunch on Tuesday but I would try and find the time later. I had been putting it off as I wasn't sure I wanted to get involved but Phil knew which button's to press and deep down I was concerned for Andy's wellbeing.

I had brought my laptop with me and had a spare hour before my shift started so before looking at the races I wanted to look at the form of the two dogs that had been gambled.

When I started in the greyhound industry the only way you could have looked up historic race results and form was by collecting the race results sheets from the tracks; having a large stack of Racing Posts hidden in a cupboard or a collection of old race cards. I had none of them.

The internet had changed all that.

You could now access results from the GRB's own website and numerous others. There were two websites that I used religiously when I was a Racing Manager. The first was the Irish Greyhound Board's which was excellent as it provided race videos for most of the dogs that would start their careers in Ireland as puppies before being sold into the UK to race. The other internet site was a greyhound database that held historic form and breeding for greyhounds all around the world.

Many a trainer had tried to have me over by allowing a new dog from Ireland to trial in as slow as possible before letting it show its true potential under race conditions. Some Racing Managers, not many, were too lazy to do a bit of research and were made to look stupid when the dog won easily in its first race. Give a trainer an inch and he will take a mile.

I remembered Richard Quinn trialling in a dog who had

wonderful race lines in Ireland under the name of Kings Star. The greyhound had raced three times around Clonmel and won all three by an average distance of six lengths. There had been an article in one of the Greyhound publications in Ireland stating this could be a star of the future. He was well named.

Two months after I had read the article, and having not run since, Kings Star had turned up at Stony Stratford after being sold with paperwork to change his name to Jog On Ricky as his new owner was a keen marathon runner and called Ricky. The rules of greyhound racing allow you to change the name of a greyhound just the once after it is initially registered.

The dogs' first two trials were average and in his third and final qualifying trial he had been poor. I had told Richard the dog would need another trial as I wasn't satisfied and in my opinion he should be going quicker than he had.

"What you trying to say Jackson" said an angry Quinn stomping round the Racing Office "are you saying I have stopped it?"

It was his usual trick, shouting loud enough for everyone to hear hoping I would call him a cheat.

"Richard, you must think I have come over on the last boat if you think I am going to grade the dog on its trials given his Irish form. On those trial times he would be running in a lowly A7. Now you have two choices, you can either trial him again and hope he improves or I will grade him on what I think he should be doing?"

I got the answer I had expected as Richard knew I had made up my mind he was trying to have me over. Yes he was cheating, but he wasn't going to get me to say it publically.

"So what grade will you put the dog in then?"

"Probably A2 and then you can go for your little touch" I teased.

The grading system is like handicapping in horse racing where the better you are the higher the grade you run in. For graded racing the highest grade for the standard four bend distance would be one, with the lowest being eleven which is used at Brighton & Hove.

Richard had allowed the dog to race in the A2, just below top grade, and it had duly obliged by five lengths with plenty of 'on you go my son's' audible from the terracing. He hadn't landed much of a gamble though as the on course bookies knew Quinn's methods and I had shown the main ring layer the Kings Star races from Ireland.

I wondered if Andy had fallen foul of the Quinn scam and that is why the gambles had hit the big firms and not the bookmakers on track?

Rainbow Warrior was the name of the first dog I put into the GRB database and immediately his race lines of form came up. He had had 11 races, winning on four occasions, all in top grade A1. It had taken him four races to win. He had finished 6th, 5th and 5th in his first three races before winning at 8-1 on 16th September.

That didn't follow the Kings Star pattern of Mr Quinn.

The database indicated Rainbow Warrior had just turned two years of age and had been born in Ireland.

I checked the IGB site for Rainbow Warrior and up his name popped. It was the same fawn dog, no name change; he'd had three races at Galway before coming to the UK. He obviously had plenty of pace and was above average ability judged on his race videos and was entitled to be graded how he had by Andy. He had won his first two races by a considerable margin before being beaten in his third and final race in June.

No clues there then.

Next step was to check his trial lines using the tracks own website. The standard distance at Stony Stratford was 440 metres and the better dogs during the summer months would be clocking close to 27.00 with the slower ones about 28.20. Rainbow Warrior had three trials, won them all and clocked 27.16, 27.12 and 27.22 respectively.

No clues there either.

The dogs' three gambled wins had come after two or three bad runs before scoring at 8-1, 6-1 and 11-2. How he had only been 11-2 for the third win after he'd finished last on his previous three runs beaten a long way can only have been down to pressure from the big firms. His last victory was just three weeks ago, the night of Andy Whelan's last meeting, it had been another A1 victory and he had started as the 6-4 favourite.

I closed down the computer and packed it away. Took the lift to the second floor and entered my sound proof booth for my shift.

The booth measured no more than eight feet by five feet and consisted of a comfy chair, a desk with lots of buttons and switches, a set of headphones and a bank of eight flat screens that showed results, betting shows, ante-post prices and a central monitor from which I was to commentate.

I sat down and got on with it but my mind really wasn't on the job.

The eight hour shift had been uneventful and the Gallery director thanked me for coming in at short notice and said he would see me tomorrow.

With my earlier investigations still fresh in the mind I decided I'd look into the second dog on the list Phil had given me; it was called Double Vision.

Following the same methodology as earlier, the results site told me in a few seconds that Double Vision was a recent arrival at Stony Stratford with two wins from his opening five races. He was a black dog who wouldn't be turning two years of age until the following February so was still officially a puppy. He was 6-1 when winning for the first time in his third race, a performance that was a marked improvement on his initial race track appearances. None of this was out of ordinary as puppies did have a tendency to improve from race to race, some of them quite rapidly.

Andy had upgraded Double Vision from A3 to A2 for his next start and the dog had run respectably to finish third behind the favourite.

His last race had been three weeks ago on the same card that Rainbow Warrior had run and won.

Starting as the 11-4 second-favourite, Double Vision had scorched to victory by 7 lengths recording an extraordinarily fast time of 26.98. The winning time was considerably faster than those recorded in top grade races on the same card. It was time for me to look at the greyhound's Irish form.

According to the Irish website he'd had two races at Galway, finishing second on both occasions before moving to the UK.

Something caught my eye though, the name of the trainer, Tommy Coyne.

I typed Rainbow Warrior into the greyhound search box and hit enter. Almost immediately his history was back on the screen and there it was again, trainer, Tommy Coyne,

I'd never heard of him.

The beauty of the IGB site is that you can click on the trainers name and it will list all the greyhounds under his care, and if you are lucky even those that have moved on to the UK.

I clicked on his name and on the screen appeared eight greyhound names. The two I knew about were there, I decided to click on the rest to see if any others had made the journey across the Irish Sea recently.

The first three obviously hadn't as they had run at Galway in the previous fortnight. The fourth hadn't run for over four months and a cross reference against the GRB site showed it hadn't run in the UK either. The fifth was only sixteen months old and so far had only had one qualifying trial at Galway a month previously.

The sixth however had.

Seeing Double was his name and he was the litter brother of Double Vision and he had run twice at Galway, finishing second on both occasions. The website videos showed that he'd run well enough without looking like beating more experienced rivals. His times suggested he was inferior to his litter brother and his races at Stony Stratford backed this up with him having failed to trouble the judge in five races in A6 grade.

Was there a link?

I wondered if Phil Clarke had ever heard of Tommy Coyne, I would ask him on Sunday.

CHAPTER FIVE

Three years earlier

"That is absolutely fantastic news; tell me more I need to know?" she was shaking as she spoke into her mobile.

Her brother had been true to his word when he said he'd go through their mother's things as quickly and as thoroughly as possible. As the eldest he had insisted being the first to read any correspondence he had found.

It had been a long and at times painful experience and by the end of it he was exhausted, both mentally and physically. His two sisters had brought him meals and tea as he locked himself away for three days in her room, only leaving at night to return to his own bed. There was only one key to the master bedroom and he attached it to his crucifix for safe keeping.

He had found the piles and piles of letters his youngest sister had sent back to Ireland to her elder brothers and sisters; his mother had tied a piece of string around them and placed the pile in the bottom corner of the trunk. It was a deep trunk and his mother was a hoarder of the highest order.

He untied the bow that kept the pile together; none of the letters had been opened. All had an Epsom postmark. Epsom had been where Auntie Bridget had lived.

He had read every letter at least once and in order according to the date on the front of the envelope. He had to stop on more than one occasion to wipe away the tears and recompose himself before moving on to the next letter. There had been just over a hundred in total. His sister's desperate pleas for help had gone unread and unheard until now. The last letter had been sent the week before she gave birth. If there had been any after his mother had not kept them.

He had almost given up hope of finding anything that would help his sister in her quest to find her son. The trunk was now empty; he had three black bags of rubbish and two piles of bits and bobs his sister's may want to keep. He doubted they had any financial value.

He sat back and leant against the bed accepting defeat, thinking of how he could tell her his search had proved fruitless.

It was then he found it, tucked into a side panel of the lid of the trunk.

There were three letters in total and his mother had read them all. Two were from Auntie Bridget and the third was unsigned.

Auntie Bridget had written to advise that the birth had gone successfully and the bastard born was a boy and in her second letter she advised that Sally-Ann had been kicked out as promised to fend for herself.

His sister had warranted one line in each of the letters that had totalled three pages each. May they both burn in hell he said out loud before asking God for forgiveness.

The final letter had consisted of one page.

Dear Agnes
I write to advise that the young child that was recently brought into our home is a strong young man and I and my husband thank you from the bottom of our heart for your help in this delicate matter. We will treat him as our own.
It was such a Christian thing to do and we are indebted to you and your daughter at this time.

The world had gone mad he thought.

There was no signature. He looked for the postmark on the envelope but it wasn't clear, any clue would help. He could make out 'stead' at the end and a capital 'E' at the start. Why couldn't it have been the date mark that had been smudged and not the area it was sent from?

He took the evening to question his own beliefs and decide on how he would break the news to his sister. She would have very little to go on but it was better than nothing at all.

He called Sally-Ann in the morning and she arranged to get a flight over the following Monday. She had wanted to do it the following day but he was due to start in his new parish in Dublin this weekend so it couldn't be any earlier. They agreed to meet at Dublin airport as there was no need for her to come all the way into the City and then have to fight through the traffic to get her flight home later that evening.

They hugged when she arrived; she was dressed casually but smartly with just a small handbag thrown across her shoulder that would have only been big enough to contain a phone, travel documents and her purse.

"Shall we sit down over there?" said her brother pointing in the direction of the fast food outlet to their right. "I need a tea, can I get you one?"

She nodded.

He brought back the drinks to the table that was in desperate need of a clean.

"Show me what you have" she said, her excitement was akin to a child opening his or her presents on Christmas day.

He pulled the envelope from the inside pocket of his long overcoat and handed it to her. She read it over and over again, the tears streaming from her eyes and she took in the text before her. She looked at the envelope in search of clues. The postmark had been dated three weeks after she had given birth.

She wiped away her tears with a tissue she had retrieved from her jacket pocket.

"Hell is too good for that woman. She gave away my son and made it look like I was happy to do so. Was there no end to her deceit? She really was a two faced bitch" she said.

Her brother tried to console her as best he could but he wasn't sure where to start. He was more than inclined to agree with her. His faith had made him blind to such things happening in his own family. His mother was a bully. She had bullied him into becoming a Priest and she had bullied her brother into joining the Christian brothers. His two other sisters had been too frightened to stand up to her, just like he had been.

"There is something I haven't told you" he said nervously.

She looked up from the envelope she was still studying. "What haven't you told me?"

"I found all the letters you sent over from England" he was crying and struggling to find the right words. "She had never passed them onto us, she had never opened them. I read them all."

He paused; he didn't have a tissue close to hand like his sister so instead used a napkin to dry his eyes.

"I am so sorry, I really am. I had no idea; none of us had. Father never spoke about it and mother had made it clear that your name was never to be brought up in the house. When asked in public we had to say you had gone to England to help a sick Auntie and you had subsequently found a job as a nanny. Apart from that we never said anything."

She shrugged her shoulders in acceptance.

"What will you do now?" he asked.

"I have a friend who I will give this information to and see what he can come up with. He has access to the all the relevant databases for schools, hospitals, doctors, electoral registers. He exhausted all the options available to him for legal adoptions and turned up nothing."

"With this" she waved the envelope "he has at least a starting point."

They parted soon after. It was just under two hours until her return flight and she decided to check in early and make her way through to departures.

It had been just over a year since she had met up with Ben; he was an investigative journalist and sometimes doubled as a private investigator if the money was right. She had given him the envelope and its contents to search for her son. He had said that it wasn't much for him to go on but he would do his best. They agreed a fee and reasonable expenses and they parted on good terms. She was confident he would find him, he less so!

The call she had received this morning from him had taken her by surprise. It was a nice surprise as she was beginning to lose hope if the truth be known. He had kept her posted regularly on his progress, which had been minimal. Time after time a potential lead had resulted in disappointment.

"Can you come around tonight? I am working this afternoon but will be home by six" she had said to him, almost dropping the mobile as she sat down at the kitchen table.

He was waiting for her as she pulled up quickly on the large shingled drive. Her four-bedroomed detached house in Cobham was far too big for one but she had no intention of moving. It was all paid for and she loved the area and the pomp of being surrounded by rich Premier league footballers and TV stars. She was a snob but would never admit it.

"Come in, come in" she said "fancy a drink?"

"A beer would be good" replied Ben.

She poured herself a wine and brought him an opened bottle of lager and a glass; he declined the glass and drank straight from the bottle. He opened his briefcase on the kitchen table and pulled out a blue cardboard folder with her name on the front.

"I think I have found him. It has been a lot harder than I thought but I am almost certain I have found your son."

He took another large drink of his lager.

"The breakthrough came when I was able to establish that the post mark on the envelope was for East Grinstead which tied in well with your Auntie's address in Epsom, just the other side of the M25. I had to get hold of all the primary school records from 25 years ago for the area and cross reference them against six or seven other databases for hospital records, birth certificates etc.

There is no record of your child's birth anywhere which made life a little more complicated. You told me you gave birth at your

Auntie's home, that wouldn't have been unusual in the sixties but it was rare from the seventies onwards so I had a look at the registered child deaths around that time and I came across a child that had died at birth a month earlier in East Grinstead."

"How is that relevant?" she said struggling to keep up.

"It became relevant because the couple whose child had died at birth had a child registered at primary school the year that we are interested in and it was a boy."

"He could have been a twin?"

"The child that died at birth was also born at home as they couldn't get to the hospital in time. I have spoken to the midwife in attendance. She is in her 80's now and she kept a record of every birth she undertook and attended and there was definitely no twin. I showed her the school records and she confirmed it was the same family and address she had been to. She showed me her own records."

"So what next?" she asked.

"I checked the electoral register and they are still living there. I have been around to the house and they are both still alive, in their early sixties and look in good health."

"What about the son, does he live there?" she asked nervously.

"No, but he does visit. I staked out the house as discreetly as I could for a couple of days. He parked up outside one Sunday afternoon so I went up to the house on the pretence that I had seen someone hit his car. The woman of the house answered the door and when I told her what had happened she said it was her son's car and she would go and get him. By the time they had come back I was hiding in the bushes but it was the same gentleman who had entered the house earlier."

The news that he had found her son had reduced Sally-Ann to a crumbling wreck, she sobbed uncontrollably. Ben let her get it all out before producing a photograph from the blue folder in front of him and handed it to her.

"Is this him?" she said studying the black and white print he had handed her.

He nodded.

"I have something else I need to tell you but I need you to confirm something for me first. Did your Auntie Bridget have any children of her own when you were staying with her that you know of?"

"Yes she did, she had a daughter called Moira who did visit when I first came over to England but I never saw her after that. She was a bit older than me and married. I guess she was probably in her early thirties. I think Auntie Bridget didn't want her to see me as my condition developed. Why do you ask?"

Ben emptied the last of his drink in one mouthful.

"I will come straight out with it Sally-Ann. If the gentleman I have found is your son, then I have to advise you that he has been raised by Moira as her own son. Your son is relatively speaking, your second cousin!"

For the first time since Ben had arrived she looked shocked. She studied the black and white print for the umpteenth time, she was certain the man looking back at her was definitely her son. A mother knows and she had no doubt.

What should she do now?

CHAPTER SIX

The Greyhound Charity Ball was the biggest event in the greyhound social calendar where all aspects of the greyhound industry, owners, trainers, bookmakers, journalists and officials came together for the night to raise money for the retired greyhounds. It was the one night of the year where politics were left at the front entrance of the Holiday Inn in Kingston.

I hadn't been to the event for two years for obvious reasons but previously had ensured Stony Stratford had been represented with four or five people in attendance. The charity was based near Sandown racecourse in Surrey and catered for 80 retired greyhounds at any one time. They do a fantastic job trying to find retired greyhounds a home or giving them sanctuary for the remainder of their life.

I had arrived early in the afternoon, allowing me time to check into my room and change into my tuxedo for the evening. I made my way down to the foyer at 5:30pm

"Good evening Joe, how lovely to see you" said event organiser Natalie-Jane as I bent down and kissed her on the cheek.

"Hi Natalie-Jane, wouldn't miss it for the world and hopefully the bad weather doesn't deter too many from being here. I understand from reading the *Racing Post* you have sold out again and you have surpassed yourself with the Auction lots?"

She looked embarrassed but pleased.

"We have some fantastic supporters Joe who come every year and we even had a waiting list this year. You are down as Phil Clarke's guest on the seating plan as he only told me yesterday you were coming and all the stationery had already been printed" she said before moving off to greet her next guest.

With complimentary glass of champagne in hand I made my way through to the function room. There were plenty of people I knew. Some shook my hand, some stopped to speak and some just blanked me. It didn't take me long to find Phil. He had obviously just delivered the punch line to a joke as those around him burst into laughter.

He beckoned me across "Ah Joe me old cocker, come and join us" he said at the top of his voice "glad you could make it."

I integrated myself into the huddle to make it six by the bar and Phil in turn introduced me to his guests. All were from the big betting firms and had no idea who I was and I them. I assumed it was a deliberate ploy on Phil's part as he liked to play mind games as much as possible. He had once told me he could gain more from a facial expression than any words spoken. We exchanged pleasantries; I told them what I did for a living and they did in return.

We were joined by a girl in her mid-twenties with long flowing blonde hair and a tight fitting red dress who I assumed was part of the bookmaking fraternity enjoying a night out at the expense of Phil. She definitely caught the attention of the other males in the group.

"Joe, let me introduce you to my daughter Alice, she is my driver for the evening and also here to make sure I don't make a complete twat of myself. Isn't that right my angel?" he said to us both with a huge smile.

"Take more than just me to stop you making a twat of yourself Dad" she replied with no hint of a Bristolian accent.

I couldn't help but add insult to injury with a little dig of my own as I shook her hand "Lovely to meet you Alice, I assume the good looks come from your mother's side?" looking straight at Phil

"Funny buggers" he chuckled as he emptied the contents of his champagne glass before adding "just as well I like the pair of you or I'd have you shot at dawn."

Phil went on to introduce Alice to the remainder of the group. I thought to myself what odds these bookie reps would give themselves of ending up being Miss Clarke's suitor for the remainder of the evening. Individually they probably made themselves favourite but I doubted they had factored in the handicap of trying to navigate a passage past her father. I smiled.

"What you smiling about Joey boy?" I was interrupted from my little daze by Alice who was handing me a pint of lager.

If only I was ten years younger I thought.

"Thank you" I said taking the glass from her hand and thinking quickly on my feet "nothing much, just thinking how strange it is to be back amongst so many people I know, I came here quite nervous as I really didn't know what to expect. Your father has incredible powers of persuasion and given it is a freebie how could I decline?"

I had expected her to just re-join the conversation of the group with her father holding court with yet another tale from his army days.

"Never be fooled by my father's actions Joey" regaining my attention as she took a sip of her glass of red wine. "He always has a plan and if plan A doesn't work he will revert to plan B, C or D. There is always a method to what others perceive to be his madness."

She had taken me completely by surprise and had my full attention.

I looked to my left and caught a glare from one of the reps. His facial expression was etched with disappointment and I guessed his price had just drifted from favourite to 10-1!

"Alice, I have known your father for almost ten years now and nothing he does would surprise me but…." I paused as I looked over towards Phil.

"But what?" she asked.

"Well.." again I paused whilst searching for the right words. "I guess I am surprised he is looking a bit far gone already and the night is still young so what is he going to be like later and I was hoping for a quiet word with him?"

"Watch and learn, Joey, watch and learn" she said just as all the guests were asked to take their seats in the main room.

As we slowly made our way towards the main function room, a

lady on our right was taking photographs of some of the late arrivals in front of a beautifully designed Santa's grotto backdrop.

With a sharp tug on my right arm Alice pulled me towards the booth and she must have used the same manoeuvre on Phil's left as we both ended up in front of the photographer with Alice in between us.

"Right you two, I want a few pictures to mark the occasion and then you can meet me by the door, you have a few minutes. Now smile" she said as the photographer clicked away before moving us on.

"See you in two ticks and be good boys" winked Alice as she walked off.

I looked at Phil totally bemused and before I could say anything he got in first.

"Ok, we have about two minutes. Have you had a look at the DVD's and come up with anything?"

The man who I was convinced was close to being as drunk as a lord was as sober as a judge and I told him so.

"What's with the act Phil, you were coming across as half pissed?" I asked.

"People are likely to say a little more if they are under the impression I won't remember a word of it come tomorrow morning. Unfortunately for them I have hollow legs and will eventually drink myself sober. I will ease back during the meal whilst plying my illustrious guests with copious amounts of wine and any other beverage they may require. They think they are getting a free ride but I have already gained a nice piece of information I didn't have before."

"Pray tell Mr Clarke?"

"All in good time young man and I trust my delightful daughter is looking after you well. So do you have anything for me since our meeting on Tuesday?"

"Tommy Coyne" I said.

"And who is he?" asked Phil. Re-joining Alice we entered the main room.

"He's an Irish greyhound-trainer. He trained both Rainbow

Warrior and Double Vision in Ireland before they came over to Richard Quinn. I need you to find out if he has sent any others over to the UK in the past. I could only trace one other which is also with Quinn but the IGB site doesn't go back that far. Can you speak to your counterpart in Ireland and see what you can come up with? He races mainly at Galway."

"I will. Stay close to Alice tonight and I will see what else I can get from these boys as I am sure there is something they aren't telling me" he fell into line behind Alice who had already worked out where we would be sitting.

There are many hardships in life but staying close to Alice was not going to be one of them.

We located our table which was in the far corner to the right of the stage and dance floor. I again shook a few hands and exchanged hellos as we made our way across the room. There was a fantastic turnout and the room, which had been prepared by Natalie-Jane and some of the other volunteers from the kennels, looked fabulous. I remember Natalie-Jane telling me a few years earlier that all the stationery and flower arrangements were donated by workers and volunteers and it meant they saved almost a £1,000 every year.

I stopped as if shot as we reached our table.

"Joe, let me introduce you to Sam Hampshire, she works for one of the exchange firms as their representative in the south" said Phil.

I shook the hand of Sam, who I guessed was probably in her early fifties. She was a tall woman and obviously one with plenty of confidence as she was showing enough cleavage to warrant a second inspection but it was the guests sitting behind her, rather than her breasts, that had caught my eye.

Phil you bastard I thought to myself.

"…and you know both Orla and Richard Quinn. Sam has a couple of greyhounds in training with them" he added as we took our seats.

What was it Alice has said in the bar earlier '*there is always a method to what others perceive to be his madness.*'

At this moment in time I could quite easily have sectioned him and thrown away the key.

The one saving grace was that Phil had at least ensured I wasn't sitting next to either of them. I looked across the table and could see that Orla looked extremely uncomfortable and was getting an ear bashing from Richard. She tried to leave but Sam put a strong hand on her wrist and she remained in her seat.

Alice squeezed my knee to avert my stare and gave me a wink in the process as I looked at her.

Sensing how uncomfortable I was with the whole situation she leant across me and planted a kiss on my cheek. She smelt fantastic, I squeezed her hand to thank her and in unison we turned to face the stage where Natalie-Jane was giving a welcome speech to everyone, explained the purpose behind the evenings events and how vital all our support was for the retired greyhounds in their care. She received a hearty applause as she always did.

The evening was a huge success; Phil stuck to the water during the meal whilst his bookmaker friends one by one became intoxicated. They had all booked rooms for the night so no fear of any drink driving on their part.

I had exchanged some small talk with Sam Hampshire about the merits of in-running betting and explained my own strategies for certain tracks which had proved profitable during the previous twelve months. She knew that I was an ex-Racing Manager as Richard had told her and in his words 'I was a smarmy bastard who deserved what I had got.' No change there then.

Although she was based in the south she rarely went to Kempton unless she had to see one of the bookmakers who had requested a meeting. She joked that she found it disheartening to go to a race meeting where only a man and his dog would go on a sub-zero Wednesday evening. I jokingly replied that she obviously hadn't been for a while as the dog didn't go anymore. She laughed, much to the annoyance of Richard.

Throughout the evening Orla didn't utter a word to me. I caught her glancing across the table on a few occasions as I joked with Alice who was great company. As far as ego's measurements go, mine had raised a few notches during the night. It was great to have the company of a good looking woman again.

It also proved to be a successful one as I claimed second prize in the raffle, a forty-six inch flat screen television. I needed a new TV.

The auction was a boisterous affair with the auctioneer, a former jumps jockey with quick wit and eyes in the back of his head prowling around the room bumping up the price by twenty and fifty pounds a time.

The lads on the table had decided, with wallets at the ready that they would all chip in and bid for a golf day at Wentworth. Bidding and being drunk is a recipe for disaster. The bidding had reached £500 when the young lad next to Orla raised his arm to take the bidding to £550. He had no sooner done it when the guy next to Phil raised the bidding to £600. Not to be outdone the first guy came back again and raised the bid to £650. In a matter of seconds the pair, who were going to be playing together, had cost themselves an extra £100. The room was in stitches.

Phil caught my eye and beckoned me to come over, which I did.

"Meet me by the bar in five minutes."

"Ok."

I returned to my seat and gave Alice a friendly squeeze of the knee which she didn't object to. I was on dodgy ground but sober enough to actually know that I didn't care.

"Would you like anything from the bar Alice? Your father wants to have a chat in a couple of minutes so can I bring you anything back?

"Just you," holding my right hand as she looked me straight in the eye.

"I do believe Miss Clarke that you are somewhat tipsy" I said mocking her.

"Far from it Joey boy" she pulled me by my tie closer to her and I could again smell the perfume she was wearing, white musk I guessed. "I am in room 176 if you are brave enough later, but don't leave it too late and I will show you how sober I am."

She pulled me closer before kissing me passionately on the lips. Not only did she smell good but she tasted good as well.

"You don't want to go anywhere near him love, you don't know where that scum has been" Richard Quinn shouted over my shoulder. Always a man for spoiling the moment I thought.

Alice loosened the grip on my tie slightly, moved me to one side with the back of her right hand and replied "I know exactly where he has been" and then stared straight at Orla and said "don't I love" and smiled.

I wouldn't want to cross Alice Clarke.

Richard hadn't expected that back and looked furious. Orla had always been the brains in the relationship and soon defused the situation. She pulled Richard back into his chair, had a quick word with Sam Hampshire and finished her drink. She rose from her seat, gave Richard the cloakroom ticket and instructed him to get their coats.

She waited until Richard was out of ear shot.

"Alice, we have only just met and you don't know me, you know nothing about me and you most certainly have no idea what occurred between me and Joe" she said looking straight at me before continuing, "we all make mistakes in our life and have to live with the consequences, some more than others. Now I wish you both good night as we" pointing to Richard as he returned with her coat, "need to be up early for the dogs in the morning."

"I think I will be leaving now as well as I need to be up for Plumpton tomorrow if it passes an early morning inspection" said Sam rising from her seat. She was about my height at just under six foot in heels and looked in good shape for a woman of her age.

I thought the likelihood of Plumpton going ahead was zero given it was still under two inches of snow and guessed she was just being polite.

"It was lovely to meet you Sam and hopefully I will see you on a racecourse soon and buy you a coffee." I said shaking her hand.

"I look forward to it" she smiled and walked off behind Orla and Richard.

Orla's words were the first she had muttered all night and they had been measured and to the point. So we had been a mistake as far as she was concerned and whereas I'd had my career taken away, lost my home and had limited access to my kids, she had just carried on as normal. So much for being in love!

I had forgotten about meeting Phil at the bar. I impulsively kissed Alice again and she responded in kind. I would be making it to room 176 I promised myself.

"Where have you been?" scowled Phil.

"Just had a ticking off from the previous love of my life and publicly informed that I was a big mistake. You really are a bastard for not telling me they were coming and an even bigger bastard for not telling me they were going to be on our table. What are you playing at?" I replied.

"I am playing games young Joseph, playing games and your presence here tonight hasn't half caused a stir in the greyhound towers."

I had stirrings of my own in the groin area and they were thinking about room 176. It was probably not a good idea to tell Phil that though.

"I will look into this Tommy Coyne fella tomorrow and will call you Wednesday. In the interim I have established that the last gamble wasn't the same as the previous four…."

"They were in a double weren't they?" I interrupted.

"Yes they were how did you know that? I knew you would spot something. That spotty kid with the garish orange tie let it slip that they had been hit. Because neither dog was a big price on the morning shows they didn't bother sending out a message to the shops to restrict bets. By all accounts they got hammered."

Some of the betting firms offer a price on the morning of certain races and on this particular occasion the odds compiler for one of the big firms had priced up both dogs at 3-1. He hadn't done his research and taken heed of the note that both dogs were on the 'be wary list'. He had subsequently been served with his P45 after doubles were placed all over the country costing his company just under £150,000.

I quickly did a calculation, remembering that Rainbow Warrior and Double Vision had won at 6-4 and 11-4 respectively. As singles the bookmaking firm's liabilities wouldn't have been high, but as a double the odds would have been just over 8-1.

"I had to take the drunken lad to one side as he had no idea that Richard Quinn was the trainer" said Phil "young kids and drink, you can't take them anywhere" he added.

"So what is wrong with the bigwigs then, do they have a guilty conscience or annoyed I am still living off their pay-out? I got completely blanked by a couple of them when I first arrived and another turned his back on me at the bar. I promise it was a pure accident when I spilt my pint on him, the glass was really slippery" I said laughing.

"You may laugh mate but you are seriously persona non grata as far as they are concerned. I told them, that in my opinion, you should go back in as Racing Manager until Andy turns up. That old fart Bill Battersby almost choked on his Yorkshire pudding. They still don't know you are helping me and I suggest for now we keep it that way."

"Does Alice know?" I asked.

"Yes, but she is the only one. I told her on the way up as I needed you to feel comfortable. I also told her about your relationship with Orla and how much Richard hates you so she was prepared. That guy really doesn't like you. You could see the evil in his eyes; I bet he has a voodoo doll or a dart board with your picture on it."

We both laughed.

"Well I was shagging his wife as you so politely used to put it so it is hardly surprising."

"I guess so, anyway I'd better get back to mingling with the enemy and thanks for coming, it will have done you the world of good" he said offering me his hand in friendship which I gladly accepted.

We said our good nights and agreed to speak on Wednesday. Weather permitting I would be at Kempton for some racing. I went back into the main function room which had become a disco; there was plenty of activity with young girls clad in very little and overweight men in tuxedo's trying to impress. There was no sign of Alice. It was time for bed.

I took the lift to the first floor. The gold plated sign on the wall opposite the lift exit indicated that room 145, my room, along with all those from 111 – 155 was along the corridor to my left. Rooms 156-199 were on my right.

Nothing ventured nothing gained, I turned right

I found room 176 and knocked on the door twice.

Was Alice on the wind up or was her invite a genuine one? I heard footsteps from behind the door; I was just about to find out either way.

The door opened with Alice wearing nothing more than a white towel and a huge smile.

"Hello Joey boy, glad you could make it" she said as she reached up and put her arms around my neck, pulling me towards her before kissing me passionately. The towel around her fell to the ground. I reached back with my right foot and kicked the door closed.

Phil had said I should stay close to Alice. I'm not sure he meant this close.

CHAPTER SEVEN

18 months earlier - Ireland

"Jesus Jamie will you stop messing with that blasted pup and come and give me a hand with the feeding?" roared Tommy Coyne.

Tommy Coyne was a man in his early seventies who had spent the majority of his working life in England like many in the surrounding area, before returning to his native Ireland 15 years earlier after inheriting a rundown bungalow and five acres of land from his uncle.

He had tried his hand at farming but found that sheep shit and cows muck were not for him.

What he did know however were greyhounds and he decided, much to the annoyance of his neighbours who thought that their sheep would be sitting targets if the greyhounds escaped, was that he would try his hand at training a few.

Despite the fact he was Irish and despite the fact his family were from the area and despite the fact he still had a broad Irish accent, Tommy had never been accepted by the locals and after 15 years of being called a blow in, he was well used to doing the opposite to what they wanted. It was all a game.

With a pick axe, spade, scythe, a few garden forks and a rickety old wheel barrow he had in the first two years transformed the top field above the bungalow. Gone were the rushes, the boulders and the privet bushes that had old wire fences growing through them to divide the neighbouring fields to be eventually replaced by rhododendron hedges and six-foot high fencing.

Trenches had been dug in hail, rain, sleet and snow to ensure that the boggy moss areas would drain and remain dry. With a clean sheet of paper so to speak he set about building what he needed to train his greyhounds. He carried bags of cement a quarter of mile when the wheelbarrow had cried enough when the puncture patches on the inner tube far outweighed the actual rubber. The sand to mix the cement came from a sandpit he unearthed by accident in the lower field, at least that was a blessing.

He worked morning, noon and night, lighting fires in puddles when the rain refused to relent. He had no help and sought none either. It was his project, it was his time and it was his money and bugger the concerns of others.

If it hadn't been for meal times his wife would never have seen him.

A win of €5,000 on a scratch card bought by his wife saw him treat himself to a second-hand tractor that enabled him to build a 300 yard gallop. The soil below the moss was peat and once he had removed the top six inches he found he had a perfect surface that only needed to be rotated to loosen it up. Having built eight kennels, assembled two rearing sheds and fenced off five paddocks, two large and three small, Tommy was ready to start his training career.

He hadn't thought about buying a dog at this stage. The ground work needed doing first.

Fifteen years later, and five years after the sudden loss of his wife, Tommy was still a contrary bugger who loved nothing more than annoying the locals, but as he said at the outset, he knew his greyhounds and not one sheep had been attacked or lost.

There had been some disasters along the way, along with some notable successes and he was regarded by his fellow trainers and breeders as someone who knows his stuff. Their acceptance wasn't important to him but he made a living from it and that made him happy.

Tommy had no owners in the kennel from the village, they had no interest and that suited all concerned fine.

Were they jealous of his success? He didn't know and didn't care. He spoke when spoken to and never frequented the village pubs which numbered two and doubled up as food stores.

The kennels, his daughter and his grandson were his world, the rest were a mere distraction. He had never told people what he did in the UK before his return and he imagined it had been the topic of many a Guinness consumed in the local establishments on a cold winter night.

"Ah granddad, give me a minute whilst I finish with Archie" replied Jamie as he put the young pup back in his kennel.

Jamie was Tommy's grandson, his only daughter Aoife's youngest son. Aoife had decided to move to Ireland when her mother had died and brought young Jamie, who was then 12 with her. She had divorced the child's father years ago and with nothing left to stay in England for with her two eldest children having moved to Dubai and America respectively, she had packed in her office managers job with an Insurance company in Reading, taken Jamie out of school and moved to the small village of Leenane on the Galway / Mayo border in the West of Ireland.

It was a massive upheaval for the pair, coming from a big city to a village of no more than 300 people where everyone knew everybody's business and even knew what they had for dinner. Jamie found it even harder having to adjust to school life in a different country and try and make new friends. He used to walk no more than 600 yards to school, now he had two 20 mile bus journeys to the vocational school in Westport. He had hated it at first but slowly came to enjoy the country life and being around the greyhounds.

Tommy had objected to her moving over as she'd expected but he was glad of the company. The winters could be a long drawn out affair. The drive to Galway to race the greyhounds was a strain, even though it was only 40 miles away. He wasn't getting any younger. The fact his grandson had shown an interest in the greyhounds rather than his computer games had given him a new lease of life. He was a shy lad but a willing worker.

"Your ma will be up with the tea in five minutes so let's get these dogs fed and out in the paddocks before she gets here."

It was a beautiful sunny final day of April. A Monday morning with not a cloud in the sky. Aoife arrived with the tea and snacks and the three of them sat down to discuss arrangements for the week. As designated driver she needed to know when and where she would be required.

"We have three entered up for Galway Thursday evening and two for Saturday. I will also try and get trials for those two pups of Pete Morris' on Saturday but will give them a gallop here later on before making a definite decision" said Tommy.

"Bernard McHugh the Control Steward is coming out from Castlebar this afternoon to earmark the three black pups that are in the back shed and the feed and sawdust man is calling later to arrange a time for delivery. Tell him Friday as he hates coming out here and the journey back into Galway will be crap" he laughed.

He leant down to pick up his tea and his doughnut.

"Who has had my bloody doughnut?" he said looking on the floor to see if it had fallen off the bale of hay that they were sat around. He caught sight of the young pup chewing on the remains of his snack.

"For fecks sake Jamie that pup will never make a racer if you keep feeding him stodge."

"Language dad" said Aoife.

"Feck my language Aoife, I was looking forward to me doughnut and just because he has been hand rearing him from birth when the mother died doesn't mean Jamie can molly coddle him as he will end up bloody soft. The next thing you'll know he'll have the dog sitting to order and giving him a paw."

"He already does, that was easy" interrupted Jamie.

"Jeez, you are having me on?" said Tommy waving his hands in the air.

"Look granddad" said the youngster dangling a small piece of his own doughnut in front of the pup that in turn sat, lifted his left paw and was promptly rewarded for his actions.

"I give up" said a now exasperated but seeing the funny side of it grandfather. Aoife was laughing also.

"You do realise young man that you will have to cut out the sugar intact for the dog once he starts racing as he will fail every dope test in the land and probably cost me my licence? And please tell me you aren't giving doughnuts to any of the other dogs?" his tone slightly more serious.

"He won't be racing granddad and I haven't given anything to the others, cross my heart and hope to die" making the relevant gestures with his hands.

"What's got Trixie all excited?" said Aoife as she could hear the house dog, a Tibetan terrier barking away in full voice.

Tommy rose from the hay bale and looked out of the window down towards the house.

"It's Bernard, he has arrived early, and you better go down and put Trixie away as the dog won't let him out of the car without biting him again. He took a chunk from him last time. Jamie you go and get the pups for earmarking."

The threesome went their separate ways.

"How are yee Tommy, beautiful day isn't it?" said an out of breath Bernard after negotiating the steep hill from the house.

"Tis indeed Bernard, tis indeed. Will be fine for the rest of the day as not a cloud to be seen on Mweelrea" said Tommy pointing in the direction of the mountain across the Killary Harbour.

"Just the three pups for me today then Tommy?"

"Just the three Bernard. They are from Pippa's last litter as we have retired her now and she will be coming down to the house shortly. She has been a great mum and every one of her four litters has thrown winners. She was home bred herself so it's been grand now to have her with us all the way through."

"She won her fair share of races for you too Tommy, and was definitely a class act to reach the Irish Oaks final for you."

"That she was."

Jamie poked his head in around the door, "Granddad, can I not watch this bit as I don't like the noise, I hated it when you did it to Archie and he sulked for a month?"

"Ok Jamie, just bring the pups in and put them in the cage by the door and I will do the rest" said Tommy pointing to the black cage underneath the window.

Jamie did as he was asked and brought the three black dogs in one by one.

"Bloody hell Tommy, these are fine animals for only 10 weeks, lovely bone structure and a fine back on them. I have seen a lot of the sire's pups over the last few weeks and these are the best I have seen, they are grand looking now so they are. The sire is throwing lots of black dogs with little or no white on them" he paused, lifting the first pup into the air admiring him from head to toe. "Actually, this little lad has no white on him at all."

"No white on the other two either" said Tommy with a wry smile. "In fact even all their toe nails are black. It's only Jamie who can tell them apart to look at."

"We better get started, I need to get to Jack Stiles place in Cornamona after this" said Bernard as he removed the relevant paperwork from the Irish Coursing Club and earmarking kit from his case.

He had just finished the first dog when his mobile phone rang. He offered his apologies and made his way outside to continue the call. Tommy could see through the window that Bernard was getting flustered but by hearing only small snippets of one side of the conversation Tommy had no idea why or with whom.

Bernard returned and again offered his apologies but before continuing took a swig from his hip flask that he always carried with him. He offered it to Tommy who declined.

"It is purely medicinal, trying to clear a bad chest cold."

Tommy thought he sounded fine but didn't say otherwise.

They moved onto the second dog and again Bernard checked the dog and earmarked both ears. The right ear contained two letters which related to him as the Control Steward whilst the left ear had a combination of three letters that had been sent down by the ICC on the naming forms. He took rough notes of the pups marking and filled in the appropriate section of the original declaration of litter form. Tommy could understand why Jamie didn't like it as it wasn't the most humane process that would leave a tattoo permanently in the greyhounds' ear that would identify him throughout the whole of his racing career and once his career was over. It took Tommy a few litters to get used to it.

The mobile rang again and Bernard looked mortified and he again apologised and took the call outside. This time the call lasted ten minutes and he was very animated, kicking the ground with his shoe and hitting the closest tree with his flat cap on more than one occasion. The swig on the flask was a lot longer this time before returning.

"Problems?" probed Tommy.

"Fecking women Tommy and I mean women in the plural sense. They do my fecking head in."

He was on a roll and Tommy leant back on the sink as Bernard emptied his deep frustrations.

"My eldest daughter is getting married in two weeks and she has turned into the devil incarnate, I want this and I want that and Auntie Joan won't come if Uncle Ted does. Sure it is all bollocks and the wife seems to think I have fecking bottomless pockets. If I had known the flowers were going to cost me a bollock I would have grown them myself."

His hat was off, his right hand was scratching his balding scalp and just when Tommy thought he had got it all out the next barrage came his way. Tommy was beginning to wish he hadn't asked.

"The caterers are just taking the piss as well. Eighty-five euro a head for feck sake for two courses and a lemon meringue pie for pudding, and why does anyone need 6 bridesmaids and every relation known to man at the reception? When I got married in England thirty years ago, it was me, the wife, best man and her best friend and then down the pub in Camden afterwards."

He tried the flask again but he had obviously emptied it.

"They will probably be divorced in two years and I will probably have to pay for that as well. Anyway I had better get back and sort it all out as the daughter is threatening to call it all off" he had added whilst rushing through the final dog.

He signed the paperwork and gave it to Tommy, shook him by the hand and rushed down the hill to his car. Tommy returned the pups to the breeding shed, left the paperwork on the side and went in search of Jamie to find the two pups he was going to gallop.

It was Aoife who took the call at tea-time.

"Oh my God……. surely not……it can't be .....he looked fine……….are you sure…………I will tell him." she had said before sitting down at the main table, head in hands, crying.

"What's up mum, why are you crying?"

"Jamie son, can you go and get your grandfather from the kennels please and ask him to come down as quickly as possible?"

Jamie put on his trainers and ran the 250 yards to the kennels and fetched Tommy who came down immediately.

"What's up Aoife, Jamie said you were crying? I've still got dogs to feed but the lad insisted I come straight down."

Aoife pulled a chair out from under the table and instructed her father to take a seat whilst she brought over the teapot from the range. She poured and set down opposite him. She asked Jamie to go up to the kennels and finish up and lock up for his grandfather.

"What's all this about girl?"

Aoife took a deep breath.

"Jack Stiles called about two hours ago wanting to know if Bernard had finished here as I he'd been waiting in for him to mark up his litter and he couldn't get hold of him on his mobile. I told him he'd left just after midday, which would have been four hours ago. Bernard's wife then called and wanted to know if he was still here as she couldn't get him on his mobile."

She took a sip of her tea before continuing.

"He's dead."

"Who's dead?"

"Bernard is."

"Don't be daft woman, he has just turned his phone off or is somewhere where the signal is crap. If I had a wife like his I would be turning the mobile off as well."

"Jack called back ten minutes ago……."

She began to cry again.

"He was coming to the village but the road coming into Maam was closed. He called Terry in the garage in Maam to ask what the problem was and there had been a major accident three hours ago. A car ran straight into one of the quarry Lorries by the Maam

Bridge turning opposite the pub. It was Bernard's car and it exploded. He had no chance. The Garda are on the way to his house now to tell his wife."

They sat in silence.

Jamie returned from the kennel, he was a good lad to have around Tommy thought to himself, and a credit to his mother. Bernard had been a good friend to Tommy since he had set up his kennels and was always on the other end of the telephone if he needed any advice. He would miss him. Was the accident his fault, was he drunk, was he on the telephone or had the telephone calls from earlier just proved one distraction too many?

He was interrupted from his thoughts.

"Granddad, I have brought down the paperwork that was by the sink, is that ok?" he asked handing over the three naming sheets, the last three naming sheets ever signed by Bernard McHugh.

Tommy nodded and took the papers.

Tommy looked at the sheets but wasn't actually looking at anything in particular, they were just pieces of paper with writing as far as he was concerned with green smudges from the ear marking stamp. Did they really matter?

He began to focus and then smiled.

"Good old Bernard, have a drink on me" he said before rising from his chair and stowing the paperwork safely away in the drawer.

CHAPTER EIGHT

Eight months earlier - Ireland

A number of opinions had been passed on the possible reasons behind Bernard's sad passing but the coroner had returned an accidental verdict.

Tommy had been interviewed by the Garda as he was the last person to have seen him before his death and he had answered all of their questions. He didn't mention the hip flask contents he had consumed or the two blazing rows that Bernard had on the telephone with his wife.

It wouldn't bring him back and if Tommy revealed everything that had occurred that day he would be digging an even bigger hole for himself than the one Bernard was now in. He had met Bernard's replacement and it would take time to build the same relationship

The funeral had been a moving affair and had been well attended. The wedding had been cancelled as a mark of respect. Poor Bernard would be turning in his grave Tommy had thought at the time.

Bernard's misfortune had presented Tommy with plenty to think about over the winter.

The three black pups Bernard had earmarked had matured well despite the inclement weather they had endured in the previous months. There hadn't been a problem with any of them. They had kennelled well together and the testing conditions in the paddocks ensured that they were plenty fit enough.

The initial schooling at home over the past three weeks had gone well and one of the litter was showing extreme promise and it was the one that Tommy had hoped would do so. Only Tommy and Jamie could tell the difference between the three and even Tommy had to admit to himself that he struggled at times to tell them apart.

Tommy had a plan but he would need to let his grandson in on it soon to be able to pull it off. He knew he could be trusted but he wasn't sure his daughter would be overly impressed with what he had lined up for her son.

Jamie had plans of his own.

The young lad informed his mother he intended to work full time on the greyhounds when he had completed his education in three-month's time and had no intention of going to university. Tommy had thought it a marvellous idea and it fitted in beautifully with his plan. His mother was far from keen but was out voted.

The dog sitting, paw giving greyhound Archie was another to have matured over the winter and much to Tommy's surprise had the makings of a decent racer. He had been slow to learn on the home gallops but the penny dropped on a cold January morning. When they had first taken him to the track at Galway for an unofficial trial he had absolutely flown round.

The beauty of rearing pups in Ireland is that you can trial them at the track where they will race without revealing who the dog is, thus making it unofficial. Archie had been the last to go around the track that day and so there were few to witness first hand his ability. Tommy and Jamie had seen enough to make the journey home an exciting one as they planned what route to take with the dog.

The following week Archie was set for his first official trial. They set off on the journey to Galway that would take them through Maam Cross, Oughterard and Moycullen. The roads weren't the greatest and at times it really was slow going as Aoife had to pull the van to the side as bigger vehicles came towards them.

"Granddad is Archie my dog or your dog?" asked Jamie as they drove in through the main gates of Galway Greyhound track.

"I registered him in your name Jamie so I guess he would be yours, why do you ask?"

"Just wondered" he replied "and am I right in thinking we don't want him to go too fast in his trial tonight" he said with a smile on his face.

Tommy turned in his passenger seat to look at his grandson and asked him "what are you up to young man?"

"Nothing" and he jumped out of the now stationary vehicle to help unload the two dogs they'd brought to the track.

Archie's trial in Tommy's view had been a disaster. The dog, who had flown from the traps in his last schooling trial had walked out of the traps, hesitated before consenting to chase and recorded a time that was about a second slower, which equates to fourteen lengths, than had been expected.

Jamie collected the dog at the end of the trial and walked back towards the paddock.

Tommy was searching for the right words to console Jamie who he imagined would be really upset given their conversation the week before. The plans they had made for his pet project had failed on the track. He just hoped he wasn't too disillusioned.

Far from it!

"That was great granddad, I am really pleased with that, can I bring him back next week as we only need one more trial before he can race properly?" the enthusiasm beaming from the youngster left Tommy speechless.

"Jamie, we can do but I think we need to do a bit more schooling with him before we bring him back, don't you agree?" said Tommy, looking for some support from Aoife. There was none forthcoming.

"He will be fine trust me granddad, we didn't want him to go fast remember?" he said taking the dog off to wash him down and give him a well-earned drink.

The following week the three of them again made the long journey to the Galway track. Tommy had given Archie a session out the traps to see if he would trap after his failings at the track the previous week. He needn't have worried as Archie came out like a natural and strode away up the gallop.

It had been enough to convince Tommy the journey would be worthwhile. Jamie was in particularly high spirits.

"Are we having a mixed trial tonight granddad with two other dogs?" asked Jamie.

"You know we are Jamie, and the dogs he is trialling against aren't very good so he should win easily if he traps out. Now would you like me to take him out so you can watch or will you do it?"

Without hesitation he replied "I'll do it."

In Ireland there is no restriction on the age that a person can parade a dog whilst in the UK you need to be eighteen. Jamie wouldn't reach that milestone until July.

Jamie took Archie to the starting traps; he was running from trap 3, with the two other greyhounds in traps one and five respectfully.

Not all greyhounds want to race on the same part of the track Tommy had advised Jamie which is why we give them plenty of schooling so they can learn where they want to run. Some prefer to be closer to the inner white running rail and would be expected to run from either trap one or two. Others go to the other extreme and run as close to the outside hare rail and would normally run from either trap five or six. Archie had run straight down the middle, never deviating his run either left or right and would be expected to run from either trap three or four depending on how many 'railers' or 'wide's' made up the six runners.

Please God let it be better than last time said Tommy under his breath.

It was, but only just.

Tommy was lost for words after the trial. Archie had again walked out of the traps and was behind by five lengths at the first bend before coming through to win with a strong finish off the final bend. The time was an improvement on the previous week which was another plus but was still considerably slower than they had both hoped.

As had been the case the week before Jamie was delighted.

"Next week can we come back for a race and he will win, I just know he will granddad?" pleaded Jamie, sensing Tommy was losing a bit of patience.

Tommy thought it was a waste of time, what with fuel costs and the race entry fee the dog would end up costing him a fortune. "I will do you a deal Jamie. If Archie finishes in the first three next week, I will give you twenty five euro's. If he finishes out of the first three we will just need to re-school him for a few weeks."

Jamie without hesitation held out his hand and taking Tommy's said "Deal."

It cost Tommy twenty five euro's as Archie flew from the traps to win by 12 lengths much to the delight of Jamie who was jumping up and down in the middle of the track from the moment the traps opened. He had just trained his first winner and the dog had run a very quick time of 29.20. He was ecstatic.

Tommy was bemused but also delighted. "Jamie, can you tell me why you were so confident the dog would win tonight you little beggar as if I had known I would have had a bet on it at 3-1?"

"It's ok granddad, mum had ten euro on for me" he said pointing in the direction of Aoife who was returning from the bookmakers waving a handful of twenty euro notes in the air.

"I suppose you backed the bloody thing as well?" said Tommy.

Tommy gave his daughter a hug and his grandson a playful slap on the back.

"One day Jamie you will need to tell me what goes on in that little head of yours and Archie's. He has a big future, you both do."

"I will, I promise" replied Jamie with a huge smile before walking off with a skip in his stride.

CHAPTER NINE

The telephone next to the bed rang for the third time.

"Let it ring" said Alice, her head close to my own with her arm laying across my chest.

We had explored each other's bodies for two hours and she had indeed proven she was more sober than I had expected. She was a passionate lover and although it had been a long time since I had been with a woman I was confident I had satisfied all her desires.

The phone rang again.

This time Alice reached across me to lift the receiver, exposing her bare left breast which was close enough for me to lick her nipple which she didn't object to.

She answered with a lazy "Hello."

She sat bolt upright

"Hi dad" she said putting one finger to her lips, indicating that I should say nothing.

"Breakfast..... of course I will be down......what time is it now?"

I looked at my watch, 9:38am.

"I took myself off to bed when Joe went over to see you by the bar. I probably had a little bit too much red wine and slept right through my alarm and early wake up call."

It was always difficult listening to one side of a conversation but she was a very good liar I thought. She had convinced me and I was in the room with her.

"Joe?" I averted my gaze from her naked body that was now sat on the edge of the bed thinking she was talking to me "No I've not seen him since last night" she turned ninety degrees to smile at me.

"Yes he was a lovely man, great company. You were right, he

was easy to get on with and yes I made sure he didn't get into any trouble."

I had to suppress a laugh. We had got on alright would be the understatement of the year. She gave me a playful punch on my thigh.

"I have no idea dad, have you tried his mobile............oh you have........and it just keeps ringing..........and you have rung his room as well........see you in five minutes?" she said before hanging up the phone.

I was laughing my head off.

"Oh bollocks! Dad needs a lift home and has been trying to get hold of you for half an hour as well" she said now laying on her front on the bed, happy for me to rub her lower back.

"Ummmm, that's lovely" she murmured.

"Well we can't sit here all day. Can you pass me my mobile?" I asked Alice.

She reached down to the floor and retrieved my trousers that had been quickly discarded only hours before. The once beautifully tailored garment was now a heap of cloth and I soon retrieved the phone. I had put it on silent before the speeches had started and left it in that mode. I had five missed calls and two text messages, one of which was telling me I had two voice mail messages.

I really must remember to take it off silent.

Phil had called me three times, one call was from Natalie-Jane and the other was a withheld number. I listened to the voice mail messages. Natalie-Jane was ringing to let me know the TV I had won in the raffle and left in the main function room was with Hotel reception. She thanked me for coming. The second message was from Phil asking for me to call him back and he was worried he couldn't get hold of me.

"All ok?" asked Alice as I deleted the messages and took the ringtone off silent.

"All good" I replied, leaning across and kissing her on lips before adding "all very good."

We both dressed quickly. Alice put on a pair of jeans and loose jumper whilst I put on my trousers and shirt from the night before.

She decided she would go out first and go down and see her father and I was to give her a couple of minutes before coming out.

"Alice, will I be seeing you again?"

She turned before exiting the door, returned to the edge of the bed where I was sat. On the bedside table was a complimentary pen and writing pad.

"Put your number on here and I will call you in an hour. Don't leave the hotel."

I did as I was asked; she put the piece of paper in her back pocket and went downstairs.

I gave Alice five minutes, made it back to my room and called Phil.

"Where the bloody have you been" he shouted down the phone "I was bloody worried?"

"Calm down Phil, I had far too much to drink last night. I am way out of practice you could say and I don't have hollow legs like yourself" reminding him of his own comments yesterday. "I put the phone on silent before the speeches" which was true "and went straight to bed after our chat by the bar" which was half true.

"Oh right, so you are still here in the hotel?"

"I am indeed, just going to jump in the shower, pick up the TV I won last night and head back home. I intend to have a look at those DVD's you gave me in more detail this afternoon and I will give you an update on Wednesday before I head off to Kempton when you will hopefully have some more details for me on this Tommy Coyne bloke."

"Cancel the Kempton buddy; I need you at the track on Wednesday night. The dogs of interest are running. Rainbow Warrior is running in an Open for the first time and Double Vision is having a trial before racing. I want you to be there to see if you can pick up any vibes from some of the locals. You weren't unpopular with everyone you know" he joked.

"What about Kempton, I need to earn a living?" I replied.

"Go on Thursday instead and Wolverhampton Friday. I really need to get to the bottom of this one mate and find Andy."

I reluctantly agreed and hung up and went for a shower.

Alice called me as promised.

"Hello Joey boy, you still here?"

"Sure am, room 145, need to check out in 25mins."

"I will be up in two minutes."

Alice had convinced Phil she needed to see someone in London and he could have the car and she would come and pick it up from him in a day or so.

"Well lover boy, I am all yours for the day and then you can drop me home later this evening as I have an early start tomorrow. So don't get any ideas about a repeat performance of last night as you will be sadly disappointed. I need a clear head and my father says you have plenty of work to do."

"Do I now?" I teased, "Do you and your father tell each other everything? I do doubt that somehow. I heard your telephone conversation earlier remember."

"We operate on a need to know basis, and last night is something he doesn't need to know. Last night is something I wanted to do, I don't regret it and we will do it again maybe sometime but don't expect me to drop my knickers as and when I see you. You have your career and I have mine. Don't get me wrong Joe, I can see exactly why Orla fell for you and seeing us together last night was eating away at her all evening. A blind person could see that."

"Wow, where did that come from?" I replied. I had seen nothing but loathing from Orla.

"Joe, as far as I am concerned sex is sex and I enjoy it and I can take it or leave it. I am a single woman but I think it is fair to say that Dad not knowing about last night is probably best all round."

I nodded in agreement.

"I missed breakfast, do you fancy lunch, or would that be pushing it?" I enquired tentatively.

"Lunch would be lovely but first I have to do something" she said grabbing me by both hands and kissing me passionately. "You are a good man Joe Jackson and I am a complicated woman. Just take things as they come, no strings"

We drove back to Wolverton via Bicester where we enjoyed a lovely lunch in a country pub. The snow was still lying heavily on the ground. There had been a slight thaw in the north but temperatures hadn't risen above zero south of Birmingham in a fortnight.

I put the first of the DVD's into the player and watched all of Rainbow Warrior's races in sequence. It was time to put my Racing Managers head on. The dog had plenty of pace and when he led out of the traps, he was unlikely to be beaten as he easily stayed the 440 metre race distance at top speed. Unfortunately his Achilles heel was that he was too inconsistent from the starting traps and more often than not was very slow away which put him at a massive disadvantage against his opponents who would be too far in front of him.

He had run most of races from traps three or four and would be deemed a 'bunny dog' by most racing managers. A 'bunny dog' being a greyhound who'd run its best races when he or she was able to gain an early lead.

Out of curiosity I again looked at his races on the Irish Greyhound website. He had led in two and won and missed the start in the other so I learnt nothing new from them.

I had been at it for almost two hours, examining every minute detail.

"Fancy a cuppa?" asked Alice who had sat next to me on the two seated sofa as I pressed re-wind and fast forward on each race three of four times. She asked what I was looking for in each of the races and I tried to explain that I was looking for something that stuck out from the races he hadn't won. In truth I was looking for a needle in a haystack and I wasn't actually sure there was a needle to find.

We spent the next hour doing the same with the Double Vision races. I learnt nothing.

I leant back on the sofa, turned off the DVD and looked at Alice.

All we had gathered was that both greyhounds had been trained by Tommy Coyne in Ireland and both were now trained by Richard

Quinn. We knew all that last week.

"Time to get you home, but where is home exactly? You didn't actually tell me as I was still picking myself up off the floor from all the other stuff" I said with a smile and added "it was really nice to have you here today."

"I have enjoyed myself as it happens and never realised you would go into so much detail. My flat is in Woburn Sands, about 30 minutes from here and we can go whenever you want. I'm a bit tired and need my beauty sleep."

There was a sarcastic comment that could have been delivered but I refrained.

The drive to Woburn Sands took less than half an hour as the A5 was nice and clear, we drove in pretty much silence. I put my hand on Alice's knee and she looked at me and smiled. Things weren't totally dead in the water then I thought happily.

"Alice, what exactly do you do as a job then if you don't mind me asking as you have told me very little about yourself but you have learnt so much about me and my past?" I asked as she gave me directions for the last 100 yards to her flat.

"Is it important?" she said turning to look at me.

"I guess not, but I thought I'd ask anyway."

I stopped the car at the point indicated. She kissed me on the cheek and said good night before getting out of the car. I drove off, she had been adamant there would be no repeat of the night before and she had stuck to her word.

I was five minutes down the road when my mobile rang, it was Alice.

"I am a Detective Sergeant with Milton Keynes CID. I will call you soon" and hung up.

I hadn't seen that coming but it explained Phil's contact within the local Police.

CHAPTER TEN

Six months earlier - Ireland

There was a knock at the front door.

Nobody ever came to the front door; those neighbours that did come to the house always came to the back scullery door and in doing so they knew from experience they were at risk of losing a limb or two with Trixie on the prowl.

Fortunately for this caller Trixie was happily cuddled up in front of the fire whilst Tommy caught up with the latest news from around the world.

Aoife poked her head around the kitchen door.

"It's the new priest come to visit."

Oh great thought Tommy, the last time a priest had come to the house was when his wife had died. He had heard from Aoife a new priest had taken up residence in the big house on the Westport Road but not for one moment had he thought the new man would be into home visits.

Aoife saw him into the living room and turned on the portable gas fire. The living room only ever saw use for birth, deaths, marriages and visitors. There hadn't been many of the latter over the previous six years. Tommy took a few minutes cleaning himself up, brushed some water through his hair and put on a pair of shoes. The priest would have frowned at the sight of his religious socks as Tommy called them, they were very holey!

"Good evening Father, welcome to our home, please take a seat and Aoife will be through with some tea and biscuits shortly" said a very polite Tommy offering the clergyman the comfy single armchair.

"Thank you Tommy, I can call you Tommy I hope?"

Tommy nodded in acceptance.

"Well Tommy, my name is Father Sean McGrath, and I am the new priest for Leenane and the surrounding area and I thought I would come and introduce myself out of courtesy as I hadn't see you at Saturday night or Sunday morning Mass over the last couple of weeks."

In fact he hadn't seen Tommy at all Tommy had thought as he tried to gauge the age of the man opposite him, mid to late sixties was his initial guess.

"I race on Saturday night's and Sunday is my day of rest so to speak as we don't do anything with the dogs. I'm not really into religion Father and I am past seeking redemption from the Lord for my past sins. Sorry and all that"

The priest smiled.

"I came to see you about the greyhounds as it happens, I am looking to buy one or two to give me an interest as things are a bit slower around here than what I am used to. I was brought up around greyhounds and some say that our family surname is a direct descendant from the great Master McGrath who won the Waterloo Cup three times between 1868 and 1871. I did some research into family trees and it is amazing what old wife tales you will unearth.

We were mad keen on greyhounds growing up in Oola in County Tipperary, we had lots of fun with them and plenty of winners, especially in the coursing field at Clonmel. My father even won the Derby believe it or not. I suppose apart from my faith greyhound racing has always been a passion that runs through the veins.

I like nothing better than having a night at the races and a couple of Guinness' and the craic with the lads. I suppose I would have probably ended up in greyhounds if I had my way."

"Had your way, I'm not sure what that means Father?" said Tommy.

"To cut a long story short Tommy I was born into a very religious family and I was expected, as the eldest, to become a man of the cloth. I have to admit that at first I did find it a struggle but my faith was strong and I have found it very fulfilling. I was moved to Harold's Cross just after my mother, god rest her soul, died three years ago, I gave in to temptation with the greyhounds and I hope the Lord will grant me this one weakness so late in life."

Tommy was refreshed by his honesty but doubted the locals would be as liberal if they were to see the Parish Priest handing over Sunday's collection at Galway on a Thursday night.

Well it wouldn't be Tommy who would be telling them.

"So how have you ended up here then?" enquired Tommy.

"My predecessor died" replied the priest

Tommy look embarrassed "Oh yeah, so he did, sorry."

His apology was waved away and they both smiled.

"The Lord works in mysterious ways and it has been decided I should come here to see out my days until otherwise notified. I am just fortunate you are on my doorstep" he said.

He stood up and walked over towards the sideboard.

"I saw this bitch run in the Oaks Final at Shelbourne Park, she ran a brilliant race and she was a credit to you" he said holding a picture of Pippa's Angel.

Tommy was beginning to warm to the clergyman. "Another biscuit Father?" he said offering the last chocolate digestive. "What would the Bishop say about you owning a greyhound then?"

"Call me Sean please Tommy, far too formal this Father stuff" he said removing his dog collar and placing it in his trouser pocket. "Knowing the Bishop as I do, he would probably ask for a share in it if it was any good."

They both laughed.

Aoife popped her head around the door and enquired if another pot of tea was required as her favourite soap opera was about to start on TV.

"That would be grand now Aoife, thank you" said Sean.

With the photograph of Tommy's pride and joy safely returned to the side board the pair sat down and discussed greyhounds past and present. The merits of using a certain sire with a certain bitch and the benefits of using Australian breeding which had become so fashionable in the past decade.

The gas fire had been extinguished and a roaring turf fire now heated the room. The tea had been replaced by bottles of Guinness and the odd whisky chaser.

"I was at Galway on Thursday night Tommy when that pup made its debut. Was a taking performance so it was. Looks to have plenty of gears" remarked the now somewhat tipsy layman.

Tommy made to rise from his chair but his brain and legs were obviously on different wavelengths as he slumped back to his original starting position. He stayed where he was.

"Ah, you mean young Archie? That would be the young lad Jamie's dog. A funny little bugger he is, more human than dog is Archie. He was hand reared on the bottle after the mother died at birth. He was the only one to survive and it was touch and go for a while but Jamie stayed with him night and day until he was strong enough to stand on his own feet. The bloody thing even sits to order for feck sake."

"Would he be for sale?"

Tommy, who was now upright, but unsteady on his feet, took a look at the clock on the mantelpiece and was surprised to see it was well past midnight.

"Would he be for sale you ask?" said Tommy with one hand on the shoulder of the still seated Sean before continuing "every dog is for sale in this kennel if the price is right, but I will need to discuss it with the owner."

The following morning Jamie's cheery mood was far too much to take for a more than slightly hung-over Tommy who even turned his nose up at the beautifully fried breakfast Aoife had prepared. Sausage, bacon, eggs, fried bread and black pudding looked extremely appetising but he waved it away and just asked for a strong coffee.

"You are looking a bit off colour granddad" he teased "and off your food as well. We may need to give the vet a call. Do you want to do it mum?"

Tommy didn't look amused as he drank his coffee slowly.

"You seemed to be getting on well with the Priest last night dad?" said Aoife, clearing away his plate that Trixie looked keen to clear. "What with your hatred of all things religious I would have thought you wouldn't have had a lot in common."

Tommy looked straight back at her and winced.

"Do you have any fecking paracetamol to go with your chat woman, I have a banging headache and if you must know the priest as you call him wants to buy a greyhound from us and one in particular."

"Really granddad, which one?" said a now very attentive Jamie.

Tommy drank more of his coffee.

"Archie!!"

Jamie jumped from his chair extremely annoyed, he was almost in tears and his mother quickly went to console him. Jamie tried to pull away, picked up his now empty plate from the table and threw it in the sink. He stood opposite Tommy who had not moved at all during the commotion.

Jamie let rip whilst wiping tears from his cheek.

"You told me Archie was mine and any decisions made on him were down to me. I have worked with him since he was a pup granddad. I have seen him through sickness and schooled him and taught him to race even though I didn't want him to. If you sell him I will never speak to you again and as soon as I can I will move away and leave you to it."

"Sit down Jamie and stop talking daft."

Reluctantly Jamie pulled up a chair at the kitchen table.

"I said that he wanted to buy Archie, I didn't say we would sell him. I told him I would need to talk to the owner, which is you, and I am now doing that. Given your reaction I would not dream of selling him outright, but listen to me now, I have done some thinking and this could work in our favour. It is something I have had on my mind since Bernard died.

I cannot carry on forever doing this and one day all this, the house, the kennels and the land will all be yours. I have seen over the last couple of years that you have the ability to train greyhounds on your own but there is only so much I can teach you. Sean, I mean Father McGrath; well he has a number of contacts in England who may be able to give you a job for a few years to learn even more. I haven't discussed it with him but if you are agreeable I would like to put a proposition to him."

"What proposition?" asked Jamie.

"If you were to sell him half of Archie you would probably get about five thousand euro's for him depending on how he runs next time. I would suggest that you should only sell him half if he could get you a job in a well-established kennel in England and also on the condition Archie went to the same kennel as you go. I am absolutely convinced that no-one else could get Archie to perform the way you have. Now if he is willing to agree to these conditions would you agree to a part sale with you going over in July when you turn eighteen? That would give you a couple more races over here with him."

Tommy rose from his chair; the coffee had obviously done the trick as he now looked completely composed. He made his way around the kitchen table and put his hand on his grandson's shoulder and said "Think about it Jamie, discuss it with your mother. You have already told us you want to go to England after your exams and we completely support you with that. This may be a great opportunity and give you some money in your pocket as well."

He gave his daughter a kiss on the cheek, placed his now empty coffee mug in the sink and made his way up to the kennels.

CHAPTER ELEVEN

Ireland

The Priests visit's to the Coyne kennels had become the talk of the village much to the amusement of Tommy and the clergyman.

"Well Sean if they are talking about us I suppose it means that they are leaving some other poor bugger alone. Sure didn't Aoife overhear the postman talking to the bread delivery man this morning in the village so it will have reached Letterfrack by lunchtime and the Bishop of Galway by tea?" he joked.

The visits had been regular over the past three weeks and the late night sessions were a once a week occurrence with the odd game of cards thrown in with Aoife making up the players. Aoife had seen a new lease of life in her father who apart from being hung over the following morning each time he had been a lot less grumpy. It made life easier for everyone.

She had resigned herself to the fact that Jamie would be going over to England in July and there was only a week until his exams. He had cut back his time in the kennels to enable him to get in some quality revision before his Leaving Cert but that would be on the back burner tonight as Archie was due to have his second race.

"My friend is coming over tonight to see the dog run and if she is happy with the performance and you agree on a price we can then start to look at getting young Jamie a position within the kennel" said Sean.

"What makes you think she can swing the second part of the deal as that is probably the most important part for me" replied Tommy, doing well to hide how anxious he actually was.

"When I spoke to her last week she said that she had already discussed it with the trainer and because of the owners and quality of dog that she has been bringing into the kennel over the last year or so then she is pretty confident that once he finishes his exams there should be a position for him as I have told her he is an excellent lad with the dogs. There is a caravan on site as well so he will always be close to the dogs."

"Excellent" replied Tommy as he made his way back down the kennels with Sean in tow.

The three black pups were the apple of Tommy's eye and he had slowly been increasing their schooling up the gallops over the previous months and they were due to have their first unofficial school this week at the track. Barry, Maurice and Robin had been named after the Bee Gee's singers who had sung *Tragedy*. He thought it apt given the circumstances behind his plan.

"So who are these little beauties Tommy?" asked Sean.

"This" he said stroking the ears of the nearest black dog "is my pension and retirement plan all in one."

"Care to explain?" said the now intrigued Sean.

"Maybe one day but these are the last litter thrown by Pippa's Angel and they are showing plenty of promise here at home but the big test will come when myself and Aoife take them to the track this week as Jamie will be at school."

"How do you tell them apart just as a matter of interest as I have been studying them for the last five minutes and they look identical in every way? Do they have any distinguishing marks at all?"

"Not a one Sean. Not a single white hair, not a light coloured toe nail not a bite mark, scar or tooth out of place they are identical triplets" smiled Tommy.

"So how do you tell them apart?"

"Well if I am totally honest I can't but Jamie can by looking at their eyes so he says and of course we have the earmarks which will differentiate them when they start racing. Let's give them a gallop and see them in action. Fancy giving me hand if I show you how to operate the drag hare? We will give them a spin out of the traps I think."

"Absolutely, be great fun" Sean replied and the pair wandered up the gallop to set things up.

Neither of them knew whether it was Maurice, Barry or Robin who went the fastest but all three showed they knew what they were doing, which is more than can be said for Sean who struggled to keep the drag hare at any consistent speed for the first of the gallops, much to the annoyance of Tommy whose foul language suggested he had forgotten he was in the presence of a priest.

"Well they went well I thought, what do you think Tommy?"

"Just grand now, just grand. There is not a bother on them and they are great grubbers, the last one we sent up was a bit blowy when he came back down so I might have to have a look at his tonsils to see if they are inflamed but apart from that they should be good to go at the track this week."

They washed the dogs down and put them away in the kennel before making their way down to the house to clean up before heading off to Galway in the evening.

"I will see you at the track later then Tommy. Here's hoping for a good run tonight" said Sean before getting in his car.

"Yes Jamie I went over him this morning and gave him a massage and his favourite breakfast as promised. He is in great shape and should run well if he comes out the traps fine" said Tommy to his excited grandson who was firing questions every couple of minutes, "now sit back and save your energy for the track, we will be there in twenty minutes."

Having arrived safely and in plenty of time, Tommy, Aoife and Jamie set off for the canteen underneath the grandstand for a bite to eat. It was a big night at the track with first round heats of an unraced stake that had seen the current English Derby champion make a winning track debut the previous year. All the big trainers from across the country were in attendance and Tommy spent his time people watching and pointing out to Jamie who was who.

"Is that really Pat Mulhall who trained Docs Eclipse to win the Easter Stakes twice and the guy with the grey hair and red jacket is that Bobby Tucker who trained Bonbon Neo to win the Irish

Derby?" said Jamie in awe.

The people watching and history lesson continued for another hour before they were interrupted by the arrival of Sean and his friend.

"Good evening you three, this is my friend Sam, sorry we are late but she got a bit lost at the roundabout at the end of the road" said Sean.

Sam shook their hands, leaving Jamie until last. "You must be the young man who I hope to be seeing more of once you have finished your exams; Sean has given you a glowing reference?"

Jamie looked embarrassed at the compliment.

"So will this young dog of yours be winning tonight or have I made a long journey for nothing?" she said pulling on his right cheek.

"Don't worry. Archie won't let any of us down I can assure you. He is in fine form, will have improved from his first run and he will make your journey worthwhile" he replied with a beaming smile.

"Well let's hope so as I have brought my cheque book. Now who fancies a drink, I'm parched?" she said heading off to the bar. The other four followed.

Archie's race was the fourth on the card.

Jamie had gone down to the paddock after the second race with Tommy to prepare the dog, leaving Aoife, Sam and Sean in the bar exchanging small talk until Aoife broached the subject of Jamie's impending move to England.

"So tell me Sam, what are you able to tell me about this trainer Jamie maybe going over to and how long have you known them?"

"Well Aoife, I have known them for about two years. They had come recommended by a colleague when I bought my first dog and they did such a good job that a few of us chipped in to buy an expensive dog who as it transpired was pretty useful. Sean may have told you I was brought up around greyhounds but I only regained my interest a few years ago through a mutual friend.

I told the trainer I had the chance to buy a possible Derby dog but it came with the proviso that they were willing to give young

Jamie a chance to continue his greyhound education within an up and coming kennel. The trainer's wife will take him under her wing as she does most of the track work whilst the trainer runs the kennels. She will show him everything he needs to know" she replied.

"Where are they based?"

"Just outside of Dunstable; so not too far from Luton Airport for him to get a flight home if he needs to" she smiled.

"Sounds good. Archie is Jamie's pride and joy as you are probably aware and I doubt anyone actually understands the relationship they have. Anyway, they are coming out on parade now so let's go outside as I have to put ten euro's on with the bookmakers for the lad."

Tommy joined them on the steps in front of the grandstand and they studied Jamie as he walked Archie around in a circle by the winning line before being announced to the expectant crowd. Aoife returned from the bookmakers pleased she had been able to bet twenty euro's on Archie at 3-1, an extra ten euros for herself.

The formalities over, the six greyhounds made their way to the starting traps. Archie was wearing a white racing jacket indicating that he was in trap three.

Tommy had everything crossed that Archie would break quickly from the traps like he had done in his first race. The dogs he was racing against tonight were the most experienced he had ever faced and he would need to produce a personal best performance to win.

"Come on Archie" shouted Aoife as the commentator announced the hare was running.

"Here comes the hare......and they're off" said the commentator.

"Three traps smartly from two and one as four and five bump. They go into the first bend and three goes round in front..........."

"Go on Archie my son, home you go" roared Tommy punching the air.

".........and three has opened up down the back straight and has taken four lengths out of the rest........."

"Oi oi Archie, home you go" the four of them now roared from the steps.

".........this is some performance from this youngster as he pulls further and further clear. Trap three wins, a huge gap back to four and one in a photo."

Tommy looked to the centre of the track where the winning time was immediately shown on a digital clock, it showed 28.78. He wiped tears from his eye and hugged Aoife who was also in tears.

"Have you seen the fecking time, 28.78 is unbelievable? That is six lengths faster than his last win. That boy of yours is a fecking genius. I'm shaking I am that excited. That was bloody, bloody brilliant."

Tommy broke into a jog as he made his way down to the paddock to greet Jamie and the dog and gave him a huge hug as he came off the track, patting the panting Archie at the same time.

"Jesus granddad didn't he run well, he was awesome? The gentleman over there" pointing at a man in his forties who had paraded the greyhound who had run from trap two "reckons Archie could be a Derby dog."

"He may well be, he may well be. Now clean up the dog, give him a good drink and put him back in the kennel and come back and join us in the bar. I have a feeling you may have a nice big cheque coming your way" said Tommy as he playfully ruffled Jamie's hair.

Tommy left Jamie to sort the dog out and made his way back from the kennels, accepting lots of congratulation's from fellow trainers on the way. Tonight's performance had made him even more determined to execute his plan in the coming months and with the help of his grandson he was certain he would pull it off.

Sam, Sean and Aoife were waiting in the bar, "Well Tommy, I think we should get the business out of the way first and then crack open a bottle of bubbly. What do you say?" said Sam.

Tommy agreed but they waited until Jamie arrived.

Jamie finally joined them but he left the adults to discuss figures as he sipped on his diet coke. Sam wrote out a cheque and handed it to Tommy and they shook hands. The sale was done.

"Now young man, I have just spoken to the trainer in England

and they will be expecting you the week after your birthday which I believe is in four weeks. The dog will have one more race over here if you want and then he will come over to race in the UK. Once you arrive we can register the dog in your name and Sean's name. Is that okay with you?"

"It certainly is."

"I need you to promise me you won't let on I have bought the dog as the bookies have a tendency to give me shorter odds on dogs in my name. I will let your grandfather explain why but for now we need to keep this as our little secret?" urged Sam.

Jamie nodded in acceptance.

"Well that's great. Let's celebrate; I suggest a toast to Archie and future successes."

They raised their glasses, the adults with champagne and Jamie and his diet coke; "To Archie and more successes."

With the cheque safely stowed in his inside pocket, Tommy and Aoife made their way back to the van where Jamie had already safely put Archie in the back.

The long trip back to Leenane seemed to take no time at all, the mist was quite heavy and the rain persistent as they came into Maam Cross but Aoife knew every pot hole and soft verge to get them home safely. Jamie fell asleep just outside of Galway, what with the excitement of winning and his studying the lad was exhausted and he had to be woken when they reached home.

Aoife made herself and her father a cup of tea and a hot chocolate for Jamie. They all set around the kitchen table. The embers in the range had been stoked and a couple of turf sods added for good measure.

They sat in silence for a few minutes.

"Jamie?"

"Yes granddad."

"When Archie trialled at Galway did you do something that stopped him from trapping?"

Jamie smiled, kissed his mother on the cheek and went to bed.

CHAPTER TWELVE

Four months earlier Ireland - July

A date had been set for Jamie to move over to England and Tommy had decided it was time he brought his grandson in on his master plan especially with Archie due to have his last race in the coming days at Galway. With his exams all finished and his birthday on Sunday Jamie couldn't wait for the move over.

"Jamie, finish up those last two and come and see me in the feed room in five minutes will you?" Tommy shouted above the music into the kennel block where Jamie was putting the last two dogs away after they had been in the paddock.

"Will do."

Jamie joined his grandfather in the feed room and they both took a seat on a hay bale and tucked into the sandwiches, snacks and tea that Aoife had brought up for lunch.

"You won't be getting luxuries like this in few weeks' time Jamie" said Tommy tucking into a doorstop ham and mustard sandwich. "You will be lucky to get a cup of tea what with the eighty dogs they have in the kennel."

"It will be grand" replied Jamie with a mouth a full of sandwich.

Tommy made himself comfortable before continuing.

"Well, I have a plan I have been working on for over a year that I am going to need your help with and the details of this plan are not to leave this room. You are to tell no-one, not your mother, not Father Sean, Sam and definitely not the trainer who Archie is going to. Is that understood?"

Jamie nodded.

The next hour saw Tommy doing all the talking and Jamie doing all the listening. The more Tommy talked the more attentive Jamie became. He did interrupt once or twice but his grandfather asked him to wait until the very end before he had any questions. When Tommy had finished he stood up and moved over to the sink and looked out of the big bay feed room window down to the house at the bottom of the hill.

"If we pull this off Jamie I will never have to work again and it will give you a great foundation to upgrade facilities here if you want" smiled Tommy, still looking out of the window.

"Jesus granddad I had never noticed that but surely we won't get away with it? It cannot be done, there are far too many checks carried out. Surely someone will notice. It can't be that simple?"

"I agree it isn't a formality and we may need a little help from elsewhere for the second part of the plan but the first part is all down to you and that is why we need Archie to go over before you do so he can settle into a new regime and new surroundings. You have yet to tell me what it is you do to stop Archie trapping. I have tried everything whilst you have been at school and he traps every time, regular as clockwork. It has me totally baffled."

"Let me finish my doughnut and I will show you" said Jamie wiping the excess sugar from his fingers onto his trouser leg.

"Ok, I will go and set the drag hare up and you go and bring the dog out" said Tommy.

Jamie collected Archie from his kennel. The dog was delighted to see him, play bowing and nuzzling into the young lads side as he brought him out on to the gallop. He safely placed the greyhound into the single trap and indicated with a wave of the hand to his grandfather they were ready to go.

Tommy had taken the drag hare about 20 yards behind the trap so it would generate some speed as it passed and would be at a safe distance in front once the trap had opened.

The pair of them had done this at least a thousand times over the past few years and their timings were almost spot on. Tommy would control the drag hare speed and Jamie would release the trap as the hare went past and the dog would come out.

For once Tommy was hoping the dog didn't come out too well. He got his wish.

The hare came past the traps and Jamie released the switch and the front of the trap flew up but unlike in his last two races where Archie had come out running, he paused slightly before consenting to chase the drag hare that was now some distance in front of him.

'Bugger me' said Tommy to himself as he pulled the now stopped drag hare from the grasp of Archie who had caught it at the end of the gallop.

Jamie gave a whistle and Archie turned on a sixpence. With a lolloping stride he made his way back down the gallop where his lead was put back on his neck and the pair walked up towards Tommy who was making his way back down towards them.

"Told you" said Jamie with cheeky grin.

The three of them stopped in the middle of the gallop and Tommy put a hand on Jamie's shoulder whilst the panting greyhounds smiled up at them with no idea as to why the two humans were in such good spirits.

"Can you do it under race conditions though lad?" said Tommy seriously.

"Of course I can" replied Jamie. "Will do it tomorrow night if you want but I doubt Father Sean will be too pleased if he has a bet on it."

"You can leave Father Sean to me."

The home gallops over the past weeks had taught Tommy an awful lot about Maurice, Robin and Barry. Whereas there looks were indistinguishable to anyone but Jamie, their racing abilities were considerably different and that was exactly what Tommy had prayed for over the winter. He was confident they would all make the grade.

Sam had called to ask if all was well with Archie for his final run tomorrow evening and confirmed the transporter who would be bringing the dog across to England would be arriving early on Saturday morning.

"There is not a bother on him now Sam. I gave him a gallop

yesterday and he seems fine. It is a hard race tomorrow mind you and I wouldn't be having a bet as he will be no sort of price. The young lad will miss him terribly when he has gone and has compiled a list of the dog's habits for the trainer. He has spoken to the trainer's wife this morning and she seems a nice girl who put him at ease a little bit" advised Tommy.

"Thanks for the warning Tommy, was going to have few quid on so will keep the money in my pocket" she had replied.

Father Sean arrived unexpectedly.

"Good afternoon Tommy, do you mind if I tag along for the trials today as I am at a loose end?" said Sean.

Tommy had to think quickly as he was only intending to trial two of the pups today but he didn't want to tell him why.

"Certainly Sean, just taking the two today, one of the pups has a bit of a temperature and off his food so will give him a rest this week to enable him to get over it. You can give me a hand and drive if you want and Aoife can stay here and have the afternoon off."

Sean seemed delighted to be so hands on and jumped at the chance and was soon loading up the dogs onto the van. They drove down the steep incline from the kennels to the main road, the Killary Harbour to their left looked like a sheet of glass with the bright sun reflecting off it. It was a beautiful day to start the pups off on their racing careers.

Tommy always liked to be one of the last to arrive at the track for unofficial trials as he hated all the waiting around and idle gossip that would transpire. He loved the camaraderie of his fellow trainers but also liked his privacy, today probably more than any other day.

"Hello Tommy" said a passing trainer, "fine looking pups you have there."

Tommy tipped his hat in acknowledgement whilst making sure he had a strong hold on the pup who was straining on the lead.

"You can follow Paddy's two dog trial if that's ok for your first one Tommy? You just giving them a handslip today from the first bend?" asked the hare driver as he made his way back to his box with a soft drink in hand.

"Yes please Seamus. I will follow him out and hold this dog in the centre of the track so he can see what it is all about when the hare goes round then I will walk onto the bend" replied Tommy.

The hare driver waved a hand in acceptance and carried on walking.

"Sean, can you hold this one and I will take the first one out but make sure you have him on a short tight lead as he may get a bit jumpy when the hare comes past?" instructed Tommy as he handed over one of the pups.

Tommy followed Paddy onto the track, but whilst Paddy made his way to the traps on their right, Tommy took the young pup through a small gap in the inside running rail and made his way across the grass to the centre of the track.

Some pups react totally differently the first time they see and hear the mechanical hare that is used for racing. Some will stand and look, ears pricked with their heads moving from side to side. Others are more animated and will jump and twist to try and get off the lead, pulling and barking at the new venture. Many an inexperienced handler has found themselves dumped on the seat of their pants when a young pup has suddenly jumped up when the hare has gone by.

The pup behaved impeccably, as did his brother when Tommy followed the same routine fifteen minutes later. Both pups were hand-slipped by Tommy at the first bend. Holding the dog between his legs, Tommy turned the pups head towards the mechanical hare that was coming from behind them. The dog was struggling to break free but Tommy held firm until the hare had passed them, at which point he let the dog go off in pursuit of the now accelerating hare.

From a trainer and breeders perspective there is nothing more satisfying than seeing a dog you have bred showing keenness on the track. Tommy was delighted.

"They went well Tommy don't you think?" said Sean.

Tommy smiled to himself. If only you knew the whole story Sean, if only you knew.

They drove home in good spirits and Tommy got the enquiry he had been hoping for. Sean coming today could work out to be a total blessing in disguise.

"Would the pups be for sale Tommy?" asked Sean.

"Every dog is saleable Sean and these are no different, I think these two are the best in the litter as I am bit concerned the other one has a few wind problems. I had the vet look at his tonsils and they are a bit inflamed. We'll need to get him looked at when his temperature comes down."

"Well I will have a word with Sam as I might fancy a share in the two if we can agree a deal. I've liked what I have seen and I was a major fan of their mother" said Sean, slowing down to avoid a coach full of tourists coming in the opposite direction just outside of Moycullen.

"I'm sure we can come up with something that suits us both but let's wait and see how they do in the next couple of weeks."

Jamie was waiting for them when they returned.

"All go well granddad?" he asked.

"Absolutely fine Jamie, they will improve for the experience but they were both keen and chased hard. They will grade I am certain with natural improvement. Father Sean is keen on them and will talk to Sam about maybe buying them after they have another go next week. How is Archie, all set for tomorrow?"

"He is smashing but he didn't eat all his food tonight so I am not sure if he will be one hundred percent tomorrow" he said with a wink to Tommy that Sean wouldn't have seen.

"Will he still run though?" asked Sean.

"He will, but I wouldn't be placing any bets on him just in case it is more than a twenty four hour bug" said Jamie. "The run will do him no harm as he is heading over on the transporter this weekend."

The race at Galway went exactly to plan and Sean had even refrained from having a bet on Archie who was made the 5-4 favourite by the track bookmakers.

The traps opened and just as he had done earlier in the week,

Archie came out the traps slowly; he was at least five lengths behind his rivals going into the first bend and although he made up lots of ground he was always going to struggle to catch the clear leader. He finished a creditable third.

"Can't win them all" said Tommy who was doing well to hide how delighted he was.

Jamie walked off the track and as pre-arranged with his grandfather tried not to look happy as he was met by the two elder men by the paddock gate.

The youngster did a brilliant impression of being disappointed.

"He just missed the kick, I'm sure he would have gone close with a level break. These things happen and I will try and work on it when I go over to England. I will go and wash him off and come and join you in the bar in a few minutes" Jamie said trudging off, head bowed.

If he didn't make it as a trainer a career in Hollywood would be an alternative.

Tommy's old legs had a spring in their step as he made his way into the lower bar and ordered a couple of Guinness's. He had lots to look forward to.

CHAPTER THIRTEEN

Ireland – August

Jamie's departure to England had taken a while to get used to around the kennels. Aoife was withdrawn for a couple of weeks and Tommy was hardly great company. The three pups' education on the track at Galway had continued. Maurice and Robin had plenty of pace but Barry was definitely the weakest of the three he had told Sean after a session on the home gallops.

"I just can't get him right. The vet has had his tonsils out and he still seems to be a fair bit behind the other pair who are just grand now" said Tommy.

"Will they still be for sale though as Sam is due over at the end of the week so she could meet us at the track for their first official trial?"

"Sounds like a plan. I will book them in for a solo trial and she can come and see how they get on and if she likes what she sees then we can talk money. I assume they will go over to the same guy as Archie? Talking of Archie, I see he is due to have his first race tomorrow evening?"

"That's right, Sam says he took a while to settle in and only came back to himself when the young lad came over. The grader has been very hard on him for his first race sticking him in top grade. I think she had a word with the Racing Manager but given the times he did in his trials I am not sure what she expected to be honest Tommy. What do you think?"

"He certainly went well in his trials Sean and it is a shame the trainer didn't get a few runs into him before the lad arrived, he was bound to be a bit home sick, the dog that is, as he was used to Jamie fussing around him all the time. Probably made him a bit soft and it was always going to take a while for him to settle in. They say he was off his food, the bugger would eat if he was hungry that is all I will say.

Let's go down to the house and ask Aoife to book these pups in for Friday shall we and I could do with a cup of tea. You fancy one?"

"I bet the young lad will be nervous tonight" said Tommy to his daughter as he finished his breakfast and put the dirty plate in the sink. "Think I will give him a quick call and see how he is."

Tommy took the cordless house phone outside; he didn't want Aoife to hear what he was going to say to her son. What she didn't know wouldn't harm her he thought.

"Hiya granddad" said Jamie as he answered the phone, he could hardly hear himself think as the greyhounds in his kennel block were in full voice.

"Have I called at a bad time Jamie, you sound busy?" asked Tommy.

"You're fine, honest, just in the middle of feeding breakfast. What can I be doing for you?"

"Just calling to see how you are getting on and wishing you luck for tonight and hope Archie comes off sound; it's the most important thing remember. Looks like a hard race, he'll do well to win and I think Sam is having a few quid on."

Jamie burst out laughing.

"That's a shame then. It's not luck he needs tonight it is a miracle of divine proportions, The plan is in place as previously agreed, three bad runs and then let him go, by which time we should get a decent price. You still want to stick to that or you had a change of heart?"

"Sounds good to me as long as you promise it won't get you into trouble and you have no way of being caught. Oh and before I forget your mother says you have to eat more than just bloody doughnuts. She has had reports back."

"I'll be fine granddad, don't be worrying yourself now and I need my doughnuts, will have a couple before his race tonight for luck. Now I better go before the boss comes back. Love to mum" he said before hanging up.

Although he wouldn't admit it publically Jamie was extremely nervous about Archie's first race. The fawn dog had gone really well in his three qualifying trials but it was the trainer's wife Orla who had taken him to the traps on all three occasions. Tonight she had said he could do it. When he had spoken to his grandfather earlier he hadn't factored in that he may not be parading, it only occurred to him when they'd reached the track.

He had been at the kennels for just over a month having arrived at the end of July and so far he had enjoyed every minute, he thought the trainer was a bit of a miserable sod and his side kick Ken always smelt of cow dung or something similar, whatever it was it wasn't pleasant. He tried to stay out of their way and stay as close to Orla as much as possible. She was good fun to be around and easy to work with. Between them they did most of the racing and trial meetings with the other pair staying behind at the kennels. It was a system that seemed to work and they were having plenty of winners.

"Good evening Jamie. How have you settled in?" asked Sam Hampshire as she joined him at the table in the canteen.

It was the first time Jamie had seen Sam since she had bought Archie at Galway a couple of months ago. He had kept his promise not to say anything about the purchase and as far as he was aware no one in the kennel knew she had signed the cheque.

"I am very well missus, I mean Sam. Really enjoying it and Orla has been great at helping me settle in" he said with a smile.

"I bet she has" she said with a touch of sarcasm. Jamie couldn't help but notice a scowl towards his mentor. "So will he be winning tonight this dog of yours as I might have a few quid on?"

"He" emphasising the word "will be doing his very best and with luck he will win" but not if I have my way he won't he said inwardly.

"Great, in that case I wish you luck" said Sam before departing.

"Now fuck off and leave us alone" said Orla loud enough to be heard whilst smiling at Jamie. "I bloody hate that woman."

Archie's race was the second last on the card, the worst part of being in the top grade is you have to wait all night before your dog gets a run Orla had said to him. The pair of them had shared the parading duties and between them they'd had a winner apiece from five runners.

"Off you go young man and good luck" said Orla as Jamie took Archie out on parade.

Orla came down from the paddock and stood by the wall near the winning line. She noticed that Ken Kelly was stood with Sam up by the bookmakers but neither looked like they were having a bet. Sam normally had her bets off course and not with the track bookmakers. She wasn't Orla's favourite person in the world but she had been backing plenty of winners lately and putting on for Richard as well and the extra winnings always came in handy. She was struggling to work out what the relationship was between her and Ken but wherever she went he wasn't far behind.

The greyhounds had been safely loaded into the traps and she watched Jamie as he made his way into the middle of the track to watch his dog run.

The race for Archie was over as soon as the traps opened.

Whilst the other five greyhounds had come out of the traps in unison, Archie had dwelt badly and was at least four or five lengths behind the fifth placed dog as they ran around the second bend. He couldn't possibly win from that far back but she studied him all the way round the track just to be sure his running action didn't deviate. Any deviation would be a sign that he may be carrying an injury. Nothing jumped out at her to suggest he was lame.

Jamie gave Archie a huge hug as he came to a stop on the other side of the track after the race had finished.

"Good lad, your turn will come in a few weeks" he whispered in his ear whilst slipping on his collar and lead and removing his racing muzzle. The pair walked back to the paddock and he did his best to look disappointed when he was met by Orla at the paddock gate.

"Is he ok?" asked Orla.

"He's fine; he has a tendency to miss the break now and again. He did it during his last race at Galway and in both his qualifying trials. He is still a pup and it may take him a couple of races to get used to the track here. We can check him over in the morning" he said before taking Archie off to clean him up and give him a drink of water.

Orla was impressed by the maturity of her young prodigy; she thought he would have been more disappointed after such a poor run but he had taken defeat in good grace, far better than Sam she thought who she had seen storm off to the bar with Ken two steps behind her. With the dog safely locked away back in his kennel Jamie pulled his mobile from his pocket and called home.

"Hey granddad, job done, dog fine, speak tomorrow, love to mum" and hung up.

Tommy put the phone down with a huge smile on his face. The lad had pulled it off and two more runs like that would see them in prime position to implement part one of their major plan. He hadn't yet started on his side of the deal and he would start to ring around a few old friends from England in the morning. He hadn't been this excited in a long time and he felt twenty years younger.

"What has you so chipper dad?" asked Aoife as she came into the kitchen.

Thinking quickly on his feet he convinced her it was Sam on the phone and they were discussing the possible sale of the pups on Friday. He hated lying to her but it was for the best, for now anyway.

Sam met them at the track. Sean had volunteered for driving duties. He was good company Tommy had thought and he was sorry he was going to be caught up in his plan but it wasn't as if he was ripping them off, well not quite he kept telling himself to ease his conscience.

Tommy removed the pups from the van and took them to the paddock where their earmarks and markings were checked. The pups were individually weighed and locked away in their allocated kennel where they would remain until they were due to trial. Sam was waiting at the bar with Sean.

"Good evening Tommy" she said offering him her left cheek to kiss in welcome which he duly did.

"Evening Sam, good journey over I hope? I hear that Archie is ok after his exertions on Wednesday, just a bit disappointing he missed the start, did it once or twice over here you know. It will come; he is a fast dog and will win plenty of races."

"I do hope so, I had a good few quid on him Wednesday but I will wait until he shows some consistency before I back him again. Anyway, what can we expect tonight from these two?" she asked.

"Anything between 18.10 and 18.40 would be good. I think Maurice will go faster than Robin. We have left Barry at home as I don't think he will make it to the track as he has a few breathing problems."

The trials were a huge success Maurice clocked 18.36 and Robin a much faster 18.06. If those times didn't result in a sale he would give up the game. "They went really well Tommy, you must be delighted?" said Sean handing him a pint of Guinness. "I certainly am, but it doesn't matter what I think, it is whether the lady with the cheque book was suitably impressed. I will give them a four bend trial next week and then they will be ready to race. What did you think Sam?" Tommy asked as he took the first gulp of his pint.

"I think we can do business, I will write you a figure on this cheque for the pair and as long as they both do a grading time next week then we can sort out the necessary paperwork" she said as she put pen to paper and handed it to him.

Tommy looked at the figure; she had offered a fair amount. "Smashing Sam" he said and shook her hand to seal the deal. "Well I need to get off and see someone down south before I fly back tomorrow evening so I will look forward to hearing how these pups get on next week, What are they called by the way?"

"Robin is called Double Vision whilst Maurice is called Seeing Double. Quite apt don't you think. I named them all after the Bee

Gee's, Barry is the other one." said Tommy. It probably wasn't the right time to tell her Robin was actually at home tucked up in bed and it was Barry who had clocked 18.36 and Maurice the 18.06. What she didn't know wouldn't harm her and she was getting a bargain at half the price.

CHAPTER FOURTEEN

September / October

"What do you mean you don't know what is going on, you work with the lad all day, surely you have some idea whether the dog is lame or not? That is three runs he has had now and underperformed. Is he eating up now, and what about the state of his coat, could he be dehydrated?"

Richard was firing the questions at Orla and they were questions she didn't have the answers to. She had been over Rainbow Warrior with a fine tooth comb after his run at the track last Wednesday and found nothing wrong with him. He had missed his start for the third race running which was normally a sign that he would have some sort of muscle problem that would be causing him pain when he would push off with his back legs when the traps open.

She had found nothing. They rarely used a 'muscle man', a canine physiotherapist who would specialise in finding underlying muscle issues. She had called one in on Saturday and after an hour going over the dog from head to toe he couldn't find anything either.

"Sam is doing her nut; some of her bigger clients have had a fair few quid on in the last couple of weeks and left their money behind on this bloody dog. I've told her I cannot guarantee what the dog is going to do and maybe she should put it down to experience. I've tried to explain to her that not every dog turns out as good as we would hope. She is backing plenty of other winners I told her to just leave this one alone, especially tonight" he said pacing around the room.

"What do you want?" shouted Orla as Ken entered the kitchen.

"A word with the boss if that is alright with you?" said Ken.

"Fine, but take it outside, I don't want to have to disinfect this place every time you come in."

Jamie was sat in Archie's kennel when Orla returned with tea for the pair of them. She had found it difficult to look at him the last couple of days after he'd caught her doing something she shouldn't have been. She had laughed it off and he'd acted as if nothing had happened. She was glad it hadn't affected their working relationship.

"I hear we have a couple of dogs coming over at the weekend from your grandfather, brothers I believe, are they any good?" she asked as Jamie came out from the kennel and ushered Archie away from the door.

"They were going nicely before I left but granddad is sending the third one of the litter over as well as company for me. He's had a few problems with his wind and granddad wanted to home him but I said I'd have him as he was my favourite, apart from Archie here of course. He has tried to get him going on the track but he struggles in the closing stages of his races. No point persevering."

"So what about Archie tonight, what do you think?" asked Orla

"I was wondering" said Jamie "do you want to parade him tonight and I will watch? Maybe I am doing something wrong when I am putting him in the traps; change of routine may work as he trapped fine for you when you did his initial trials."

"Don't be daft Jamie, you do it; he's your dog. You have just been unlucky, his time will come." It was exactly the answer he had been hoping for and he would be ringing his grandfather as soon as he got a spare five minutes away from any listening ears.

"Orla, I just need to give my mum a call and ask for some clothes to be sent over with the transporter at the weekend. Will only be a couple of minutes, is that alright?" She waved back at him from the feed room indicating it was fine and he took himself off to his caravan to make the call. "Hi mum, is granddad around, want to have a quick word about the pups coming over?"

"He is up at the kennels son. I will go and get him and ask him to call you back. Is everything ok over there and when will I be seeing you, I'm missing you?"

Tommy rushed down from the kennels and called Jamie straight back. "Good morning Jamie, what news do you have for me on this bright sunny day. All well with the dog for tonight I hope?"

"All fine granddad; Archie is bouncing. You can tell mum I have cut back on the doughnuts. Will call you tomorrow but have to go now" said Jamie who then disconnected the call.

Tommy sat down at the table and handed the phone back to Aoife with a huge smile on his face as she brought him over a cup of tea. Over the last few weeks he had been able to catch up with a few old friends in the UK who he knew would be able to get some sizeable bets on the dog for him. It had been an emotional couple of days hearing about old friends who had passed away and whose funerals he had missed.

He expected the dog to be a decent price tonight after his recent poor performances and now that Jamie had called he needed to ring a few guys to tell them the bet was on.

"Aoife love, can you bring the last two in from the big gallop for me and I will go back up after I have made a few calls? Thanks for the tea" he said raising his mug in appreciation.

Tommy made three calls in all. They were all short and to the point. It was like riding a bike for Tommy, he hadn't done this for seventeen years but he still had the respect of the call recipients. His word was his bond and they trusted his judgment. Should the plan fail he would make sure he settled his debt within the week.

Roll on the 8:46pm race at Stony Stratford tonight.

The Quinn kennel had been flying of late; they'd had two winners already on the card tonight, both newcomers who had recently come over from Ireland. Orla noticed that Sam and Ken were in good spirits but neither of them had been to collect from the track bookmakers. They made their way down towards Richard who was stood by the perimeter wall. They were in deep conversation when Orla joined them.

"Do we back it or not Richard, I am not having a penny on it but there are a few of my guys who have made a few quid on the first two tonight who might want to play up their winnings? He is a big price at 7-1" asked Sam who was checking a text message on her phone at the same time. "Another one asking" she said putting the device back in her pocket.

"Look Sam, as I said to you before I couldn't back it until it starts trapping and even then I would still be reluctant. I have had a look at his last three races and his last race at Galway and he definitely has an issue somewhere. Orla here had the muscle man in at the weekend and found nothing wrong with him. You can back him at your peril but I wouldn't be."

The group of four turned their attention back to the track where the dogs, including Rainbow Warrior, had come on parade for the next race. Jamie had a tight hold of his charge who was wearing a black racing jacket with a white number four on its side. The six greyhounds were now behind the starting traps waiting for the starter to give the instruction for them to be loaded into their respective trap.

With the last dog safely in, the starter moved to the front of the traps. It was a final check to ensure all six greyhounds were facing in the right direction, Happy they were, he waved his yellow flag to indicate to the hare driver high up in the grandstand roof he was happy for the race to begin. Orla looked intently at the occupant of trap four. She noticed how still he was whilst the greyhound either side of him scratched at the bars on the front of the trap.

The noise from the mechanical hare intensified as its speed increased. Orla still focussed on Rainbow Warrior. She noticed his fawn head dip lower in his trap as the hare came past the traps and tripped the switch on the rail that released the expectant hounds from their temporary incarceration. It is a beautiful sight she thought, seeing a greyhound surge into his or her initial stride, pushing with their rear legs and grabbing the sand with their front paws, accelerating with their eyes fully focused on what they enjoyed chasing.

Archie as she now called him had timed his start to perfection and was poetry in motion as he passed the group with all four feet off the ground. He was at least two lengths clear of his nearest pursuer as he went around the first bend, his long perfect stride in the back straight saw him accelerate away from his toiling rivals who were just a blur as the fawn dog extended his advantage.

"Go on Archie, do it for Jamie" Orla roared and punched the air as he safely negotiated the final bend and the run to the winning line in splendid isolation.

Jamie was ecstatic as he collected the dog at the pick-up, bending down to give him a massive hug and whisper in his ear. He felt like he was floating on a cloud as he made his way back to the paddock where Orla met him and gave him a huge kiss on his lips. Apart from his mother he had never been kissed and went red with embarrassment.

"That was great wasn't it?" he said as they walked side by side back to the paddock.

"It was bloody fantastic and I am sorry for kissing you like that, just got caught up in the moment. It won't happen again" said Orla as she brought over a bowl of water for the dog.

"Not a problem" said Jamie with a smile, "not a problem at all."

Orla re-joined Richard down by the perimeter wall and his sullen demeanour wasn't going to dampen her mood. He was alone with no sign of Sam or Ken. "You could at least smile, Archie is potentially the best dog we have in the kennel and you look like a rat has crawled up your trousers. Get a grip will you?" she said.

"Sam didn't have a penny on it and it returned at 8-1" he said with a whisper, turning to lean his elbows on the white painted wall. "She reckons I should have known he'd win and she has put off a few of her clients from backing it as well."

"Well that's tough shit isn't it? Now make sure you cheer up before we go back in the van. Young Jamie is over the moon and I don't want you ruining it for him."

"You are a bloody genius Jamie, an absolute bloody genius" said Tommy who had been waiting with fingers crossed for his grandson to call.

"He was brilliant granddad. I am not sure how far he won by but he won really, really easily, at least six lengths I'd guess. How did you get on with your side of the plan?"

"All sorted. No idea of the figure won yet but it will be bigger next time so we need to stick with the original plan. Is that still ok with you?"

"No probs. Love to mum."

Three weeks later

The new pups had settled in well and having Jamie around had made the transition from Ireland to England that much smoother. It was unusual to kennel two dogs rather than a dog and a bitch together but Orla had agreed to it once Jamie had convinced her it had never been a problem back home.

Archie had reverted to type in his last two races and Jamie had heard a blazing row between Sam and Richard at the track the previous week after he had trailed in a well beaten fifth after missing the start.

The pups were due to have their second trial at the track tonight, both solos, and Archie was scheduled to race again. Given the atmosphere around the kennels he wasn't sure whether tonight's plan was a good idea but he changed his mind when his grandfather rang to say Sam was actually in Ireland for a couple days staying with Father Sean.

"If you are sure it is safe to go tonight then I will do my bit and you can sort your end. I will let you know how the pups get on. They went ok last week but should improve tonight" said Jamie as he let Robin off for a gallop up the straight whilst talking on the phone.

He had been caught by surprise when Ken had come up from behind unannounced. He smelt him before he had heard him. "Who's that?" he asked as the big black pup ran back down towards them. Jamie had to think quickly. As of yet none of them had been able to tell the dogs apart by sight only. "It's Maurice, due to have a trial tonight. Thought I'd try and tire him out a bit so he doesn't go too fast."

He now had a predicament. If Ken went back into the kennel block he would see that Maurice was tucked up in his kennel with Barry and he would want to know why he had lied about the dog he now had on a lead. He needed to get him away from the kennels so he could get Robin back into the caravan without him seeing. "Ken, I think Richard was looking for you earlier. I saw him wandering off to the bottom field about five minutes ago if you want to catch up with him."

"Oh right, cheers, better get down to him then."

The field in question was in the totally opposite direction of the kennels. He waited until Ken was out of sight before running back to the caravan, putting Robin inside and locked the door.

"Alright Jamie, you look a bit flustered. All ok?" asked Orla as she came up behind him.

Jamie was only eighteen but if anyone else caught him by surprise today he doubted he would see his next birthday. He was a bag of nerves.

Richard was relieved Sam was away in Ireland. She had called in the morning and he had again reiterated that Rainbow Warrior wasn't a betting proposition and hopefully that would be the end of it. He had considered taking the dog to another track for a trial to see if his starting problems were just confined to Stony Stratford but Orla had talked him out of it. Waste of time and effort she'd said. He took up his normal position on the perimeter wall and stubbed out his cigarette as Orla joined him as the dogs were entering the traps.

"Well, so what do you think of his chances?" he asked.

Orla shrugged her shoulders, indicating that she was as much in the dark about which Rainbow Warrior would turn up as he was. He would let us know in ten seconds she thought as the hare made its way around toward the traps. He flew out, and just as had been the case three weeks previously he made the opposition look decidedly inferior, whilst on paper they were far from it. His official winning margin of five lengths looked decidedly more. The dog was becoming an enigma.

Ken wandered down from the steps by the bookmakers towards where Orla and Richard were still stood. "Six to bloody one, Sam will go mad you do know that don't you? Twice he has won at a big price and she hasn't had a penny on."

"Shut up Ken will you. I'm running the kennels remember, not her and if you still want a job in the morning I suggest you get out of my space and start putting some of the dogs on the van. Now I have a trophy to go and pick up" said Richard as he made his way to the centre of the track with Orla where they would have their picture taken with Jamie and Rainbow Warrior.

Tommy was waiting anxiously for Jamie to call, the longer it took the less likely he thought Archie had won. He had arranged for the bets to be placed in the UK again and he imagined he stood to make a few quid if the feedback he had received was anything to go by.

Sam's mobile rang in her jacket pocket. "Yes Ken, what is it?"

Tommy looked across the table towards his guest who had arrived about an hour earlier with Sean. Whatever was being said to her down the phone had markedly changed her mood from a jovial one to one of anger. She was now stood up and stopped to look directly at Tommy.

"What price, did you say?"

She ended the call with a thank you and returned to her seat. "Archie just won again."

"Brilliant" said an excited Sean "what price and how much did you have on him?"

Tommy knew the answer to the second question before she had uttered another word. Her body language and facial expression did the speaking for her.

"He was 6-1 Sean and I didn't have a penny on. Did you Tommy?" she asked.

Tommy hadn't expected the dog to be that big a price but he had no reason to lie to her. It wasn't as if she would pay him back if he'd backed a loser was it. "As it happens Sam yes I did, had a couple hundred on him and the 6-1 is a very nice bonus as I thought he would be shorter. If anyone could get him to win it would be young Jamie. I was hoping he would have called by now as the pups were trialling tonight but I am sure he is busy still working and will give me a call later." Tommy sensed that Sam was far from happy that she was the only one who hadn't backed the dog and her demeanour worsened in the next five minutes when she received three text messages. She didn't reveal their contents but she brought her stay to a premature end and thanked Tommy and Aoife for the hospitality before following Sean out to the car.

"What was all that about?" Aoife asked her father "She was pretty damn rude."

"No idea but I wish Jamie would give me a call" he replied.

He finally called just after 10:30pm.

"He won" he said with excitement.

"Yes I know, I was getting worried I hadn't heard from you."

"Sorry. There was a trophy presentation for Archie's race and we had three more races to parade after. He ran really well and I understand he was 6-1 so we should see a nice sum coming our way. How did you know?"

"Sam got a call here at the house from someone called Ken. Put her in a right bad mood so keep your head down for a couple of days. I told her I had a bet on Archie but not how much. She didn't have a penny on apparently. How did the pups go?"

"They went alright, Maurice was a lot faster than Barry but the times weren't great. If I am honest I thought they would have gone a lot quicker given you'd have expected them to improve considerably on what they did last week. They will be having their last qualifying trial on Monday so we will take it from there. As long as they do a qualifying time they should be racing for the first time Saturday week."

"Well give Archie a big kiss from me and we'll talk next week."

"Will do, love to mum."

CHAPTER FIFTEEN

October / November

"Morning Sam, I didn't know you were over?" said Aoife as she pulled a barking Trixie away from the back door to allow her entry. The last time she had seen Sam was the night she had stormed out after receiving a call from England. Jamie had called the following week in tears after she had torn a strip off him at the track when one of the pups had been beaten on its debut. The more time she spent with this woman the less she liked her.

"Is Tommy around?" asked Sam.

"He is up the kennels, it's feeding time."

"Could you get him for me, I'd like a word?"

"No I can't. If you want him that urgently you can go and get him yourself, other than that you can call back later when he is finished" said Aoife in a tone that even surprised herself.

Shocked at the forcefulness of Aoife's response Sam turned on her heels and made off in the direction of the kennels. She could see Tommy in the distance; he had a greyhound in either hand leading them to the paddock nearest to the kennel block.

"Morning Tommy" she said as she came up behind him as he ensured the paddock gate was securely closed. "Oh hello Sam, I didn't know you were over. How are you?" he said whilst walking back into the feed room.

Sam got straight to the point. "Talk to me about these gambles you have been having Tommy. I had a meeting with the head of the GRB integrity team on Tuesday and he tells me that there have been a couple of right touches landed on Rainbow Warrior. Imagine my surprise when he told me, especially as I am the one who bought the dog from you and I haven't had a penny on him either time."

She studied his face for a reaction. Her unannounced visit had been deliberate to catch him off guard. The meeting with Phil Clarke from the GRB had been hastily arranged and he was promising to follow this through until he got answers. She would help where she could but not if it jeopardised her own current agenda that was reaping a nice tidy return. He didn't flicker; she would have to try harder.

"I am led to believe the bets are being placed all over the country and the only information I have been able to glean from some extensive digging is that the tip for the dog is coming from Ireland and only when it wins. Now from my perspective I am extremely disappointed. The disappointment is not that you have been having the bookmakers for a good few quid but the fact I have had to find this out from someone else. If you had included me in on the bets then maybe I could have helped out along the way as well as making a few quid for myself and a few friends and clients. Rather than having this conversation on the telephone I thought I'd come ask you in person to see whether my assumption that you are behind this is correct. So tell me I am wrong?"

Tommy had listened to every word she had said but had shown no emotion in acceptance or denial of her accusation. The fact she thought she could come into his home and lay down the law about what he did or didn't do in his eyes was taking the piss. He stood with his back to the sink with Sam directly opposite him waiting for a response. He could see that she was bubbling up inside and he had his grandson to think of as well. He'd tell her enough to get her off his back but not everything. He still had an ace up his sleeve and he would be playing that when it best suited him.

"Not exactly sure what you are accusing me of Sam as I have only ever told the two people who have backed Archie on my behalf when Jamie has told me he fancies it" Tommy replied.

None of what he had just said was untrue and she couldn't prove otherwise. He had only told two people and he had no control over who they told. He was only interested in getting his money on and who he did it with was none of her business. Granted he wasn't telling her the whole story but he wasn't going to give her everything. He was also telling the truth that he only ever bet Archie when Jamie said so.

"So you haven't been spreading the word to back the dog then?" asked Sam who didn't seem convinced. "So who have you told, I want to know?"

"Feck off Sam, I am not telling you that. Take my word for it or get out of my kennels!"

Sam was so used to getting her own way but in the last twenty minutes she had twice been rocked by people who had no qualms about standing up to her. It wasn't something she took kindly to and she reacted in the only way she knew how, with threats.

"You let me know the next time it is going to be gambled or I will make sure you don't get a price. I know where some of these bets are being placed, if they see any money for the dog they will contact me and I will make sure the price is shortened. The choice is yours. Include me or it will cost you. Do I make myself clear?" she said pointing a finger at Tommy

"Jesus woman, I don't know what world you are fecking living in. You seem to forget that young Jamie owns half of that dog and if I was so inclined I would tell him to pack his bags and bring the dog back with him tomorrow and there would be fuck all you could do about it. Now get off your high horse and I will let you know next time Jamie tells me the dog is well and we will pretend that we have not had this conversation. Now I have work to do. You know the way out" Tommy said and walked off down the corridor to get the next pair of dogs out that needed paddocking.

The pups had proved a major disappointment since qualifying to race two weeks ago. Jamie had fully expected them to improve on their final qualifying trial but both had been well beaten and the times they had recorded were not improving significantly either. None the less the Racing Manager had taken no chances with Maurice, aka Double Vision and graded him quite highly in the youngster's opinion.

Sam had a large bet on him the first night he had run much to Jamie and Orla's surprise and she had been in a foul mood when the young pup could only manage a very creditable third. She had torn into Jamie the following day. He filled the same position last week and tonight, he was hoping to break his duck at the third attempt.

Orla had noticed that there was a definite atmosphere in the air when Jamie and Sam had been in the same vicinity since and broached the subject with Jamie after kennelling that evening. Anyone who pissed Sam off was a friend of hers she had thought.

"So come on then, spill, what's the story between you and the wicked witch of the west then?" asked Orla as she planted a can of drink in front of him on the canteen table.

"She was over in Ireland at the start of the week and granddad told her that if she shouted at me again then he'd put me and Archie back on the next boat home. She has bitten off more than she can chew if she thinks she will get the better of him" he said as he opened his drink and raised it to his mouth.

Orla had assumed parading duties for Maurice for his race whilst Jamie led another runner from the kennel, a newcomer having its first race. Ken and Richard were stood up by the bookmakers as the greyhounds came on parade and watched to see what the prices were on offer for the pair.

"Sam has had a few quid on the pup" said Ken.

"Which one, we have got two in the race. Double Vision is 6-1 and the newcomer Docklands Dottie is 7-2 on her first start" replied Richard.

"Dottie, she left her money behind on the other one when it first ran remember a couple of weeks ago. She told me she thinks it is a good thing."

Richard thought it highly unlikely that Sam would have given that amount of detail to Ken who was becoming more of a nuisance by the day and his infatuation with everything his biggest owner did and said. Richard himself had told Sam he was disappointed with the newcomers last trial time but he had been with many of his dogs over the last couple of months and they had still won first time. He wasn't backing them and he was getting a few quid from her when they won so he was in a no lose situation.

At the current rate he reckoned he could pay off all his gambling debts in the next three or four months. Maybe then he wouldn't be as reliant upon her as she was becoming very tiresome with her moods when dogs were beaten. She had only yesterday called to say that she wanted himself and Orla to come as her guest to the Charity Ball at the end of the month. He had agreed but not yet told Orla.

The dogs were safely loaded into the traps and the two men took themselves down the steps from the bookmakers to the perimeter wall where they were joined by Sam who had just arrived. They exchanged quick hellos before focussing their full attention on the dogs coming out of the starting traps eighty yards to their left. Between them they didn't utter a single word in the next thirty seconds.

'and it's another win for the in-form Richard Quinn kennel as Trap three wins' announced the commentator.

Richard looked to his right and those stood around weren't smiling. Trap three had been Double Vision and he had won easily from the kennels other runner. Sam stormed off closely followed by Ken. Richard stood and shook his head in disbelief before making his way slowly to the paddock to help Orla and Jamie with the runner in the next race.

Although Jamie hadn't been the one to lead Maurice up on the night of his first victory he was delighted all the same. It hadn't been expected and he knew that his grandfather wouldn't have had any money on him. They'd had a long discussion at the start of the week about the second part of their plan and had decided to put its execution on hold as the pups were not performing as they'd hoped.

After tonight's run they may need to have another think about it.

"Stop fussing, I can't talk now, I will give you a call later" said Sam into her mobile as Ken walked towards her.

"Who was that?" he asked.

"A client" she said abruptly to indicate that it was none of his business "so what news do you have for me?"

Sam had found Ken a great ally, even more so in the last few weeks when she had been made to look a fool with the victories of Rainbow Warrior. If Richard wasn't going to be keeping her up to speed then she needed the information to come from someone else from within the kennel. He had also over the years helped her out on more delicate matters and he had been rewarded handsomely. He knew which side his bread was buttered.

Phil Clarke called her less than an hour after Double Vision's victory reading her the riot act as she was the named owner. There had been plenty of money for it but not the same volumes as had been placed on Rainbow Warrior when he'd won. She had been straight on the phone to Tommy in Ireland and he had denied being involved. Phil had told her the bulk of the bets had been placed in the Oxford area and that area only.

The call she had received earlier was from the Racing Manager Andy Whelan. He had also proved to be a willing ally but he was an ally who was getting itchy feet. It was not only her to whom Phil Clarke was giving a hard time. Any investigation that the GRB started would reflect badly on him and Clarke had a reputation for leaving no stone unturned. She had reassured him that he had nothing to worry about and that she had it in hand. The gambles on Rainbow Warrior however had resulted in some unwanted GRB attention as far as she was concerned.

It had been three weeks since Rainbow Warrior's last victory and he, along with a few others in the kennel had been hit by kennel sickness. It hadn't been bad enough to stop him from running but his performances had been well below his normal levels. He had even led on one occasion before being overtaken near the winning line. There had been no call from Tommy to advise a gamble was imminent until this morning and it was in two races time on tonight's card.

Andy had told her that the big firms had sent a representative to ensure the price on Rainbow Warrior wasn't too high. She had a word with the on track bookmakers and asked them to keep it as high as they could but they said it wouldn't be possible. There was no chance of them getting the 8-1 price that had been available in the morning.

Jamie was confident of victory as he loaded Archie into the traps. The kennel sickness had really knocked the stuffing out of his pride and joy and it had taken him a week longer than expected to come back to full health. He had shown signs of a revival on Sunday when he had given him a gallop and by Monday he was raring to go. He'd rung his grandfather on Tuesday to tell him everything was ready for Wednesday.

The opposition was very similar to those he had raced against the week before and with his improvement in health there was no reason he wouldn't leave them trailing behind he thought. He didn't disappoint. Archie flew from the traps and stormed to a facile victory of over ten lengths as his rivals bumped and crowded each other at the first bend. After tonight's performance it would be all systems go for his grandfather's master plan next week.

Sam looked on with a huge smile on her face as Jamie walked Rainbow Warrior back towards the paddock. Her mobile had been beeping non-stop for the last two minutes. She didn't need to read the text messages; they would be from some very happy clients who would have had some big bets on Rainbow Warrior on her say so. Over the last three months she had built up a reputation for tipping winners and she was being rewarded accordingly. She had a substantial bet of her own on the dog tonight but her return would just about cover what she had lost previously. Tommy Coyne would think twice about crossing her in the future she thought to herself.

The mobile rang in her pocket; she looked at the screen to see it was Andy Whelan again. She ignored it. She'd had a six month fling with the guy and it had served its purpose. He had become too clingy and his fussing was only going to bring attention to themselves if she didn't put an end to it as quickly as possible.

She knew he wouldn't take it well, she had been with plenty of needy men, she preferred it that way as she could manipulate them to suit her own needs and dump them without a care in the world. Andy had been different. He was the one who had given her the idea in the first place and she had given her body as payment in return. Whereas she had always come across as the one in control she had let Andy think he was the one calling the shots, by doing so he had got what he wanted.

He was a fool to himself though if he thought she didn't have a backup plan. Sam always had something up her sleeve in the event of an emergency.

She put the mobile back into her pocket and walked towards the bar.

No one got the better of Sam Hampshire, absolutely no one.

CHAPTER SIXTEEN

I didn't have the greatest night sleep, more out of frustration that there hadn't been any clues gained from watching the DVD's than anything else. I had spent another two hours on them after dropping Alice off in the hope that something would jump off the screen and say 'look here', the clue is here. Was it possible Phil was on a crusade to prove a point when there wasn't anything to be proven and we should just take our hats off to Richard Quinn and Company for beating the bookmaker's?

Phil was rarely wrong so I would keep on looking.

Alice hadn't called.

A shift in the office on Tuesday was probably what I needed after the last two days to concentrate the mind and things took a turn for the better when Barry Brown chased me up the stairs before entering my booth.

"Hi Joe, how do you fancy a bit of race track commentary this weekend? Kris is still struggling with his teeth and no one else can get to Crayford Saturday. All yours if you want it, just let me know after your shift today" he said.

"Cheers Browner, love to, really like Crayford and I know the General Manager quite well from a few years back. Think I still have his number somewhere. Shall I call him or will you do it?" I replied.

"You do it mate, might be a few sessions in it for you as Kris is going to be on the side lines for a while and his new missus isn't exactly enamoured about him working Saturday nights."

I called Stan the General Manager straight away. We exchanged pleasantries and we confirmed timings for Saturday night and what he expected me to do. The extra money would come in handy as would the experience I thought.

I gave my best ever session in the booth that afternoon.

I hadn't known what to expect on my return to the track at Stony Stratford, I had taken comfort from some of the kind words at the Ball the previous Sunday and used them as the motivational tool to get myself in the car for the short drive to the track. I was really nervous as I turned into the car park.

The first race wasn't due to start until 7:30pm but the trials before racing, which Phil wanted me to be there for to see Double Vision run would normally begin on the hour so I arrived in plenty of time.

I had never paid to get into the track but I did on this occasion.

It could have been no more than five minutes before word had got around that I was on the premises. The old guy on the turnstile would have made a great spotter for the Apache Indians, sending out smoke signals to the natives that an outsider had infiltrated the tribe. He had obviously forgotten I had once been their Chief. I smiled inwardly.

Having obtained a list of the greyhound's trialling before racing I took my place on the steps in front of the restaurant. I had brought my own stopwatch out of habit and waited for Double Vision who was the third dog due to trial over the standard 440 metre trip.

He was down to have a solo trial, a trial on his own.

It was Orla who took the dog from the racing kennels which were situated up a steep set of steps on the corner of the first bend. She didn't see me and I made no attempt to attract her attention. Whereas once I would have watched her every move with affection and desire, it was the strapping black dog she was leading to the starting traps rather than my former lover, with her brown hair tied up in a pony-tail with a red ribbon that I was keen to see.

'We all make mistakes in our life and have to live with the consequence*s*' had been her words. I doubted I would forget them.

Having safely been loaded into the traps, Double Vision visually looked to have trapped well and was accelerating as he passed me into the first and second bend which he negotiated with flowing ease at 30mph. He stretched out well between the second and fourth bend before tiring slightly in the final fifty metres.

I checked my stopwatch, 28.02, a lot slower than I had expected or appeared on the eye, but it had been a while since I hand timed a trial and maybe I pressed 'stop' too late or started it too early.

I waited for the steward in charge to announce the time over the public address system.

"Time for Double Vision 27.98."

I still had it, whatever 'it' was.

"Hello Mr Jackson, fancy seeing you here."

I turned to my left and was greeted by the smiling face of Foxy who was holding out his right hand in welcome, which I shook.

Foxy was a character of Stony Stratford dog track who over the years whilst I was Racing Manager had owned greyhounds with any number of trainers. He'd had some good dogs and some bad ones along the way but he had never once given me a moment's problem, unlike some owners.

He was a Turkish Arab whose descendants had settled in South Shields before slowly making their way down the East Coast. His real name was Makbule El-Mohammad and he owned a string of Electrical Supply shops which funded his love of greyhound racing. He was a big punter and a good one to boot and the nickname had come about due to his love of gold or orange corduroy trousers which he was wearing again tonight. Everyone knew Foxy and everyone referred to him as Foxy.

He had once tried his hand at racehorse ownership but said he preferred the spit and sawdust of the dogs to the pomp of Newmarket and Ascot.

"Hello Foxy. Good to see you" I said genuinely.

"Fancy a pint and a bit of warmth?" he said pointing towards the bar.

"Yeah why not, after you."

We turned to make our way towards the restaurant entrance and into the bar; the crowd was beginning to build but not sufficiently enough to stop us spotting the rotund figure of Paul Colley, flanked by two security guards, earpieces and all, making a beeline towards us.

This could be fun.

There were no hellos, no warm handshakes and definitely no smiles.

"You cannot be in here, leave immediately before I have security remove you forcibly" said a furious Colley.

The smoke signals had obviously reached the Chiefs tepee and he was after my scalp but fortunately the Cavalry arrived just in time.

"Do we have a problem?" boomed the distinctive voice of Phil Clarke.

Colley had been caught off guard; he hadn't seen Phil coming as he'd been totally focused on me.

"This man is barred from this track and every other track in the country as you well know for issues I will not discuss here" replied Colley as he composed himself.

Go on I thought, spill the beans, let's get it out in the open and move on.

"Total bollocks Paul" replied Phil "shall we take this to your office or would you rather I made you look a dickhead in public? You choose."

He chose the office.

I made my apologies to Foxy and said we would catch up later.

"If you are having a bet later have a few quid on Sand Dancer in the 9:24pm. He's mine and should go well" he said as we parted.

I thanked him and followed Colley and Clarke, flanked by the hired heavies.

The office where I had been fired hadn't changed in the slightest. A picture of the track was on the wall, the filing cabinet with a dent in the bottom draw of three filled the corner and the coffee stain on the floor hadn't been cleaned. The track may have new owners but they hadn't invested any money in the place that I could see. The track looked tired and in need of a major makeover but that wasn't my concern.

"Now look here........" started Colley.

"Shut up and sit down Paul" instructed Phil "and get rid of these two numb skulls whilst you are at it" pointing to the voiceless guys in black.

Phil had a great way with words.

Colley waved for them to leave but asked them to stay in contact by radio in case they were needed.

We all took a seat.

"Now listen here Phil, you can't come in here and tell me how to run my track. I will be having words with your boss in the morning. I'm not having it, you hear" said Colley trying to gain the upper-hand.

Phil was smiling, "Tell you what Paul, you feel free and whilst you are at it make sure you give your bosses a call and ask them to have their legal team on standby."

"What are you on about?"

You can't beat a bit of argument tennis for entertainment. I hadn't said a word since I had entered the room and I was starting to develop neck ache as they exchanged volleys across the desk.

Phil leaned forward on his chair and put his elbows on the desk, he had taken his tone down an octave to deliver the blow that knocked the wind out of his opponents sail, "Well Paul it is quite simple really. This guy" pointing at me "has served his two years that he should never have had to serve in the first place. But because of your gutless behaviour and complete lack of support he was hung out to dry. Now please bear in mind I could have done the same to you and this track when these gambles have been landed. I haven't and you still have a job. If you lose your BMS contract you will close, make no bones about it."

He paused. I smiled. That told him.

He hadn't finished though.

"However, if you wish to persecute him even further then I will recommend he takes his compromise agreement back to his solicitor and I will happily highlight the section that is most relevant and recommend he sues the pants off you. I will also with great pleasure sign another affidavit as a witness to your harassment here this evening. Shall I continue or is that enough for you to be getting on with?"

Paul said nothing and slumped back in his chair, fully chastised.

I walked out.

"Well that went well don't you think, fancy a pint?" said Phil as we made our way back down to the bar.

"You cut it bloody close, where the hell were you?"

He pointed to the corner of the restaurant where he had seen me arrive earlier.

"So what did you think of the trial?" he asked

"It was rubbish if the time is correct. There must be something wrong with him unless the track is running very slow. I know there will be plenty of salt in the sand to stop it from freezing because of this cold weather but Jim the Clerk of the Course knows what he is doing so it won't be any more than -30. He has clocked 27.98 today; if you take off the going allowance for the slow going he will have clocked 27.68. That is over 70 spots, where one spot is a hundredth of a second, slower than his last win. He must be carrying a slight injury to have run that slowly."

"I see the brother is running tonight as well as Rainbow Warrior" said Phil.

I had been a bit slack, I hadn't noticed the yet to win litter brother Seeing Double was running in the second race. He would need close scrutiny.

"The big firms are taking no chances tonight I notice, they have priced up Rainbow Warrior as 6-4 favourite in the Open Race. There are some good dogs in there Phil but he should win and it will put him in good shape for The Golden Lead Competition that starts next week."

Phil, ever the cautious one, looked around to see who may be listening.

"There has not been one bet on him tonight with the big three but plenty of money for the others at nice prices from the known faces. It is as if someone knows it isn't going to win. We have got everyone here tonight for this one dog. We have the stipendiary steward here who saw the dog come off the van. She oversaw his microchip check, his identity check and even locked the padlock on his kennel door. We have put a security guard on the door to make sure that no one goes near the kennel. We have kept the kennel either side of him empty.

Once he has run, win, lose or draw, we will take a sample from him and if he doesn't take a wee we will take a bloody sample. I had operations in Northern Ireland during the troubles that had less precision planning than this."

"Really, how about the exchanges, is there much activity to indicate that the dog is not going to win?"

"Too early for the exchanges, this race is only going out to the betting shops tonight. It is the big Sky Sport meeting's that will see the heavy hitters playing early."

"I bet Richard Quinn loves all this attention?"

"Don't get me started on that man, he is doing his nut. The wife told him to go and sit in the van and stop making a scene. He had the stipendiary steward in tears over something else. He doesn't seem to realise how serious this is."

It was Orla who led up Seeing Double, he was the splitting image of his brother that had trialled earlier, and the pair of them had been aptly named. It was impossible to tell the difference from this far away.

Unlike his brother however Seeing Double lacked the instant acceleration and pace to trouble the judge in the lowly graded race he was running in, finishing a well beaten fifth behind the well supported favourite, much to the delight of those around us in the restaurant. He would do well to win a race of any kind I thought.

Rainbow Warrior's race was the fifth on the card.

I wanted to watch this race from outside and left Phil, who was busily answering calls and texts from colleagues around the stadium, in the restaurant.

"What do you fancy then Foxy?" I asked as we stood in front of the bookmakers who were putting their prices on the board.

'Seven to four Rainbow Warrior' shouted one of the three

bookmakers in attendance.

Foxy was studying his mobile and looking at the prices that the online exchanges were offering for this race.

"Greedy bastards" he whispered.

"Why is that?"

"Rainbow Warrior is currently 3.85 on the exchanges which is the equivalent to 11-4 in normal betting terms and it is drifting like a barge and they are backing trap six Two Ton Tessa. They are only offering 7-4 here. Someone knows something and it is always the bloody same with this dog. It is a no bet race for me. I have done my homework on this one and I make Rainbow Warrior a clear favourite on times and ratings."

"You see those guys over there?" he said pointing to two men on mobile phones who were in deep individual conversations, "They are here from the big firms to keep the price on Rainbow Warrior down as low as possible as they have been hit three or four times in the last few weeks. They haven't had a bet here yet but are probably waiting for instructions."

I took a longer look at the men in question who were now facing me. Both had been guests of Phil's at the Ball, the one on the left had fancied his chances with Alice. He saw me, acknowledged me and carried on with his call.

The greyhounds came on parade; it wasn't Orla who paraded this time but a young kennel hand who was in charge of the black jacketed trap four runner. I checked the race card, I didn't need to, I knew the form of the greyhound off by heart but it was the first time I had noticed the owner's names; Fr S McGrath and Mr J J Mulcahy.

A greyhound owned by a Priest, how unusual.

The greyhounds were taken to the traps, there had been no bets of any note placed on Rainbow Warrior and his price remained at 7-4.

'The hare is on the move' boomed from the overhead loudspeaker.

The traps opened and Rainbow Warrior, like he had done on

previous occasions, was the slowest to start by two or three lengths.

'Six leads from three with two back in third' said the commentator as the dogs entered the first bend.

'They go down the back straight now and six still leads from three, there is trouble between two and five as four begins to make ground' he continued.

'Coming off the final bend six is still holding three but keep an eye out for the four who is still finishing. Four is still coming but the six will hold on to make all by a length. Six beats four with three back in third' and the microphone fell silent.

I looked at the greyhounds as they ran all the way around to the pick up where the kennel hands who had paraded them were waiting to collect them and bring them back to the paddock. Rainbow Warrior was the first to reach them.

I watched as the young kennel hand expertly put the lead on his charge in one flowing movement. He removed his racing muzzle and kissed the dog's head. He didn't look in the slightest bit disappointed that his dog had just been beaten, just happy to have him back safe and sound to race another day.

I went back to sit with Phil.

"Well that was some run, he would have won by half the track if he had trapped out" said Phil with a pint in hand.

"He certainly would have done. He is a serious dog Phil but probably better suited to a big galloping track like Hove. He could be a serious Derby contender if they keep him fit and cut out the trapping issues. He was very strong to the pick-up."

"Well the guys are up at the kennels waiting to do the sample now. We will put the hurry up on it with HFL who test the samples but I doubt anything will come of it."

"Ok."

"I have ordered you a pint of lager, be here in a minute."

"So did you obtain any information on Tommy Coyne for me?" I asked accepting my drink from the waitress.

"I did and I didn't" he replied

Phil put his pint down and pulled out two sheets of typed paper from his inside pocket.

"I'm not sure this will be much of a help but this came over by email this morning" handing me one piece of paper "and these are the dogs that have come over in the last 18 months" he said handing me the other.

I looked at the first sheet and it contained details of Tommy Coyne. He was 73 years of age and it gave his address as Leenane Village, County Galway. He had five dogs in training at Galway and was mainly a breeder who reared his pups on before selling them. He had no cautions against his name and his biggest training success was with Pippa's Angel reaching the Irish Oaks Final.

Pippa's Angel rang a bell. I checked the race card and she was the mother of the two black dogs Seeing Double and Double Vision.

The second sheet showed he had sold into the UK six dogs to four different trainers. Three had gone to Richard Quinn, the three on the card tonight and three to other trainers. The last of which had been about two months ago. That dog was now running in the Midlands at Monmore Green.

I put the pieces of paper down and looked across to Phil.

"Well that doesn't tell me a lot and I have never heard of the village, I assume it is close to Galway?" I said slightly frustrated.

"It is almost in Connemara matey, forty miles from Galway City. I looked it up on the internet and it is a really small village where they made a film with Richard Harris a few years ago called '*The Field*'. Not a lot goes on by the looks of things. Mainly mountain sheep farming and it attracts a few tourists during the summer. The salmon fishing close by is highly recommended."

Phil and the remainder of the GRB staff who had made the long journey to the track left after the seventh race but I stayed to finish my pint, I wanted to catch up with Foxy and see how his dog ran in the next.

We stood together in the betting ring.

Sand Dancer opened at 4-1 and Foxy was the first in with four creased fifty pound notes.

"Ticket 27, £800 to £200 down to Foxy" called the bookmaker to his clerk behind his betting pitch who was writing down each of the bets struck; indicating that should Sand Dancer win then Foxy would be collecting a thousand pounds.

I followed him with a mere twenty pounds but the price had shortened from 4-1 to 3-1. I stood to win eighty pounds.

The pair of us moved back to where we had met earlier by the restaurant. It gave us a great view of the greyhounds running from the traps at full pace into the first bend.

"If he traps he wins" said Foxy as he zipped up his black leather jacket and tucked in the scarf that was keeping him warm in the biting wind.

"What happens if doesn't trap then?" I asked as I turned to acknowledge his confident prediction.

He smiled back at me, "He still wins, but not by as far!"

We both laughed and both cheered two minutes later as Sand Dancer flew from the traps to win easily. I thanked Foxy for the tip and he said to stay in touch. I intended to.

I collected my winnings and made to go home when I bumped into the person I had always referred to as the village idiot.

"Why don't you just fuck off you aren't welcome here Jackson" sprayed Ken Kelly.

"Oh dear Ken, are we still a bit bitter and twisted? Tell me, did you ever get Orla into bed or did you get the message after the fifty rejections that she wasn't interested?" I said mocking him.

"What?" he grunted in reply.

"Go away Ken and play with the traffic or something slightly more dangerous. I have got your number and your time will come. We both know those photographs that stitched me up were phoney and one day I will find out who put you up to it as you haven't the brains you were born with to think it up."

"You know nothing mate and I have moved on to someone a lot classier than Orla. Got a few quid she has, looks after me she does. You are just a loser" he said before walking off.

I really had missed the place.

CHAPTER SEVENTEEN

I hadn't been to Kempton in over two weeks and it was nice to get back on the racecourse.

Hannah and Louise welcomed me with a warm smile as I came through the main entrance showing them my annual members badge as I passed. The crowds at Kempton for midweek twilight and evening meetings were often sparse which is probably why the staff could be so familiar with their clientele. They did a good job under the circumstances and I dreaded to think how many layers of clothes they were wearing as the temperature still hovered around zero.

I had studied the runners on tonight's eight race card for about three hours. I had a tendency to leave the two-year maiden races alone as most of the runners were having their first ever run so there was little or no form to go on. At this time of year trainers were keen to get at least one run into a horse that had missed the whole of the summer racing for one reason or another so I had spent much of the time in the morning studying form and watching videos and race replays of the horses in the four handicaps over a variety of distances.

The first two races on the card were of little interest to me, two well-bred two-year-olds owned by a Qatar oil magnate won impressively at short odds. I was watching the racing from the comfort of an Executive Box in the Clubhouse Stand as two horses flashed past the line together in the third race and the judge called for a photograph. I looked at my computer screen and the exchange prices that had briefly been suspended at the finish were live again after the photograph had been called. The betting suggested the fast finishing favourite had just got up to deny the game front running outsider. The camera angle always seems to favour the horse nearest to the grandstand and so it proved to be as much to the delight of the few punters in the crowd the favourite was announced the winner.

"Christ that was close" said Bill Hoskyns with whom I was sharing the box; "didn't think he was going to get there."

"Backed the winner then, must have been a nice price in running?" I said.

"I backed the favourite after he missed the start and his price drifted from 5-2 to 5-1 and I backed him again at 16-1 as they turned in as I thought the front one would stop. Made forty thousand on the race so very happy" he was puffing out his cheeks and looked mightily relieved.

"Well done Bill" I said whilst thinking at the same time what his mood would have been if the result had been different. With the amounts he was betting there really was a thin line between success and failure.

I decided to stretch my legs and made my way outside where the wind chill must have made the temperature well below zero now. I reached the parade ring where the first four finishers in the previous race were being led away by their respective handlers. A small group remained; I guessed they must be the winning owners who were just about to receive their prizes from the race sponsors.

A familiar face dressed in a dark long overcoat welcomed the winning owners onto the covered presentation platform with genuine applause. It was Sam Hampshire. I waited until she'd finished her sponsorship duties to say hello.

"Cold enough for you?" I asked her as she made her way up the steps from the parade ring towards the Owners and Trainers Bar that ran alongside it.

She appeared to do a double take before recognising me.

"Oh hi Joe, sorry I was miles away. How are you?" she said without actually stopping.

"Fancy a coffee or are you rushing off?" I asked out of politeness.

"Coffee would be good" she said with a smile and we made our way into the sparsely populated main food hall.

I purchased the drinks and brought them to the table. It was ideally positioned below a TV screen to watch the next race which was due off in ten minutes.

"This must be one of your rare visits?" I said jokingly referring back to our conversation at the ball.

She laughed as she put her steaming hot drink back down.

"Not out of choice, we are sponsoring the whole meeting so I am here to do the presentations. Thankfully it is only a six race card tonight so halfway there."

The conversation was interrupted on a couple of occasions as she answered calls from clients. I took the time to watch the replays of previous performances of horses running in the next race. The betting suggested it was a hard race to call.

"Give me two minutes Joe, just going out to have a bet on the favourite. That was the owner on the phone and he really fancies it" she said before quickly departing towards the betting ring.

"Brrrrrr, its cold out there" she said upon her return holding her betting ticket.

"I was at Stony Stratford last night, the Rainbow Warrior dog Richard trains ran a fantastic race considering he missed the start. Could be a serious dog if he learns to trap consistently?" I said changing the subject.

She paused before replying in a tone which suggested she'd rather I hadn't brought it up.

"He is proving costly to follow shall we say but you are right he is extremely fast. I thought you said you didn't go dog racing anymore?"

"Fancied a night out and met up with a few old friends. Strange about Andy disappearing don't you think?" I said as the last of the horses entered the stalls for the fourth race. We watched it together. Sam said very little until the horses entered the long home straight.

"Come on Poor Pete" I heard her mutter as the well-backed favourite, the horse she had backed, came with a surging run on the outside of the field.

"Come on Poor Pete" she now roared at the screen above us as the horses entered the closing stages. He looked sure to win until being overhauled by a fast finishing outsider in the final ten yards.

The betting ticket she was holding was crumbled up in her gloved hand and dropped to the floor. Without any emotion she rose from her chair and offered me her hand. "Well I'd better go, duty calls. Thank you for the coffee Joe."

I smiled in acknowledgement but waited until she was out of sight before picking up the discarded betting ticket. I was shocked to see she had just lost £250.

My mobile vibrated in my pocket, I pulled it out and the display indicated a withheld number.

"Hello" I said into the device.

No one spoke, I said hello twice more before the line went dead. It was the third such call this week.

The runners for the next race sporadically made their way into the parade ring. I was looking for one horse in particular that I would be backing in the forthcoming five furlong handicap. Fawlty Towers was the horse's name and he looked well, far better than he had three weeks earlier when he had tired quickly in the final furlong after setting a ferocious pace. I was hoping he would last out a bit longer this evening.

I made my way into the food hall and purchased a portion of chips and a couple of coffees to take back to the box. The horses had started to make their way to the start by the time I had settled myself in front of my computer for the race ahead. I placed my bet on Fawlty Towers and watched as one by one the horses were loaded into their respective starting stalls which were situated on the far side of the track directly opposite the main grandstand.

There were still three or four horses to go in when all hell broke loose at the start.

It was difficult to see with the naked eye what was going on and the big screen was no longer showing the horses in the stalls. I retrieved my high powered binoculars from my bag to get a better look but I was none the wiser as two big green sheets had been erected in front of the stalls. This was normally a sign that a horse had been injured and to give the horse and vet some privacy a screen would be put up to keep any activity out of the public gaze.

I turned my head to the left and noticed all the horses had been removed from the stalls and were now making their way back towards paddock. That was unusual.

I could make out the stalls handlers running to and from their jeeps on the inside of the racetrack and to my right a tractor was making its way towards the scene.

"Just going to go downstairs Bill to see what is going on" I said.

He waved a hand in acknowledgement.

I had just reached the paddock when I bumped into one of the working cameramen. We had a chat occasionally over a coffee so I quickly asked him if he knew what was going on.

"We've got a swimmer in the lake" he replied before rushing off.

I must have misheard him. Why would anyone want to swim in the lake on a night like tonight? I saw Hannah standing over by the main entrance, maybe she would know something.

"Hi Hannah, do you know what is going on?" I asked with a smile.

"There has been an accident at the start with one of the horses, it's not looking good and no one can get hold of Jim the Clerk of the Course, he slipped off early to miss the traffic. We are just hoping the fire brigade can get here in time."

Now I was completely confused, why would you need the fire brigade for an injured horse?

"Why do you need the fire brigade, is the horse stuck in the stalls?" I asked.

"No he isn't. He came out under the stalls and panicked"

I must have looked totally bewildered. She looked around to make sure no one was listening before adding "the horse panicked and jumped onto the ice and has fallen through into the lake, the horse is in the water and they can't get it out."

So that is what he meant by a swimmer.

I returned to the box to let Bill know what was going on and I had no sooner finished when an announcement was made over the

PA system advising that the remainder of the meeting would be abandoned. We packed up our belongings and went our separate ways. With a clear run I would be home in just over ninety minutes.

I thought about giving Alice a call but she had said she would call me so I knocked the idea on the head. In fairness I really needed an early night so I would be going straight to bed.

CHAPTER EIGHTEEN

I recognised the blue Honda Civic parked outside my flat and a double check of the number plate confirmed my initial view.

What the hell was she doing here?

I didn't have long to wait to find out. I had no sooner retrieved my computer bag from the back seat of the car and pressed the key fob twice to lock it when she came up behind me, her brown hair no longer tied up but flowing.

"You are a fucking bastard Joe Jackson; how the bloody hell could you do that to me?"

"Good evening to you too Orla" I replied with a smile "do what exactly?"

"Don't you bloody smile at me you bastard, I have had nothing but grief from Richard since Sunday evening and you turning up at the track last night didn't go unnoticed! You stay out of my life for two years and then you pop up twice in a week" she said with tears in her eyes.

I hadn't expected her here and I definitely hadn't expected the tears.

She asked me to stay out of her life or had she forgotten that very important detail.

"Come inside, I am not having this conversation out here for the world and his wife to hear and apart from that it is bloody freezing" I said pointing her in the direction of the flat.

We walked the short distance from where the cars were parked in silence. I was getting too old for surprises. I needed a clear head and I even found myself looking in every direction for a hidden photographer, after all, I had been stung once before.

I retrieved the house keys from my pocket and opened the front door, thankfully the timer on the central heating had kicked in and the main room was warm enough to have caused a thaw on the inside of the living room window as I noticed a small pool of water on the window sill as I pulled the curtains closed. I put my jacket on the back of the settee and checked the telephone for any messages. There was one, I would check it later.

"You want a tea or a coffee" I asked Orla who stood in the hall with her arms crossed and black marks around her eyes where her mascara had run.

She was still beautiful, panda eyes and all.

"I shouldn't be here. He will kill me" she said.

I couldn't help but think her beloved husband may well kill her but I was probably ahead of her in the pecking order of life terminations. She was right; she shouldn't be here but more importantly how did she know how to find me 'here' in the first place. Apart from Ella and her family I had told no one where I was living. Even SIS had my old address and Phil only a telephone number which was ex-directory.

"How did you find me?" I asked.

"I followed you home last night after you left the track. I saw you talking to 'our friend' Ken in the car park as I was loading up a dog in the van" she replied.

I hadn't noticed anyone following me home but in fairness I hadn't expected anyone to either.

"What in the van?" I asked.

"No, I was in the car. Richard came to the track after all the dogs had been kennelled in the car and I said I needed to do a bit of shopping so he drove the van home."

"Did you sleep with her?" she asked in a more controlled tone.

I ignored the question.

"I'll make some coffee and take your coat off if you are staying. If not the door is behind you but please pull it closed after yourself as it costs a fortune to heat this place" I said turning my back on her and walked into the small kitchen.

I didn't hear the front door open or close. I filled the kettle and flicked the switch.

Orla was the master of flicking switches, she used to turn me on and off as and when she wanted and like a light bulb I would light up every time she entered the room. Our six month relationship was all about her it seemed at the time, everything was geared around when she could and couldn't see me. Over the last two years I had realised I was just a pawn in a life game of chess, where every wrong move was ultimately punished.

Hindsight is a wonderful thing.

How we came to be together is as much a mystery now as it was then. She was the bubbly wife of a greyhound trainer, not yet 30, with shoulder length brown hair and green eyes and I was the track Racing Manager. I had employed them from their previous track about two years earlier. Richard was being touted as an upcoming trainer who could get the best out of any dog and he could, but his interpersonal skills were pretty non-existent. He wasn't the best communicator in the world but he left that side of the business to Orla.

I had not sought out Orla Quinn to have an affair. It could be argued however that she did and I had been a willing target.

When one of their dogs had shown massive improvement on its previous runs, I, as senior officiating steward had called for a kennel representative to come to the Racing Office over the PA system. I made my way down from the steward's box and Orla was waiting for me by the locked door.

"Have you called me in to slap my wrist or spank my bottom?" she had joked.

I laughed and opened the door and went through first, as I did so she put her hand on my right bum cheek and squeezed. I turned to look at her and she just smiled back.

"Nice arse" she said.

"Have you been drinking Orla, what you playing at?" I had said with surprise and a bit of annoyance that she might have been seen.

I stood with my back to my desk and what came next could not be found in any Racing Manager manual for possible stewards enquiries!

She moved closer towards me and pulled on the cord of the fleece jacket I was wearing, "Cut the crap Joe, I want you as much as you want me. All this flirting over the last six months is doing my head in so what I want to know is if you are all mouth and no action or whether I am wasting my time because believe you and me I am very ready, willing and more than bloody able" she had said moving her hand down to the front of my trousers, gently caressing my now semi-erect penis through the cloth.

She was taking a massive risk.

I was shocked but I hadn't pushed her away.

She had been right; I had wanted her for months but had not thought about doing anything about it. She was happily married as far as I was aware and so was I. Maybe I was far more naive than I had actually thought and hadn't realised the signals I was sending out. My antennas were definitely out of sync.

Without thinking about the possible consequences or even contemplating rejection I put my hands either side of her face and slowly pulled her towards me, I kissed her slowly at first and she responded and our tongues soon intertwined. It wasn't passionate but it was vigorous and it felt great. I slipped my hand under her top to caress her left breast which was ample whilst she unzipped my trousers with her right hand. She got down on her knees and her mouth took over from the good work that the hand had started and slowly and expertly brought me to a sexual climax I had never experienced before.

It was a moment I will never forget.

I had no idea if we were noisy nor did I care. I was hot and flustered and completely taken aback. I had not expected it, I had not sought it and I hadn't stopped it and had enjoyed it. Orla, stood up, realigned the bra that I had removed, smiling at me as she did so. I tidied myself up, tucked in my shirt and grabbed a cup of water from the dispenser in the corner of the room.

"You wanted to see me Joe?" she said in a serious voice and emotionless face.

We both burst out laughing.

The kettle boiling brought me back to reality.

I brought two coffee mugs through to the main room with a couple of chocolate biscuits and sat them down on the small table.

"I put one sugar in, hope that's ok?" I said raising the mug to my mouth.

She nodded. I noticed she had removed her jacket and had made herself comfortable on the settee with her boots removed and legs tucked up underneath her.

"Why are you here Orla?"

"I don't know."

"You come here shouting the odds and it was you remember who dumped me and cut all ties. You didn't come to the track from the day you dumped me to the day I was sacked. I don't hear from you for over two years. I wanted to know how you were, how you were coping and not once did you do the same. You even blocked my telephone number to incoming calls on your home number and mobile. The last time I heard from you was to tell me to come and see you and you didn't turn up. You bloody set me up and I have no idea why or what I did to deserve it."

She was crying. Were the tears genuine or an act, I didn't know anymore.

"It was the photographs Joe, they were so embarrassing."

I suppose from her perspective they probably were. I remembered the contents of the brown envelope I had taken off the floor of Paul Colley's office. The first showed us kissing passionately in the car in a secluded spot just outside of Luton; you could clearly make out both our faces.

The second showed her with her head in my groin and it didn't take a rocket scientist to work out she wasn't looking for a lost contact lens. The third and fourth were the most damning. They clearly showed us having sex on the back seat of my Mondeo, a small tattoo on her fully exposed right breast was on one and another tattoo on her lower back clearly proved it was her in control.

I had memorised those photographs, not in a sexual way but because I had looked at them about one hundred times wondering how we had not spotted the person taking them.

We had both been oblivious to the fact anyone else had been around the car, caught up in the moment, the danger of being caught had added to the thrill. We hadn't heard anything and we hadn't seen anyone but the time and date on the photographs in the bottom right hand corner tallied with one of our weekly meetings.

"I was in the photograph's as well you know, don't you think I found them embarrassing?" I replied.

"Jesus Joe, give it a rest. It wasn't your tits or images of me riding like a top class jockey my husband was going to pin up all around the track and post on the internet was it?" she said angrily.

I relaxed back into my chair with coffee in hand.

"The photographs were evidence enough that I was screwing around but Richard had got hold of my mobile phone records as well and seen how many times we had been in touch over the past six months. He wanted your blood and that bastard Ken didn't help either.

Richard didn't have a clue about us but that slime ball must have followed us one day as he knew about our secret meetings. He said he knew all about me and you and if I gave him a blowjob he wouldn't tell Richard. I told him to go fuck himself.

A couple of days later Richard turned up with those bloody photographs and copies of my mobile bill telling me I was to end it now or face the consequences. He was frightening, eyes bulging. You know what his temper is like. I had no bloody choice, I had to ring you and end it."

"So who took the photographs?" I asked

She shrugged her shoulders "No idea!"

"So why did you text me and ask me to come and see you the week after? One week you are telling me it's all over and you can't see me again, the next you say you want to see me. Why did you get Ken to turn up instead, could you not have warned me?"

She looked genuinely confused.

"I didn't."

"You bloody did, how else do you think those photographs were taken?"

"Joe, you don't get it. Richard had taken the phone off me the day I rang you to tell you it was over. Richard was with me when I made the call and took the mobile straight off me. He kept showing me the texts you were sending and all the missed calls. He was furious because you had made him look a fool and that scumbag Ken was egging him on. That's why we blocked the number eventually. I didn't text you, I didn't have the phone so how could I?" she said defiantly.

One of the final pieces in the two year puzzle had just been fitted.

The day I had been photographed with Ken had been the day I had received the text from Orla asking me to meet her in our normal meeting place as she needed to see me, the text had finished with *'Two kisses and don't text back as Richard around.'* It was how she would end a text if I wasn't to reply.

"So if you didn't text me, who did? Was it Richard?"

She didn't even need to think about it.

"It couldn't have been Richard if it was the following week as we went over to Ireland for a fortnight to buy some dogs. He didn't bring the phone with him as he made a point of leaving it at the kennels."

Was she lying to me to cover her own tracks?

Whoever had sent that text was the person who had set me up and Ken didn't have the brains to think of it himself and he couldn't have taken the photographs either.

I had been late because of traffic on the M1. Orla's Honda was already there when I pulled up. I got out of my car and went straight around to the passenger side and got in. Ken was sat where I had expected Orla to be.

"Alright Jackson, bet this is a surprise?" he said grinning, his balding head awash with grease and dirt. God he needed a wash I thought at the time.

I jumped out of the car and made my way back to my own.

"Oi Jackson, your lover asked me to give you these" he said waving a brown paper bag.

That was my biggest mistake as I should have known Orla had nothing of mine, we had been meticulous in ensuring that we left no clues. I took the bag from him and took out the contents. There were four bundles of fifty pound notes with yellow bands around them, the yellow band indicating that each bundle contained two thousand five hundred pounds.

"What the fuck are you on Ken this isn't mine?" I said angrily and gave it back to him.

It was a ten second interaction which had convinced my bosses I had been on the take.

So who had taken the photograph?

"You didn't answer my question earlier Joe?" said Orla interrupting me from my thoughts.

"Orla, it doesn't matter if I did or I didn't. You made your choice and if I am quoting you correctly from Sunday you actually said we had been a mistake and you have had to live with the consequences of that mistake. So please forgive me if I decide to keep my private life private. I didn't think it was a mistake at the time and for the last two years I have been trying to figure out what I could have done to make things work. You however on Sunday made it pretty clear I was living in cloud cuckoo land."

For the first time I was getting angry, it was about time I let out exactly how I felt.

"Don't get me wrong, I am glad to see that your life is on an upward curve and you are training plenty of good dogs and big winners but please do not expect me to welcome you back into my life with open arms. I would have done anything for you but as it happens I lost everything. I no longer sit in on a Tuesday night when the big meetings are on television hoping to get a small glimpse of you or check your Facebook page for little bits of information. Yes I did do it, how sad am I?"

It suddenly occurred to me I had never actually spent a night with Orla and woken up beside her the following morning unlike Alice last Monday.

Oh god what would Alice say if she was to walk in now?

Had my relationship with Orla only ever been about sex? Every time we met we had sex and it was always good as she was good. Whether it was in the car or at her house when Richard had been away Open Racing or on a night when she stayed at home and he had gone to the track and I made sure I had the night off. We had almost been caught once in my office whilst having sex on the desk. It was like one of those scenes you see in the movies when pens and pads are thrown all over the place in the heat of passion. We just couldn't keep our hands off each other. Fortunately my office had a self-locking door and could only be opened from the inside or with a key.

Nobody seemed to have a clue we were seeing each other or if they did they just said nothing.

In a nutshell I had made a huge mistake thinking with my groin and not my head and was I doing exactly the same thing again by inviting her in now for coffee. Was there a photographer outside the window I couldn't see? Was Orla aware I was actually looking into the gambles that were going on in her kennel?

I think my outburst shocked Orla and she made to leave.

"Yes Joe I did say it was a mistake and I have had to live with the consequences of our actions but the mistake was not seeing you, the mistake was not leaving Richard for you" she said bending down to pick up her boots and put them on, struggling to do so as she wiped more tears from her eyes.

Alice had been right when she said Orla was envious of me, seeing me enjoying myself with a beautiful woman on my arm. She was jealous enough to risk being caught coming here tonight. I'd been in her shoes when we'd broken up and thinking straight and applying common sense were two things that were not high on the agenda.

"So where is Richard this evening as I assume he doesn't know you are here?"

"He is at Hove and won't be back until after midnight, he has a runner in the last."

I remained in my seat as she struggled to put on her heavy overcoat.

"I have tried to call you for the last four days but every time you answered I didn't know what to say so I hung up"

"That was you with the withheld number?"

She nodded.

"I was told so many bad things about you Joe. Tales about the women you were sleeping with when you were with me, the back handers you were taking and that you were only with me for the pillow talk so you could back our runners. They showed me the pictures of you and Ken and it all made sense until............." she paused.

"Until what?" I urged

She sat down on the arm of the settee.

"Until I realised it wasn't the Joe I fell in love with and what they said didn't add up. We rarely talked about dogs when we were together and they said you were involved in many of the kennel gambles which gave their argument credence. When they mentioned gambles that had happened after we had split up I became suspicious so I spoke to Emma Goulding who you were supposedly seeing as well. She said it was all crap and you only had eyes for me. In her words you were all loved up" she said with a smile.

So much for us being discreet!

"I was" I said and my reply pleased her and she again relaxed.

"About six months ago Ken and Richard were having a big disagreement in the kennels and Ken let it slip that he had stitched you right up with some photographs and Richard should be thankful for what he had done for him. We had never discussed the photographs with anyone. Richard was so appalled by them that he made a point of burning them in front of me. To be honest Joe our marriage is a sham and always has been. I am convinced he is seeing Sam, the woman at the ball on Sunday, and to be honest I don't care. She is bringing in plenty of money and new owners and he is slowly paying off the debts he has incurred. He is leaving me alone in the bedroom and we are more business partners than husband and wife."

I always had Richard down as a shrewd punter but obviously not if he owed a few people.

"Have you been faithful or have you been looking elsewhere?" I asked out of curiosity given first-hand experience of her sexual appetite.

"I had a fling with one of the other trainers for about three months but it didn't last."

I hadn't expected her to be so honest. I had suspected she would but had preferred not to know.

"So are they still plotting gambles then?" I asked tentatively changing the subject, hoping she might let something slip whilst she was in the mood that might help me find Andy.

"Oh yeah, they were having it right off for months before Andy disappeared. That's why Richard is in such a bad mood at the moment, apart from bumping into you. He can't buy a bloody winner and the Racing Manager they have in at the moment is being really hard on us."

There are always two sides to a grading argument. Was the new guy being too hard or was Andy being too easy?

"How was he having it off then?"

She removed her jacket and as she sat back down I caught myself looking down her cleavage.

She smiled obviously aware of where I was looking.

"I'm not exactly sure but we'd been having a lot of first time out winners of late that Sam has been putting the money on for him in the betting shops. Not major amounts to cause a stir but enough to pay off a few people when they were all added up. We have almost got our head above water and then the winners started to dry up."

I would need to have another look at the DVD's in the morning to see if I could find anything. I was tempted to ask about the bigger plunges landed on Rainbow Warrior and Double Vision but I didn't want to make it look like I was digging, hopefully she would let something slip.

She did.

"Did you see all the bigwigs from the GRB last night at the track?" she asked.

I nodded.

"I had to send Richard back to the van before they took away his licence he was so animated; they are treating him like a criminal. The fawn dog we have, Rainbow Warrior, is the biggest freak of a dog I have ever known. Every time he wins he is gambled and Richard has never had a penny on him. He has told the stewards he could never back a dog that inconsistent from the boxes."

I nodded in agreement and from a gambling perspective it would be foolish to have a large bet on a dog who needed to lead to win. Somebody was foolish though and they were winning.

I decided to play a bit dumb.

"Is it the one owned by a priest? Never known a dog owned by a priest before."

"Yep that's the one. He came over with the young lad who is working for us and owns the other half. The lad reared him from a pup apparently and he is over here for a few years to learn the UK greyhound industry before going back to Ireland to take over his granddads kennels. I am his mentor, Sam set it up."

"Oh right, who is granddad then?" I enquired.

"Tommy Coyne. You have probably never heard of him."

Little did she know!

"Orla, you still haven't told me why you are here? Against my better judgment it is actually nice to see you, but why now, it is just opening old wounds?"

She looked uncomfortable for the first time since arriving at the flat.

"I really don't know. I needed to see you; I wanted to explain to you why I had to stay with Richard for the sake of the kids. He told me that as long as I ended it with you he wouldn't take it any further. When Phil Clarke came and saw me and asked me to speak on your behalf when you were sacked I couldn't do it. I believed the gossip; I believed the contents on the Ken Kelly photographs. It wasn't Richard who was behind your sacking I do know that but he wasn't disappointed either as you can appreciate.

I suppose I am here to say sorry Joe. I can't turn back the clock but I do not regret for one moment what we had. I just regret we got caught and I wasn't more careful. This maybe of absolutely no consolation but I did love you. It wasn't the intention at the start, it was just about sex and the danger but seeing you on Sunday made me realise how much I actually did and how much I missed you. I hadn't been in contact as I had no idea where you were or how to get hold of you and in fairness why would you want to hear from me."

"So how did you get my mobile number then?"

"I got it from Natalie-Jane. I told her you had enquired about a dog but I had left your number on the table at the Ball and did she happen to have one. I think she got it from reception as she needed to get hold of you as well about something."

Good old Natalie-Jane I thought.

For two years I had gone over in my head what I would do if the opportunity arose for me to be alone with Orla. Would I rip her clothes off or throw her out the door? I didn't want to do either.

I got up from my seat and picked up her coat and opened it up for her to slide her arms in.

"Orla, I think you should go now and I thank you for your apology."

She looked disappointed but didn't argue. I walked to the car with her and watched as she drove away. She offered up her cheek for a kiss but I shook her hand.

I had a gut feeling I would be seeing her again.

CHAPTER NINETEEN

The banging on the front door woke me from a deep sleep.

I reached out for the small alarm clock on the bedside table. The luminous figures showed 2:28am.

There was more knocking on the front door.

"Alright, alright, I'm coming" I shouted as I struggled with the belt on my night robe that had been hanging on the back of the door.

Who the bloody hell could be knocking on the door at half two in the morning. Jesus, maybe it is Richard come to do me in after Orla's visit. I had no peep hole on my solid front door or any glass either side to catch a glimpse of any possible attacker. The chain on the door had been broken before I had moved in so I would have to resort to good old voice communication.

"Who is it?" I shouted at the door.

"It's me, now open the bloody door its freezing."

It was Alice, but she wasn't alone.

I beckoned them both in and turned on the central heating dial that was situated close to the kitchen door. The flat was very cold and the heating timer wasn't due to kick in for another five hours. I asked the pair to take a seat whilst I put on some clothes.

When I came back into the room they were still standing.

"This is Detective Chief Inspector Baker of Surrey Police" Alice said introducing her companion who stood at well over six feet and looked to be in his early thirties.

He offered me his gloved hand which I shook.

"No wonder my father gets so infuriated with you, don't you answer your phone or listen to your messages?" Alice said sternly.

I instantly remembered that there was a message on the answering machine that I hadn't listen to. Orla's unexpected visit had thrown me off guard and I had gone straight to bed after she'd left.

I searched for my mobile which I had again put on silent whilst working at Kempton. I picked up the house phone and dialled the number to my mobile, it may not ring I thought but it will vibrate.

"What are you doing Joe?" asked Alice.

"Trying to find my mobile and you will need to be quiet as it will only vibrate" I replied.

The phone rang and rang before going to voice mail. There was no phone in the flat. Alice was beginning to look impatient and DCI Baker was moving from foot to foot.

"Give me two seconds."

I put on a pair of shoes and ran out to my car. The absent phone was on the passenger seat where I had left it. Orla's arrival really had thrown me.

I took the mobile off silent as I walked back to the flat; I had eight missed calls and three voice messages. Three of the calls were from Alice and four from Phil. I would check the messages later.

"Got it" I said to the pair who were still standing and looking rather annoyed.

"Sir, please take a seat" said DCI Baker.

I did as asked and the pair sat next to each other on the settee. Very cosy they looked.

"Joe, there is no easy way to tell you this but Andy Whelan has turned up dead tonight" Alice said in a well-rehearsed manner.

"Where, how?"

"There was an incident at Kempton Park yesterday evening involving a horse in the lake……"

"Yes I know I was there" I interrupted "but what has that got to do with Andy?"

"As I was saying, a horse fell through the ice at the track yesterday evening and it took two fire crews to retrieve him. The horse had become entangled in some debris under the surface which was hampering the rescue effort. A diver was sent in and discovered that the debris was actually a weighed down body.

Initial investigations at the scene have established that the body is that of the missing Andy Whelan who was reported missing five weeks ago by my father." Alice advised.

"How do you know it is Andy?" I asked.

"We recovered his wallet from his inside jacket pocket sir that contained his driving licence and some bank cards" interjected DCI Baker "we are pretty certain it's Mr Whelan but we would be grateful if you could assist us with a formal identification? I understand from my colleague DS Clarke that he, Mr Whelan, had no immediate family and that you worked with him for a number of years?"

I got up from my chair.

"I need a stiff drink" I said going into the kitchen and pouring myself a large whiskey. I came back with the near empty tumbler and looked at Alice.

"Does your father know?" I asked her.

She nodded.

"If the body that has been discovered this evening Joe is Andy's then DCI Baker and his team will be heading up the investigation. In our journey up here tonight I briefed him on the help that you have given to my father on another matter."

The pair rose from the settee and made to leave. He handed me his card and asked me to give him a call to arrange a convenient time for the formal identification in the morning. The post-mortem will be taking place as we speak he advised but it was probably best if I got a good night's sleep.

I was still in shock. Why would anyone want to murder Andy?

"Give me a couple of minutes" Alice said to her colleague as he went on ahead to the car "I want a quick word with Joe."

Alice came back into the flat and closed the door behind her.

"Hiya" I said with a feeble half-smile.

"Hiya back lover boy" she said with a huge smile that would warm up any room.

"How you been?"

"I'm good, been a long day and dealing with cases like this are never easy. I just wanted to check you are okay. Dad has asked me to arrange dinner for tonight for the three of us to get together. He wants to get to the bottom of these gambles still and now more than ever if it was Andy in the lake. He is convinced you are the key to unlocking what is going on and so am I. It cannot just be a coincidence.

If it is Andy that turned up last night, and I am almost certain it is, then I am no longer on the case. The Surrey guys will only be interested in how the body turned up in the lake and that is their priority. Dad and I have been convinced for a while now that Andy would turn up dead, he just didn't have the characteristics of someone who would take off without telling someone."

"Dinner sounds good" I said "I have a few things I want to look into on the DVD's tomorrow first but my whole day will be determined by when and where the identification is taking place and if DCI Baker has any further questions for me. You sort the venue and I will be there."

"I can do better than that, how about I pick you up and drop you back? I can stay over afterwards if you like and dad will be none the wiser" said Alice with a cheeky grin.

"I'd like that very much" I replied, bending down to kiss her.

"Ummm, god that feels good" she groaned. "Can you do me a favour though and make sure you leave the heating on, this place is bloody freezing?"

I laughed.

Alice was only a few steps from the car when I called her back.

"You do realise that Andy must have been in the lake since the day he went missing don't you?"

"What makes you think that" she said, slightly intrigued.

"I was at Kempton on the day that Andy sent a text to your dad; that was the Thursday. The reason I remember it so well is because I got all the way down to the track for the Friday afternoon meeting and it was called off. The lake had frozen overnight when temperatures dropped down to nine below zero in Sunbury. It was all over the Racing Post on the Saturday and on the news with the geese skating from one side of the lake to the other. The lake has been frozen ever since."

"Interesting, I will let DCI Baker know" she said as she got in the passenger side of the unmarked Police car.

"One other thing, you need to find out who drove his car to Holyhead if he was in the lake?"

"We will make a copper out of you yet" she said before the pair drove off.

I went back to bed.

CHAPTER TWENTY

I was able to get through to Detective Chief Inspector Baker at the first attempt when I called just after 10am, He sounded like he had been up half the night and in fairness he probably had. The news of the body in the lake was the main headline on all the news and sports channels. No names had been released and the paparazzi were desperate for any little snippet that would give them an exclusive over all of their rivals.

"Thanks for calling Joe, if you can come down here after 1pm I should be able to tell you where the identification will be taking place. I am surrounded by journalists and TV crews at the moment as you can imagine so I would be grateful as discussed earlier that you do not say anything to anyone."

I was watching the main news as we spoke and I could see him in the background on his mobile talking to me.

The General Manager at Kempton was being interviewed so I turned up the volume to hear what he had to say, in fairness there wasn't a lot he could say as he was probably in the dark like everyone else. He was keen however to inform everyone that the horse that had jumped into the lake was making a good recovery from his lengthy paddle and that he was confident that racing would continue as normal with the next race meeting scheduled for Monday afternoon.

The one man and his dog had made their way to the track and had slipped into camera shot; the dog wearing his unmistakable tweed jacket. Now that did make me smile.

I had an hour to kill, probably the wrong word to use under the circumstances before I would need to head off. No time like the present to have another look at those trial DVD's.

What exactly was I looking for?

Orla had said that they had been having a lot of first time out winners over the last three months. I had all the trial sessions on disk going back to July and I didn't want to look at all of them if it could be avoided.

Ideally I needed a complete list of all of Richard Quinn's dogs in training, he probably had about sixty. Once upon a time I would have known every single one of them and every detail about them but I was going to have to do this from scratch. It was going to mean an awful lot of internet searching and cross checking from one site to another.

There had to be an easier way.

There was but it wasn't an option. One call to Orla and she would be able to rattle off every dog in their care, kennel by kennel, tell me whether it was a dog or bitch and how old it was. All the information I would need was just one call away.

I needed a plan B and that plan was to call Phil. So I did.

He didn't answer when I called so I left a message and he called back within five minutes.

"Glad to see you got my message from last night" he said with a huge hint of sarcasm which I should have expected given the four missed calls and messages.

"Don't start Phil; I had a few distractions last night and an unexpected visitor which threw me a bit. I left my mobile in the car. It happens, sorry."

"Distraction eh, hope she was worth it mate, anyone I know, about time you got your leg over?"

I almost choked and pretended to have a coughing fit.

"Sorry about that Phil, bit of toast went down the wrong way. It was Orla Quinn as it happens and before you say anything it was nothing like that but I will explain another time. She did however let slip they were having a lot of first time out winners before Andy disappeared so I thought I would do some research as I have an hour to spare. She has no idea we are looking into this but she did say Richard is livid because he has never backed Rainbow Warrior and I actually believe her."

I waited for a response but none was forthcoming so I carried on.

"You said last week you had all the dogs in the kennel tested a few weeks back and they all came back clean with nothing untoward?"

"Yes I did and yes they did" he replied.

"Do you have by any chance a list off all the dogs tested as I have no idea what dogs he trains now? A list will save me hours if you have one" I said with my fingers tightly crossed.

"As it happens yes I do. I am at my desk now, what is your email address?"

I told him.

"Ok, email has been sent. I assume Alice mentioned to you about us all meeting for dinner this evening when she woke you from your beauty sleep this morning? That will teach you for not answering your phone" he said laughing.

"Yes she did."

She also mentioned a few other things such as what I would be getting for pudding and breakfast in the morning but Phil didn't need to know that.

"See you later then buddy and good luck with DCI Baker, he can be a right bastard by all accounts when he is tired" Phil said before hanging up.

Was there anything that Phil didn't know? Yes there was and I wasn't going to be the one to tell him. I just hoped the DCI had got some sleep before our meeting later.

I checked my email account and Phil's email was one of two emails I had received since last night, the other was from Orla. How did she get my email address?

I opened her email first. It wasn't very long but she continued to surprise with her methods of gaining my contact details.

Hi Joe, sorry for the surprise visit last night, it was lovely to see you. I wouldn't have blamed you for throwing me out but thankfully; you didn't. I got your email address from the

piece of paper you left by the computer printer when you were making coffee, sorry, I couldn't help it as I'm a nosey cow. I know you probably don't want to stay in touch but this is my email address if you do. Don't worry about Richard reading any replies as he hasn't mastered the art of turning on a computer yet lol
Yours O xx

I would let her stew.

Phil's email had all the details I needed and a little bit more besides. The sampling steward who had sent through the list had been very thorough and split the dogs in the kennel into three categories; racing dogs with the last race date, retired dogs with the date they were retired taken from the GRB database and those that had yet to race and were trialling only.

I printed off the list of racers; there were forty nine in total. Three of those had come over from Tommy Coyne and I knew all I needed to know about them so I crossed them off the list.

It took me just over forty five minutes to go through the list and Orla had not been kidding when she said they had been having lots of first time winners. In fact of the forty six names on my original working list, twenty five were dogs that had recently started their racing career at Stony Stratford in the previous four months. Of those twenty five, eighteen had won their first ever race, with three of the other seven having run in the same race as one of the other newcomer winners. The percentage of winners to runner's first time out was phenomenal.

I searched for my calculator in the desk draw to work out the exact figure. With runners in twenty two races he had trained eighteen winners for just over eighty per cent. That figure was unheard of at any track.

There was one other stat that was amazing, not one of them had been the favourite when winning.

I checked my watch; I had been sat in front of the computer for over an hour and a half and hadn't even looked at the DVD's yet. That would have to wait until I got back from London.

DCI Baker called as I was just passing the Staines turn off on the M25, the traffic was horrendous as it always was on Friday and I was doing plenty of cursing out loud as the lane dodgers cut me up more than once.

"Hi Joe, I am still at the track so if you come here I will drive us to the mortuary for the identification if that is alright with you?"

"Ok. I've just gone past junction thirteen" I said wishing he'd called two minutes earlier so I could have exited the biggest car park in the world.

I had to convince a Policeman on the gate that I did have good reason to want entry and pointed to DCI Baker who was stood by the side of his car waiting for my arrival. There were still television crews on site hoping to be the first to release news of any developments.

DCI Baker drove the short distance to the hospital where the body had been taken. He informed me that the Forensic Medical Examiner had confirmed life was extinct by the lake and that the post-mortem had taken place this morning. I tried to take in everything he was saying. He looked like he hadn't slept and the two day stubble was decidedly untidy. I was sure he had bigger things to worry about than having a shave.

We waited in the hospital reception until we were joined by a member of the mortuary staff who asked us to follow her. We didn't say a lot as we made our way along a maze of corridors and double doors. At a time like this there wasn't much that could be said.

"Thanks for doing this Joe" DCI Baker said as we stopped outside the mortuary and were asked to wait for a moment as the staff member went in alone. She returned almost immediately and held the door open for us to join her inside. I had seen plenty of films and television programmes with mortuary scenes and had wondered if it would be any different in reality. The answer was no.

The clinical smell hit the back of the nostrils immediately. There were a couple of stainless steel work tops to my left, a chair and a bin straight in front of us and a hospital trolley with a blue sheet on it to our right. With DCI Baker by my side we moved towards the trolley whilst the staff member made her way around it to be opposite us.

"Are you ready?" she asked.

I nodded and she slowly pulled away the blue sheet to reveal just a head, it was Andy's head. I looked to my right towards DCI Baker and nodded and then turned to my left and throw up in the bin.

The whole identification process had only taken moments but my recovery considerably longer. I was brought a cup of water and a few paper towels to clean myself up. I didn't envy people who had to do that job on a regular basis.

DCI Baker was just finishing a call when I met him outside; the cold air had never been more welcome than at that moment.

"Is it all you need from me as if so I'd like to get back and miss the traffic?" I asked.

"It is Joe. I have just called my superiors to confirm your positive identification of Mr Whelan and they will be holding a press conference this afternoon at 4pm. Until then I would be grateful if you could keep all this information to yourself and please call me Alex."

"How did he die Alex?"

"I can't tell you that yet but he had been in the water for some time. The information you gave to DS Clarke earlier this morning about the lake freezing was confirmed by the General Manager of the track and the Clerk of the Course when we interviewed them so we have at least established a date of death. Forensically there won't be a lot to go on I wouldn't have thought but it is safe to say we are looking at a murder enquiry rather than a suicide."

"Why couldn't it be suicide?"

"He had been weighed down to make sure he couldn't float back up. He couldn't have tied the weights to himself and made the knots so secure. Our job is to now establish how Mr Whelan ended up in the lake at Kempton Park and who put him there."

I wished him luck and made for home.

It was just gone four by the time I got to the flat, my stomach was telling me I was hungry but my mind kept bringing back visions of

Andy on the hospital trolley. The mind won the battle and the stomach would need to wait a few hours.

My mobile beeped twice in my pocket indicating I had a text message.

Pick you up at six lover boy x

I had two hours to go through the DVD's, tidy up and get a shave and a shower before Alice arrived.

I brought the laptop down to the small table and put the first of the DVD's into the machine and logged onto the Stony Stratford track website to access the trial results.

The first trial I was looking to find had been run on August 2nd. I found the relevant meeting on the DVD menu and then checked the result sheet to see what trial the first dog in question, Maverick Max, had been in. I pressed the fast forward button to number 22; it had contained three dogs and been run over 440 metres.

I watched the trial twice and there was nothing out of the ordinary. Maverick Max had been slow away, had a clear run throughout and finished last. I checked the trial result sheet and it confirmed he had finished eight lengths behind the trial winner. It was no disgrace to be beaten by dogs with plenty of track experience and on closer inspection of their respective results they were dogs of a much high calibre and ones he wasn't expected to beat.

I decided to find details on the dog's previous trial.

It had trialled the previous week in a solo. I found the trial on the DVD. I watched it three times and checked the result sheet. Maverick Max had clocked a time of 28.20.

No he bloody hadn't.

I dug out my stopwatch from the overcoat I had worn to the track on Wednesday evening, re-wound the disc to the start of the trial and pressed play. The traps opened and I started the stopwatch and watched Maverick Max as he ran just one circuit of the track. I pressed the stop button as the dog reached the finishing line. I looked at the time on the dial and did it all over again.

The dog who had supposedly clocked 28.20 had in fact clocked a much faster time of 27.90.

Andy had been a very naughty boy.

He had been cheating with the dog's trial times which meant when it came to grading he was putting a dog like Maverick Max, who was capable of recording times of 27.90 in with five other dogs who were incapable of going any faster than 28.15.

The art of grading is to ensure that the six dogs are of similar ability, the one constant in that process is timings. When a dog has its initial qualifying trials the Racing Manager needs to determine to the best of his ability the level of grade the greyhound should fit into. The bands of grade normally range from A1 for the fastest greyhounds to A9 for the slowest.

The time differential from one grade to another is normally ten to fifteen hundredths of a second. Other variables need to be factored in as well such as whether the dog had met any interference in his trial which may have affected his final recorded time. Another variable would be previous track experience and Irish track form if applicable. Richard Quinn and Kings Star being a case in point.

I went back to the initial trial I had looked at and timed that one as well.

Andy had given the right time for the winner but when I timed Maverick Max on his own he was again a lot quicker than the time officially recorded. No wonder the Quinn's were having so many first time out winners, they had been plotted up in races they couldn't fail to win.

I looked up the race form for the dog's race. Andy had put Maverick Max in a race two grades lower than he should have been in but he had been really clever with it.

On the recorded trial times Maverick Max had been put into an A7 graded race when in fact he should have been in an A5. The race Andy had graded Maverick Max in had consisted of one other dog making his race track debut whose last trial time was 28.11. Two of the dogs had won their most recent races in A8 and for this race had been upgraded to A7. They both had a best time of 28.12.

The final two dogs in the race had had their most recent runs in a higher grade of A6 but both were out of form and hadn't won for a while with the best time between them being 27.96 six weeks ago.

So on paper Maverick Max was the slowest dog in the race but the paper was full of lies

I looked up the race result and wasn't surprised to see that Maverick Max's winning time was 27.86 and he had won by three lengths and his starting price was 7-2 third favourite.

Surely somebody had spotted what was going on?

I spent the next hour looking at four more dogs on the DVD's. Now I knew what I was looking for the process had become so much easier and all four dog's trial times had been manipulated. They had a solo for their second trial and then been beaten by much better dogs in their final qualifying trial. They all had the same modus operandi and the recorded times were all wrong. No wonder Richard was struggling to get winners now, the dogs were now racing in the right grade against greyhounds of similar ability.

I had made a breakthrough and would tell Phil later over dinner but two questions began to nag at the back of my mind.

Why had Andy done it and why had no one else spotted it?

CHAPTER TWENTY ONE

Alice turned up ten minutes earlier than planned as I was in the process of getting dressed. She looked stunning with her blonde hair tied up and in a tight strapless black dress that showed off all her curves. It was just as well I had turned the heating on or she would have frozen to death.

"Didn't realise we were going formal, I will just go and put a suit on" I said whilst hurrying off to the bedroom to change out of my dark blue jumper.

"How did it go today?" Alice shouted from the living room.

"It wasn't pleasant" I said whilst walking back into the room tightening the knot on the purple tie I had put on.

"It does take a bit of getting used to, I threw up the first time I did it" said Alice who was now stood in front of me straightening my tie.

Detective Chief Inspector Baker had been telling tales out of school.

"That's better Joey boy, you do scrub up well" she said as she kissed me on the lips.

She drove a white Audi A3 sports back and she drove it at speed. We picked up Phil from the train station in Milton Keynes and then onto a little Italian restaurant I had heard of but never been to. The waiter knew Alice by sight and he beckoned us to our table, it was already busy and a hive of activity.

"Did you see the press conference this afternoon Joe?" asked Phil as he sipped on his glass of water whilst studying the wine menu.

I averted my gaze from the menu where the Fettuccine Alfredo looked delicious.

I had been so engrossed in going through the DVD's that I had forgotten about the press conference DCI Baker said would be taking place at 4pm.

"No I missed it, what did they say?" I asked as I put my menu down to give Phil my full attention.

"It was what they didn't say that is more important" Alice joined in.

"They confirmed the body that had been discovered in the lake was Andy's who had been missing for four weeks. Initial enquiries had established that he'd been in the lake since the day h'd gone missing. They were treating his death as murder and were seeking any information the public could provide in assisting them with their enquiries" said Phil.

"So what aren't they telling us then?" I said looking at Alice.

It must be a family characteristic as she looked all around to see if anyone was listening.

"He had been weighed down and death had been caused by two blows to the back of his head and in the view of the coroner he was dead before he was put in the lake and….." she paused as the waitress came to the table to take our order. I didn't bother to say I knew he had been weighed down.

I had settled for the Fettuccine Alfredo whilst Alice and Phil both chose Zitoni Toscanini. We ordered two bottles of white wine.

"You were saying Alice?"

"Oh yes, and whoever hit him was taller than him as the blows according to the coroner's report had come from above. He had no defence wounds so he wasn't expecting it.

Phil looked angry; he had already screwed up one napkin and was annoyingly tapping his side plate with a knife.

"What's on your mind Phil, spit it out?"

He paused as if looking for the right words. He had liked Andy, I had liked Andy and what I was about to tell him would almost certainly not improve his mood.

"I want to get to the bottom of these gambles; they have to be the reason Andy is dead. I asked him for help and he was reluctant at first but I am now convinced he had found something out and he would have told me. The Police aren't going to be interested in them and I suppose I shouldn't be but if we can get the answer to them maybe we will find who killed him."

It was a passionate statement but one I was about to blow a massive hole in.

"Phil, do you remember those gambles at Bristol about fifteen years ago involving that gang from Cardiff that ended up with four or five of them being locked up for money laundering, GBH and intimidation?" I asked.

"Vaguely, before my time, but I did hear about it. What about it?" he replied.

"It was a really clever scheme that went on for months. One of the guys had a contact in Ireland and he was bringing a dog a month over to the UK. The dog would have its three qualifying trials and then scoot up in his first race. It would be backed all over the country. The dog would then be put up for sale on the basis it was a potential star and would be sold for a massive profit."

The waitress arrived with our meals and I asked if I should continue now or wait until we had eaten.

"Please go on" said Alice settling her napkin in the top of her dress.

"Well, it was all going fine until they sold one of the dogs to an owner who wanted his money back and then another to a guy who had a few heavies of his own!"

"Now I remember, wasn't the Racing Manager cheating with the trial times?" said Phil.

"Yes, but it was slightly more complex than that" I said before consuming a mouthful of delicious pasta.

"It was complex in that the dog that came from Ireland had no form but had recorded really fast unofficial trials and had been running unofficial races on the flapping tracks in the West Country. When they started trialling at Bristol the Racing Manager had recorded times a lot slower than the dog had done. In his first race he came out and won by ten lengths at odds on 4-5. He was backed all around the country as I said. They won thousands.

It was the next part that eventually caught them out. The Racing Manager who had cheated with the trial times then cheated with the winning race time, saying the dog had won in a time half a second quicker than it had. So when the dog was put up for a quick sale the following day at what some perceived a bargain price it sold within the day. It was far from a bargain and the gang made a fair few quid on its true value."

"So how were they found out?" asked a now intrigued Alice.

"Well Alice, when the new owner of the fourth dog who had paid thousands for it found out his dog wasn't as fast as he was led to believe he decided to go and ask for his money back."

"Did he get it?" she asked.

"No, he ended up eating hospital food through a straw for three months" said Phil as he poured himself another glass of wine "he was given a massive beating and dumped in a lay-by on the A38."

I nodded at Phil in agreement.

"The gang had a brilliant money laundering scam. They were using drug money to buy the dog and place the bets on it. That cleaned the money and they were also making a profit from the sale of the dog. Unfortunately they sold one of the dogs to a gang leader in Manchester who was a keen dog owner. When he realised he had been sold a dud like the other guy he sent his boys down to get his money back.

They got it eventually but only after they had broken both of the Racing Managers legs to get the information they needed. When the Racing Manager recovered, despite threats of violence to him and his family, he told the Police everything and the Cardiff crew were caught and convicted for the beating they gave the guy who ended up in hospital. They could never pin anything on the Manchester gang."

Phil looked at me and knew I was building up to something.

"So are you saying Andy was cheating with the trial times on Rainbow Warrior and Double Vision?"

I put my knife and fork down on my now empty plate, the food was delicious. I wiped around my mouth with my napkin and had some of the wine. I hadn't actually timed the trial times on those two. Job for tomorrow.

"Phil, since the start of August Richard Quinn has had eighteen first time out winners in twenty two races. So far I have been able to check five of them and all of them have had their trial times manipulated to such an extent the dogs have been plotted up to win. There have been plenty of little gambles going on under the radar but the big ones have taken all of your attention."

"Are they the gambles that Orla told you about last night?"

Alice looked straight at me; if looks could kill I would be six foot under. I hadn't told Alice Orla had come to the flat. Why I hadn't I didn't know, I hadn't done anything wrong but I was guessing I was going to have to do some severe grovelling to get the pudding she'd promised.

"So Orla came around did she, when was this?" said Alice who could do sarcasm as well as her father and without letting on she was annoyed.

I was feeling really uncomfortable but I wasn't going to lie if I could help it

"She was waiting for me when I came home from Kempton last night and rather than having a scene in the street I asked her into the flat. She stayed for an about an hour, had a coffee, told me a few things and then went home."

Alice wasn't going to drop it.

"So what did she want that she was waiting outside your flat? A cosy hour together to go over old times and rekindle old love?" she made it sound like she was teasing but her piercing eyes suggested otherwise.

Oh great, I had two women now who were jealous of each other and me in the middle.

"If you must know Alice she came around to apologise for not speaking up on my behalf when Phil was working on trying to save my job. She was feeling guilty and she now believes Ken Kelly had been responsible for me being framed. She was embarrassed by the photographs that had been taken and then she left."

"What photographs?"

I guess Phil hadn't told her about them and I definitely wasn't going to elaborate.

"Photographs of me taking a payment from a kennel hand of Richard Quinn" I said,

My response seemed to satisfy her but she looked annoyed and wouldn't look at me. Breakfast for one it was going to be then.

Phil brought the conversation back to Andy and I was thankful he had. "So are you saying that Andy may have been part of a gangland coup and the heavies have come and 'done him in'?"

I shrugged my shoulders, I had absolutely no idea. "I will get over to the track for the meeting next week and see if I can get anything from Foxy. He has his head well screwed on and his ear to the ground, he might be able to help me as he knows nearly everyone at the track".

"Maybe you should try and get close to Orla and see what else she knows" said Phil.

Alice looked up from her dessert menu and her facial expression suggested she was daring me to accept her father's suggestion.

"I don't think so Phil, you will have to find another way as I am not going there again."

We ordered desserts and another bottle of wine, I had had enough for the evening and with Alice driving Phil and his hollow legs had the bottle to himself. "So what is your next plan of attack then Dad? Now it is a murder case Surrey Police won't be telling me much, we have passed down our missing persons file and the information that came down from North Wales with regards his burnt out car."

"I'd forgotten about the car" said Phil. "We need to find out who drove the car?"

"Leave it with Surrey Dad; they know what they are doing. I mentioned it to DCI Baker in the car this morning after Joe reminded me and he will need to request the information from them. I suggested getting as much CCTV coverage as possible and passenger lists for any sailings that night just in case the driver got a ferry. He said he would get some of his team onto it but I would be surprised if they kept me in the loop."

"What do you know about Sam Hampshire Phil?" I asked.

"Not too much, she works for one of the exchanges as an on track manager. She has a few dogs with Richard Quinn. If we ever have any integrity queries with regards the greyhounds I normally go through her as they have no designated greyhound team. She is very good at her job and held in high regard amongst the other bookmakers. She manages most of the track bookmaker accounts, especially the big hitters. Why do you ask?"

"Orla mentioned that it's Sam who has been putting the bets on Richard's dogs for him and collecting as well."

The mention of Orla's name again made Alice scowl.

"It is possible I suppose and as long as she isn't betting on the exchange whilst working I doubt she could be accused of any wrong doing."

"Maybe not, but can you find out if Andy had any betting accounts online with any of the firms, including the exchanges without setting alarm bells ringing? I can't imagine Andy would have been taking such a risk without some financial gain. It wouldn't make sense would it? The area where his new flat is wouldn't be cheap! I couldn't have afforded it and I know what he would have been earning. I am the first to admit I didn't know much about his life outside of work but he never talked much about any punting exploits."

"Are you certain he was cheating with them?" Phil asked hoping that I was wrong.

"I am almost certain Phil; I will do two or three more in the morning as a final check before I go on to Crayford tomorrow night. It's my first ever live commentary stint you know, really nervous. I will let you know how I get on with the DVD's."

"Fancy some company tomorrow and some morale support?" asked Alice to my complete surprise.

"I'd be delighted, I can have a word with the General Manager and see if he can reserve you a table as I will be up in the commentary box for most of the evening. You sure you won't be bored?" I asked hoping she wouldn't be.

Phil settled the bill and we made our way back outside, the weather had started to turn for the better and small tufts of grass could now be spotted through the melting snow. There was still a chill in the air but it definitely wasn't as cold as it had been, with a bit of luck there would be a complete thaw in the coming days as predicted by the weather forecasters. Five weeks of no turf horse racing in the south of England was more than most regular punters could suffer.

Alice drove at a more sedate pace with Phil in the car, dropping him off at the station before heading back to my flat in Wolverton.

There was a definite atmosphere as we drove in silence.

We pulled up outside of the flat; I had convinced myself Alice wouldn't be coming in so made to get out of the car as soon as we had stopped. I wasn't going to push my luck. Alice reached out with her left hand and grabbed my right arm as I unclipped my seat belt.

"Do you still love her? I mean do you still love Orla?" she seemed flustered.

I turned and looked straight at her, the street light enabling me to see her face clearly.

"I did love her yes but I don't love her now. What we had was not what I thought it was or had hoped it was. So no, I do not love her but I won't hate her either. I hope that makes sense."

She unclipped her own seatbelt and opened the door.

"Well what you waiting for Joey boy, are you taking me to bed or what?"

How could I refuse!

CHAPTER TWENTY TWO

The love making had been slower than the Sunday before. Alice had a body that I wanted to explore every inch of and so I did, much to her delight. She had a small tattoo of a dolphin on her inner thigh that proved overly sensitive and forced her to tense uncontrollably as I brushed it first with my fingers and then my tongue. The pitch of her groans were all the indication I needed that she did not want me to stop, so I didn't.

She had reciprocated the pleasure and some and I was woken from a deep sleep with her gently messaging my manhood to a full erection.

"Ummm, morning big boy, I think he is ready to go again" she said as she raised herself up on her elbows, put her knees either side of me and slowly lowered herself onto me. It was a ride that Frankie Dettori would have been proud of.

Starting slowly, she increased the tempo at halfway. Her breasts swung first forward and then back before my eyes as she found the perfect rhythm with her willing mount, she strained every sinew in a dramatic climax. It had been a close run affair but she had come first, but only just. There had been no need for her to use the whip and I was thankful she had not decided on a flying dismount. She had fallen forward into my embrace safe in the knowledge that I wasn't letting go.

At the start of the week she had said sex was sex and she enjoyed it, at this moment in time she could enjoy it all she wanted as long as I was part of the package.

We slept through until just after 10am. I rose first and made some coffee and threw a couple of croissants in the oven for good measure. I had planned a full English, my speciality, but the days running order was already behind schedule but I wasn't complaining.

I brought the quickly prepared breakfast through to the room as Alice was sitting upright typing away on her mobile. Her tongue was sticking out slightly to one side as she concentrated on what she was doing.

"All ok?" I asked.

"Indeed, everything good. That was DCI Baker" she said pointing to the phone "I sent him a text last night to ask if I could be kept in the loop without causing too big a problem with his superiors as dad had reported Andy missing originally. He said that shouldn't be a problem as they needed as much help as they could get."

"That's good."

"Joe, I have been thinking about something dad said last night and don't bite my head off but I think he might have a point with regards Orla."

Oh here we go. I wondered what reaction I would have got if I had said I was thinking about Orla after a night of love making.

"What point?"

"Orla is obviously still smitten with you and if you touch a hair on her head I will chop your balls off" she said in a serious tone "but I think she might be able to help us in finding out if the gambles were linked to Andy's disappearance and murder. DCI Baker reckons the car fire isn't linked and it will be some joyrider who nicked the car and dumped it before getting on a ferry to Ireland. It happens all the time by all accounts and they don't have the resources to follow it. I did however request the passenger lists last week just in case from North Wales Police and I should have them in a couple of days."

I was sat on the edge of the bed and I could see that Alice, although not keen on me getting close to Orla, wanted to get a result and find Andy's murderer.

"Alice?" I reached out to hold her hand "I saw the look on your face last night when Phil said Orla had come around here. You were fuming, and now you want me get close to her. Are you sure? If I give her any type of come on she will have my trousers around my ankles before I can say 'where's your husband'."

We both laughed and we both knew it was probably true, me more than Alice.

"I was annoyed because you hadn't told me. I trust you Joe and if you trust yourself then it won't be an issue. Just don't sleep with her, please?"

I had no intention of sleeping with Orla but getting that across to Orla could prove difficult. I hadn't told her Orla had emailed me and it was probably best left that way. I would have to find a way of getting in contact with her in a way she would believe. I have only known Alice six days and already I was lying to her. Will I ever learn?

"I will go to the track on Monday for the main trial session and see if I can get her to call me. She normally works the trial sessions and Richard stays at the kennels. I can leave a message on the van under the windscreen wiper or something."

Alice thought it was a good idea and reached across to kiss me.

"Time for a shower; as a gentleman I will let you go first as I want to have a look at two more dogs on the DVD's to confirm what I uncovered yesterday. The towels are in the airing cupboard next to the bathroom and there is plenty of hot water if you want a bath. If you go for the bath option I will come and scrub your back like a good lover boy" I teased before leaving her to get up.

I could hear the bath running as I searched for the first dog on my list on the DVD. I was meticulous in that I cut no corners, following the same routine as I had done yesterday.

Poll Rating was the next on the list, a strapping black dog as it turned out who I had seen run at the track last Wednesday. He had run in the same race as Foxy's dog Sand Dancer which was an A2 graded race. Andy has started him off in an A8 only three months prior, no wonder it won its first race by six lengths.

True to form Andy had manipulated his last two trial times and plotted him up to win his first race.

He had done the same with Docklands Fred in his trials as well. That made it seven from seven dogs I had looked at and it was evidence enough for me to stop having to look at anymore.

I turned off the computer and joined Alice in the bathroom and scrubbed her back as promised. I could really get used to this.

Stan the General Manager welcomed me at the Crayford main entrance and he had reserved a table for Alice by the bar which wasn't too far away from the door I would go up through to do my commentating from, it meant I could grab a couple of minutes with Alice after every race.

I bought us a drink from the bar; we had an hour before the first race so I had a whisky to calm my nerves. I had just finished it when I caught sight of a familiar face, it was Foxy. I beckoned him over to our table.

"Hello mate" he said with his infectious smile "what brings you here and who is this beautiful young lady?" he said to Alice grabbing hold of her hand and kissing it.

How did I introduce Alice? Girlfriend, friend or lover?

Alice saved the day.

"Hi, I'm Alice, I am Joe's squeeze for the night and he has hired me at £250 and decided to bring me here. What a gentleman he is" she said with a huge smile.

We all laughed and Foxy took a seat as I went back to the bar and bought him a pint. I found the pair in deep conversation when I returned. The upper floor at the track was already beginning to fill with restaurant diners and owners who were sat with their respective trainers. All had come with hope and expectation of backing, owning or training one of the winners on tonight's card.

"Foxy has a runner on tonight's card Joe" said Alice "Sand Dancer in race eight, you saw it win at Stony Stratford on Wednesday apparently?"

I had and it had run well. The tight contours of the track at Crayford would suit it down to the ground. "Do you fancy it tonight then Foxy?" I asked.

"If he traps he will win but it is a hard race."

There was no time like the present to ask him the question I thought he would know the answer to and as neither of us had yet broached the subject of Andy's death, it gave me the ideal opportunity to bring it up now.

"Very sad news about Andy?" I said.

Foxy drank some of his lager, wiping the froth from his moustache.

"He was a bloody fool and he was going to get caught sooner or later but I didn't think he would end up dead."

I hadn't expected such a direct answer.

"How do you mean he was a fool?" I replied. Alice said nothing and just listened, her coppers instinct kicking straight in.

"Him and Quinny were having it right off and the bookies must have been in on it as well as a blind man could work out he was having too many winners. Tony 'the timer', we called him that because he timed every trial, told me about three months ago over a Chinese he thought there was something fishy going on. He was clocking totally different times to those being announced."

"So why didn't he do something about it?" I asked.

"He did!"

"Like what exactly?" said Alice, speaking for the first time.

"He backed them all; he had sixteen out of seventeen winners. He was going around all the betting shops in Oxford putting on a forty quid here there and everywhere. He and the wife have been on a cruise for the last six weeks all paid for by his gambles and he will be gutted when he gets back to find that his nice little earner is no more. Thing is, the bookies never took a bean on track for any of the dogs but I heard someone was having it right off apart from Tony with the high street bookmakers as they were backing to small stakes. Anything over fifty pounds in a betting shop on a dog race at Stony Stratford would set alarm bells ringing so they must have been putting less than that on each time. If the grapevine is to be believed they were putting on all over the country from Perth down to Folkestone and from deepest Cornwall to Yarmouth."

That tallied with what Orla had said.

"So who has been putting the money on then?" I asked more in hope than expectation.

"No idea mate. Andy wasn't a punter! He had no interest in punting but the whisper on the street was that he was seeing some bird who was pulling all the strings. He was receiving payment in kind if you know what I mean. Andy wasn't exactly a charmer mate was he and with his gammy leg and sullen personality there had to be another reason he was getting his leg over."

"Do you know who she was?"

"Not a clue, I was the last to know about you and Mrs Quinn mate, you were given the nickname of Lloyd amongst the boys in the ring so I don't get involved in any of this alleged pillow talk" he said and winked.

"Why Lloyd?" asked Alice.

"Because he was a dark horse. You know as in the bank advert?" he said with a smile "none of us had a clue he was playing away from home."

He looked across and mouthed a 'sorry mate'.

They both laughed as I made my apologies as I had work to do. They wished me luck.

The commentary box at Crayford wasn't a commentary box. It was small area at the far end of the racing office situated between two three tiered filing cabinets. I had two options to view the racing. I could do it from a TV monitor that had seen better days or lean out of a window no bigger than a porthole on a ship. I bet Tony 'the timer' wasn't facing such cramped conditions on his cruise ship.

The Racing Manager welcomed me and went through what he needed me to do. He had a reputation for being one of the best in the business at one of the busiest tracks in the country. I had met him once or twice in the past at racing manager conferences set up the by GRB. He had a good team around him and the working atmosphere was a jovial one.

Having welcomed the crowd over the PA system and advised them that there were no non-runners I cleared my throat to announce the runners for the first race.

'Here are the runners, owners, trainers and weights for the first

race on this evening's card, an A7 contest to be run over the standard three hundred and eighty metre trip.'

I flicked the micro-phone to off as I waited for the trap one runner to be brought to the podium to be introduced to the crowd. Once in the correct position I turned on the microphone again.

'In trap one wearing the red jacket is Mr Bannon, owned by Miss D L Hodges, trained by Jean Hodges, tonight's weight is thirty point eight kilo's'

I followed the same format for the next five dogs.

With one minute to go before the start of the race the six greyhounds and their respective handlers made their way behind the traps which were to my immediate left. Looking out of my porthole I could see the last greyhound entering the traps. I was nervous and kept telling myself just say what you see, nothing fancy. Just call what you see in front of you.

'Joanne's Pride in trap six is the last one to be safely locked away. The starter is checking them over, she waves her flag and the hare is on the move.'

You can do this Joe.

'Here comes the hare and they're off. Three traps smartly from four and six shows good pace on the outer as they go into the first bend. There is trouble in behind as one and two bump and three and four kick four lengths clear of six, two, one and the badly crowded five who tails the field.'

I shifted my body position to get a better view.

'As they come into the penultimate turn three still leads four but six is flying behind them and is only a length adrift, the rest can't win. They turn for home and four has his head in front but three is battling back, it's on the nod, that's close.'

I turned off the microphone and the Racing Manager took over by announcing over the tannoy that there would be a photograph to determine the winner.

I had really enjoyed it.

I stepped from around the filing cabinets to be greeted by four smiling faces giving me a small round of applause.

"You sure you haven't done this before Joe; that was perfect?"

said the Racing Manager just before announcing that trap three had prevailed by the minimum distance of a short-head in the photograph.

What a buzz I felt and I wanted more of it.

I only managed to pop down to see Alice on four occasions throughout the night, Foxy was doing a wonderful job of keeping her entertained and she obviously hadn't told him she was a Detective Constable. I'd had to sleep with her to find that out!

Sand Dancer had finished a gallant second after failing to lead. I doubted Foxy would be too disheartened as Crayford wasn't the easiest track to run at if you hadn't had a trial there before. Stan the General Manager came to see me after the ninth race to ask if I fancied a regular Saturday shift. Kris had become unreliable and the Racing Manager was pleased with the work I had done tonight.

It had been a good night.

Alice was full of herself on the long drive back to Wolverton.

"Ok for me to stay at yours again tonight, I have had a couple of wines and probably safer if I drive back in the morning. Is that okay with you?"

"Absolutely, the flat will be cold mind you as I didn't set the timer."

"Idiot" she said in return but with a smile.

She had an interesting night with Foxy. He told her many tales of scandal and mystery that had occurred in the greyhound world at Stony Stratford. It was common knowledge apparently that Orla had cheated on Richard again with another trainer. Ken Kelly was constantly bad mouthing me and telling everyone who wanted to hear I wasn't as smart as I thought I was. In fairness he was probably right.

"He reckons Richard is having it off with the woman who was at the ball, you know the one with the big tits and bleached hair? Sam I think her name was. Anyway she seems to be calling the shots and bringing in the big dogs into the kennel. She owns the Double Vision dog you were looking into and the brother whose name escapes me."

"Seeing Double."

"Sorry?"

"Seeing Double is the name of the other dog related to Double Vision."

"Well I bet you didn't know she didn't have a penny on the night it won at 6-1? She was at the track that night and she went absolutely berserk with Richard and the young lad who paraded it as they had backed another one in the kennel. She went around all the bookmakers to ask who had backed it with them and according to Foxy no one had. The young lad was in tears and Orla had to take him home."

"So how did Foxy find out; did Tony 'the timer' tell him?"

"No, it was Billy the bookie" she said and burst out laughing.

We drove in silence for about twenty miles.

"If rumours are to be believed Andy was having his end away with a woman whose identity is unknown whilst Richard is knocking off his biggest owner behind Orla's back. The same said owner didn't have a penny on her dog which is being investigated by your father when it won. Also, Foxy reckons a few people were aware Andy was up to no good with his grading. Have I missed anything?" I asked.

"We found out Orla had a fling with a trainer which is now over and that Tony 'the timer' is going to be very upset when he gets back from his extended holiday." We both laughed.

"Oh, and there is one other thing" said Alice.

"What's that?"

"We found out you are a very good commentator and you have more friends in this sport than you actually realised. Now I am going to get some sleep, some bastard kept me up all last night and I need some kip" and with the jacket from the back seat turned into a makeshift pillow she closed her eyes and slept all the way home.

CHAPTER TWENTY THREE

Against my better judgement I sent Orla an email on Monday morning after Alice had gone home, she had popped out briefly on Sunday and picked up some clothes and returned at lunchtime. We had gone out for lunch and done the things most new couples did. I was assuming we were now a couple but hadn't actually raised the subject. I was going with the flow and seeing where the current took me.

The email to Orla had been brief.

Hi Orla, it was good to see you too albeit unexpectedly and I am happy to stay in touch if you want.

I had received a reply almost immediately.

Can I come around tonight O x

I replied that she could but not until 7pm.

Alice and Phil were putting me in an awful position, they both knew how I had felt about Orla and maybe this was a test but for me it was going to be purely a business arrangement. I may have to tell her a few home truths and that may not be ideal.

I dropped Alice a text to let her know that Orla was coming around tonight and she had replied about an hour later with a two word reply. *'Behave yourself x'*.

Phil called for a catch up; he had been busy this morning talking to the big bookmaking firm's integrity departments to establish if Andy had any betting accounts. He had drawn a blank on the first six and was waiting on two more to come back to him.

"How about the exchanges?" I asked.

"One of them is a no but I have turned up something interesting on the other, the one that Sam Hampshire works for" he said in a tone that suggested it was more than interesting.

"Go on, I am all ears?"

"There was a betting account at the address where Andy was living in Towcester that was registered in the name Andrea Whelan.........."

He waited for me to comment but I just listened.

"There was £25,250 in the account."

Again he paused.

"The office guys think it was a genuine typing mistake that wasn't picked up when the account was opened. The relevant paperwork he sent in to verify his identity was in his name. He has never placed a single bet on the account and all the deposits into the account had been cash deposits. There were no debit cards registered on the account for him to make withdrawals but he had made three cheque withdrawals totalling £5,000 over the last three months prior to his disappearance. None of them had been cashed."

"You have been a busy boy this morning" I said.

"I haven't finished yet. All the deposits were banked by one of the exchange reps on a weekly basis over a four month period and they varied from £500 to £2,000 in value."

"Have you spoken to Sam Hampshire, isn't it her area?" I asked.

"No, it's my next job, I have spoken to the head of integrity and he is all over this and is due to have a meeting with her tomorrow as she is in Ireland at the moment. It was one of her guys who banked the money."

"Do me a favour Phil and call him back and ask him to cancel the meeting and don't speak to her if you can help it. Something isn't sitting right with me. Foxy said something Saturday when I was at Crayford that has set a few alarm bells ringing, it isn't anything concrete but I am due to meet Orla tonight and if I can't get anything from her then you can speak with Sam. Just give me thirty six hours if you can" I was pleading.

"I will try but I can't promise anything. He does owe me a favour so I will have to call it in" he said before disconnecting.

Everyone at some time or another seems to have owed Phil a favour.

Orla arrived at dead on seven. I had checked the entries for tonight and seen that Richard had a couple of dogs entered up at Nottingham with one running in the last race on the card at 10:30pm.

She was dressed to impress, low cut top exposing plenty of cleavage, her hair tied up in a bun and a skirt. It would be a safe bet that she had no knickers on under there but maybe I was being a little unkind. She was caring a bottle of white wine. She leant forward and I moved slightly to her right and gave her a peck on the cheek.

She looked disappointed.

I took her coat from her and hung it on the hook by the front door, I had put a pizza in the oven and that would be ready in about twenty minutes.

"Hi Joe, something smells nice" was a good ice breaker to start.

"Just a pizza, thanks for the wine" I said taking it from her and leaving it on the coffee table.

This was going to be harder than I thought as she sat down opposite me; I instinctively looked between her legs as she sat down awkwardly on the settee. I would have lost the bet. I had prepared a speech about how I wanted this to pan out but I hadn't expected Orla to turn up looking so provocative.

"Orla, we are only going to talk tonight, we will have a pizza and a couple of glasses of wine but I am not going to sleep with you. You look stunning and under any other circumstances I would not resist you or want to but I am in a relationship now and I do not want to jeopardise that at all" it had come out better than I thought.

"I hadn't expected you to" a response which had caught me off guard.

"Good, very good in fact" I said slightly surprised.

We spent the next twenty minutes talking about how her day had been and some of the dogs in the kennel and what her plans were for Christmas which was less than three weeks away now. Christmas was one of the busiest times of the year in the kennels she had said and the normal routine was to be up at 4am on Christmas day and be finished by lunchtime for the kids to open their presents under the tree.

The timer on the oven pinged to signal the pizza was ready. I brought it through with two plates and opened the wine. So far so good!

"What do you know about Sam Hampshire Orla?" I said as I put the last crust back onto my plate.

Orla finished chewing, cleaned her hands on the tissues close by and then smiled at me.

Without a hint of anger she replied "I think she is screwing my husband for a start."

I hadn't expected her reply especially after meeting Sam at Kempton earlier in the week. I couldn't put her and Richard together at all. She seemed to be way out of his league.

"Do you have any proof or are you just guessing?"

"I have no proof but I haven't been looking for any either. She can't stand me, always putting me down and when Richard isn't around she has a little dig saying I am not good enough for him and he could do better. She wound me up so much one night I told her she should sleep with him if she thinks he is that wonderful. She went to slap me but thought better of it when she saw I had a leather dog lead in my hand. Can do a fair bit of damage with one of them I can tell you."

Maybe I needed to reassess my initial thoughts about Ms Hampshire.

"So how long has she been in the kennel then?"

Orla looked puzzled.

"Why the interest in that bit of strumpet, her hair has had so much bleach through it will fall out one day and those boobs of hers will have cost a few quid I can tell you. You can't beat the real thing" she said jokingly pushing her own forward.

I knew from first-hand experience that Orla's were her own and if I ever needed reminding I still had the photographic evidence tucked away in a box.

"I saw her at Kempton the other night and don't know much about her apart from she likes a bet."

"She likes a bet alright and she hates losing. She has been with us, let me think; must be close on about two and a half years now, just after we started seeing each other. To be honest I was more pre-occupied with you than taking much notice of any new owners. She was a friend of one of our current owners and bought a couple of graders with him. They weren't much good from memory but she has been with us ever since."

She was in full flow so I let her continue.

"Then she got lucky with that good staying dog that won the Summer Cup at Stony Stratford and got to the St Leger Final at Wimbledon about two years ago. She has brought a few of her bookmaking colleagues into the kennel in a mixture of syndicates and individual owners and they are buying good dogs which means Richard is out most nights of the week" she said winking at me, uncrossing her legs.

'Remember Joe Jackson, behave yourself.'

"Well that is all good news then isn't it? Good dogs give you a chance of winning good races and the prize money that goes with it. Has to be a win win situation?"

She sighed and nodded in agreement.

"The thing is, she is taking over the place, buying dogs in from Ireland, talking to the racing manager, or should I say was talking to the racing manager and the final straw was bringing the young kid over from Ireland" she said leaning forward to refill her glass.

"Is he no good then this kid and what is the deal there?"

"When Rainbow Warrior came into the kennel his Irish form made him look like a bloody superstar, the time he clocked around Galway at such a young age was brilliant. He came over before the young lad and was given a month to settle in. We couldn't get the dog to eat when he first arrived and he dropped loads of weight and condition. He only started coming back into his coat at the start of August after Jamie, that is the young lads' name, came over."

I remembered Rainbow Warrior's races from the Irish website, I am sure he wouldn't have been a cheap purchase.

"Well the deal Sam set up was for the dog to come here and for us to take young Jamie on as a type of apprentice under my wing. He has nothing to do with Richard and in doing so it didn't put

Ken's nose out of joint. Jamie owns half the dog and the village priest owns the other half."

"Is Ken still sniffing around you then?" I asked remembering his comments from last Wednesday.

"No thank god. He is all over Sam like the plague, right little lapdog he has turned into. Still a slime ball and I wouldn't trust him as far as I could throw him. I think he is working on Sam and a few other owners to help set him up in his own right. John Williams is packing up and looking to rent out his kennels. Ken reckons he's got first refusal."

I laughed. "He told me the other night he had moved up market."

"So how you doing with this young Jamie lad then, not corrupting him I hope?"

"He is doing alright, he is very good with the dogs and works hard, very shy though and I think girls would frighten him. Does his work, comes racing, comes in for his meals and then goes back to his caravan. I did embarrass the hell out of him one day though" she just about got that out before she burst out laughing. When she laughed a large dimple would appear on either cheek.

It took her a while to control herself; every time she tried she started laughing again. She managed to compose herself at the fourth attempt.

"We were racing at Swindon one night, think it was for the Produce Stakes and we stopped off at Chievely Services on the M4 on the way back and I sent Jamie into to get us a take-away. Unbeknown to him I had arranged to meet the guy I was seeing in the car park. I pulled the van up next to his and he got in the back for a quick fondle. Anyway Jamie came back quicker than anticipated as the food stores were closed. He couldn't see me in the driver's seat and saw the side door open and panicking he rushed round….."

She burst out laughing again and it took three attempts to finish what she started this time.

"He opened the side door to see me bent over a dog cage and the fella doing me from behind. He looked mortified the poor lad."

I burst out laughing, it was typical Orla.

"What did he do?"

"I should have invited him in as I was as horny as hell" she joked "but he just shut the door and said through the door 'pick me up from the petrol station missus when you're ready, I need some grub'."

I was still laughing. You'd have thought Orla would have learnt from being caught with me but she was obviously fearless, an adrenalin junkie who lived life on the edge. There was one thing I had never asked her when we were together and until just now it had never occurred to me.

"Had you had an affair with anyone else before me Orla?"

"A couple, one before I married Richard and one about six months after at the last track we were at. It was why we had to move, Richard couldn't cope with the subsequent gossip."

I really had been a bloody fool, I was just another notch on her battered bedpost and my bitter disappointment must have shown on my face as she tried to rescue the situation.

"I didn't love them though Joe, it was just sex. With you I felt for the first time that I was actually in love. I was kidding myself it would last but it didn't mean I didn't want it to" she looked genuinely upset but I wasn't falling for it.

Right on cue Alice called at just after eight to see how things were going. We had pre-arranged the call, more as a safety net for me rather than anything else. I was surprised however to learn that she had decided to park outside to catch any unexpected visitors with a telephoto lens lurking in the bushes.

Alice had already disconnected when I said into the phone "see you in about an hour darling."

"Is that her?" Orla's mood had changed instantly.

"If you mean Alice, yes it was. I am picking her up from the train station in an hour" another lie. I was becoming as good as Orla at this.

She made herself more comfortable on the settee; her glass of wine was now out of her reach so I got up and passed it her, she nodded in thanks.

"I am pleased for you Joe, I really am. You deserve to be happy and she is a pretty girl. Does she know I am here tonight?" she asked.

"She does."

There was an uncomfortable silence for about two minutes as we both sipped on our wine.

"So what did poor Jamie do about your situation at the services, did he say anything?"

"In fairness he has kept his lips sealed. The guy I was seeing ended it the following day and hasn't been able to look at Jamie since. It is quite funny."

I needed to get some more information out of her about Rainbow Warrior and Double Vision if I could. The more information I could get the less likely I would need to see her again but in fairness I was actually enjoying her company. I hadn't expected that to happen and she had already checked her watch once so I need to get a move on without being too obvious.

"I thought that Rainbow Warrior ran a serious race last week, was desperately unlucky. I see he is entered up on Wednesday night for the first round of the Golden Lead. How much is that worth to the winner now? It used to be £6,000 from memory."

"Still the same I think. He is a very fast dog Joe, his initial trial times at the track had us seriously thinking he was a Wimbledon Derby dog for next year but he has got serious problems coming out of the traps. Sam went for a right gamble first time out but he walked out of the traps and he does that more often than not. When he does trap h's the fastest dog at the track. If he can put three consistent runs together he could win the competition."

Orla could speak passionately and clearly about the dogs, she knew her stuff, it was just a shame about the baggage, which included me that she had acquired over the years. I was certain she could make it in her own right as a trainer. Whereas Richard would be lost without her to steady the ship, I was sure she didn't need him as much as she thought she did.

How I was going to bring Double Vision into the conversation was going to be a little trickier than Rainbow Warrior, so I decided on an outright lie.

"I was stood with Foxy on Wednesday evening when Double Vision trialled, he reckons he is a nice dog for the future but probably lame given the time he did" I asked and was sure Foxy wouldn't mind me using his name, I doubted Orla would be speaking to him anytime soon.

"He is another mystery dog, Sam owns the brother as well who is pretty average. I thought he must be lame as well but Richard checked him over the following day and he was fine. Just as well we have earmarks as we can't tell the difference between them. We had right fun and games the last time he won as his micro-chip had migrated through his body and the scanner couldn't find it anywhere."

Up until a few years ago the only way to identify a greyhound was from his earmarks that had been tattooed into the dog's ears about three months after birth. Irish bred dogs have earmarks in the left and right ear whilst UK bred dogs just have an ear mark in the right ear. The government brought in legislation that said all racing dogs had to be micro-chipped and this needed to be done before a greyhound could trial in this country.

It is a painless exercise that is carried out by the track vet who would inject a small chip into the base of the neck. A note of the micro-chip number is made and registered with the GRB and the National database.

The biggest problem with micro-chipping racing greyhounds is that they are constantly active and the chip every now and again would migrate around the body, it would normally turn up somewhere. On other occasions the chip has been faulty and just wouldn't register when scanned.

When a greyhound is brought in at kennelling on a race or trial day a member of the racing office, using a scanner about a foot long will scan the dog and then check his earmark. Once scanned, data will appear on a screen that will tell the official the name of the dog, its earmarks, who trains it, the race or trial it is due to race in that day and its last racing weight. When the greyhound is placed on the scales, as long as his or her weight is no heavier or lighter than one kilo compared to his last racing weight he will be allowed to run, the exception to this being if he or she is only trialling.

On the rare occasion that a chip does migrate the Racing Manager will revert back to the earmarks and body markings as a form of identification.

The dogs are also scanned before they race by the senior paddock steward before they leave the kennel area to go out on the track.

Over the years there have been hundreds of dog races that have seen the wrong dog run due to human error; the introduction of the micro-chipping has cut these occurrences massively

"So how did they let it run without the micro-chip?"

"Andy was in charge and he did it with the earmarks. The dog is pure black and has no distinctive markings so he only had the tattoos to go on."

"So has he been re-chipped now then?" I asked.

She paused as if something had triggered a long lost memory.

"Now there's a funny thing and one of the reason's Richard kicked off last Wednesday. I brought the dog in to be re-chipped as it hadn't run since it had won and the office said it needed to be done before it trialled. I thought they meant I could do it on the night but by all accounts they wanted me to bring it in separately. Anyway, it was all a fuss about nothing as when they scanned him the original chip came up on the scanner."

"That's unusual isn't it?" I said as I had never heard of that before.

"I thought so but that blonde tart of a stipendiary steward had a right flap on what with Richard ranting and swearing and all her bosses in attendance wanting to sample the fawn dog. As I understand it Andy should have completed a form and sent it onto the GRB to say the chip had migrated and sent them the new micro-chip details. They didn't put the chip in that night as the vet hadn't brought any with her. I understand it is up to the GRB to inform the administrators of the National database when a new chip is in place.

We are now back where we started with the original chip. It has been known to happen with faulty chips but it worked fine last week. The new guy they have in charge had no idea there had been a problem previously as Joan the senior paddock steward who retired two weeks ago hadn't told him. Joan and the new RM didn't get on. They thought I was talking through my arse so I let them get on with it."

There was something about the information Orla had just given me that was setting an alarm bell ringing in my head. Her demeanour suggested it was part and parcel of everyday life in the greyhound world. She had given the information freely and without any pressure which was normally a sign that she had nothing to hide.

"One other thing that is a bit strange about Jamie is that he brought a retired dog over with him, sleeps in the caravan with him and they go off for a walk and a gallop every day. I was talking to him about it the other day as it happens during trials. I asked him why he didn't put it in one of the kennels to give him a bit more room. Wasn't having any of it. Very protective he was."

"Did he say why?"

"In a roundabout way he did but he got a bit flustered. The pup had its tonsils out about five months ago and the operation was a bit of a disaster, scarred the wind pipe so makes it difficult to breathe when he is racing. They gave him unofficial schools but he was no good. His granddad wanted to send him out to be homed but Jamie nursed him back to health but insisted on bringing him over as a pet.

He doesn't half like a packet of jam doughnuts as well, seems to live on them and there isn't a pick on him either" she added.

We had been sat talking for almost two hours and it had been really enjoyable. It was obvious she was lonely and apart from the dogs and kids didn't have much of a social life. She had surprised me when she said she was going to make the best of a bad lot with Richard for the sake of the kids. Thankfully her mother was a more than willing babysitter which meant she could get away now and again, such as tonight.

I helped her up from the settee. She put her shoes back on whilst I fetched her coat from the hallway.

"Can we do this again sometime, I had a good evening?" she said.

"I can't see why not" a reply that came out unexpectedly easily.

She smiled.

"You are a good friend to me Joe, I won't go over what has already been said but I am truly sorry how things turned out" she said as she put her hand on my left cheek. I left it there.

I helped put her jacket on as she turned her back towards me.

"Do you think we will ever be close again?" she asked.

"Never say never Orla; anything is possible but now is not the time to discuss it or for you get your hopes up. I may see you at the track on Wednesday" I said leaning down to give her a peck on the cheek.

I didn't walk her to the car. I could just about make out Alice's Audi parked in the darkness to my left. Orla didn't turn around until she got to her car; she turned around and gave a small wave which I did in return.

I had already closed the door before she had driven off.

Alice waited five minutes before coming to the door.

"Hello Joey boy, I assume you behaved yourself?" she teased before putting her arms around me to kiss me.

"Yes I did, I was the perfect gentleman" I said with a smile.

"Glad to hear it, so what did you find out?"

"Surprisingly more than I had expected to. Can you take two or three days off, say Thursday to Saturday this week?"

I had automatically assumed she would want to come with me, was it a mistake?

"I should be able to, I am due lots of leave, why do you ask?"

"How is your Irish accent; we need to go to Ireland?"

"Why Ireland?"

"I need to go and see a man about a dog."

CHAPTER TWENTY FOUR

I had rung Phil late on Monday evening to tell him I was off to Ireland, I was hoping he would pick up the bill and he offered before I had even had the chance to ask. Alice listened on in the background. Orla had planted the seed in my head and I needed to go and do some digging at the root of where this all started.

It had taken me twenty minutes to convince Alice we needed to go and once I had convinced her I then had to repeat myself with Phil, he was dubious to start with but when I said I intended to ask Alice to come with me to make sure I did not step out of line he seemed to warm to the idea.

"It's a bit far-fetched mate but if you think it is worth a trip to the back end of nowhere then go for it" Phil had said.

Alice had already started to look up flights on the internet. I was working tomorrow in the studio and it was too late to cancel and I wanted to be at the track on Wednesday night to see if I could get any more information out of Foxy.

Phil rang back about ten minutes after we had finished our last call to say that the meeting his contact at the betting exchange had arranged with Sam had been put off for a week. That gave me some extra breathing space. Especially if I was barking up the wrong tree!

I had already given my word to Stan that I would cover Saturday night at Crayford so we needed to be back in the UK no later than 4pm on Saturday.

Alice had rung her boss to confirm a couple of days leave whilst I tried to find Leenane Village on the internet. I found it eventually.

"Ok, so it looks like the best place we can fly into is Knock in County Mayo. There is a flight that leaves at 10am on Thursday from Stansted that gets us in at 11:30am. They have a car hire facility and we will need one of them. According to the route planner it will take us just under two hours. The flight back on Saturday leaves at 2:15pm and gets us in just before 4pm" said Alice reading from her Police notebook that had become very handy.

"So where do we find this guy in Leenane then, according to the details your dad gave me his address is Leenane Village, County Galway and that is it?"

"We will have to ask when we arrive, there can't be many Coyne's around, never heard of the name before."

With the tickets and car hire booked, it was agreed that I would pick Alice up at just after six on Thursday morning. She gave me a gentle kiss goodnight before heading for home; she was on the early shift tomorrow and needed her beauty sleep.

The bleak weather that had brought the country to a virtual standstill at times over the previous six weeks had abated and life and transport had returned to normal. My return to the track was a lot easier than the week before. I pulled into the car park just after 7:15pm, it was busier than the previous week, the good quality racing on show tonight had a tendency to see punters travel the extra few miles and with the weather distinctly milder, a few office parties had also swelled the numbers in attendance.

I paid to get in. I thought about something sarcastic to say to the snitch on the turnstile booth after his exploits last week but thought better of it. I was here tonight for two reasons and two reasons only. The first was to see Rainbow Warrior run and the second to see Foxy.

With Rainbow Warrior not due to race until the fifth race it was a fair assumption that I would be seeing Foxy first. I found him by the bar talking to his trainer, I stood back as they finished their conversation before moving in before anyone else did. He welcomed me with a drawn out 'Hellllloo maaaate, how are you? Impressive piece of commentating Saturday son, very good indeed."

I thanked him and beckoned for him to join me outside away from listening ears. I had been around Alice and Phil too long.

"What's up Joe? Why all the cloak and dagger stuff?"

"I need a favour but it is strictly between me and you, I know that I can trust you otherwise I wouldn't be asking but it has to remain between us."

"Sounds serious, you better spit it out."

I spent the next twenty minutes telling Foxy something I hadn't told Phil or Alice. If my plan went pear shaped the only person that could be implicated was me. Given Foxy's popularity and contacts I knew he could do what was required with minimum of notice and with little fuss.

He listened without interruption until I was finished.

"That is doable, when will you know if you need me to help?"

"Next Wednesday morning at the latest, I will need your mobile number though." He called out his number to me and I typed it into my phone and let it ring. The phone rang in his hand and I cancelled the call. "I have saved your number and mine will be on your phone now as a missed call."

I offered him my hand.

"Thanks for this mate, I owe you" I said with sincerity and left him to study the runners for the second race as our conversation had seen us miss the first.

I saw Orla in the distance as she stood at the top of steps by the paddock, she smiled but didn't wave. The young lad Jamie was working with her tonight which was hardly surprising as his dog was due to race later. Richard, Ken Kelly and Sam Hampshire were in deep conversation by the wall that separated the terracing from the sand of the race track. It was Ken who saw me first and gave me the finger and mouthed some expletive which thankfully I could ignore as I could not hear it. Richard just scowled and puffed on his cigarette whilst Sam turned around and decided to walk back up the terracing in my direction, she looked annoyed.

"Good evening Joe, what brings you back here? I understand from Ken that you are actually banned from the track" she said in a tone I took to be mocking.

Two can play at that game.

"There's the thing now Sam, good old Ken never was the sharpest tool in the box and I wouldn't believe anything he says. He has a tendency to exaggerate his own importance" I smiled.

"What has Ken got to do with anything, I asked you a straight question?"

"Yes you did and I gave you a straight answer. It is actually none of your business why I am here tonight but just for the record my ban as you so politely put it expired last week. As you have taken the time to come and see me I thought I'd ask how you were getting on with renting the John Williams kennels, I believe you are setting Ken up as a trainer?"

She looked over her shoulder towards dumb and dumber down by the wall. The scowl hadn't left her face by the time she turned back to face me.

"I don't know what you mean" she said with a grimace rather than the intended smile. She would never play poker.

"Well there you go then, my apologies. It was just I was told earlier this evening by a good source that you were financing his new venture and Ken was already looking for owners" I said knowing whatever chance Ken had of being set up on his own was now dead in the water.

Revenge is like Gazpacho soup. Best served cold.

"Well it is lovely to see you again Sam" I said and turned to walk away.

I got about a yard before I felt a pull on my right arm. This wasn't the same pleasant Sam I had met at Kempton the previous week. This was the Sam Orla had warned me about.

"I'm not finished talking to you" Sam said through gritted teeth "stay out of my business Joe if you know what is good for you. I do have influence you should know. I am very good friends with the head of the GRB and I am sure it wouldn't take much to have you banned again."

I reached across with my left hand and released her fingers from the grip on my arm and looked her straight in the eye.

"You have finished talking to me and if you touch me again you will be eating baby food for a month. You aren't the only one who can make threats Sam. The thing is I have nothing to lose by carrying them out. If you think I haven't worked out you had something to do with the photographs of me and Orla you must think I came across on the last ferry. What I haven't worked out yet is why, but I will, trust me, I will as Ken didn't do it on his own" I said looking for any type of reaction. I was angry, she had made me angry.

"You can't prove anything and Ken won't say anything, I am too important to him."

For the first time she looked completely out of control of the situation she now found herself in. I wasn't sure where my outburst had come from. She didn't deny the photographs and seemed to take pleasure from it, but her body language indicated she had no idea whether I was bluffing or deadly serious. Unlike Sam I could play poker; she may hold a pair of Queen's but was I holding a pair of aces or a pair of twos? Would she be brave enough to find out?

She didn't say another word and walked off back down the terracing towards the pair by the wall. I had missed the second race as well as the first but did back the winner of the third thanks to a tip from Foxy, making a nice profit of one hundred pounds. The greyhounds were just being loaded into the traps for the fourth race when the mobile went off in my pocket, it was a withheld number.

"Joe" said Orla down the line, she sounded extremely anxious.

"Hi, what's up?"

"Don't drive home, get Alice to pick you or get a taxi or something but Ken is after your blood and he is going to be waiting for you in the car park he is absolutely raging. Apparently you have really stirred up a hornets' nest with him and Sam. Just be careful, please?" she said and then rang off.

I had intended to get my revenge on Ken but I hadn't bargained on a beating in the car park if I could help it. I could leave the car here and get a taxi home but if Ken was in as bad a mood as Orla had indicated I would be returning to a burnt out shell or four slashed tyres at best the following morning.

I needed to find Foxy and ask for another favour because of a more immediate dilemma I now found myself in. There was no point me getting a taxi as Ken could just follow me and I didn't want him knowing where I lived. I couldn't go out in the car park alone. It was too dark and too busy; he could jump out from any number of cars or vans. If someone walked out with me he could still bide his time and follow me back to Wolverton.

I explained the predicament I was in to Foxy.

"Jesus mate, it hasn't taken you long to piss a few people off has it? Give me until the sixth race and I will come up with something."

I waited on the steps overlooking the track. Rainbow Warrior and Jamie were on parade for the fifth race, the first heat of the Golden Lead. I moved ten yards to my left to be in front of the track bookmakers. Rainbow Warrior had opened as the favourite at even money and looking at the other runners in the race it seemed quite generous as he was by far the fastest dog in the race. I invested all the money I had won on race three on the favourite.

The result was never in doubt once the traps opened. Rainbow Warrior trapped best of all and simply destroyed his inferior opponents by at least five lengths.

I collected my two hundred pounds from the track bookmaker and moved back to my step, there was no sign of Foxy.

He appeared just before the sixth race.

"All sorted, you can go home after this one." He pointed to a guy standing by the exit "Jack will take you to your car."

Jack had been one of the heavies who had escorted me to Paul Colley's office the week before; I wouldn't pick a fight with him.

"What's to stop him following me home though?"

"This" he said, pulling out a set of ignition leads from his pocket.

We both laughed and I didn't dare ask how.

Jack walked two steps behind me as I made my way back to the Mondeo. Ken was crouching behind Richard's distinctive white transit van. I wouldn't have seen him if I hadn't known to look.

I gave Jack a tenner for his help which he accepted with a grunt and a smile. I drove towards the exit and could see Ken running between cars as he made his way towards his own car. Once on the main road I headed towards the A5. I would normally turn right onto the dual carriageway but on this occasion I turned left; just to be on the safe side.

I was probably driving faster than I normally would but by the time I got home I was confident I hadn't been followed.

I wondered how long it would take for Ken to realise the cause of his engine problems.

CHAPTER TWENTY FIVE

There had been no unexpected visitors overnight and my car appeared in one piece. I did have a check around just to be on the safe side. All the wheel nuts were in place and I found no piles of tacks hidden under the tyres. We arrived at Stansted in plenty of time for our flight to Knock and took a leisurely stroll around the Departure lounge shops before boarding.

We had obviously chosen a day when a nun's convention was taking place in the Emerald Isle as we were surrounded by them. A few wise cracks about the merits of the Sound Of Music and their bad 'habits' resulted in an untimely elbow to the ribs from Alice. I needed to move smartly to avoid a repeat dig when I started to sing 'Sisters are doing it for themselves'.

I had spent much of the flight bringing Alice up to date on the events at the track the previous evening and the threats from Sam and from the village idiot.

"You don't like this Mr Kelly much do you?" she had teased.

"What can you mean? I sarcastically replied. "What's not to like about him? He smells and he's a liar" I refrained from mentioning that he perv's around cars taking photos whilst others are enjoying themselves.

We had no plan of attack for our flying visit apart from to meet Tommy Coyne on the whim that we were looking for a greyhound. Our story which we had rehearsed in the car was that we were on holiday and he had been recommended to us. We were going to have to make it up as we went along. If we got an opportunity we would also go and see the priest who part-owned Rainbow Warrior. As of yet we knew nothing about him apart from he was a priest. He was probably just caught up in the middle of this just as Orla was convinced Richard was.

"How do you fancy getting married?" I threw into the conversation just as the Captain announced that we were on our final approach for landing.

"I beg your pardon?" said Alice looking stunned.

"I think our way in with the priest is to go to the parochial house and pretend we are looking to get married in the local church. We can say this is where we got engaged."

"Oh right," she replied puffing out her cheeks and relaxing her shoulders.

"I am useless at accents, can you do them."

"Now tobesure I can now" she said in a perfect Irish accent. Was there to be no end to this woman's talents?

The flight had been pretty uneventful apart from the landing.

Visibility out of my window was zero; there was no land to be seen, no runway or airport buildings. We could feel the plane descend and the under-carriage had been lowered into place.

'Cabin crew ready for landing' said the Captain.

The two nuns immediately to our left held their rosary beads out and I was close to joining them in a few 'Hail Mary's' as something caught the bottom of the plane.

"Jesus what was that?" said a woman two rows in front of us. She was oblivious to the looks she was receiving from the portly sister to her right who I could see mouthing the Lords' prayer at an increased rate.

"That's just the top of the tree's" said someone from behind us.

Within a matter of moments we were on the ground, bouncing up the runway with wing flaps and brakes being applied expertly in equal measure as we came to a stop before turning and making our way slowly back to the airport terminal.

We grabbed our bags from the overhead locker and made our way to the exit. I had to suppress a laugh when the first thing I saw on reaching daylight was a statue of the Virgin Mary in a small alcove.

I could have sworn she winked at me.

Alice acted as navigator as we first made our way through Castlebar and then onto Westport. We stopped on the main high street and grabbed a sandwich from the bakery and a drink before continuing on our way.

"According to the directions I have printed off we need to take the next left towards Leenane and then just stay on this road for about twenty miles" Alice said.

The weather had cleared and it was a beautiful winter's day. Frost was still evident on the grass verges not yet reached by the sun. The roads were excellent and we made good time, admiring the beautiful scenery along the way.

"That mountain over there to our left is called the Devils Mother" advised Alice, her map and directions having been replaced by a tourist guide she'd picked up in the car rental suite.

We reached the Galway / Mayo border and were greeted with a completely new road surface, the smooth black tarmac and crisp white lines replaced by loose chippings, no road markings and bends that needed my full attention.

"Stay on this road and the village is two miles away."

I grunted an acknowledgement.

After about a mile we took a sharp left bend and in front of us was the stunning Killary Harbour.

"Wow" we said in unison "what a beautiful view."

Alice had consulted her tourist guide once again and advised that the Killary Harbour was Ireland's only fjord and it formed a natural border between counties Galway and Mayo. It was sixteen kilometres long and its base was situated in Leenane.

"Not far now" she said.

We passed what we assumed was the Parish Church on our left hand side and a couple of houses with Bed and Breakfast signs on the gateposts; we hadn't considered where we would be staying. With the Killary on my immediate right we dropped down a small incline. There was a large car park opposite a Sheep & Wool Museum on our right with a couple of village pubs immediately in front of us over what looked like a newly built bridge.

"Did you see any kennels?" I asked Alice as we pulled up

outside the pub.

"Not a thing. Maybe we could ask in the pub. Somebody will know. Park the car back up in that big car park and we can walk back."

Having parked up we made our way across into the village, safely negotiating a couple of sheep who were meandering down the road without a care in the world. There were two pubs to choose from, one next door to the other with a petrol pump separating them. Neither looked overly busy so we chose the one on the left.

We entered through the double doors; there were four people inside, one behind the counter and three customers. They stopped in mid-sentence as we entered the open fire heated bar; they studied us up and down before returning to their respective drinks and continued their conversation.

"How are yee" said the lady behind the bar "can I be getting you a drink?"

"That would be grand" said Alice in her best Irish accent; "a pint and a half of Guinness please."

The barmaid indicated she would bring them over so we took ourselves over to the open fire and removed our coats.

"Leave the next bit to me" I said.

The barmaid brought over our drinks and asked if we were just passing through and where we were heading and where we had come from.

"Actually we are looking for the Coyne residence" I said.

She smiled and two of the customers at the bar burst out laughing.

"Ah now, would that be the Coyne's of Glan or the Coyne's of Aasleagh or even the Coyne's of Derraheeda?"

"Don't forget the Coyne's of Nancy's Point and Letterbrickaun" said another at the bar.

I was becoming annoyed at being the butt of their obvious in-joke.

"Jesus son there are more Coyne's in this village than in the Bank of bloody England. I am a Coyne, these two are Coyne's and she" pointing to the barmaid "was a Coyne. You might want to be a bit more specific."

"Tommy Coyne, the greyhound trainer" interrupted Alice.

That wiped the smile of their faces.

The one guy who hadn't spoken as of yet finally joined the conversation and it was obvious from his tone he was no fan of Tommy Coyne of Leenane Village.

"What do you want with that fecking blow-in, him and his fecking dogs? Waste of good grazing land building kennels up there. His Uncle Mick god rest his soul will be turning in his grave" he said downing the dregs of his pint before walking out of the bar.

The barmaid had sat down beside us, warming her hands from the blazing coal fire; "take no notice of that hot head, lost a couple of sheep up the mountain this morning; was the drink talking. You will find Tommy's place just up the hill. You need to turn right out of here, after about 200 yards you will see a bungalow up on the hill, go past the front gate and after another 50 yards you will come across a driveway that takes you up to the house. Go up there and park outside, and wait."

"What are we waiting for?" asked Alice.

"You are waiting for his daughter Aoife to come and get Trixie in. Trixie is the house dog who has a tendency to bite anything that moves and especially English girls who are putting on an accent. It was good, I will give you that, but you need a little bit of work on it" she teased leaving us to finish our drinks in peace.

We thanked the barmaid for her hospitality and said we may pop back in a bit later.

"Good luck now, and be wary of that mongrel, he will have your toes off if you give him half a chance."

Was she referring to Tommy Coyne or the dog?

We found the kennels easily enough with the directions given. We would never have found them otherwise. We negotiated the steep hill up to the house and were chased all the way up the drive by what could only have been Trixie. There was a light on in the bungalow and we waited as instructed. Presently a woman in her late forties came out and retrieved the dog, put him inside and came across to the car.

"Can I help you?" she said leaning in the through the car door window Alice had opened.

This was going to be the first bit we had rehearsed and it was down to me.

"I do hope so. We are looking for the greyhound trainer Tommy Coyne. He has been recommended to us and as we were passing we thought we'd pop in and see if he had any dogs for sale."

"You better come with me then. Dad is up in the kennels. I am his daughter Aoife and you are?"

"My name is Joe and this is my fiancée Alice."

"Lovely to meet you, now if you want to follow me the kennels are at the top of the hill."

I locked up the car and the three of us made our way slowly up towards the kennel, Aoife leading the way. I couldn't help but notice how pristine the kennels were when she brought us inside but there appeared to be no electricity linked up. There were plenty of camping lamps but no light switches or dangling bulbs.

"Dad, where are you?" shouted Aoife.

"Just coming; what's with all the noise woman?" a voice said from down a corridor.

I wasn't sure what to expect or who to expect as Tommy joined us in the kennel kitchen but what came next hadn't been rehearsed or even considered.

"Hello Joseph, what are you doing here?" asked Tommy.

CHAPTER TWENTY SIX

"You look like you have seen a ghost" said Alice.

"I think I may have done" I whispered as I lowered myself onto one of the hay bales that doubled as seats in the feed room. I felt like a boxer who had been knocked on the side of the head by a punch he hadn't seen coming. I obviously looked as shocked as I felt.

Aoife took her cue from her father to leave the three of us together in the ever darkening room.

"Put the kettle on love, we will be down in five minutes. Tea ok for you two I hope?" said Tommy.

Alice watched as Aoife made her way down the hill to the house through the big window, "can somebody please tell me what the bloody hell is going on here?"

"Take a seat Alice and I will try and get my head around this myself" I said beckoning her to join me on the hay bale.

Alice came over to me whilst Tommy remained standing; he looked older than the last time I had seen him which was hardly surprising as I was still in school. I recognised his steely jaw and his receding hairline and his distinctive Irish accent. It was different to those in the village earlier; I guessed it was probably because of the time he had spent in England.

"So when did you become Tommy Coyne then? I assumed you were dead?" I asked.

Tommy moved over to the corner of the room and turned off the gas lamp, "That was the idea, best we go down to the house; it will be more comfortable down there and warmer. It gets very cold up here and the dogs are all locked up with their pyjamas on and I would rather not disturb them."

Alice was becoming very irritable and more confused by the minute and I was not sure what I could tell her to comfort her as I was as baffled as she was. We had come here with a basic plan of attack which had been thrown out of the window the moment Tommy had walked in from the kennel corridor.

Reluctantly we followed Tommy down the hill, passed the parked car and entered the house through the backdoor. There was no sign of Trixie but we could hear him. Aoife had a made a pot of tea and there were potatoes and a joint of bacon cooking away on the range.

"Will you be joining us for dinner, we have plenty?" asked Aoife.

"They will" said Tommy abruptly and without any type of consultation with myself or Alice.

We all pulled out a chair from around the kitchen table and Aoife joined us, acting as mother, pouring tea into her best bone china cups and matching saucers. A selection box of chocolate biscuits had also been laid on.

"Ok, as I asked earlier can someone please tell me what the bloody hell is going on? You two", pointing to myself and Tommy "obviously know each other so Joe can you please tell me why we have come all the way here if you already know each other?" said Alice.

"Do you want to go first or shall I?" asked Tommy. I took the lead.

"Alice, I don't know Tommy Coyne, I know this man as Thomas Brady and I was under the impression he was dead as I have not seen him for fifteen years."

"Seventeen years, it is seventeen years" interrupted Tommy.

Had it really been that long? I quickly did the maths in my head and given I had just turned thirty four it would have been seventeen years. How time flies.

"So why did you think he was dead? You aren't making any sense Joe" said Alice.

"Alright alright, let me do the best I can from memory and then

Thomas, I mean Tommy can fill in the blanks. Is that ok?

All around the table nodded in acceptance.

"You remember I told you on Friday in the restaurant about the gambles that had been landed at Bristol all those years ago. Well Tommy was one of the guys who would be putting the money on in the shops in the West Country and with all his contacts around the country they made absolute fortunes. Tommy was the brains and it was his network of contacts that put the bets on and collected any winnings."

"So he was a money launderer?" said Alice.

Tommy looked annoyed and his daughter put her hand across to stop him from speaking, allowing me to continue.

"Unknowingly yes he was. He was under the impression the money he was dealing in was clean genuine gambling money coming from a high rolling bookmaker who was privy to lots of inside information from the racing stables in the south-west. Tommy, for use of a better word, was a facilitator, he would put on for a fee and should the gamble pay off he would take another fee for collecting. He would be doing all the legwork as you couldn't get the amount on in one hit that was wanted. Is that correct Tommy?"

Tommy nodded but said nothing, allowing me to continue.

"Tommy was a winner whether the horse won or lost, he just made more if it won. Well, when he was approached by his bookmaker contact to back these dogs that were running at Bristol he didn't give it another thought. He collected the money, put the bets on, took his fee and collected when the dogs won. As it turns out it was easy money as the dogs couldn't lose. He had no idea however about all the other skulduggery going on until it was too late.

"How do you know all this?" asked Alice interrupting again.

"I am coming to that."

I finished my tea and Aoife refreshed my cup, the next bit wasn't going to be easy.

"You will also remember I told you one of the guys who had bought one of the dogs was badly beaten and ended up in hospital and the Racing Manager at Bristol had both his legs broken by the gang from Manchester trying to get the information they needed to get their money back?"

She nodded.

"The Racing Manager was my father!"

She hadn't seen that coming and it wasn't something I'd discussed with anyone. I wasn't even sure Phil was aware of the link as it had never been brought into conversation.

"Go on Joseph, tell her everything now you have started" urged Tommy.

"When the case finally came to court my father was given a lenient sentence on the basis of the evidence Tommy here had given. My father had been put under severe pressure by the head of the gang because of gambling debts he had accrued. He was a good man, a good father and a hard worker but a god damn awful punter. The bookmaker he owed the money to handed the debt over to the gang boss in Cardiff. They dragged my father into their scheme to cheat with the greyhounds and promised to write off his debt if he did so."

I could feel the tears starting to fall down the side of my cheek, Alice put her hand in mine and squeezed. In the words of Magnus Magnusson of Mastermind I had started and needed to finish.

"They didn't write-off the debt and kept coming back time after time. When my father heard about the man who had been badly beaten and left in the lay-by he confided in Tommy about his part in the gambles. They had known each other for years; Tommy was a regular punter in his own right at Bristol and made a good living from it as well. I had spent many a night sat on the steps with him when my father was working. I learnt so much from him. Tommy had told my father to stop and tell the authorities but he was too frightened of the gang and when he heard of the beating it made him even more scared. Not just for him but for my mother and me. They had threatened to harm us both unless he carried on.

Eventually it was the gang from Manchester rather than Cardiff that inflicted the harm. They came around to the house one night and in front of my mother took a baseball bat to his knees until he told them who was behind the gambles. It broke my father's resolve. He was in hospital for months and it was Tommy here who called in the Police and gave them more details about the gambles. It took them months to track down the ring leaders and the heavies but they did and they were convicted. Until today, I had not seen Tommy since the court case."

"So what happened to you Tommy?" asked Alice.

Tommy stood up and took his cup to the sink, rinsing it under the running water before putting it on the side.

"Young lady it changed my world but I have no regrets. I had been interviewed by the Police for what seemed like weeks and they were treating me like a criminal. I had nothing to hide as I hadn't knowingly done anything illegal. I managed to convince them eventually I had no idea the money I had been betting with was dirty. I hate drugs; I hate anything to do with drugs and violence. The Police told me they had heard there was a contract out on me because of the evidence I had given and I should disappear as quickly as possible as they couldn't guarantee my safety. I had been left this place by my Uncle a few years earlier so we upped sticks overnight, cleaned out the bank account and moved here. We told no-one, not even Aoife here so as not to endanger her, not that anyone knew we had any children as I had always kept my home life private.

When we came here we had coal bags for windows and sheep eating grass that had grown through the floor boards in the bedroom. Everyone around here referred to me as Tommy Coyne, Mick Coyne's nephew so I let them assume I was Tommy Coyne. It took my wife a lot longer to get used to living here but she did eventually. Between us we invested every penny we had into re-building and making this place home. She made new friends, invented parts of her past, like where we had come from and what she did. We needed to keep ourselves safe as these guys would stop at nothing to gain revenge. I imagine like you they think I am dead and I'd rather it stayed that way."

Aoife had joined him by the sink and put her arms around him.

"So what happened to your father?" asked Aoife looking at me.

“He killed himself, threw himself in front of a Great Western train at Bristol Parkway the day after my nineteenth birthday” I said without any hint of anger. “Mum left him, he had lost his job and his integrity and he couldn’t go on. He had hit the bottle quite hard and I had left home to work at Stony Stratford the year before. I suppose it didn’t help that I was doing a job that he loved, working around the greyhounds.”

Alice was learning more about my life sat around this table than I had ever told Ella, and I had been married to her. It was a part of my life and past I was happy to blank out.

“Dinner will be ready in about half an hour. I have made up the spare room so you can stay here tonight and I have left a couple of towels on the bed” advised Aoife quickly changing the subject.

“We couldn’t possibly impose, we will get a ....”

“No arguments, you are staying” interrupted Tommy “I won’t be having any village gossip in a B&B asking your business here especially when I don’t know why you are here anyway. Now go off and get yourself cleaned up and we will see you back here in thirty minutes. My girl here” planting a kiss on Aoife’s cheek “makes the best cabbage and bacon in County Galway.”

I’d retrieved our overnight bags from the car and managed to side step Trixie before he caught hold of my leg as I ran back into the house. Alice had changed into a green hooded top and jeans and had freshened herself up in the bedroom sink. She was applying some eye make-up when I came back in to the vast bedroom after taking a shower

“Well, I’ve learnt an awful lot today Joey boy, you alright?” she asked still looking in the mirror.

I sat on the edge of the bed and let out a huge sigh. Was I alright, what was the exact definition of being alright? Confused I definitely was but I wasn’t sure about alright.

“I think we need to tell Tommy the whole truth and see where it takes us. He is too smart not to see through any lies we might try and tell him. He did say one thing towards the end that stuck out for me and that was he doesn’t like drugs and violence. Andy met a violent end and I think we need to tell him that and gauge a reaction.

The two dogs that were heavily gambled are definitely his style but they have only been gambled on certain dates and in certain races and when they have they have won. Does he still have his connections after all these years? Orla is convinced that Richard has no idea about the Rainbow Warrior gambles landed and we have little to go on with regards the Double Vision gamble apart from what Foxy told you on Saturday evening.

"I think it is fair to assume that Sam is the money behind it so maybe we need to start there and see if the Priest is a diversion or if he actually exists. What do you think?"

Alice nodded in agreement. "Let's go in for dinner and see where the conversation takes us. We will either hit a brick wall or find the key to all this" she said.

Tommy had poured a Guinness for me and a white wine for Alice and invited us both to take a seat at the dinner table.

"So tell me young Joseph what brings you here and don't give me any bollocks about wanting to buy a pup?" he said laughing whilst looking at Aoife.

"It is quite simple Tommy, or do I call you Thomas? It is too confusing for me to get my head around so I will stick with Tommy. An old colleague of mine is now dead and I want to find out why and who did it. If you can help me along the way then that would be great but if you can't I will just keep on digging. My biggest concern from your perspective is I understand your grandson Jamie works for a trainer who keeps popping up in my enquiries."

"I'm listening" said Tommy as Aoife began to serve.

"Over the last four months there have been four major gambles on two of the dogs that you have sent over to Richard Quinn. Andy Whelan turned up in the lake at Kempton last week dead; he was helping a friend of mine with his investigations into these gambles. Knowing you of old Tommy I would say these gambles are right up your street but I do not believe for one minute that you would condone any sort of violence.

So here is my problem Tommy, I am not convinced Andy's

death is directly related to your two dogs but I think there is a connection. If I can find the connection I may well be able to find who killed him and why."

"And what is the role of this beautiful young lady?" he said trying to smooth talk Alice.

"I am a Detective Sergeant along for the ride. Our visit to Ireland is not official; it is a fishing trip so to speak. I have no jurisdiction over here or sought any either. I am purely here as a second set of eyes and ears for Joe who is my partner."

It was nice to know we had established a relationship status I thought.

"Struck lucky there Joseph, a woman with beauty and brains, a rare combination so it is. So what is it you think I can be telling you that would be helpful to your unofficial investigations? What I will tell you is I had nothing to do with any violence or that young man turning up dead. Our young Jamie called me over the weekend to tell us the news and I have told him to keep his head down and just carry on with his work" he said looking at Aoife who seemed unaware of the conversation they'd had.

Tommy had been right about Aoife's cooking, it was delicious and we helped ourselves to a second helping.

"What can you tell me about the other owner of Rainbow Warrior? It says on the race card he is a Priest, does he exist?" I asked.

"Sure Father Sean exists alright but he is away down the country at the moment visiting his sister. Will be back tomorrow evening in time for Mass. Lovely man so he is, was brought up around greyhounds just below Limerick in a little place called Oola. His father was a big owner back in the day, owned a winner of the Clonmel coursing Derby no less, as proud as punch of it as well. There is a big picture on the sideboard in his house out on the Westport Road. He bought half of Archie, well actually Sam bought half of Archie after his second win at Galway."

"Archie is Rainbow Warrior's pet name" interrupted Aoife just before I was about to ask.

"Must have paid a few quid for it? I said.

"That she did but the dog was worth every penny. Little win machine he is. Will win the Golden Lead Competition you know that is on at the moment and will be really suited to Wimbledon for the Derby next year. Raw speed and all the credit has to go down to young Jamie. Reared him from a sickly pup to where he is now. The night he won at Galway was simply awesome. Fancy another Guinness, I'm having one?" he asked.

"Yes please. Isn't it a bit strange for someone to pay so much money for a dog and then put it in someone else's name? I got the impression from my meetings with her she would want all the glory. Surely there is more to it than that?" I said accepting another bottle from him.

"Now funny you should say that Joseph, as Aoife here said exactly the same thing but I don't care whose name it runs in as long as we got paid. The pups we sold her she was happy for them to run in her name. I think she said she thought that Archie would be better graded if it ran in the name of a priest rather than her own. I could have told her she was wasting her time as the dog was always going to be top grade."

I instantly remembered the three trial times Rainbow Warrior had recorded when he had first started at Stony Stratford and Tommy was right, he was only ever going to be a top grade performer or a dog that would race away at other tracks in Open races and competitions.

"Sam comes here quite often you know, at least once a month to have a look around and to see if we have anything worth buying. She stays with Sean at the parochial house for a couple of days before heading back. I don't think there is any funny business going on, just a mutual interest in the dogs. They have been friends for years and he used to point out dogs for her at Harolds Cross and Shelbourne Park when he was based in Dublin. She did say one night when we had a few that she had been brought up around the dogs but she only got back into them a few years ago. She definitely has a few quid. I knew her father-in-law from years back, I didn't let on though. He used to be a major punter at the likes of White City and Wembley dog tracks before they closed. His son took over the business but stuck mainly to the horses and a string of betting shops."

"So is she a big punter then do you know?" I asked.

"She definitely likes a bet and hates losing from what young Jamie has told me. She had a right go at him the night Maurice won, I mean Double Vision. I do know she doesn't back on track, she told me all the bookmakers at the track are her clients and they have an unwritten rule to keep the price high so she can get a better price off course."

I bet Phil would be delighted to hear that when I told him. If Stony Stratford BMS contract had been under serious threat because of the big gambles being landed then they would be in even more trouble if the bookmakers had been manipulating the starting prices.

"So tell me about these Rainbow Warrior gambles Tommy, what is going on there?

"I can't be telling you something like that!" he exclaimed and laughed at the same time. "Young Jamie will ring me up and tell me tonight is the night and I will ring a fella, and that fella will ring a fella and that fella will ring a couple of fella's" he said with a massive smile on his face.

I wasn't sure whether it was the effect of the Guinness or the fact he was getting it off his chest but he loved the fact I was digging in the dark for crumbs of information.

Alice had been very quiet taking everything in, "So how many fellas are we talking about then?" she asked.

"Well the first time around I'd guess there were about eighty around the country. You have to remember I've been out of the game for so long that half my contacts were either six foot under or retired from the game. This gambling lark is a young man's game, betting on the internet and on their mobile phones. I got hold of one contact in London who still liked a bet and one in Glasgow and they did the rest. The deal was I provided the information for twenty per cent return. I have left it to them to see me right and they have done so far."

"What if it had lost?" I asked.

"They don't Joseph young man, they don't. A person like me is relied upon to provide guaranteed winners. The people laying out the money only want winners. The first gamble was the test. If it won then they would be willing to get more of their 'fellas' to put the money on. You need to remember we are dealing in small amounts so as not to raise suspicion. The first time the bets were placed with only two or three minutes before the start of the race in the betting shops. The dog won at 8-1 and we won just under thirty thousand."

I again quickly did a calculation and Tommy was better off to the tune of six thousand pounds. Not bad at all for a nights work.

"You couldn't guarantee they would win though surely?" asked Alice as Aoife placed a homemade apple pie with steaming custard in front of her.

"Agreed" accepted Tommy "but that was part of the gamble. If Jamie tells me it will win then I trust his judgement and no one knows Archie better than him."

"So does he tell you when it isn't going to win?" I asked.

"Maybe, maybe not" he said and winked at Alice.

We all tucked into our dessert on Aoife's instructions, again the food was delicious and I reluctantly declined a second helping on fear of bursting the button on my trousers. Alice was unable to finish hers.

Tommy opened two more bottles of Guinness. We were running out he had observed and asked Aoife to pop into the village to get some more. Alice offered to go with her as she needed the fresh air and left myself and Tommy alone in the kitchen.

"I am sorry to hear about your father, he was a good man, the betting will get the better of most men unless you know your limits" he said with sincerity.

He was right and I thanked him for his words.

"So how about the second gamble; was it eighty 'fellas' again or more?"

"Jesus Joseph it was a lot more and by god that Sam woman threw her teddy out of the pram when she found out we'd had it right off and not told her about it. I didn't tell her the whole story though. She told me she'd make sure his price was a lot shorter from now on unless we included her in the gamble. Bossy cow, almost told her to go and stick it up her arse and I'd bring Jamie straight back over here."

"How many then?"

"There must have been at least two hundred give or take ten or twenty, I got a nice few quid out of it and the price of 6-1 was better than we had hoped. He shouldn't have been any bigger than 4-1 in my mind."

"So why didn't you bring Jamie back then?"

"You don't half ask a lot of questions and it is only because I know you that I am telling you anything. I need to tell you this so you will believe me when I say I had nothing to do with the guys death. Is that clear?"

I smiled in acceptance.

"The third gamble was the hardest. Archie had a spot of the kennel sickness for a couple of weeks so his bad runs were easily explained and we just let him run within himself on those occasions. Jamie then rings at the start of the week to say that the dog was now bouncing and we were good to go that Wednesday evening. I rang Sam on the morning of the race to say Archie was primed but she was to keep her stakes low so as not to attract attention and ruin the price for me. She gave the impression she knew that and it would just be her who would be backing it to try and recoup what she had lost.

It was then she told me she'd had a tip off that the GRB integrity team were all over the gambles now. On his recent form he should have been at least 10-1 so I put the word out to the fellas that the gamble was on. Sam called me from the track to say the big firms were in attendance and her guys couldn't keep the price up as high as we would want so we'd have to settle for whatever we could get. We got 11-2 and the same two hundred and a few others got on as late as possible. We made a few quid but not as much as I had hoped."

Tommy had been behind the first three big gambles that had Phil all a fluster and the big firms running for cover every time Rainbow Warrior had set foot on the track. I had quickly tallied up and estimated they had won about £150,000 between them and at twenty per cent Tommy was looking at a clear £30,000 without any outlay.

I had been right to be suspicious of Sam as well and if we were to get to the bottom of this she needed to be taken out of the loop.

The ladies returned from the village with Guinness and Lager aplenty. It looked like being a long night and Tommy appeared to have hollow legs just like Phil. I could see me being drunk under the table quite literally at this rate. I brought Alice up to speed on what had been said whilst she'd been out and whilst Tommy was on a toilet break.

"I think your father is going to be happy in one way and disappointed in another. Tommy is behind the big gambles on Rainbow Warrior, he has openly admitted it and he hasn't done anything wrong that I can see, just an old style betting coup with no paper trail. We haven't discussed Double Vision yet. I am convinced he has nothing to do with Andy's death though" I said before Tommy returned into the room wearing his overcoat.

"Right you two love birds, I am going over to Father Sean's now to feed his cats, should have done it hours ago. Do you want to come with me or help Aoife with the washing up?" he said.

I retrieved our jackets from the bedroom and Aoife lent Alice a scarf to keep her warm against the wind that was coming off the Killary.

Tommy acted as tourist guide as we turned right over the village bridge, pointing out who lived where and who was related to whom. He gave the impression he had little time for his neighbours and they him. We carried on walking past the Sheep and Wool Museum we had passed earlier. There were plenty of sheep on the side of the road seeking refuge from the wind and the next big house we came to was the parochial house. I hadn't noticed Trixie following us until Tommy had given him a stern order to stay outside of the gates. He obviously acted on his best behaviour when his master was in attendance.

"We will go in the back way" said Tommy, shining his torch

down the side of the two storey building which was way too big just for one. He found the key to the back door and the cats were waiting patiently by their bowls to be fed. He found the food under the sink and fed the expectant animals.

"Whilst we are here I will show the photographs of Father Sean and his father, I am sure he won't mind. Just follow me; it's in the room on the right."

We followed Tommy down the corridor into the room and the sideboard was covered in greyhound photographs from yesteryear. There was one of the Clonmel Derby victory and other coursing and track trophies won. They must have been taken after he had joined the priesthood, I looked at the dates and they had been taken over thirty years ago.

"This is his favourite" said Tommy handing me a silver photo frame with a group photograph surrounding the winning greyhound on the podium.

"Why is this his favourite, I would have thought the Clonmel Derby winning one would have taken centre stage being the most prestigious?" I replied.

"I am not really sure, he got really maudlin here one night after a few whiskies and said that this was the last one that they had taken before his father packed in owning greyhounds. It was all very sudden. I asked him why and he just changed the subject."

I took another look at the picture, you could clearly pick out Father Sean at the back of the group with his dog collar and his father was holding the dog.

"Who are the rest of the people in the photograph Tommy do you know?" I asked as one in particular had caught my eye.

"Bring it over here and where is Alice?"

I didn't actually know and I was beginning to wonder myself.

With photograph in hand Tommy proceeded to point out each of the individuals, "The guy on the left is his younger brother Marcus, the two girls sat on the front of the podium are his sisters Dolores and May, the guy to the right of the dog's head is the trainer and next to him is Father Sean's father. At the back on the right is the trainer's son with Sean's youngest sister Sally-Ann stood in front of him."

I took the picture from him and switched on the table lamp to generate more light. I couldn't be sure but I was sure I recognised the guy at the back. Alice joined us at the ideal moment as I wanted to take a photograph and I didn't have that facility available on my phone. She looked decidedly flustered,

"Who was the trainer Tommy?" I asked on the off chance.

"The trainer of that particular dog was Padraig Lowry. You will have heard of his son Tomas, he won the English Derby two years running about five years ago with Yogi's Eclipse. Bloody fast dog that one. He trains in a place near Cahir, probably the best trainer in the country at the moment. Miserable bastard though."

"Oh right, you won't tell Father Sean if I take a picture will you, I feel like I am intruding?" I said.

"Crack on, not sure what help a picture from thirty years ago will do you but I doubt very much he will mind" he said as Alice zoomed in with her phone to take four or five different pictures.

With the images safely stowed away on her mobile we followed Tommy out as he locked up. The wind had really picked up in the preceding half an hour with waves crashing against the car park wall as we walked past. The sheep hadn't moved and didn't stir as Trixie wandered off in front of us.

Tommy declined my invitation of a pint in the pub we had been in earlier with an inaudible grunt and upped the pace as the rain and then hail began to fall heavily.

We settled back in around the kitchen table and Tommy acted as barman again. A mixture of the sea air and the salty bacon we'd had for dinner gave me an unquenchable thirst. I had decided to give the Guinness' a miss and stuck with the lager.

"Slainte" said Tommy raising his glass.

I was desperate to get another look at the pictures Alice had taken but we hadn't yet raised the subject of Double Vision, or Maurice as Tommy had called him. We did know the big gamble had been landed with a double bet involving the two dogs the night before Andy had gone missing.

"So is Jamie the brains behind the Double Vision gamble then? I understand Sam didn't have a penny on that night as well, did she do her nut on that occasion?"

"It had nothing to do with me or Jamie; we didn't have a penny on. The dog is only a pup and he had disappointed me if I am honest, I thought he would go a lot faster in his initial qualifying trials as he had shown as much promise over here as Rainbow Warrior without being as explosive. I know Sam had a big bet on the first time he'd run" said Tommy.

I suddenly remembered that I hadn't looked at the initial qualifying trials of Double Vision in as much depth as I had all the others. If he had followed the same pattern as the previous newcomers then Sam was probably confident the dog should have been in a lot higher grade than Andy had put it in and punted accordingly.

"I think that could have been one for Tony 'the timer'" I replied, thinking back to what Foxy had told us about the still cruising punter. If he was convinced the dog still had plenty of time in hand he may have continued to back it despite it having been beaten twice. Having won at 6-1 he would have made a tidy profit.

As Tommy had been so forthcoming with the information on the gambles that had been landed with Rainbow Warrior I thought it only fair I bring him up to date on what I had gathered from studying all the DVD's and filled him on what Richard Quinn had been up to over the previous four months. Tommy listened with interest as I talked him through how Andy had fabricated all the trial times and plotted the dogs up to win first time out. He almost spat out the last of his drink when I told him the win percentage.

"Jesus, how had nobody spotted that?" he said.

I had been asking myself the same question for a couple of days and it made me decidedly uneasy especially with Alice here. The number of winners and the prices of those winners should have set alarm bells ringing with Phil a long time before Andy had disappeared. A sequence of results like that were his bread and butter and what he was being paid to investigate. Had he taken his eye off the ball or had I missed something.

He was normally a great judge of character and one

conversation with Orla had only confirmed my initial thoughts on Sam. How had he not seen it?

I looked across to Alice and she smiled back. She wasn't saying much and looked to have something on her mind. She had been very quiet since we had returned from the priest's house. I assumed she was tired after the long day. I checked my watch; it had just gone 10pm.

The information about the gambles Sam and her crew had been landing had really annoyed Tommy, a couple of 'fecking woman' and 'cheeky bitches' had crept into the conversation.

"She'll do well to get the better of me that fecking woman with her posh clothes and fancy jewellery. She has the fecking cheek to tell me I need to tell her when a dog is going to be gambled and not give me the heads up when she is winning week after week. Well she better watch out next week. Wait until I talk to young Jamie tomorrow. Golden Lead or no Golden Lead the dog isn't winning but she will be told otherwise. She will learn through her pocket."

I think I had gained an ally.

"So what about the gamble you landed with the two dogs a few weeks ago?" I asked.

"That, young Joseph, had been in the planning for over a year and I have one more lined up and if you promise me here and now you won't tell anyone, I will tell you exactly how I pulled it off. I have one last payday and then I am retired for good. It will make me enough money to live off for life and let young Jamie run this place as he likes" he said in his most serious tone of the night.

"Is it illegal because if it is I cannot and will not condone it?" I replied.

He sucked on his bottom lip, the alcohol intake had definitely started to kick in and I could see he was contemplating whether or not to tell me.

Eventually he did, it wasn't exactly above board but it wasn't something I was going to tell anyone about.

The guy was a genius.

CHAPTER TWENTY SEVEN

We took ourselves off to bed just after. Alice had become very withdrawn and I had enough information to dissect for one night as it was. I did however want to have another look at the pictures she had taken on her phone.

"You're very quiet?" I said as I got in beside her.

"Just tired, been a long day."

She handed me her phone and I had a long look at the pictures she had taken. The third was the clearest and I handed it back to her and asked her if she recognised anyone in them. She didn't seem to be overly bothered and put the phone away.

"Ok, spit it out, what's on your mind, you have been very quiet since we came back from the priest's house so what is it?"

She said nothing and just looked at me.

"You can stare as much as you like but I do know something is on your mind. Is it something I've done or said?"

Tears had started to creep from the corner of her eye as she reached out to rest her head on my chest, "I did something I shouldn't have this evening Joe and I am not sure how to deal with it, be it from a personal or professional point of view. From a personal perspective I am disgusted and from a professional angle I have put myself in a very difficult position."

"What could you have done my love?"

She got out of bed went over to her overnight bag and came back with a brown padded envelope. I had seen a similar envelope two years ago. Surely she didn't have the photographs of me and Orla. I could feel myself sweating.

"When you and Tommy were looking at the pictures downstairs

I went in search of the toilet as I was desperate. I couldn't find one downstairs so I went up. The first room I went into was obviously a guest room…."

She wiped more tears from her eyes.

"I did a bit of nosing around whilst I was up there as there were a lot of women's clothes on the back of a chair and hanging on the front of a wardrobe. I thought it extremely strange to see so much woman's clothing just laying around, there were even more clothes in the wardrobe, it was full of them in fact, not cheap stuff either, designer labels! As I moved a few things around an envelope fell out and spilled the contents on to the floor, it was full of photographs and other papers. I have put them all in here" she said still holding the brown padded envelope. "The photographs shocked me and disgusted me, I wish I hadn't found them but I have and I really do not know what to do? What made it worse were the papers I found with them, detailing where the pictures were taken and when."

I can imagine the contents would have upset her especially as I hadn't told her about them. I held my breath as she brought the pictures out of the envelope. There was no way I could talk my way out of these, she was already jealous of Orla and these will have hurt her.

I wasn't in any of them.

There were six photographs in all. The images were clear, timed and dated as mine had been. They weren't explicit in a sexual way but they told a story. Alice passed me the papers and their contents were just as damning. I looked across at her and she looked distressed and completely lost for words. I looked at the pictures again and the words that accompanied them.

"It gets worse" she said jumping out of bed again and retrieving a package covered in toilet paper.

She slowly removed the wrapping to reveal a mobile phone. I tried to turn it on but nothing happened. It was the same make as Alice's and she quickly removed the battery from her own and replaced the one in the phone I was holding. Almost immediately the screen lit up and it was ready to use. She took the phone from me and quickly pressed a few buttons to bring up the text messages. It was the last one that immediately struck a chord.

Tings aren't always as they look at the start. Donut boy has deep pockets and the solution will b in touching dist.'

It was the text Andy had sent to Phil.

I could now understand why Alice was in such a quandary, she had removed vital evidence in a murder enquiry and not taken the necessary precautions to secure any forensic evidence. She had no warrant and no jurisdiction either but I guessed she was far from concerned about that. The photographs however were a different matter altogether.

"Did you do the battery changing at the house?" I asked.

"Yes."

It did answer one question though and one I had been reluctant to discuss with her. For a man who knew everything and everyone Phil had turned a blind eye when it came to investigating the smaller gambles that had been going on at the track and the decision to do so hadn't been by choice. The papers and photographs proved beyond all reasonable doubt Phil was being told to look the other way. I had no idea who the woman in the picture was but Alice's reaction made it pretty clear it wasn't her mother.

"We will need to talk to him on Sunday when we get back and get to the bottom of this. You arrange it in the morning with him but do not let on what we have found whilst we are here, you will just incriminate ourselves and it is best he doesn't know" I said trying to take control of the situation and reassure her at the same time.

"What are we going to do next?" she asked.

"Tomorrow we are going on a long drive to Cahir to see the young man in the picture and if Tommy will have us we will come back here tomorrow night as we are going to need his help. Sam is pushing all the buttons here and we always seem to be one step behind her. The photographs of your father are similar to the ones I received and I know I was innocent. She didn't deny being responsible for them.

"There could be an easy explanation as to what is going on with your father in these but we will let him tell us rather than jumping to any conclusions. What I haven't worked out yet is what she is gaining from all this. Is it about power, control or money?"

Aoife's excellent culinary skills were seen again at breakfast, it was delicious and I was glad of it as we had a long day ahead of us. Alice had asked if she could use the computer to print-off directions to the Lowry kennels and a few of the pictures she had taken whilst I walked up with Tommy to the kennel block and helped out as best I could with morning feed. A young girl was already working away when we arrived and Tommy introduced her as Siobhan.

"Of course you can stay again tonight, I had a great time and I can introduce you to Father Sean as he may pop around for a quick one after Mass" said Tommy.

"Thank you but can you not let on who we are as I'd rather Sam didn't know we were here, especially if Jamie is going to stop Rainbow Warrior next week?"

"Jesus that reminds me, I must quickly run down to the house and give him a quick call before I forget. I'll teach that woman to feck with me."

I saved him a journey by handing him my mobile. I listened intently as he gave his grandson instructions and debriefed him on what was said last night. He handed the mobile back to me but not before he reminded him he wasn't to say a word to anyone, especially Sam.

"Right, you heard all of that. Jamie has your number if he has any problems from here on in and you can call him if you need any more information" he said. "Now go off and do what you have to do as I have work to do and a couple of pups to take off to Galway for schooling with Aoife."

It would take us at least four hours to reach the outskirts of Cahir according to the internet directions so we hit the road just after 10am. Aoife had told us to take it easy until we reached Galway as the roads from the house to Maam and then Maam Cross weren't the greatest, surrounded on either side by bog land and deep ditches. You will have never encountered roads like them she had said to me as I got in the car.

The journey to Galway took just over an hour with Alice again putting her excellent navigational skills to full use. There were one or two wrong turns taken which she blamed on poor signage. We discussed the implications of the photographs and decided there was no point worrying about them until we had spoken to Phil. She had set up a meeting for Sunday evening and he would meet us at her flat in Woburn Sands.

"So why are we going to see this trainer exactly?" she asked.

"We are going because of the photograph you have printed off. If his father is alive then even better but he looked sixty if he was a day and the son would be going on that age now."

"And what will you ask him?"

"Oh that bit is easy. I want to know if he is still in touch with his son!!"

Alice looked at me as if I had gone mad, it wasn't something we had discussed and I could be completely wrong but the facial features, the height and slant of the head to one side were very distinctive. I wanted to see if there were any similarities in the flesh.

"Does he know we are coming?" she asked.

"Yes he does. Tommy is going to ring him at lunchtime and if we don't hear from him then we can assume we can just turn up. He doesn't know why we are coming though as I didn't tell Tommy."

We had been driving for just over three hours when we came to a small village called Oola.

"Isn't this the place Tommy said Father Sean came from?" I said as we passed a row of bungalows on our left. Every other telegraph pole and lamp post had a poster of a candidate for a forthcoming election.

"I honestly can't remember Joe, I was slightly pre-occupied" she said looking up from the directions.

I slowed the car as we passed the village church and pulled up outside a row of shops that consisted of a supermarket, betting shop and a hair salon. I grabbed a copy of one of the pictures that Alice had printed off earlier and wandered into the bookmakers. We hadn't heard from Tommy so I assumed he had got hold of Tomas

Lowry who would be expecting us. "Wait here, back in five minutes" I said to Alice.

With picture in hand I went up to the counter of the bookmakers where a young man was tucking into a large sausage roll. There were four or five punters in the shop watching the closing stages of a hurdle race from Newbury. Given the lack of animation between them I assumed none of them had backed the winner.

"Can I help you?" asked the cashier

"Oh I do hope so young man" I said in as posh an English accent as I could muster. "My name is Neville Higginbotham and I am a lecturer at Dublin University. I am doing a paper on the history of Irish greyhound racing and I have this picture that I have been sent for my research and I am trying to trace one of the owners or speak to anyone who may have known them" I said handing him the picture.

He took one look at it before calling out to a customer who was minding his own business in the corner of the shop drinking a cup of tea.

"Hey Jimmy" he shouted "get your arse over here and see if you recognise anyone for this lecturer gentleman will yeah."

Jimmy, a man of at least eighty; deserving of more respect, started to make his way slowly to the counter. I decided to meet him halfway and pulled up a chair for him to settle into.

He took the picture from me and pulled out a pair of scratched glasses from his inside jacket pocket. He mumbled something to himself before handing the picture back to me.

"That's the McGrath family; I was there that night at Clonmel when it won; never missed a meeting in those days. They came from the village you know, owned the big house as you come into the village from Cashel. It was sold a few years ago to some Yank when the mother Agnes died. The father died years ago. Go speak to Dot in the Post Office next door, she will tell you more about them, right village gossip she is."

I thanked Jimmy for his time and paid for a cup of tea the cashier had brought down for him.

I left the betting shop and indicated to Alice with an open palm that I would be five more minutes before heading into the food store that contained the Post Office. There was only one customer in the shop I could see so I went straight up to the counter.

"Hi, are you Dot? I have just spoken to Jimmy in the betting shop and he said you may be able to help me. I am a lecturer at Dublin University and I am doing a paper on Irish greyhound racing and one owner in particular who came from this village, a Mr McGrath. Did you know him?" I asked handing her the same photograph I had shown Jimmy.

She moved the glasses that were hanging around her neck onto the bridge of her nose.

"Yes, that's him. What do you want to know and who did you say you were again?" she said studying me closely.

This accent lark was proving hard to maintain so I needed to be careful what I said, "Higginbotham, Neville Higginbotham of Dublin University. We have no records of him; Mr McGrath that is; owning anymore dogs after this one and wondered if he had died or moved away? Jimmy tells me the family still lived here until a few years ago and it has left a huge hole in our research and the part that Oola has played in the history of greyhound racing."

That was enough to loosen her tongue and I got the impression very quickly that once she started it was going to be very difficult to stop her. She was a living gossip train with no driver to pull the brake as she was going downhill.

She went through the family history child by child until she came to the youngest. She paused momentarily before continuing.

"I guess it was around the time this picture was taken, let me think. My Janice was fifty last year and she went to school with Sally-Ann and you say this picture was taken thirty four years ago? That would make Janice and Sam both seventeen. Sam moved over the UK at that age as she didn't finish school. She went over to help a sick auntie apparently but none of us believed that. It was just a story Agnes wanted us to believe."

"I'm sorry, who is Sam?" I asked.

"The youngest daughter?"

"I thought her name was Sally-Ann?"

"It is. Sally-Ann was known as Sam because of her initials, Sally-Ann McGrath, S A M" she said, looking at me as if it was a blatantly obvious thing to assume.

No wonder she and the priest were so close, they were brother and sister.

"So why did Agnes, her mother, make up a story about her then?"

"Because she was pregnant that's why. A good catholic family like that in an area like this, the scandal and embarrassment of a child being born out of wedlock would have been torture for Agnes, especially with her eldest being a Priest. I don't think she has been back since. I've not seen her anyway, didn't even make it back for either of her parent's funerals. I know my Janice was desperately upset that she never stayed in contact."

"Are you absolutely certain she was pregnant? I mean, could she not have had a sick auntie and just not bothered to come back" I asked hoping I was wrong.

"Young man, in a small place like this I can tell you what most people have for their breakfast, dinner and tea and the reason I know that is because I have sold them the food. Young Sally-Ann went to England for one of two things and helping her supposed sick auntie wasn't one of them. It was either for an abortion or to have the baby and my money would be on the latter as even that old battle axe Agnes, God rest her soul, wasn't that big a hypocrite."

"So who is the father then?"

She looked at me blankly and shrugged her shoulders; the runaway train had run out of puff as far as information went.

I was convinced I knew who the father was and he was expecting me at his kennels twenty minutes ago.

CHAPTER TWENTY EIGHT

"What are you looking so happy about" asked Alice as I got back in the car, "you've been gone ages?"

"We have just had a major breakthrough and I just need to confirm it with Tomas Lowry and then we can head back" I said as I pointed the car in the direction of Cashel.

It took us no more than twenty minutes to find his kennels and he was waiting for us as we pulled up sharply.

"You're late and I have dogs to get ready for racing" he said with no warmth whatsoever.

He was well over six foot in height with little or no hair on his head. He definitely had a presence about him and was entitled to do so given his training successes. We exited the car and I offered my apologies for our lateness. I didn't expect to take up much of his time.

"So what can I do for you? Tommy called me and asked me to spare you five minutes as you were passing so what can I be doing for you?" said Tomas.

He hadn't asked us to introduce ourselves or offered his hand in welcome so I got straight to the point.

"Could you take a look at this picture for me please" I said handing him the piece of paper that had become well-worn.

He looked at it and then at me and Alice in turn before handing it back.

"Is that it? You just wanted me look at a picture of a trophy presentation that was taken over thirty odd years ago?"

"Not quite. I am sure you know who the dog is and who the owners are but I was wondering if you could tell me why Mr

McGrath never owned another dog? I think I know but I would be grateful if you confirm it for me and then we will be on our way. I promise you will never hear from me again and that whatever you tell me stays on this driveway. I am here because a friend of mine in the UK has been killed and another is being blackmailed and I want to find out why."

He looked angry, "I have no idea why he packed up and why should I tell you anything?"

"It is quite simple really" I took a deep breath as I was trusting my judgement and if I had got it wrong it would have been a very wasted journey, "how would your wife feel if she knew you had another son as I can almost guarantee she doesn't know."

"You are deluded" he replied but didn't deny it.

"Am I, are you really willing to take that chance as I am pretty confident that the young girl who you are stood behind is the one who is doing the blackmailing and I will take a wild guess the reason her father, who was a prominent greyhound owner at the time this picture was taken, ceased owning dogs was because his greyhound trainers son had got his youngest daughter pregnant?"

He said nothing.

"I will also take a wild guess that you had no idea you had a son? I have met your son and he looks exactly like you do in that picture."

He snatched the picture back out of my hand and looked at it again. "You're wrong. I do know I have a son. Sally-Ann's father came and saw my father about six-months after he was born to tell him. He told us that the child had been adopted. My father got the impression it was eating away at Mr McGrath and he thought I should be told. I had only been married about six months when I slept with her and it was only the once. I regretted it the moment it happened but Sally-Ann was a very attractive girl and very persuasive. She still is."

The fact he knew he had a son had completely thrown me, I had based our whole visit on the premise I could use it as leverage without resorting to the underhand tactics of blackmail which I wouldn't do. I was so caught up in my own thoughts of this particular bombshell I had missed his last comment. It had passed me by but it hadn't Alice.

"What do you mean, still is?" she asked. "Is she blackmailing you as well?"

He stopped, turned and walked back towards us.

"Follow me" he said.

We walked out onto the main road and followed him at a brisk pace for about 100 yards where we stopped outside a large open field where six or seven greyhound pups were playing merrily. They saw Tomas and headed straight for the fence that divided them from us, yapping and play fighting, seeking his attention.

"Make it look like you are interested in the pups, the trees around here have eyes and ears it would sometimes appear" he said putting his fingers through the wire fencing for the pups to try and nibble on.

"She came and saw me about two years ago. I didn't recognise her at all. She made out she was interested in buying a couple of dogs that were for sale. I welcomed her into my house and we talked about all my recent success and how she had always been a big admirer of my training. I lapped it up of course as you would. She then dropped an envelope on the table and told me to have a look."

He was visibly ageing before our eyes.

"As soon as I saw him in the picture I knew who it was, it was like looking into a mirror over thirty years ago. It was my son. At this point I still didn't know who she was. As I'd said, I had been told that he'd been adopted but had no idea with whom or in which country. I have three daughters of my own and none of them were ever interested in the dogs" he said as he stopped to light a cigarette.

"I asked her what she wanted as if it was money she had come to the wrong place as all mine had gone on university fees and expanding this place over the years. The bottom has fallen out of the economy as everyone knows and selling pups and winning big races just about keeps food on the table."

We walked on a bit further to the next paddock and again the pups hurried over to meet their master at the fence.

"'I don't want your money Tee Jay' she'd said and that is when I realised it was Sally-Ann. She was the only person who called me that. I was christened Tomas Jack but most people referred to me as just Tomas, not her. She said she wanted me to give her some good dogs to run in the UK for a little project she was working on."

"What project?" I asked.

"She didn't say, just that she needed a good dog for her and some friends to have some fun with. It took me about three months to find one who was half decent and when I did it was sent over. It got to the St Leger final so it was pretty useful."

"It didn't stop at one dog though did it?" I asked.

He looked down towards the floor; his body language told me it hadn't been.

"She threatened to show my wife the photographs and tell her about the baby. She also said she would leak it to some influential owners within the kennel. My wife has no idea about the baby which is bad enough but it would ruin my reputation and without that I am nothing. I guess I have sent over another four since, all good dogs as well."

"I would rather continue sending them over than risk losing what I have so if you are going to go after Sally-Ann you are going to have to do it without my help, I'm sorry."

I could have threatened to do exactly what she was doing but it would serve no purpose. His involvement as far as I could see was in no way linked to any of the gambles or Andy's death. He had been manipulated for her gain, just like it appeared that Phil had been. Who else did she have a stranglehold over? Had she been blackmailing Andy Whelan as well?

"Have you been in contact with him yourself since she has been back in contact?" I asked.

I had put the question to him at our furthest point from the kennels but it took him until we had walked back to the car before he provided an answer. "No I haven't been and Sally-Ann has warned me I am not to start looking for him after all these years. I have no idea of his name or where he lives. She says he doesn't need me in his life so I guess she has seen him. It doesn't mean I don't want to though, it just means under the circumstances I won't."

I thanked him for his time and gave him my word his secret was safe with me. I intended to keep that promise. It was something he'd had to live with for over thirty years and probably for the rest of his life.

The drive back to Leenane had been a slow one and had taken just over four hours. Aoife had warned us to take it easy once we got to Maam Cross as the road markings were non-existent and the sheep did have a tendency to sleep in the middle of the road if the mood took them. Alice had rung ahead and spoken to Tommy to say we would be back as soon as we could but could he not mention to Sean that we were staying over if he could possibly avoid it. He agreed without question.

We arrived just after seven. The rain that had started to fall just after leaving Galway had intensified as we negotiated the last long hill down into the village. We pulled upside the house and Aoife called Trixie in before we got out of the car. Tommy was up at the kennels making sure everything was secure as another storm was forecast overnight.

We settled down around the kitchen table and Aoife brought over a pot of tea and advised she had a shepherd's pie in the oven and it would be ready in about an hour if we wanted to get cleaned up. It smelt great and I was starving. I wanted to speak to Tommy first to bring him up to speed without divulging any of the information Tomas had told us earlier. It was imperative that Sam did not know we were here and if the priest was going to be coming around we needed to watch what we were saying.

"Good evening you two, had a good day?" said Tommy as he removed his wellington boots before entering the kitchen.

"Yes thanks Tommy, very productive" I replied.

"Father Sean will be here in about an hour. So why isn't he to know you are here?"

"You remember the picture you showed me last night of the

trophy presentation, well I recognised someone in it so I asked a few questions in Oola today and to cut a long story short it would appear that the woman we have been referring to as Sam is actually Sally-Ann McGrath. She is Father Sean's sister!"

"Well that would explain why she visits so much but why is that important?" he asked.

From his perspective I could see it wouldn't have meant much and I had promised Tomas Lowry I wouldn't say anything about his infidelity of years gone by. I looked towards Alice for some help.

"Tell him" she said.

"Tell me what?" said Tommy

"Last night, when we went over to Father Sean's, Alice disappeared for five minutes looking for the toilet. She went into one of the guest rooms and saw lots of women's clothes, being a bit of a nosey parker she took a look in the wardrobe and she came across loads more. Whilst moving things around a large envelope fell out onto the floor and spilled out its contents. There were photographs and some other papers. Alice didn't tell me any of this until we went to bed which is why I am telling you now."

I could see that Tommy was angry and Aoife looked far from impressed.

"Please let me finish. I know how it looks but it wasn't our reason for coming here and I am sure I speak for Alice when I say she apologises for snooping but I am glad she did as I think we have had a breakthrough of some sort. Alice can you go and get the pictures and papers please."

Alice looked reluctant to do so but did as I asked and returned with the brown padded envelope momentarily.

I removed the pictures and paperwork and handed them to Tommy who studied them with Aoife who had pulled up a chair beside him. He looked at each in turn and read what was written, occasionally looking in my direction as he did so.

"So what is the purpose of these and who is this gentleman?" asked Aoife.

"Last night I told you about all the first time out winners Richard Quinn was having and the gambles that were being landed and you said that surely somebody within the industry should have picked up on it. Well the person whose job it is to investigate the gambles is in that picture and he is Alice's father. It would appear he is being blackmailed. We will be speaking to him on Sunday when we get back and ask him for his side of the story.

Phil, he is the guy in the picture, asked me to look into the gambles involving Rainbow Warrior but he has not said anything to either of us about being blackmailed. The only reason Alice took the envelope from the house is because she panicked and was in shock."

"I am so sorry Tommy" said Alice.

Tommy said nothing and again studied the pictures.

"What else aren't you telling me Joseph?"

I didn't want to tell him about the mobile and I wasn't going to.

"Many years ago when I was Racing Manager at Stony Stratford I had an affair with a trainer's wife and I had photographs taken of me allegedly taking a payoff from a kennel hand. Those pictures led to me being sacked and whoever took those pictures has taken these ones as well of that I am certain.

If you look closely enough at one of the pictures you can make out a reflection in a van wing mirror of a man taking the picture. He is sat in a car opposite and you can just about make out a number plate" I said reaching across for the picture to which I was referring.

I had studied the photographs for about half an hour this morning looking for any clues whilst Alice was in the bath. I hadn't mentioned anything to her as I wanted to leave it until tonight. She had the means to check the number plate when we got back and I also didn't want it to distract from our visit today. I needed her to be fully focused on what we were doing and after the way she had picked up on what Tomas Lowry had said it had proved to be the correct thing to do. We couldn't do anything about Phil until we had spoken to him, we had agreed on that.

Alice took the photograph from me and studied it. She asked Aoife if she had a magnifying glass or an old pair of spectacles that she could borrow to get a better look. Tommy passed her his. Holding the lens above the picture that was now flat on the kitchen table, she moved it gradually up and down until she could clearly read what I had seen.

"Got it, I can read the whole bloody thing" she said with a smile. "I can trace this when I get back, we will make a copper of you yet Mr Jackson."

"So what now?" asked Tommy.

"Father Sean has never mentioned to you that Sam is his sister and there is obviously a reason for that and that is between them. You cannot let on that you know or that we have these pictures or who we are. When he comes around tonight I want you to say how well Rainbow Warrior is and that you are going to be having a big bet on it Wednesday with your contacts."

"But I'm not, I have already discussed that with Jamie remember?" said Tommy.

"You know that and I know that but he doesn't and I want him to tell Sam so that she has a big punt on it. I will work the rest out when I get back to England. I want to be able to get under her skin especially when she has lost some money and take the control away from her for once. As I said to Alice last night she is pulling all the strings and I am convinced that she was blackmailing Andy as well. If she was, did it have anything to do with his death?" I said, knowing that the mobile phone I had in my possession wasn't proof enough in itself. In fact if I was found with it I would suddenly become a prime suspect in his disappearance.

"Tell him we are potential new owners and continue to call me Joseph" I said whilst laughing.

Father Sean arrived just after we had finished Aoife's delicious shepherd's pie and jam roly poly with steaming custard for pudding. He only stayed for an hour as he said he didn't want to intrude whilst Tommy and Aoife had visitors. It was obvious from the conversation that he loved greyhound racing, a true enthusiast who liked a bet within reason. Tommy slipped into the conversation that Rainbow Warrior was in great shape and that he would be having a good sized bet on Wednesday when he contested the semi-final of the Golden Lead.

“How big a bet?” asked Sean.

“It will be a big one. Jamie says the dog is absolutely flying. I have looked at the trap draw and he should be no bigger than even money with the bookmakers” said Tommy with a straight face.

“Brilliant, I will let Sam know and she can put some on for me.”

He said his farewells and we took ourselves off to bed. It had been a really long day.

We had only been in Tommy’s company for just under two days but it had been great to become re-acquainted, he and Aoife had been the perfect hosts and the trek to the back of beyond as Phil had described it had been worthwhile. We had a couple of hours to spare before we needed to head back to Knock. Aoife had written down a list of places we should see before we went. Alice borrowed a pair of boots and we took a walk up to a place called Ashdoo, it was a waterfall that could be seen on the mountain called Bing she had said. It was clearly visible from the kennel block but had taken us forty five minutes to reach on foot.

The walk had been worth it though. The recent rain had ensured that the mountain streams were in full flood and the water roared as it cascaded over the waterfall into the pool below before continuing its meandering journey down through the village. It was a breath taking view from here down to the Killary, surrounded by steep mountains on either side with only small dots of white representing the houses and bungalows. It was so peaceful with no other humans in sight, just sheep. Thankfully the walk back was all downhill.

We said our goodbyes and headed for the airport but not before promising Tommy and Aoife we would be back.

“You have Jamie’s number if you need anything for Wednesday. Let me know the fall out. That fecking bitch won’t get the better of me” he shouted as we pulled away, chased by Trixie.

CHAPTER TWENTY NINE

Orla had already checked the results on the internet and knew Richard would be coming home in a foul mood. Of their last twenty runners they had only had one winner and none since she had seen Joe earlier in the week.

'God I miss him' she muttered to herself as she checked on the kids before taking herself off to bed. She wanted to be asleep before Richard came in.

He had gone to the track on the Saturday night with ten dogs in the van and he would have been hopeful of having at least one or two winners. He had stormed into the bedroom and switched on the light.

"Stop pretending you are asleep and get your arse downstairs we need to talk" he shouted.

Orla dressed slowly and made her way to the kitchen and was surprised to see that not only was Richard waiting for her but Sam and Ken were as well.

"What the fuck are they doing here?" shouted Orla.

"Give him your mobile" said Sam.

"Fuck off and get out of my house. I am going back to bed" said Orla turning to leave the kitchen.

Ken blocked her path whilst Richard searched through her handbag for her mobile. It wasn't in there as Orla had it in her trouser pocket. She should have turned it off but she hadn't and it went off as Richard rang it. He took it from her and handed it to Sam. It wasn't password protected so Sam went through it. Whatever she was looking for wasn't on there. She threw the phone back to Richard.

"Have you been in touch with him again?"

"With who?"

"Jackson, that's who" said Ken speaking for the first time "someone tipped him off that I was waiting for him in the car park on Wednesday and that could have only have been you. It cost me just over two hundred quid to get the car fixed and that loser will pay."

"If he is a loser then I am not sure what that makes you but no I haven't been in touch with him. How could I? I don't have his number" said Orla, delighted that she deleted her recent call to him from her call list.

"I will be watching you and don't think I won't be" said Sam.

"Who the bloody hell do you think you are, you old tart? I am not frightened of you. These two may be your little puppets and jump at your every word but don't think for one minute that you scare me…………."

"Stop it Orla" shouted Richard.

"Stop what Richard? Ever since this woman has come into our kennels she has taken over with this dummy lapping around her heels. He tried it on with me so many times and you still trust him. If he was the last man on earth I wouldn't touch him with two barge poles. I might catch something."

Orla could see that Ken was getting angry but it was the first time that she had publically belittled him in front of anyone other than Richard.

"Is this true?" asked Sam looking straight at Ken.

"What of it, you said yourself that she is a slapper, why shouldn't I have a bit of it; every other fucker has. I hear she is a right goer?"

He was just about to continue when Richard launched himself at him from across the table landing a punch on his chin in mid-flight, knocking Ken to the floor. Richard picked himself up and hit him again before being pulled off by Sam. Orla had done nothing, she just stood and watched. For the first time that she could remember Richard had come to her defence. Ken picked himself up, blood trickled from a cut lip and judging by the mark around his eye he would have a lovely shiner in the morning.

"You come anywhere near my wife and next time it won't be a fist I will hit you with, have you got that" said Richard as Orla held his now red fist under a running tap of cold water.

"You don't know the half of it Richard, without me................" Ken began but he didn't finish what he was saying as Sam shouted him down and told him to wait for her in the car outside. He tried to argue but his protests fell on deaf ears as Sam got her way. With Ken out of the room, she came over to see how Richard was whilst looking at Orla with disdain.

"The winners will come, trust me on that" she said, "I will be having a big bet on Rainbow Warrior on Wednesday so that should ease some of your money problems Richard, if not I can give you some to tide you over."

"We don't want your money Sam now please leave" said Orla.

Sam looked towards Richard hoping that he would counter act Orla's request. There was nothing forthcoming so she left the pair to it. Orla made the pair of them a mug of coffee and brought them back to the table, his hand now wrapped in a wet tea-towel and a bag of frozen peas.

"What has happened to us Richard? Is there something going on between you and Sam that I should be aware of? Are you having an affair with her?

She had said to Joe when she had met him that she didn't care what Richard was getting up to or who with. Seeing his reaction tonight had made her realise that she did care for him. She may not love him like she thought she loved Joe but he was the father of her children and he was a good father. He did his best to provide for them and he knew he had his faults.

"I will never be enough for you Orla will I? I try my best but I would never be unfaithful to you. All I know is greyhounds, I am crap with people; we both know that but you hurt me so much when you had your first affair and then when you slept with Jackson that killed me. Those photographs were so clear and Sam bringing so many good dogs into the kennel has been the perfect distraction to our problems. Our relationship is purely business and that is it. She was having an affair though and I only found that out a few weeks ago. Ken and his big mouth let it slip and if she finds out she will probably leave the kennel and we cannot afford that.

I promise you that all these gambles that have been going on with Rainbow Warrior and that black pup have absolutely nothing to do with me but because of it I thought we were being harshly graded, but I don't think we are."

"She isn't having it off with Ken surely?" said Orla in shock.

Richard put down his now empty coffee mug and played with the handle.

"God no, it wasn't with him, it was with Andy Whelan and by all accounts she had been for about six months. She is very protective of Ken though for some reason" said Richard.

"Are you certain or is it Ken talking bollocks again? I thought Andy was gay?" said Orla, inwardly delighted that it wasn't her husband who Sam was trying to get her claws into.

"I am pretty certain he isn't making it up and it would explain a couple of things as well. Firstly the number of winners we were having and the bets she was landing and also why we aren't having any now. We aren't being harshly graded now; we were just being easily graded previously by Andy."

"I don't understand?"

"I am not sure I do either but I am off to bed and we will just have to work harder to get us out of this mess won't we?" he said with a smile, the first time she had seen him smile in months.

"Well I better come with you then" she said and smiled in return, taking him by the hand and leading him up the stairs to her bedroom.

CHAPTER THIRTY

I had intended to arrive at Alice's flat in Woburn Sands well before Phil was due. She welcomed me with a kiss and took me through to the kitchen where she had been preparing dinner.

"I am no Aoife in the cooking department but I can prepare a decent roast" she said whilst putting the joint of beef back in the oven. "Dad rang earlier, should be here in ten minutes."

Phil arrived in good spirits. "Okay boys and girls, how was your trip to the Emerald Isle? Useful or a complete waste of time and my money?" he joked.

Alice suggested we went through to the living room as dinner wouldn't be ready for at least an hour. She led the way. I sat myself down beside her with Phil opposite.

No point messing around I thought, let's get on with it.

"Whilst we were away we actually learnt lots of things. Firstly you will be glad to know I have found out who instigated the gambles on Rainbow Warrior and they are just a good old legitimate coup but I will come back to the details shortly. We also found out details on Sam Hampshire we didn't know previously and we also came across these" I said pulling out the brown padded envelope from under the cushion I was sat on.

Alice said nothing as Phil opened the envelope to reveal the photographs and the papers that went with them. I didn't know what I was expecting him to say or do. It was blatantly obvious he'd seen them before. He didn't look shocked or take much interest in what had been written down.

"Where did you get these?" asked Phil, putting the envelope down on the table beside his chair and picking up his drink.

"Who is she dad, who is the woman in the picture that you are in deep conversation with and giving money to? She looks like a prostitute. Have you been doing the dirty on my mother because if you have I swear I will chop your nuts off?"

"Where did you get them?" he asked again more forcibly, he looked and sounded angry.

"Answer my question Dad and I will tell you?"

He sat back in his chair and took his time before responding.

"The girl in the picture is Melanie Giles and you are right, she is a prostitute but no, I haven't done the dirty on your mother. I served with her father in Northern Ireland; he was like a brother to me until he had both his legs blown off by a roadside bomb outside of Londonderry. He had fallen on hard times since I left the army and I used to bung him a few quid now and again but I hadn't heard from him for ages until Melanie contacted me about four months ago.

She called to say that Dave, that's her dad, was in danger of losing his house and the MoD have cut back his benefits and he had built up a lot of debt and could I help, She said he needed about two grand to see him right. I had no hesitation; you never desert a fallen comrade. You just don't. She gave me details of where I was to meet her to give her the money as if I went around to the house Dave would just turn me away as he hated charity.

About ten days later a brown envelope similar to this arrived in the post at work. I was bloody shocked when I saw them and read what was written. They didn't look good and given my position the press would have had a field day. You can see the paper headlines now 'Bookies man scores with odds-on certainty'.

I immediately rang the number I had for Dave and his wife answered it. I asked if I could speak with him as I wanted to get to the bottom of it and imagine my surprise when she told me he had died three years earlier. He suffered complications during routine surgery apparently. I had no idea. I wouldn't have missed his funeral for the world but they kept it just to family she told me."

He looked extremely annoyed with himself for being sucked in.

"So what did Melanie have to say?" I asked.

"I have no idea; I haven't been able to find her since. I have had someone make discreet enquiries for me but he has turned up nothing. I can cope with losing the money but I feel like such a fool for not being more vigilant."

"So at what point did the blackmailing start then as I assume that this wasn't the last of the letters you received?"

"Who says I have received anymore?"

"I do Phil. There is no way whatsoever a man as vigilant and thorough as you would have missed all the winners Richard Quinn was having unless you were told to ignore them. Did you bring me in on this to help find Andy Whelan or find out who was blackmailing you because I can answer the latter now but I have no idea why Andy Whelan turned up dead, not yet anyway?" I said.

He considered his answer carefully.

"A bit of both I suppose. Yes I was being blackmailed but I did look into the gambles as I wanted to have some ammunition of my own should I find out who was behind them. I couldn't see anything inappropriate; the dogs looked like they were being graded correctly but just kept on winning. I knew something like this was right up your street and I didn't know where to start. Alice was keeping me posted on all your progress but once Andy turned up dead the goal posts were moved. As I said before the Police are only interested in this as a murder enquiry now but I still had these bloody pictures hanging over me."

I remembered our initial meeting and how personally he was taking Andy's disappearance. No wonder he didn't want his bosses knowing I was helping him.

"So Alice kept you posted on everything did she?" I said looking straight at her for some reaction.

"Pretty much!"

"Joe can I have a word with you in the kitchen please?" interrupted an angry Alice.

I followed her into the kitchen and moved over to the sink.

"I have a rough idea where you were just about to go with that Joe and if you think I slept with you and went to Ireland with you just so I could keep a close eye on you then you are wrong. In fact you would be very very wrong. I had no idea my father was being blackmailed and I was shocked by the pictures, disgusted in fact. Do you think I made that up, did I plant the mobile as well?" she said with tears in her eyes. "Now is not the time or the place to tell him about you and me. I want there to be an 'us' more than I thought possible but you have to trust me on this. I believe what he is telling me, call it a coppers instinct or a daughters intuition but between us I think we are getting somewhere now let's go back in there and tell him what we know. What do you say?"

I had believed him as well but her outburst had been very persuasive.

"Sorry about that Phil" I said as we re-entered the room "now where were we. Oh yes, I was just about to tell you who was blackmailing you."

"Yes you were."

"You and god know how many others are being blackmailed by Sam Hampshire. She has you in her pocket, she has the bookies at the track pricing up the races as she wants; she stitched me up I think it is fair to assume she probably had Andy Whelan for something as well. Ken Kelly does as she says and Richard Quinn would appear to be frightened of losing her out of the kennels.

The one bit of good news is that we may have a lead on who has been taking the photographs. There is a number plate on one of the pictures and Alice is going to run it through the Police National Computer tomorrow when she goes back to work. The PNC check will tell us who the car is registered to and I think we should do some digging into him and maybe pay him a little visit. If you want to keep the blackmailing quiet you need to keep the Police out of it.

We also found out the priest who owns half of Rainbow Warrior is the brother of Sam and she goes over to Ireland regularly. A seed has been planted with him that Rainbow Warrior will win on Wednesday night and hopefully he will feed it back to Sam in the coming days so she can do her bit and manipulate the bookies to price up accordingly so he is a bigger price than he should be. I get the impression he has no idea what his sister is up to."

"You can't do that, the firms will go ballistic, they have lost fortunes already and you told me you'd tell me who was behind them" said Phil.

"Keep your hair on, the firms will be getting some of their money back on this one as it won't be winning. I can't tell you how I know but I have been assured he won't and I trust my source. Do you agree Alice?" I asked.

"Trust him on this one Dad."

"Right, you wanted to know about the gambles? Well the simple fact is the gamble landed on Double Vision when he won at 6-1 had nothing to do with Sam or the bloke who has been cleaning up on Rainbow Warrior. I think it may have been one of the bigger punters at the track who was following his own instincts. He had cottoned on to the times being manipulated and was betting accordingly.

Sam was far from happy by all accounts she wasn't in on the Rainbow Warrior coups and threatened to shorten the price in future races if she wasn't told. On Wednesday you need to forewarn the big firms and your bosses you have this matter under control. We need her to get as much money on as possible."

"You do know they will still want to test the dog on Wednesday after it races? How do I explain it if he returns a positive for some drug when I have convinced them it won't win, can you tell me that?"

I hadn't thought of that as Tommy hadn't told us how it wouldn't win. Trust in Jamie were his words, trust the young lad.

"It won't I promise" I said crossing my legs as the fingers would have been too obvious.

"We also need to get a meeting with Sam's bosses and when I say we I mean you, me and Alice. We need to find out who has been banking the money for Andy Whelan and where they were collecting it from in the first place. It should be easy enough to do as they have a paper trail for those sorts of things. One of the guys I bet alongside at Kempton regularly puts cash into his account via one of the exchange reps and he is given a receipt every time. Alice's presence may add a little weight. It is imperative Sam doesn't know we are looking into her."

I hadn't yet mentioned the mobile Alice had found and I wasn't sure now was the right time to bring it into the conversation.

"So who has been having the big gambles then Joe, can I not put a stop to them to keep the firms off my back?" Phil asked.

"I wouldn't worry about them Phil if I were you. They are a thing of the past" I said hoping Alice wouldn't contradict me or remember Tommy had said he had one last gamble planned before retiring for good. If she had remembered she said nothing, which I was grateful for.

"So do we have anything that can link her with the other gambles and Andy, surely we can tie her into those?" asked Phil.

"Nothing concrete but I am working on it. I might need to get hold of Orla again and I will do that tomorrow. Alice needs to check the car registration and you Phil can start on Sam's bosses. I suggest we enjoy the dinner Alice has prepared and start afresh again in the morning. I only have one day booked for work this week at SIS and that's on Friday. Do we have anything on Andy's car that turned up at Holyhead?" I said.

"Oh god that reminds me" said Alice "give me a minute and I will bring those passenger lists down from upstairs."

There were four ferry sailings from Holyhead to Ireland, two to Dublin and two to Dun Laoghaire that had sailed within twelve hours of the car being left in the car park. If whoever had dumped the car was in fact just a joy rider then we'd be looking for a needle in a haystack but if we were lucky a name would jump off the page.

We took a list each. The sailing to Dublin had consisted of mainly freight traffic, 65 trucks, 26 cars and 34 foot passengers. It was the busiest of the four sailings so it shouldn't take us long.

We repeated the process for all four lists, passing them between us as three sets of eyes were better than one. Alice completed her set first and drew a blank and passed her final listing to me. I almost missed it but there it was shining like a beacon from the page.

"You beauty, I've bloody got you?" I shouted out loud.

They both rushed over to see what I had found.

"There you go, third from the bottom on the foot passenger list, 02:30 sailing from Holyhead to Dublin. They both looked at the piece of paper and the name in capital letters I had circled in blue ink."

"It says GRATH, thought we were looking for Hampshire, Kelly, Quinn or McGrath?" said a dejected Phil as he returned to his chair.

"Take another look Phil. Alice can you pass me over my mobile please as I need to call DCI Baker?"

Phil had taken the paper back from me and still couldn't see what I had seen whilst Alice brought over my phone. Phil passed the list to Alice to see if she could make out what I thought was blatantly obvious. She handed it back to me still none the wiser.

"God you two are bloody useless and maybe I will make a copper after all!" I said whilst laughing. "All the names are in capital letters, surname first in the left column followed by the initials in the next column, in this case the initials are S A M C."

They still both look puzzled.

"Are you two deliberately playing dumb? Look at the two names above Grath and the one below" I said turning the page towards them to look again.

"Donald, Fee and Pherson" said Phil.

I looked to the ceiling for inspiration before adding; "Now look at the initials?"

"MMC, FMC and GMC" said Alice slowly reading from the list that was shaking in my hand.

The pair looked at each other and then back at me, their facial expression suggested they thought I had lost the plot.

"Jesus you two are hard work. The MC is part of the surname and not the Christian name. You have McDonald, McFee, McGrath and McPherson. Grath SAMC is Sally Ann-Mc bloody Grath. That bitch was on the boat. Check another of your lists and see if it follows the same pattern."

We again took a list each and we all found a name following the same pattern. Neill NMC, Ellistrim NMC and Leod SMC.

I found DCI Baker's number in my mobile and dialled.

"Good evening Joe how are you?" he asked.

"I am very well Detective Inspector and I think you may well be by the time I finish this call" I said with major excitement.

"Please call me Alex, a lot less formal and it works better for me" he replied.

"Ok Alex, when can I come and see you as I may have a breakthrough on the car dumping at Holyhead? I understand you think it will have been joyriders but I think you are wrong. I think I can put a name to the person driving the car. Are you able to get hold of CCTV coverage from Holyhead as if you can I will have the proof I need?"

"Slow down Joe, slow down. We are looking for a murderer remember, not a car thief? I can't just go and request information like that on a whim without something more concrete. My superiors will have me back on traffic duty. You will need something more substantive for me to get North-Wales back involved."

I had the mobile phone but did I tell him that?

"If I can get hold of something else will you then request the CCTV footage for me? I honestly think it is linked to Andy's disappearance" I pleaded.

"Joe, if you can link the two then yes I will request it but only if it is a strong link. At the moment we could do with any lead as so far we have nothing. We have no idea how he got onto the track let alone into the lake. The track has 24 hour security which has thrown up nothing. It has six-foot perimeter fencing running all around it. Unless he could fly, was invisible or was a horse he couldn't have got past security.

We are expecting CCTV coverage from the surrounding area in the next day or two. The petrol station has CCTV and there were new traffic camera's put in on the Sunbury roundabout the week before the incident to catch offenders in the yellow box. We will need to go through all that lot first and hopefully turn up something. Thanks for the call Joe and stay in touch. Good night."

I disconnected the phone and placed it on the table. I was dejected, I'd really thought we'd made a breakthrough but I understood he had more pressing matters to investigate.

I would have to do some more digging starting first thing tomorrow.

CHAPTER THIRTY ONE

Phil hadn't stuck around for long after dinner the previous evening; I assumed it was more out of embarrassment than the excuse given that he wanted to get started on arranging a meeting with Sam's boss as quickly as possible. We had discussed and agreed an approach we would use without raising too much suspicion at the exchange. It had become pretty obvious she had friends in high places and must know where all the skeletons were buried to have obtained so much influence. Only last week she'd said she could have me banned again, after what I'd learnt in the past couple of days I didn't doubt it.

We all had our own jobs to do and had agreed to keep in touch as and when we had any information that would prove beneficial. I had emailed Orla when I had got back to the flat and was delighted to see she'd sent a reply just after seven this morning. Being trial day at Stony Stratford she would have been up early to get the dogs prepared. She agreed to pop around at seven this evening.

With little else on I decided to look back over the qualifying trials of Double Vision I had neglected to do previously. Sure enough Andy had manipulated his trial times just like the others and it was fair to assume that Tony 'the timer' had benefited handsomely when he won at 6-1 on his third start.

Phil called just after ten, he sounded happy enough with no hint of being uncomfortable with last night's revelations. It was probably a huge weight off his shoulders but he would never admit it.

"Morning matey, meeting all set for 2pm this afternoon if you can get your arse down to Kempton. Alice can make it and reckons she will have the details from the car in the picture by then" he said.

"Kempton's not on today so why are we meeting there?" I replied.

"You're getting a bit slack in your old age? What with all the bad weather the British Horseracing Authority have put on three extra all-weather meetings this week, one at Kempton today, one at Lingfield tomorrow and Southwell are racing now on Thursday. Bookmakers footing the bill because of all the revenue they have lost in the last month or so. We can kill two birds with one stone as it happens, the guy who deposited all the money for Andy is working at the track.

Lewis, he's my contact, has agreed to meet us there but he needs to pick up the paperwork for all the deposits on the way. He is fuming so we need to make sure we are on the ball."

"Yes we do. I will be there don't worry. I need to be back here before seven though as Orla will be popping around."

"You don't waste much time mate, how did you get hold of her that quickly? I was working on this virtually all last night when I got back and yet you get her round just like that. Is there something you aren't telling me?"

I couldn't gather from his tone whether he was mocking me or being deadly serious. I had let my guard down as I still hadn't told either of them that I had Orla's email address.

"I called Tommy's grandson on his mobile and asked to speak to her. I assumed they would both be at the tracks for trials" I said without hesitation.

"Oh right, see you later then" he said and disconnected.

I was late arriving and found the three of them waiting for me in the restaurant on the top floor of the grandstand. Phil has managed to secure a table on the lowest level overlooking the betting ring. From a privacy point of view it was ideal as the few diners that were in attendance preferred to be nearer the winning line at the opposite end.

There were only five bookmakers in attendance and the crowd was sparse as was normally the case when hastily arranged extra meetings were put on for the benefit of the betting shops.

Phil rose to his feet as I arrived and introduced me to Lewis who was in a half sitting half standing position as I shook him by the hand. Alice remained seated but smiled as I sat down beside her. She even managed a quick squeeze of my thigh for good measure.

"Right, now we are all here let's get down to business. Shall I start and are we all agreed that what is said here stays here?" asked Phil looking around the table.

We all nodded.

"Lewis, as you are aware I have been looking into, for some time now, the 'gambles' that have been taking place at Stony Stratford without any success whatsoever. About three weeks ago I asked Joe here, as an ex-racing manager, if he could help, to see if he could establish any patterns that would get the big firms off my back. I am glad to report he has and they are now a thing of the past."

Not quite Phil.

"Whilst undertaking his investigation the same name kept cropping up and that was Sam Hampshire. We are led to believe she has some control over the bookmakers and Joe here also has a strong belief she was instrumental in his sacking at Stony Stratford but has no idea why. As we discussed previously over the phone he was dismissed after being framed taking a back-hander. Now you may ask why I am so convinced he was framed, well that is simple. About four months ago I received a package blackmailing me. Until yesterday I had kept it to myself and told no one."

I hadn't expected Phil to tell him that but he was laying his cards on the table. We needed Lewis' help and Phil knew that without it we were stuffed. He paused momentarily to take a large sip of water.

"Whilst investigating the bigger gambles Alice and Joe came across the same photographs by accident amongst Sam's belongs in Ireland. Now if needs be I will pass what I have over to the Police and they can investigate it. It will undoubtedly bring bad publicity on me but also on your company. We have not established any link between Sam and Andy's disappearance and him turning up here in the lake. Now I don't know about you but I'd rather leave the Police out of it but Alice will tell you they will leave no stone unturned if it helps them. Isn't that right?" he said looking towards her for confirmation.

Alice nodded.

"Do you have anything to add?" Lewis asked me.

I wanted to make sure that whatever I said didn't come across as holding a grudge against Sam who I had convinced myself was behind the photographs taken of me. I also didn't want to say anything that I couldn't prove.

"Everyone who knew Andy assumed he wasn't a gambling man. I worked with him for nigh on ten years and I have spoken to a number of regular punters since. None of them had him down as someone who liked a bet. Phil tells me Andy had over twenty thousand pounds in his account but never had a bet. Does that make sense to you as it doesn't to me? Also, whilst I was in Ireland I was told by a very trusted source that Sam openly admitted being able to control the starting prices for her and her clients. That in itself is concerning but what is of interest to me however is the control she seems to have over so many people."

He studied the three of us before opening a rather large blue flap over folder.

"I have no reason to believe what you have told me" he said looking at me "but I have known Phil for far too many years to mention for him to dream up such a story about blackmail and photographs and envelopes in wardrobes without there being some semblance of truth. I will tell you what I can and we will take it from there" he said pulling out a sheet of paper and handing it to Phil.

"On this sheet are twenty separate deposits made into Andrew Whelan's account over a five month period. All are cash deposits and all were banked by the same individual at a branch in Romford. I have had our payments department cross-reference every one of them just to be sure."

"So who banked them?" I asked.

Lewis turned one hundred and eighty degrees in his chair and looked out of the window. He looked left and then right before spotting who he was searching for.

"The guy over there with the blue and yellow waterproof" he said pointing towards the fence that separated the betting ring from the turf race track.

I recognised him immediately.

"Does he know you are here today?"

"No, he doesn't even know what I look like. I had his picture emailed through to me this morning from the guys who do our security passes because I didn't want to ask on track who he was, I wanted to be able to identify him. He knows of me but not what I look like. I will let him get this race out of the way and give him a call and ask him to come up" he said as the last of the runners was safely loaded into the starting stalls.

It took Owen five minutes to find us in the restaurant. Lewis introduced himself first and then the rest of us. I thought he over egged the importance of the presence of a Detective Sergeant before he'd even removed his jacket.

"Take a seat please Owen. I need some information on money that you have been banking in the last couple months" said Lewis handing him the sheet of paper with all the deposits on them.

"If you say I banked them then I banked them. It's the bank I use. What is all this about? I have collected lots of money over the years and not had a problem. I've not been robbing if that is what you are insinuating. Every penny has been banked and my boss Sam will confirm it?" he said.

"Calm down Owen I know that. You're not in any trouble it's just we are investigating the person you deposited for" replied Lewis trying to reassure him.

Owen relaxed back into his seat.

"So where do you collect the money for Andy Whelan from?" asked Phil.

"What do you mean where did I collect it? I collected it here on the track" he replied in a manner suggesting he thought Phil was trying to catch him out. He again shuffled in his seat

"You mean here on this race track?" I chipped in.

"Yes here, where else would it be. My shifts are split between Lingfield and Kempton and I always collect it off him here. I haven't had any for a while mind" he said checking the piece of paper Lewis had handed him earlier. "The last time was at the end of October as it says here."

Alice decided to join in the conversation. "So when was the last time you saw him?"

Owen looked at us as if we were all stupid, he didn't come across as the sharpest tool in the box but at this present moment in time we weren't making any sense to him.

"I saw him about twenty minutes ago buying a coffee in the food hall, he offered to buy me one" he replied and sat back in his chair.

I looked at Phil, Phil looked at Alice and Alice looked at me. Lewis just looked at the three of us.

"Let me get this straight, the person who gave you the money you have collected and banked into the account of Andy Whelan is here tonight, on the race track down in the food hall drinking a coffee?" I said trying to get my head around what he had just said.

"Yes, but he isn't in the food hall now, he is down there in the betting ring on the third betting pitch from the top. Never misses a meeting here. Regular as clockwork he is."

"Owen, it can't be Andy Whelan!" said Lewis, "the guy whose account you have been depositing money into was pulled out of the lake here ten days ago. You remember the night the horse jumped in, all the fuss on the news and in the papers?"

"Yeah, I know all about that, I freeze my nuts off here remember all winter whilst you work in a warm office. I always found it strange though when Sam would ring me up and ask me to collect the money from him. I reckon he must be one of her bigger clients as he never gives it to me in the betting ring, always before the first race out by the parade ring."

"What was strange about it?"

"Dunno really, I write him out a receipt every time I collect the money and give it to him in the name of Andy Whelan with his account number like I do all the clients but everyone else in the ring calls him Mark!"

He really wasn't bright.

"Do you want me to introduce you to him?" he asked Lewis.

"No, just point him out to Joe here for me" he said and Owen duly obliged. I knew instantly who he was. I wonder what Sam had on him?

"Can I go now, I've got a race to call into the office and I don't want to miss the start?"

The four of us sat around the large table in silence taking in what he had just told us. None of it really made sense but did anything about this whole situation really make any? The guy Owen had pointed out was an employee for one of the three big firms who had asked Phil to carry out the investigation into the gambles in the first place.

Phil was in deep thought; he was tapping away with a spoon on a coffee saucer when he was brought back to full attention by a returning Owen.

"I have just checked my receipt book and I came across one I'd scrapped for that Andy Whelan guy. When Sam calls asking me to collect money I normally write up a slip straight away so as not to forget when I get to the track, I can be a bit forgetful like that" why didn't it surprise me I thought. "Well this one I didn't need to collect as Sam turned up unannounced and collected it herself from the guy down in the ring. She also collected the other amount I was due to collect so I have two wasted slips in this receipt book" he said passing the book to Lewis.

Lewis flicked through the receipt book and paused on one receipt in particular before continuing. He then passed the book to Phil for him to peruse.

"Thanks Owen. Before you go, I see from this book that apart from Andy Whelan you seem to collect a lot of money normally on the same night for one other client. Is that person here this evening as well?" asked Phil.

"No, the same guy gives me the money for both accounts, I told you that didn't I?" he replied.

I had no recollection of him saying it and judging by the expression of the others they hadn't heard him say it either. I took the receipt book from Phil and saw immediately why he had asked the question. There were plenty of receipts for Andy Whelan and the date the one had been scrapped was extremely significant, it was the day Andy had disappeared. It was the name on the other receipt which had really caught his eye and would have meant little or nothing to Owen. It was a receipt for £1,000 for account holder Sally-Ann McGrath!

I handed the receipt book back to Owen and he once again departed.

"What's got you two so worked up?" asked Alice as Phil and I both puffed out our cheeks.

Lewis was again fiddling with his folder and pulled out three sheets this time and studied them before speaking.

"I knew the name rang a bell and I'd seen it before" he said as he read the contents of the three sheets of paper for a second time. "Sally-Ann McGrath is the email address that was used for the withdrawals from Andy Whelan's account. He wrote to us to advise his original email address was now defunct and could we change our records to that of his girlfriend" he said handing over the sheet of paper to Alice.

"On this second email he has asked for a cheque withdrawal of £2,500 to be posted to his home address in Towcester. That was sent to us at the end of September whilst the third email asks for another cheque to be sent out and it is dated the middle of October."

"I thought there were three cheques sent out?" I asked remembering what Phil had told me.

"Yes there were, hold on a minute there should be another piece of paper here somewhere" he said pulling out all the papers onto the table. "Here we go; the third payment request was made by telephone by on course representative Sam Hampshire to the customer services team who arranged for payment to be sent out on November 1st."

"Can she do that?" I asked slightly surprised.

"Of course she can, the customer service team would act upon her request as long as she sends in an email."

"Did she?" asked Phil.

It was becoming very apparent that Lewis wasn't the most organised person in the world and after five minutes of searching he had to admit defeat. He would request a copy when he got back to the office he said.

"There is something we haven't told you Lewis and in light of what you have just shown us it is probably best we tell you now. Sally-Ann McGrath is Sam Hampshire; they are one of the same. I have proof Sam was Sally-Ann McGrath. Would it be possible for you to ring your office now and ask them two questions? The first is can you find out the postal address for the account and the second is has she made any withdrawals in the last two months?" I asked.

Lewis dialled a number and got through to a colleague in the integrity department. I hadn't seen him make a note of the account number when Owen had handed him the receipt book but he rattled it off and asked the questions. He hurriedly wrote down the answers on the back of a sheet of paper. He thanked his colleague for his help and turned towards me.

"She is an Irish client and the account was set up online. Her postal address is Leenane, County Galway and in the last three months she has made no withdrawals. She does have a healthy balance of just over fifty five thousand pounds which is pretty unusual for an Irish client as they normally bet in euros."

I looked across to Phil, if ever we needed confirmation Sam was behind all of this then we had just received it.

"It is the same person Lewis. The place where we discovered the pictures of Phil were in Leenane at her brother's house. He is a priest by the way" I said with a smile.

"Oh god, if this gets out the press will have a bloody field day. Is she linked to the disappearance or the murder though? You haven't got anything to link her with it have you? I will get onto the office and close this account and get onto to my boss to see what we do next as she can't continue doing what she is doing."

I had the phone that would link her but I needed it as back up for when I met DCI Baker.

"Do nothing, not yet anyway. Give us a week to see how she will react as we have a few other things we are working on so best not arouse her suspicion. I assume Andy's account is closed and the three cheques were never cashed?" I said.

He looked blankly back towards me and added both points to his 'to do' list.

"You are forgetting something Joe. Owen is bound to tell her I was here asking questions this afternoon with you guys so you don't have the complete element of surprise. She is bound to ring me so any suggestions as to what I should tell her?"

"Sure. Tell her you were helping the Police with their enquiries and you cannot tell her any more" added Alice.

We had been in deep discussion for an hour and a half. I felt we'd made some progress but nothing that DCI Baker would consider a significant lead. Lewis needed to get back to the office and carry out some more internal investigation and liaise with his boss. I added one more job to his 'to do' list and that was to find out what Sam had most of her bets on. I guessed it was greyhounds but something on paper would be beneficial.

"Wow" said Phil "I think I need a beer."

Alice hadn't said much throughout the proceedings but had been busy writing away in her little book any relevant points one of us may have missed. She was studying them when the waitress returned with a drink for all of us.

"Right then, as I see it we have established the money being banked into Andy's account was not given to Owen by Andy himself. It raises one question immediately; did Andy know he had an exchange account? We also know the same person who was depositing money into his account was also putting money into Sam's Sally-Ann account. Why?

We also know Sam was here at the track the night Andy disappeared to collect the funds for both of the accounts but the money she collected for Andy's wasn't deposited? And finally and probably most importantly of all we know she makes the rules up as she goes along and seems to be able to do anything without being questioned" she concluded by closing her notebook.

She had summarised the afternoon's proceedings perfectly. She was right; we had no idea whether Andy knew he had an account. Sam had the way and the means to set up an account in his name without his knowledge but why would she. How could she get access to the funds without him knowing about it, the cheques would come out in his name and had done? Was I being totally stupid?

"How could she access the money in the account?" I put to Phil and Alice.

"Easy, if they have a joint account she can deposit the cheques and if the account only needs one signatory for a withdrawal she can take it back out with no questions asked. Simple enough to do, I did it once, cleaned out a boyfriends account after I'd found out he was two timing me when we were at University" said Alice with a huge grin.

There was definitely an evil streak to Miss Clarke.

"I will need to have a word with the boss of the guy in the betting ring to see what the story is there. Some of these bookies clerks like to have a lumpy bet or two but it wouldn't explain putting money into those accounts unless he was paying out on bets she'd had. I guess that's possible" said Phil.

"Why not just give her the money?" I asked. "As for Sam being here on the night Andy disappeared it doesn't really help us much."

Alice's mobile rang and she answered it almost immediately. "Hey mate, what do you have for me?" she said.

She pulled out her notebook again and quickly wrote down the information being relayed to her. The conversation was pretty one sided with Alice adding the occasional 'ok', 'that's great' and 'brilliant' in reply before ending the call. She looked like the cat that'd got the cream.

"Well that's a result" she said as she took a sip of her diet coke. She was officially on duty so no alcohol for her. "That was one of the guy's in the office who I asked to run the number plate check and he has come back with a name and address but he also did a little extra digging and has really come up trumps for us."

"The name of the car owner is a Ben Henry and he lives in Godalming which is just below Guildford on the A3. He is a freelance investigative journalist now with a list of minor offences against his name. He was arrested but not charged in the phone hacking scandal a couple of years ago. According to the internet he was accused of illegally accessing the mobile and email accounts of two racehorse trainers in Newmarket during the Bravest Edge scandal. Does it mean anything to either of you?"

"It does to me" I said "Bravest Edge had been ante-post favourite for the Epsom Derby all winter and was owned by a very prominent Arab consortium. Two weeks before he was due to make his seasonal reappearance one of the tabloids reported the horse had been struck down with a severe case of colic and was a major doubt for the big race in six weeks. The trainer had denied there was any truth in the rumour and the consortium had released a statement saying all was fine. In the interim some bookmakers had decided to offer a considerably higher price for him winning the Derby. The odds they offered were so much higher than those of the big three firms they took over ninety per cent of all bets made on the lead up to the Derby.

Suffice to say the horse didn't make his reappearance two weeks later and never made it to the race track ever again and the bookmakers made a right few quid. There was one bookmaker in particular who really cleaned up. I remember reading about it afterwards in the Racing Post. The trainer of the horse sued the tabloid as he was convinced the only way they could have got the information was by hacking. There had been only one email from his vet with the horses' prognosis and the paper had virtually printed it word for word. I think they dropped the suit in the end."

Alice had a phone you could access the internet on and she typed 'Bravest Edge gamble' into the search engine. A list of results came up and she handed the phone to me, "Any of them ring a bell?" she asked.

I pointed to the second one whose heading said 'Surrey bookie Bravest as Edge misses Derby.'

Alice hit the relevant button and the archived story came up on the screen so I read it from start to finish looking for the bookmaker's name. It was hard to believe it happened over six years ago. They had named the bookmaking firm in the opening paragraph as Hersham Racing but I had to wait until the final paragraph before I came across the company owner, Sid Hampshire.

Now that was one hell of a coincidence and I didn't like coincidences.

I passed the phone back to Alice and thanked her and told the pair my initial thoughts and they agreed it was unlikely the two were not related. I knew a man who'd know so I called him.

"Hi Tommy, it's Joe, sorry to bother you but just wanted to rack your brains. When we were over you said you used to bet with Sam's father-in-law years ago when he stood at White City dogs, can you remember what his son was called and what they traded as?"

"Sure can. They traded as Hersham something or other, probably Hersham Racing. I remember that because of the trainers who trained in Hersham and his son was called Sid. He's dead now though, hit by a big truck on the M25 a few years back. I went to the house once for a summer party, big place in Cobham."

I thanked him for his time and confirmed things were in place for Wednesday evening.

"Well as you probably heard Tommy confirmed it. Sid was Sam's husband. So how do we tie Ben in with Sam?"

Alice had received an email to her phone whilst I had been speaking to Tommy and she again looked pleased having read it.

"Oh it just gets better. Ben Henry had been arrested for trespass after trying to take photographs of the England captain's wedding three years ago, he had camped up a tree for three days apparently and also for trying to sell topless photographs of a member of the royal family taken whilst they were abroad on holiday. He got off with a warning on both occasions. It would appear that he is available to the highest bidder but I'd imagine he'd be on a final warning before having the book thrown at him."

Phil and I looked at each other. If Ben Henry had been the man behind the lens when I was photographed in the car with Orla I really should be thankful the images hadn't appeared in some seedy publication or all over the internet.

"We need to pay this guy a visit and I suggest we do it tomorrow" I said and we all agreed to meet back here at the track at ten in the morning.

CHAPTER THIRTY TWO

It was hard to believe it had only been a week since I'd seen Orla as she arrived just after seven. I had always found her attractive but she seemed to have a renewed glow about her and I hadn't really thanked her for tipping me off about Ken in the car park.

I welcomed her with a kiss on the lips rather than the cheek, old habits die hard I suppose and I apologised almost immediately and she smiled and told me not to worry. I could still taste her lipstick as we took a seat opposite each other.

"Thanks for the tip off last week, he was waiting in the car park but with a little help from a friend I was able to evade him" I said with a smile.

"I heard. Ken is still squealing about how much it cost to get his car fixed."

I had decided to cook a meal, I hadn't felt the need for such a long time but I wanted her to relax as much as possible as I was going to ask her do something she may not want without the promise of something in return. It was the 'something in return' part that could prove to be the stumbling block. I settled on spaghetti bolognaise and a bottle of wine. I'd even brought out the foldable dinner table from under the stairs. I had resisted candles as it would have sent out the wrong message. The fresh smell of pine from the Christmas tree I'd bought on the way back from Kempton filled the room. I had dressed it sparsely. The lack of tinsel and baubles was easily made up for with the two sets of lights that now flickered away merrily in the corner.

"Dinner won't be too long, hope you're hungry as I have made far too much" I joked.

"Sounds good to me, it's funny you making me a meal. In all the time we were together you never had the opportunity but you are now. Quite romantic in a funny sort of way don't you think? I guess food used to be the furthest thought from our minds" she said.

She had a point, we never really did the conventional stuff people in love would do such as eat and wake up next to each other. I had hoped it would come along later but it didn't and it wouldn't be now.

"So tell me Joe, why am I here tonight? I have put on my best underwear but am I safe to assume that you won't want your wicked way with me this evening. Damn shame really as I'm as horny as hell, I always am when I'm around you" she said with huge grin.

Behave yourself Joe Jackson, behave.

"I need your help Orla to get my revenge on Sam Hampshire" I said. It wasn't exactly how I had wanted it to come out but it was exactly what I meant.

"Revenge for what exactly?"

"I am convinced she is behind the photographs that got me the sack and she was behind the photographs taken of you and me in the car. I can't tell you just yet how I know all this but I will I promise. She is also the reason I believe you were having so many winners before Andy died, I think she was blackmailing him."

She burst out laughing.

"What's so funny?" I asked having not expected such a reaction.

"She wasn't blackmailing Andy you idiot, she was sleeping with him. Richard told me on Saturday after he had punched Ken in the kitchen. Flattened him he did, it was great. According to Ken they'd been an item for a few months at least. At one stage I thought he was going to say she was seeing Ken himself. How revolting is the thought of that, yuk?"

Foxy had said weeks ago the rumour mill was rife that Andy had a woman on the go so why hadn't I considered it was Sam. I would never have put those two together so I couldn't even blame hindsight for missing it.

I went into the kitchen to finish making the dinner and Orla joined me with her glass of wine in hand. She couldn't resist running her hand across the top of my bum. It felt good but the stern look I gave was enough for her to raise a white tea towel in retreat. We both smiled and under any other circumstances I would probably have succumbed. Not tonight.

Whilst I mixed in the bolognaise sauce Orla looked after the pasta that was coming to the boil. Dinner was becoming a team effort and she was good company.

"So how can I help, I really hate the bitch and I really would like to knock the smile of her face just the once?" she said. "Even Richard is getting a bit fed up with her. She rang him from Ireland yesterday to say she'd bought a dog from a bloke at Clonmel and she'd see him at the track on Wednesday to give him the paperwork."

I wondered if the man had been a certain Mr Tomas Jake Lowry!

I explained over dinner what I needed her to do. There were certain elements of my master plan we tweaked as we went along but she was confident she could do her bit with the minimum of fuss. It was going to be all about delivery and timing. To have the maximum effect I needed to hit Sam from a number of angles all at the same time.

With her help, input from Foxy and Jamie delivering an under-performing Rainbow Warrior I was confident we could push Sam out of her comfort zone. What I wasn't so sure about was how she would react. There was also the mongrel Ken to worry about, he had already made his intentions clear with regards my future health

"So what is in it for me, not that I won't help you anyway?" she asked and I was glad she was willing to do so without asking too many questions.

"I promise you that once all this is over that the GRB will be off your back for good with regards the gambles on Rainbow Warrior and Double Vision. I know who is behind them now but we can't do anything until after Wednesday. So when they come to test the dog just treat it as you would normally.

Tell me more about Richard hitting Ken, I'm intrigued?" I said as I topped up her glass.

"It was all over pretty quickly. Richard came home in a right mood from the track and Sam and Ken were in the kitchen. Sam asked to see my mobile as she reckoned I'd called you to tip you off about Ken's car park surprise. Fortunately I've learnt how to delete calls since our affair. It all got a bit heated and Ken called me a slapper so Richard thumped him and split his lip. He has a lovely black eye as well. You can't beat a bit of family loyalty to raise the anger levels, like a lion protecting its prey. Some people will stop at nothing to protect their family you know, take a bullet; throw themselves in front of a bus to push away a child who had wandered into its path. Family makes you do the strangest things when you least expect it. Actions have consequences but they are irrelevant when your family is in the equation."

I was watching her intently as she spoke, her words were so true. She smiled back at me and wiped some sauce from the edge of my mouth with a napkin. It was an intimate moment that required no words. I reached across the table and held her hands and squeezed.

"I so loved you, I would have done anything for you but I can now see I was living in a dream world rather than reality. The pride with which you just spoke was in total admiration of Richard, I could never compete with it and I shouldn't want to" I said and smiled.

"I know you did and I loved you too and tonight will be the last time we should meet before we take it one step further than we should. Richard surprised me Saturday; I didn't know he had it in him. I have been so horrible to him over far too many years and I need to put my family first rather my own needs. If I can get Sam out of our lives then we may stand a chance but she has too much influence. She is so protective it is scary, he can do no wrong!"

The one answer that had eluded me for the past two years had just been provided. It wasn't the actions of our affair that had angered Sam and resulted in her having me framed. It had nothing to do with control or financial gain as had been the case with Phil; it was the fact I was in the process of breaking up the marriage of her son. She was trying to protect her son, the son who had no idea who his biological mother was.

Richard was the split of his father at the same age, I was surprised Alice hadn't spotted it but she'd only spent one night in his company at the Ball, I'd known him years. I had spotted it immediately in the photograph in the priest's house. The visit to Tomas Lowry had just confirmed it and the information I obtained in Oola had been an added bonus. I had asked Orla over dinner whether Richard's parents were still alive and she confirmed they were. There had been no mention about him being adopted or any other siblings. He was an only child she'd said and he visited his parents at least once a fortnight.

Orla and Richard had known each other for twenty years. They had gone to secondary school together and had first gone out when she was fourteen and he sixteen. He only became interested in greyhounds because of her she said. Her father was a greyhound trainer and he'd given Richard a weekend job during the summer months. When he left school he worked for them for about five or six years in all before getting a job with another trainer which meant he could live in. He eventually took over from him and that is where they were based now.

They'd got back together about eight years ago and had been together ever since. I was surprised I didn't know anything of this and disappointed I had never taken the time previously to even enquire.

I asked her to bring his parents to the track on Wednesday as a surprise for Richard. It would be a massive surprise she said as they didn't go racing often. She was going to invite them to stay overnight and have a day with their grandchildren which they hadn't done in quite a while due to the workload at the kennels. She would tell Richard afterwards it was part of a new beginning for them and hopefully it would be.

It wasn't for me to tell Richard or Orla who his real mother was and I had no intention of doing so. We spent another hour enjoying each other's company talking about old times and the chances we had taken. I was confident I had regained a friend and hopefully in time we could be open about our friendship without comments from others. I didn't walk her to the car but we did share a very long embrace before she left.

"Thank you for tonight Joe I have enjoyed myself, I really have. I will see you Wednesday" she said before walking away and not looking back.

I watched her drive away and shut the door.

I took the dirty dishes to the kitchen, no time like the present to wash them up. I had just finished putting the last glass away when there was a knock at the front door. I had a quick look around the room and spotted Orla's gloves next to the computer. I picked them up and opened the door.

Whatever or whoever hit me did so with precision accuracy.

CHAPTER THIRTY THREE

I had no idea how long I was out for.

My hands were tied behind my back; my mouth had been taped shut forcing me to breathe through my nose. Another piece of tape had been placed across my eyes but hadn't completely blocked out the light into my right eye.

My head hurt but not as bad as my rib cage. I could feel my fingers and my legs still had movement, albeit restricted. It was safe to assume they had been bound as well.

I heard movement over my left shoulder. I was slowly recovering my senses and lay perfectly still. No reason to give the intruder the opportunity to inflict more pain. The movement was coming from the bedroom. I could just make out the Christmas lights reflecting off the white painted walls from my position on the floor. A quick recollection of my own furniture layout put me behind the two-seater sofa Orla had been sat on earlier. I moved my knees in unison slightly upwards. I got no more than two inches before the excruciating pain from my ribs made it impossible to go any further.

Something smashed on the floor and I heard a set of footsteps coming from behind me.

'Don't move Joe' I said to myself.

"Wake the fucker up and ask him" the man now stood above me said. "We have got to find it or she will go nuts, why didn't you dump it in the lake when you had the bloody chance. Try his pockets again."

So there were two of them, definitely a good reason to play dead. Someone got down on their knees and rolled me over onto my back. The pain was unbearable and only increased as my arched back pointed northwards with my hands now on the floor. I wanted to scream but I daren't. The person searching my pockets said nothing but he didn't need to. He was that close that I could smell him, it wasn't a smell of aftershave, deodorant or body odour, it was the smell of stale urine and disinfectant. I know someone who smelt like that and he didn't like me very much. Ken Kelly.

"Nothing" he said "maybe he gave it to the slapper when she left?"

"Try all the cupboards and put your bloody gloves back on, have I not taught you anything. I will give her a call now."

"What you calling the slapper for?"

"Not her you bloody idiot."

I was pretty confident who 'her' would be and he had proved most accommodating as far as listening in went by sitting on the chair next to me. Still I didn't move. He nudged me with a foot to check for life and continued to do so as he waited for his call to connect; I was rocking slowly from left to right. I used the next nudge to roll onto my side. The relief I felt was instant.

"Hello............no I can't find it ....we've checked there as well......no he is out for the count.........he isn't going anywhere...............so what do you want me to do with him..........are you sure.......fine?" he said before ending the call.

I could hear my mobile ringing in the kitchen but it went unanswered. Almost immediately the house phone rang. The answerphone would kick in after the third ring. I so wanted to answer the call but that wasn't going to happen.

"Hi lover boy, guess your mobile is on silent again. Just checking everything went alright. I will be around in ten minutes so you can fill me in with all the details, bye."

Oh my god Alice, don't come here now, please.

"Now what do we do and who was that?" asked Ken. "That wasn't Orla's voice so the dirty bastard has got two on the go again" he added.

"Look mate, I'm only going with the information I was given earlier and there was no mention of another bird alright. Let me think for a minute will you."

"We can't get him out of here now without being seen and whoever that was will be here in a minute. Shall we wait and take her as well? Kill two birds with one stone so to speak" Ken said whilst laughing.

"You really are thick aren't you Ken?" said the anonymous voice in an angry tone "Giving him a kicking is one thing but if you think I am giving some woman a pair of size 10's to the chest you've got another think coming. Get your stuff and we'll wait in the bedroom out of sight."

"What if she has a key?" said Ken.

It was the first sensible thing I'd heard Ken say. I knew Alice didn't have one but they didn't but hopefully it would make them rethink.

"Bollocks, good point, let's get out of here for now and wait in the car, he isn't going anywhere. Grab his keys and we can let ourselves back in and get rid of him later if she doesn't have one."

I could hear the pair make towards the back door that led out into the small garden which would give them access to the alleyway which ran behind the six terraced houses of which I was right in the middle. I was just about to make myself more comfortable when I heard returning steps. I didn't know whose foot it was that landed the blow to finally knock the wind out of my recovering sails but I could hazard a pretty good guess.

I never heard Alice's knock on the front door or the glass being broken to gain entry.

I woke with my head in her lap with her looking down towards me, her tears falling onto my face. Stood directly behind her was Orla, she was also crying. I could see both their lips moving but I couldn't hear what they were saying. So this is what heaven is like, maybe I had been a good boy after all!

The tearful Alice was moved to one side as a bearded man in a fluorescent green and yellow jacket now held my head, I could feel myself being lifted slowly. Something was restricting my neck movement. I was suddenly aware my hands were no longer behind my back but instead on my chest. I had something attached to my finger. I tried to speak but nothing came out, I was feeling totally disorientated. The movement stopped, the people around me became blurs and I slowly closed my eyes.

Alice was by my side when I woke up. She was asleep; her head laying on the edge of the hospital bed, both her hands clasped my left hand. I surveyed my surroundings. The cubicle I was in had the curtains drawn all around; I had tubes connected to my arm and other cables running from my chest to a number of machines that beeped away to my right. I could hear noise, I had never been happier than to hear a beep beep beep.

I was almost horizontal, I tried to move but it was too uncomfortable. The pain from my ribs made movement almost impossible. I squeezed Alice's hand, there was nothing from her at first but the second squeeze did the trick.

"Oh my god Joe, I thought I'd lost you" she said and burst into tears. She stood up and went to cuddle me, a manoeuvre that proved not only difficult to do but also painful as she put pressure on my side.

"I will get a nurse" she said as I winced in pain and she was out of the cubicle before I could stop her.

She returned almost immediately with a nurse and a smartly dressed man.

Alice pulled her chair back towards the hospital bed. The tears fell freely from her eyes and I noticed her nose was red raw.

The nurse gave me the once over and asked if I felt well enough to answer a few of the Policeman's questions. He remained standing on the opposite side of the bed to Alice.

I nodded my head slightly, even that hurt, any sort of movement seemed to cause pain.

"Don't you be tiring him out now do you hear?" she had said to Alice in a broad Northern Irish accent.

"Joe, this is Detective Sergeant Goddard from the Major Crimes unit, he needs to ask you a few questions about what happened last night, he is happy for me stay whilst he does" she said with a smile and squeezed my hand again.

"Can you tell us what happened last night Mr Jackson?" he asked.

"Who did this to you Joe, do you know? I will get the bastard who did this" Alice added before I could reply and received a stern look from DS Goddard. She apologised.

"Plural Alice, it is bastards but can you tell me how I ended up in here and what is wrong with me first please. The rest can wait."

"All in good time Joe, just answer the couple of questions and then I will tell you" she said.

"Take a seat and I will tell you what I know" I said to the detective who pulled up a chair.

Alice handed me a drink of water before I started.

"Orla had just left and then there was a knock on the front door. She'd left a pair of gloves behind so I thought it was her coming back for them. I opened the door and something hit me in the face very hard. I didn't see it coming or who delivered it. The next thing I remember is waking up on the floor behind the sofa bound and gagged with a massive pain in my ribs. I was all taped up and in too much pain to move, not that I'd have got very far. It took me a minute or so to gather my bearings."

"You say they, there was definitely more than one?"

"Yes, there were two. I played dead. They were looking for something but they couldn't find it" I knew it was the mobile but did he really need to know. I thought about it and decided he didn't. He was bound to ask and he did.

"So did you see either of your attackers through the small opening in the tape?" he asked and I assumed he was writing the question down in his notebook for future reference.

"No, but I smelt one of them."

"How do you mean smelt? Not sure what you mean?" asked the confused looking DS.

"They may have tied my hands and legs and taped my eyes and mouth but they left my nose and ears alone. One of my attackers was Ken Kelly but I don't know who the other one was but he was the brains. Ken has a distinct aroma about him, he stinks. I heard the two of them talking openly and it was definitely Ken. They obviously thought I was still out for the count thank God."

"So what happened next?"

"The other guy made a call to say they couldn't find what they were looking for and then Alice left a message on the answer phone to say she would be around in ten minutes."

"Yes we heard the message" he said and looked towards Alice. Her eyes again began to well up with tears. "And do you know who he was calling, did he mention a name at all?"

"I've no idea, sorry." I did have a bloody good idea but I couldn't prove it. "Alice's call probably saved my life as they decided to leave and wait out in their car until she'd gone."

"I've just one more question; we couldn't find any keys to the property. We found none in your possession when you were brought in and my colleagues have been unable to locate any at the property. DS Clarke tells us your car is still parked in the street?"

"They took them; they were coming back later to get rid of me if Alice didn't get in. They thought she may have a key."

DS Goddard looked straight at Alice and beckoned for her to leave the cubicle with him. Whatever he wanted to say he wasn't going to say within my earshot. He popped back in to ask if there was anything else that I could add and help with their enquiries before he left.

"Yes there is, Ken wasn't wearing gloves all the time. There must be some finger prints of his around the place. Especially the bedroom, I heard him break something in there."

"That is very helpful. Our Forensic guys are going over the place now and I have informed them your keys have been stolen so they will make sure the place is secure when they have finished. They will padlock up the doors until you get an opportunity to change the locks. I will be in touch" he said, leaving me alone with Alice.

The Irish nurse called Beverley came in again to do her observations and wrote down the results on the clipboard at the end of the bed.

"How did I end up here and what is wrong with me, I ache

everywhere?" I asked.

She spent the next thirty minutes telling me what had happened after she'd turned up at the flat.

Alice had arrived and got no answer when knocking on the front door. Just as she was about to drive away Orla pulled up beside her and said that she was returning for the gloves she had left behind. There was no jealous stand-off between the pair I was glad to hear. They had both noticed my car was still parked up and the flat lights were on.

They tried the front door again and got no response.

"When did you leave then?" Alice asked Orla.

"About half an hour ago, just before nine."

Alice had checked her watch and it had just gone half past.

They had tried looking through the closed front curtains and even the letter box to see if there was any sign of life in the flat. Alice called my mobile again. She could hear it ringing but there was still no movement.

"Let's try around the back" Orla suggested and the pair eventually found the ally that ran behind the terraced houses. The gate was locked so Alice had to scale the six foot wall with the aid of a leg up from Orla. Their presence in the garden triggered the security sensor by the backdoor, flooding their surroundings in bright light. They tried the back door but it was locked. The kitchen blinds were only half closed and it was difficult to see in but they could make out my mobile on the kitchen side.

"I don't like the look of this" Alice said to Orla "I can't see or hear anything. The bathroom light isn't on so he isn't in the bath and he wouldn't go to bed with the lights on. His car is still outside and his mobile is in the kitchen just by the cooker. I'm going in."

She bent down and grabbed the nearest heavy object she could find, half a red brick. She removed her jacket and asked Orla to hold it against the pane of glass in the door and then smashed the glass, the jacket protecting the pair of them from any splinters that may have flown in their direction. With brick still in hand she broke off the jagged edges in the pane of glass making a hole big enough for her to open the door and let them in.

"You were motionless on the floor Joe, there was blood all around your face and your hands and legs had been tied. I thought you were dead. I panicked but Orla stayed so calm, she brought out a blanket and removed the tape. I was shaking, all the training I've done and I didn't know what I was doing. She called the ambulance and the Police arrived almost immediately. A neighbour had called them thinking you were being broken into with all the noise we were making. I was so scared" she said and started to cry again.

The nurse returned with some medication which I took without question.

"You've been out for about twelve hours but you should make a full recovery. The doctors say you have three cracked ribs. They have put twelve stitches in a cut to the back of your head and you will need to see a dentist as you've two front teeth missing. You have a lot of bruising and you need to take it easy for a bit until everything settles down."

The discomfort I had been feeling had eased slightly after the medication and I pulled myself up into a slightly more upright position and Alice moved a couple of pillows behind my back.

"I can't stop now; one of the people who did this was Ken. He doesn't know I know as I was playing dead on the floor remember. As I said there were two people, one I didn't know and Ken. They came to the house looking for the phone we took from Ireland and thanks to your call they left without it. I didn't tell DS Goddard that. I am convinced the call he made was to Sam. He said I need to call 'her'."

"It doesn't matter now. You need to take it easy and rest" she said leaning across to kiss me on the forehead.

I had a sudden flashback from the previous night's proceedings.

"I have been such a fool Alice, get hold of Orla and get hold of her now. She is in real danger. Ken said I may have given the phone to her. The only way they could have known she was at the flat was if they had been waiting outside or followed her. I doubt they will stop until they have it. Orla said last night that Sam had gone back to Ireland and wouldn't be back until Wednesday. I am guessing she has gone to her brother's house and found the pictures and mobile are missing" I said.

"What about Tommy and Aoife, are they in danger as well?" asked Alice.

I hadn't thought of that or the safety of young Jamie either.

"Do you have my mobile?" I asked.

She did and removed it from her pocket. She had turned it off. I hit the power button and waited for it to return to life. "Who are you calling?" she asked.

"Jamie first and then Tommy" I replied.

Jamie answered on the second ring. "Hello" he said.

"Hi Jamie, it's Joe Jackson, is Orla with you, just answer yes or no without raising suspicion as I think she may be in danger" I said in as composed a voice as I could muster.

"Yes."

"Can she speak?"

"Yes."

"Great" I said with a huge sigh of relief "can you put her on for me please?"

"Joe are you alright?" she asked with plenty of emotion in her voice "I was going to call Alice later but I didn't take her number."

"Orla listen and please listen very carefully. You were followed to the flat last night and Ken is one of the guys who beat me up. I want you to be very careful for a day or so and stay as close to Jamie as possible and look after him until I work out what to do. Stay out of Sam's way when she gets back on Wednesday as well."

"She's already back, flew back in late last night. She is coming to the kennels tomorrow morning for a meeting with Richard."

"Oh shit" I said and meant it. "Still proceed as normal for tomorrow night; I need to put an end to this before anyone else gets hurt. I am sorry."

"Sod being sorry" she replied "I can look after myself. Ken hasn't said a word to me this morning; normally he can't resist saying something sarcastic so maybe Richard's punch knocked some sense into him. Just get yourself better. Got to go now, Richard's around" she said before hanging up.

I had just told her nothing had changed for tomorrow night but at the present moment in time I had no idea how I was going to stand let alone walk into the track.

"Joe, you have got to rest" said a more insistent Alice.

"One more call, just need to check how Tommy is" I said as I looked his number up and then dialled.

I was just about to speak when Alice took the phone from me.

"Hello Tommy, its Alice. Joe was badly beaten up last night at home and is now in hospital with a few cracked ribs and lots of bruising. Being the idiot he is however he wanted to check that everything was still set for tomorrow."

She handed the phone to me, "He wants to speak to you."

"Jesus Joseph where the feck have you been, I have been trying to get of you all morning? Tomas Lowry called with a message for you yesterday and I forget to call you. He said it was urgent and that I was to tell you that she has been to visit and he told her to go and get stuffed. Does that make sense?"

"Now what is this about you being beaten up?" he added as an afterthought.

"Tommy I will be fine. Did Sam come and visit you at all whilst she was over?"

"She didn't but Sean came over this morning, he was ever so upset. They had a huge row yesterday afternoon and he said he'd never seen her like it before. He has a black eye no less, a priest with a black eye have you ever heard the likes of it? She'll be saying a few 'Hail Mary's' after that I'd imagine. He said he'd banged it on a door but looks like a slap to me. He was muttering something about a phone she'd lost."

"You didn't mention anything to him about us going to his house did you?" I asked already knowing the answer.

"Now, I can't be sure about that. We had a right old session on Saturday night so we did after you'd gone home. Aoife tore a strip off me Sunday morning so it must have been a real late one. It would have been the drink talking but Sean would do you no harm" he replied.

I was sure Father Sean wouldn't but his sister was a different matter altogether.

"I spoke to Jamie this morning and everything is fine so fingers crossed everything goes okay. So who beat you up?"

"I will tell you when I come over next. Love to Aoife" I said and ended the call.

I handed the phone back to Alice; the pain from my ribs was unbearable in the current position. She fetched the nurse and between them they rearranged my bed so I was again almost horizontal.

"Right, give me a couple of minutes and I will be straight back, just have a couple of calls to make. The Forensic guys were still at the house the last I heard and I'll ask how they are getting on. I will try and get hold of DCI Baker. Dad is on his way up from home. You said they were looking for the phone. How come they didn't find it? I have the pictures but you insisted on keeping the phone, where did you leave it?"

"Try the angel on the top of the tree; I taped it to the inside of her skirt!"

CHAPTER THIRTY FOUR

"Hello Joe, who have you been upsetting then?" said DCI Baker as I opened my eyes and looked towards the chair Alice had occupied earlier.

"Hi Alex, where's Alice?" I asked.

"She had to pop out but will be back in a minute, she has gone down to the main entrance to meet her father. She called me earlier and reckons this kicking you've had is linked to Andy Whelan turning up in the lake. What makes you so sure of that?"

"What time is it?"

He checked his watch and advised it was just past two o'clock.

"Can we wait until they turn up, they can fill in any of the blanks that I may miss? I asked.

He nodded and didn't have to wait long as the pair soon entered joined by a nurse. I noticed it was a different nurse to earlier; she was a lot older and a lot less friendly.

"The doctor will be around in fifteen minutes and there really should only be two of you here at any one time and turn that phone off" she said to Phil who was just about to make a call.

None of us bothered to argue with her. She gave strict instructions to them not to tire me out and advised that when the doctor came only one person could stay behind.

"Joe, I am so sorry this has happened to you. It's all my fault, I shouldn't have got you involved" said Phil who looked genuinely shocked as he settled into the chair on my right, leaving DCI Baker as the only man standing.

Alice had done a brilliant job of telling the pair of them what I had told the Detective Sergeant earlier, it was a relief not to have to repeat myself. I sat and listened and only once had to correct her, she openly held my hand and whether Phil had noticed or not I wasn't sure and didn't care. She had been back to the flat and the Forensic team had finished their work and the place was now secure. They had gone over the bedroom for prints and found a few. Alice had asked for Ken's name to be run through the Police National Computer database. He had no previous crimes against him she said so they'd have no fingerprints on the system for him to cross reference.

"Once we finish here I will arrange for him to be picked up and brought in for questioning" said Alex. "We can take his prints then and compare them to what they have from the flat."

"Don't, not yet" I said much to their surprise.

"Why ever not" said Alice "he has to pay for this and you were so confident that it was him earlier."

"Don't worry Alice, it was him alright but for the first time in this whole bloody mess we have the upper hand. You were here earlier when I spoke to Orla. Ken had turned up at work; if he was going to skip the country he would have done so by now. We need him to get to the bigger prize and I believe he is stupid enough to lead us to it if we play this correctly."

"Would you care to let me know what you are on about please?" said Alex.

"Alex, when I rang you on Sunday you asked me to provide you with a concrete lead as to why I thought Sam Hampshire and the car turning up at Holyhead are linked. What I didn't tell you at the time was that we, Alice and I, had been in Ireland last week doing some digging of our own."

"And what did you find?" he asked.

"These" said Alice handing the Detective Inspector the pictures of Phil and the accompanying letters. He studied them and looked at Phil.

"The photographs have been staged, just like the ones that saw me sacked a couple of years ago. There is more and I apologise for not telling you this earlier Phil but I needed to keep this up my sleeve. Did you get it Alice?"

Alice moved her hand into the inside of her jacket and pulled out a mobile, it was Andy's.

"The people who came to my flat yesterday were looking for this" I said handing it to Alex, "it is Andy's and if you check the last text message it was sent the day he disappeared and it was sent to Phil. This phone was with those pictures and papers and they were amongst the belongings of Sam in Ireland."

The Detective Inspector tried to turn the device on but the battery was still flat. Alice took it from him and replaced it with her own and he was able to read what we had in the bedroom at Tommy's house. He took his time reading through the messages, stopping periodically to look at the three of us. I had only looked at one message and that was enough.

"Most of these texts just have one or two words on them do they mean anything to any of you? Poll Rating, Maverick Max, Double Vision, Rainbow Warrior, there are loads of them!"

"They are all dog names and I bet all those texts have gone to the one number. Phil, do you have Sam's number on you?"

Phil turned on his phone, if the nurse came back in now it wouldn't just be me who would be in need of a hospital bed. He found what he was looking for and handed his device to Alex. He compared the numbers and confirmed they were the same.

"Why didn't you bring this to me earlier?"

Alice was just about to speak when I interrupted her; there was no reason for her to get into trouble. "If I had brought this to you I would have immediately made myself a suspect. Think about it. I go to Kempton on a regular basis which gives me opportunity, Andy took over my old job which some would say was motive as I didn't exactly leave on the best of terms."

"So what makes you think I will believe you now? You could be making this all up and staged your own beating to put me off the scent" he said but didn't believe it.

"Don't be bloody stupid" shouted an angry Alice "and I suppose I staged the break-in as well Alex?"

He waved her away; he knew he was talking nonsense. "Sorry Joe."

"You still haven't told me how any of this links to Andy Whelan ending up in the lake. All we have here is circumstantial evidence. We can arrest this Ken Kelly chap and charge him for attacking you as long as we find some prints but unless he confesses to putting the body in the lake we can't tie him into it. We can't charge this Sam woman for blackmail either unless you can prove she sent the letters and pictures as you haven't actually made any payment to her."

I knew he was right and the only way I thought we could link her was through Andy's car. I was convinced she had used her maiden name to get on the ferry and she had driven to Holyhead. Tommy had confirmed that she had been in Ireland around that time.

"What about the car?"

"I wondered when you'd ask about the car" Alex said with a smile, "one of my officers decided to run the number plate through the local council's database and it came up for an outstanding Fixed Penalty Notice, the car was caught in the yellow box on the Sunbury roundabout by the new camera that had been installed the day before it turned up in Holyhead. I haven't seen the images yet but I am told there are two people in the car, both men."

"That's good news isn't it, and we also know Sam was at the track that night as well?" I said, my mood improved markedly.

"How do you know?"

I let Alice explain about the meeting we'd had at Kempton yesterday, was it really only yesterday? Phil interrupted to confirm that Lewis had come back to him with answers to the two questions I'd posed. Sam hadn't made any withdrawals from her account and most of the bets were lumpy ones on greyhound racing. He also advised that she hadn't sent an email in for the third withdrawal request and someone would be getting their wrist slapped. Both accounts were left open but Lewis was monitoring them.

"Is there anything else you haven't told me or is that it?" Alex said hoping that we had no more surprises for him.

"Just one thing" I said with a cheeky grin. He looked back with a small degree of annoyance.

"Have you three forgotten I am in the middle of a murder

enquiry?"

I asked him to pass me the envelope containing the pictures and handed him back the one that contained the number plate of Ben Henry's car. Alice took it from me and pointed it out to him.

"What about it" he asked "is it relevant?"

Alice explained she'd had the number plate run through the Police National Computer and it gave them Ben Henry as the owner. His name was then put into the database and it showed he had been arrested a few times over the years but never charged, minor offences such as trespass. It was the mention of the Bravest Edge case that aroused his interest. "I remember it. How was he involved?" asked Alex.

"He was accused of hacking the trainers email and phone accounts but the case was dropped as they couldn't prove it. He was the guy who wrote the original expose. The person who made all the money from the scandal was Sam's husband, he was a bookmaker" I said.

"I definitely remember it now but how does it help us with the body in the lake?"

It always came back to the same question.

"He can't talk his way out of these photographs; he probably hasn't even noticed he is in them. I have a plan that may make him talk and it isn't blackmail, just friendly persuasion but I will need your help and the help of Phil and Alice to do it. I also need that CCTV coverage from the port just to put my mind at rest."

"Not more amateur detective work surely, my boss will go crackers but so far you have turned up more than me so let's hear it" he said with a resigned smile.

"I need you to set up a meeting with this Ben bloke at a neutral venue for tomorrow, I would suggest Oxford Services as it is big and open and not far from here. Alice tells me he is an investigative journalist. I am sure a bright man like you can think of some way of getting him there, you read stories about Police leaking stories to the press all the time" I said whilst smiling.

"If you can arrange it for just after noon I should be out of here by then but I definitely need another night's sleep as I am too sore to go anywhere. If I can't walk tomorrow I will be coming out of here in a wheelchair as I need to be at Stony Stratford for racing" I added.

"Joe, you can't expect to be up and about tomorrow, you need to rest, what if you get attacked again?" said Alice.

I smiled at her. "I will be alright as you will be pushing the wheelchair. Can you arrange it for me please Alex and you will need to come to the track as well for racing, nothing will give me greater pleasure than seeing Ken arrested. It adds to the master plan."

"Master plan; what master plan?" said Alex with concern.

I never got a chance to explain as the nurse came into the cubicle with the Doctor but he did have the final say.

"Joe, the CCTV coverage you wanted from the port. I requested it this morning" he said and winked at me as the nurse ushered him out.

CHAPTER THIRTY FIVE

As expected I was kept in overnight for further observation. It was proving difficult to get comfortable. The doctor explained that it was only with time and rest that the pain would begin to ease. My ribs had taken a severe kicking and the discomfort I was feeling would only get worse before it got better. Alice had taken a picture of the bruising on my side and shown it to me. I had quite literally been kicked until I was black and blue.

I had been lucky that none of the ribs had actually been broken or splintered.

I felt little pain from my head wound but I was reliably informed I'd be wearing a hat for a few weeks until the stitches were removed. Alice had been shopping and bought me some pyjamas from a local supermarket. I'd never owned a pair in my life which she was surprised to hear as she helped the nurse put them on for me.

She left just after six and said she'd be back in the morning to pick up the 'invalid'. Alex had set up the meeting with Ben Henry for noon tomorrow at Oxford Services on the M40. Phil was staying with her overnight she said but was going down to London early to pick up his car before coming back. He'd taken my beating pretty badly. Alice had left strict instructions with the ward sister that I was to have no visitors unless agreed by her first as there was still an on-going Police enquiry.

I slept better than expected, the medication had done its job and the stiffness had eased a little. I was no longer connected up to any tubes or cables; they had been removed after the doctor's visit yesterday. I manoeuvred my body so I was more upright and reached across for my mobile which was turned off on the bedside locker. If I made a call the nurse would hear me so I sent a text to Foxy asking for one more favour if he could and told him what it was. He responded almost immediately and said no problem.

Alice arrived just as the doctor was doing his rounds. I was going home whether he said I could or not I had told her and she had told me to stop trying to play the hero and take it easy. Fortunately I was given the all clear, Alice was handed a few pieces of paper, one of which was a prescription. I was told I could get the stitches removed in ten days. In the interim there was to be no lifting and if I could help it no driving until the bruising had started to relent. I thanked him and the nurses and went on my way.

Alice had the key to the padlock that secured the flat, I would need to get the locks changed tomorrow but for now I wanted a bath, a shave and a change of clothes. I had needed her help with all of them. She packed a couple of days clothes into a sports bag and took them to the car as I followed her slowly. At least I hadn't needed the wheelchair.

We arrived at Oxford Services just after eleven thirty. Alex had called Alice on the way to say he was bringing the images from the station of the two men in the car and he also had a picture of Ben Henry to identify him. He wanted us to stay outside until he had made contact and then we were to come in. Phil was to come in from the left entrance and Alice and I from the right.

I called Phil to tell him where we were parked and he pulled up beside us in his silver Mercedes about five minutes later. He looked tired and flustered as he jumped into the back seat of Alice's car. "All ok?" she asked.

"Nope" he replied and passed over a brown envelope to me, "take a look inside."

I opened the envelope; it was hard backed with 'do not bend' printed on the front. There was a picture inside of Phil and the prostitute; it was a smaller version of the one he had been sent previously. Attached to the back with tape was a note; it was short and to the point.

'Do not investigate the gamble at Stony Stratford on Wednesday night or this picture will be circulated.'

"When did this arrive?" I asked as I handed it to Alice.

"It arrived in the post yesterday morning but I haven't been in the office since Monday. I got the train home after our meeting and then came up to see you in the hospital yesterday. I popped in for five minutes to collect my mail before driving here" he said. He sounded tired and for the first time since I'd known him, defeated.

"The post mark says Hounslow and it was stamped on Monday" said Alice.

"Dammit, Sam was in Ireland on Monday so she couldn't have posted it to arrive on Tuesday" I said with a great degree of anger.

"Hold on. Hounslow is next to Heathrow. Didn't you say that Sam flew out on Sunday and came back unexpectedly early on Monday?" said Alice. "If she posted this at the airport it wouldn't have been sorted until Monday so it could still be her!"

Alice's phone beeped twice on the dashboard. "Right, let's go, Alex has made contact."

Phil helped me out of the passenger seat. We had parked far enough away not to be seen but a little bit further than I would really have wanted in my current condition. I took slow painful steps and held onto Alice's hand all the way as we came in through the main entrance. I could make out Alex sat in the middle of the coffee lounge, Ben Henry was sat with his back towards us. He was caught off guard as I pulled up a seat on his right whilst he was speaking to Alex. Alice did the same on his left. He looked at both of us and made to leave but suddenly found a pair of strong hands on either shoulder, they were Phil's.

"What's all this about?" he said in a strong Liverpudlian accent.

"Just a couple of questions if you don't mind now we have your attention" I said "I don't think I need to introduce myself and nor does Phil who is behind you."

"Get lost, I'll have you for this" he said pointing a finger at Alex.

"Tell you what. How about you listen for two minutes and then maybe we can come to some type of agreement mutually beneficial to us all. What do you say?"

"As I said, get stuffed. I have nothing to say to you and definitely not in front of the old bill. No chance, no way" he said as he again made to leave his seat without much success. He was making a lot of noise and people on seats close by were starting to look and stare.

I needed to shut him up so I pulled out the photograph that had first brought him to our attention and handed it to him.

"Nice pic, who's the bird?" he said looking up at Phil and smiling. That was a big mistake as I saw Phil squeeze harder on each shoulder causing Ben to wince in pain.

"Now, you know who the woman is as you took it as you are in it. You are obviously very good at going unnoticed but made a massive mistake in not checking your wing mirrors. Not checking your mirrors can cause accidents and you are now in your own personal car crash and we are here to rescue you."

He studied the picture closely, I handed him a small magnifying glass I had brought with me just in case. He didn't use it; he just threw the picture down on the table and smirked.

"So what, you have a picture with me in it. Doesn't prove anything" he said with confidence.

It was time to put my poker face on and see if he would bite. I stood up briefly to stretch my back and sat down again.

"The picture has been taken and used to blackmail my friend behind you. Blackmail is a very serious crime as you are aware and you have a long list of minor offences against your name so you aren't exactly known for your good behaviour. I am sure the Police can charge you with some offence which will stick but I want the name of the person who you took this picture and the pictures of me for?"

He smiled. "You've got no chance but I have to admit I did enjoy taking your ones, I could have made a few quid from them" he said looking straight at me. Alice looked at me in puzzlement; now wasn't a good time.

"Why not, I am offering you the opportunity to stay out of

prison and maybe a few quid as well just for one name? I will get it eventually so why not save us all this hassle? As I said blackmail will get you at least a few years. Smart man like you should know a good deal when they are offered one."

"I won't tell you because I don't want to end up eating hospital food like you. Did you not realise getting back with the bird you were with on Monday would get you a beating. How stupid must you be?"

"Oh right, so you followed her on Monday to my place and then let the heavy mob loose on me?" I said knowing he wasn't in the room with me. His accent really was unmistakable.

"Now look here" he said again pointing a finger "I may sneak around taking photographs of people having sex down country lanes and dig into people's pasts for financial gain but don't try and pin any violence on me. I am good at what I do and I get handsomely rewarded for it, yes I sail close to the wind and have had a few close shaves with the law but I don't get involved in violence. What happened to you had nothing to do with me. I just rang to tell them where the trainer's bird had gone and saw your car parked outside. I put two and two together like" he said in a manner which suggested he should be applauded.

"Did she pay you?"

"Not yet but she will, she always does."

He knew as soon as he said it he'd made a huge mistake. He tried to retract but knew he had no way back. I stood up again and I'd no sooner sat down when Alice received a text. She was shocked when I said it was for me. She opened it and handed over the phone, it was a picture of us all sat around the table. It was of good quality and would be much better when it was enlarged.

"You might want to have a look at this" I said handing the image to Ben Henry "I will show this to Sam Hampshire later and tell her how helpful you have been with our enquiries, just before they arrest her for blackmail. I will tell her you set up this appointment with DCI Baker and he invited us along for the ride. I will also tell her you have given us all the negatives and told us you found her son."

I made to leave my seat and beckoned for the others to join me, Phil let go of the journalist's shoulder. The once 'cock-sure' journalist remained seated, I had played him at his own game and the picture he was now looking at was causing him serious pain and anguish. He was damned if he did and damned if he didn't.

"Ok, I will talk. What do you want to know?"

I sat back down, Alice pulled out a small tape recorder from her pocket. I wasn't the only one who could spring a surprise as it hadn't been discussed before-hand and she'd taped everything up to this point. Phil pulled up a chair and sat down. I suggested we had some coffees and handed Alex a twenty pound note if he didn't mind ordering them. We waited until he returned and let him ask the first question.

"Do you know anything about the disappearance of Andy Whelan?" he asked.

"I know nothing. I told you I don't do violence, I just know Sam is not a woman to be messed with. I used to deal with her husband years and years ago, he was a bookmaker until he got killed. I used to go around digging up dirt on people who owed him money. He had some high ranking punters you know. Lords, Colonels, MP's, you name it they bet with him and his dad before. Well some of them thought they could rack up big gambling debts and not pay because they were part of the landed gentry. I'd get a call to follow them and dig up some dirt. A photo with a mistress here and a rent boy there soon saw them settle."

"Well about four years ago Sam gives me a call, offers me five grand and expenses to find her son. It was all a bit weird like and the baby she had, had been given to one of her cousins to bring up as their own. They'd lost a child at birth and were just handed this one. Nobody questioned it but I found him eventually. It was bloody hard work I can tell you. It took me about a year in all, I almost gave up."

"The child was Richard Quinn" I said. The revelation completely surprised both Alice and Phil and Ben nodded in agreement.

"Who is Richard Quinn?" asked Alex and I explained he was a

trainer at Stony Stratford whose wife had come to my flat on Monday evening before I was beaten up. I would give him all the gory details later if he wanted them.

"Well then about a year later she gives me another call to do some digging into you. She never said why but she wanted something she could hold against you. Knowing Sam it would be for financial gain, it normally was. She had just started owning dogs at the track where you were manager. I couldn't find anything; you were as clean as a whistle. At the same time she asked me to follow her son's wife. She had a bit of a reputation and she thought she was putting it about a bit and in Sam's words *'she wasn't having some slapper do the dirty on her son, she will toe the line whilst I am around.'*"

He stopped to drink some of his coffee whilst we listened intently.

"Then low and behold I catch you and his wife down a country lane going at it like rabbits in the back of a Mondeo. I clicked away, gave her the photographs and she paid me as promised."

I looked across towards Alice who no longer looked puzzled but very angry. I mouthed across 'tell you later' but that didn't improve her demeanour any. "The pictures of you and that rather revolting man with the cash hand over was all her idea. I was really surprised that anyone fell for that."

So was I but they did.

"So what about me, who set that up?" asked Phil who had remained extremely quiet.

"That was all her I promise, I was given a time and a place and told to take the pictures. You were just one of many I've had a call for in the morning. I turn up, take my shots and give her the pictures. I always hand deliver to her house in Cobham."

"Like who, who else have you done on her say so? Alice asked.

"I can't tell you that but his boss" he said pointing to Phil "has two mistresses and an illegitimate child by a Colombian nanny Sam is aware of."

Well that would explain why she was so confident of having me banned again when she spoke to me last week and why the authorities had been so reluctant to believe me when I said I'd been framed.

"There is one other thing and I can't prove this but I need your reassurance that you will protect me as even inside she will come after me if she knows I have spoken to you?" he said almost pleading.

"Go on, I'm listening" said Alex "but I am making no promises."

"Well, there was a rumour, but it was only a rumour that Sam's hubby was playing away from home and she found out. Word has it his car being hit by a big truck was actually no accident. She has access to a few heavies who do jobs with no questions asked."

All four of us looked at each other, he hadn't told us anything that would lead us to Andy's killer but I reckoned we had enough to put an end to her blackmailing. It was ironic that should Archie lose as planned tonight then there would be nothing for Phil to investigate anyway.

"Is that it, can I go now?" asked Ben.

"That's all but I will be back in touch so don't leave the country" said Alex who didn't actually have anything to hold him on unless Phil wanted to make a complaint which was highly unlikely at the moment. I was sure Ben Henry knew that as well. He seemed scared of Sam though which should work in our favour.

"Not a word to Sam about our meeting" said Alice "her phone is being monitored so we will know" she added as he started to walk away. After the production of the tape recorder it wouldn't have surprised me if she had arranged it.

"My lips are sealed."

Alice still looked furious so I took her to one side as Phil handed Alex the envelope he had picked up earlier. Only three of us had handled the picture, four if you now included Alex. He said he'd take it away with him and give it to forensics to see if they could get anything from it, be it a finger print on the tape or any other DNA.

"So were you going to tell me about the photographs of you having sex in the car or should I just wait until they are dropped through my letterbox?" she said punching me on the left arm. I guessed my sympathy time limit had expired where inflicting pain was concerned.

"No I wasn't going to because it isn't relevant. Should I have done? Yes probably but what good would it have done? I'm sorry, that may not mean much but I am, truly."

We joined the other two back at the table and Alex explained what he was going to do with the picture Phil had given him. He would put the hurry up on it and see if anything comes back. He didn't actually have anything of Sam's to compare it to so that could be a problem. I told him I'd think of something.

"Who took that picture earlier by the way?" asked Phil "It did the trick and stopped the cocky git in his tracks."

"That was my mate Foxy. I sent him a text from the hospital this morning and asked him to do me a little favour. He was to take the photograph when I first stood up and send it to your phone Alice when I stood up again. Worked like a dream don't you think?" I said and we all laughed.

I had been so caught up with what we had achieved over the last hour that I had almost forgotten about the images Alex had brought with him of the two men in Andy's car who had been caught on camera near Kempton Park. He had three in all. The first two weren't the greatest but clearly showed the number plate of the car. The third was better and clearly showed the two occupants in the front. They were both men and the slime ball Ken Kelly was in the passenger seat.

"That's Ken Kelly on the right" I said as I passed the picture to Phil who nodded in agreement and handed the images back to Alex.

"Progress at last" he said "any idea on the other man?" We both shook our heads.

"You will be glad to know Joe North-Wales are couriering down the CCTV coverage for the ferry crossing you requested and it should be at the station now. It will include the ticket office and the foot passenger walkways. They have the car footage as well but I have told them to hold onto that for now. If you want to pop down tomorrow you can have a look at it to your heart's content. So what is the plan of attack for tonight young Sherlock? I have to admit you were rather impressive earlier getting him to open up. Think you might be in the wrong job" he said and laughed.

"Rainbow Warrior's race is the third on the card at eight o'clock. If you Alex can meet up with Phil at seven thirty in the car park he will arrange you access through the paddock entrance. Alice and I will come in through the main turnstile at quarter to eight. I will call Phil when we are in.

I expect Sam will be stood up by the bookmakers watching the betting and we will idle up to Foxy to make some small talk. Richard normally stands down by the perimeter wall and Ken will either be with Richard or Sam, I imagine Sam. Orla is going to do her bit just as the greyhounds come out on parade. She is going to tell Richard she got held up in the traffic after a hair appointment.

We don't do anything until the race has been run. Phil has already been onto the big firms and told them not to restrict any bets on the race despite the big hits they have suffered previously on the dog. Foxy has a couple of little jobs to carry out and that about covers it."

"So I wait until after the race and on your signal before I arrest Ken Kelly then?" asked Alex seeking clarification.

"Yes please" I replied.

CHAPTER THIRTY SIX

There was no point Phil going all the way back into London so we went for lunch at the same place we had originally met three weeks earlier. It was less than two weeks until Christmas and we struggled to get a table and we'd have to wait an hour to be seated. We were in no hurry we told the waitress. We made our way to the bar and I ordered him a pint whilst I stuck to orange juice. I found standing a lot more comfortable than sitting so we remained where we were.

"I'm getting too old for this mate" said Phil "there was no need to do what they did to you. I did some research into the Bristol coup whilst you were away in Ireland, why didn't you tell me it was your father who was the Racing Manager?"

I shrugged my shoulders as I put my glass back down on the bar; even that hurt. "I don't know really, didn't think it was relevant. I guess I was surprised by what I had found that day, what with all the times being manipulated and Richard Quinn having so many winners."

"Surprised that he'd had them or surprised that I hadn't spotted them?" he asked.

"A bit of both I suppose. I now know but why didn't you tell me? You do know that I would have helped you if you had. If anything it would have made my job easier knowing where to start. You were very clever bringing me to the Ball that night. You put me straight in the line of fire hoping that I would deflect the bullets that were shot at you. It gave you leeway with your bosses. They suddenly became more worried about me being on the scene rather than the big gambles that were going on."

I watched his face for a reaction, he didn't argue.

"Am I right in thinking that it was Sam Hampshire who was the first to raise the alarm bells about the Rainbow Warrior gambles?"

He shook his head before replying. "It was my boss with the two mistresses. I guess Sam was a bit pissed off she hadn't been invited in on the gambles and decided she wanted to ruin it for everyone else. He came into see me after the second gamble on Rainbow Warrior and told me to get to the bottom of it and asked me to liaise with Sam, which I did. Then the third one went in and I thought he was going to come through the ceiling from the room above. You've seen him, he isn't exactly slight!" a comment that made us both laugh.

"In the interim I still had those pictures of me with Melanie that would really take some explaining along with the smaller gambles I was being told to ignore. They were only minor in comparison, four or five thousand spread in the surrounding area and Oxford. Then the other bloody dog won at 6-1 and Sam was screaming blue murder telling me it had nothing to do with her even though the dog was in her name. Thinking back now I should have realised she was more involved than she was."

"I am almost certain she had nothing to do with that one and Foxy is going to confirm that tonight. Tony 'the timer' is back from his cruise now" I said.

"By this stage I was pulling my hair out so I decided to go and see Andy unannounced at the track. We had a right slanging match and I told him I was fully aware of the smaller gambles and I would eventually come back to them once I had got to the bottom of the bigger ones. He swore blind he had no idea about the Rainbow Warrior gambles. He had a DVD on his desk of the dog and we went through all his races and he asked me straight out would I gamble a dog that consistently missed the break. I remember his exact words 'bloody hell Phil this dog even sits down and gives the paddock steward a paw at kennelling if she asks him so how can anyone be confident that he is going to win is beyond me'. I had to agree with him. I told him I wouldn't let it drop and he should think seriously about his position as if it carried on the track would close."

I burst out laughing, it was that simple and none of us had picked up on it. Tommy was right, young Jamie was a genius.

"What's so funny about the track closing?" he asked.

"I wasn't laughing at that, I think I know why Rainbow Warrior wins when he wants and after tonight you won't need to worry about it. You may want to have a few quid on him to win the Derby ante-post though" I said with a smile and asked the barmaid for a refill.

"So what happened next then?" I asked.

"I stayed up at the track. The firms had all sent a representative to keep the price down as low as possible. They hadn't put out a warning message to restrict bets on either dog so we conveniently arranged for one of the trainers to be held up on the M1 so his dog was a non-runner. The track bookmakers had his price too short though and not one bet was placed with them. Eventually they eased his price from evens to 6-4 but there still wasn't any money for it.

As you know the dog won and we thought we had limited the damage that the high street bookmakers were being hit for. His price in the morning had been 3-1 but all those bets were settled at 6-4 because of the non-runner. We thought we had reduced the liabilities massively. We thought wrong. I received a call from my boss on the way home to say the bookmakers had been taken to the cleaners again and he was having his ears chewed off and he wanted to know what I was going to do about it."

"What did you say to him?"

"I told him I would get back to him. I made a call to the firm that had supposedly been hit the hardest and asked him what the exact problem was. He didn't tell me much and seemed rather coy and said that they'd had bets for Double Vision winning as well at 11-4 for about £15,000 around the country. For the amount they make that was a pittance, it was only at the Ball I found out that the amount had been in doubles with the other dog."

"They had really cleaned them out then?" I said with a smile, fair play to Tommy.

"The other firms had been hit as well. I reckon they must have gone for at least £250,000 between them. I tried ringing Andy at the track but he was still racing so I left a message. I then received that text message I showed you and never heard from him again."

I didn't know what to say. It was obvious that Phil still felt some guilt about Andy's death. I wasn't sure what I could say that would convince him otherwise. Andy had knowingly got himself involved in cheating. Maybe he had threatened to come clean or had asked for a bigger cut, I doubt we'd ever know. I did know however that after tonight Sam Hampshire would no longer be able to blackmail him.

The waitress came over to tell us our table was ready and we followed her. We spent the whole meal going over our plans for tonight.

CHAPTER THIRTY SEVEN

Alice hadn't joined us for lunch. She'd said it was because she needed to catch up on some work at the station and see if Forensics had any results back from their visit to my flat. I should have told her everything from the start and given the opportunity I wouldn't lie to her again. Phil hadn't been as blind as we'd thought to our growing relationship. I took his 'she's old enough to know what she is doing' as an endorsement. He hadn't warned me off her and it would have been too late now if he had.

We arrived at the track just before seven thirty; Phil had driven. Alice was already there with another man sat in the back of Alex's car.

"Evening Joe, evening Phil, this is my colleague DC Tilbury, he has been brought up to speed and will follow you two in" Alex said pointing to myself and Alice "he is back up just in case someone wants to add to your bruises. He will be keeping an eye on Ken Kelly. Right, shall we get on with it?"

We went our separate ways. Phil and Alex towards the paddock entrance whilst Alice, DC Tilbury and I walked slowly towards the turnstile. We were just about to enter when Orla came up from behind me and made me jump. "Hiya, just to let you know we are here......." she started before pausing. "Bloody hell Joe, are you alright. You look bloody awful."

She looked genuinely shocked. I had looked in the mirror before we'd left Alice's flat. There was no way to disguise the swelling and bruising around my right eye or the slowness of my walk. I had been able to cover the bandage around my head though with a black woolly hat that came down over my ears.

"I'm fine honest. Are his parents with you?"

"Yes, already to go. I'm to come down to the wall just as they come on parade."

I smiled and touched her arm in thanks. "See you in there."

Sam was exactly where I had expected her to be by the bookmakers. I walked directly towards her but stopped to talk to Foxy briefly where we embraced like long lost friends before continuing in her direction. Ken was stood beside her, he was smiling. I put my hands in my pockets as I stopped beside them.

"Good evening you two, any chance I can have a quick word Sam, in private like without this twat around? I have a business proposition for you" I asked looking straight at Ken.

"Leave us be Ken, go and join Richard down by the wall and I will come down in a minute to watch the race. I'm intrigued as to what possible proposition this man could have."

Ken didn't want to go anywhere but he went all the same.

"What do you want Jackson? I see you have recovered from your kicking but I did tell you to stay out of my business the last time we met. Just a shame that little tart came back by the sounds of it?" she said without the hint of concern.

"What tart would that be?" I said and smiled at her. I checked the prices on the bookmaker boards. Rainbow Warrior was the clear even money favourite. "Nice price that dog of Richard's, I understand your brother owns half of it?"

She said nothing as she looked directly at me.

"That's right Sam, or should I call you Sally-Ann, I understand that you are having quite a bit on it as well tonight, what with your fake account and Andy Whelan's I'd imagine that you hope to win a fair few quid. Oh and look, it is starting to drift in price as well; it is 5-4 now. At what price will your money be going on?"

"None of your fucking business. Get out of my way as I have to talk to the trainer" she said and started to walk away.

"Do you mean the trainer or your son?"

That stopped her straight in her tracks and she walked back towards me. "What did you say?"

"You heard me, Richard is your son and he doesn't know. You

only framed me because you didn't want me to break up his marriage. You are a control freak Sam but it is all over for you now" I said as the bookmaker shouted out that Rainbow Warrior was now 6-4.

"You know nothing. I was right when I said you needed to be taught a lesson but that buffoon Ken can't do anything right. You have nothing on me, you lost your job because you were taking back handers so stop trying to blame someone else for your errors."

"Is that right?" I said taking my right hand out of my pocket; a signal for Phil and Alex to stay where they were. They had positioned themselves in a window seat in the restaurant so they could see everything. "I had a very interesting conversation with a gentleman called Ben Henry this morning who told me you had set me up and many others as well." Alex may have given the journalist assurances his name wouldn't be mentioned but I hadn't.

"Ben who, never heard of him?" she replied as the dogs came out on parade.

"Oh I think you have, Ben Henry supplied you with the photographs that got me the sack and the ones you are blackmailing Phil Clarke with. I bet you were really upset to find them missing when you were in Ireland as well as Andy's mobile. I know that is why you sent the boys around on Monday" I said "I heard the call to you from my flat."

"I have no idea what you are talking about, now if you don't mind I have a dog to go and watch" she said as she barged past me and headed towards the perimeter wall.

'Seven to four Rainbow Warrior' shouted the bookmaker in the direction of Sam who took no notice of him.

Sam had got to within a couple of feet of Richard and Ken when Orla rushed down towards them with Richard's parents alongside her.

"Hey Richard, look who I found wandering in the car park. Isn't it great to see them? I have asked them to stay overnight as they haven't seen the kids for ages" shouted Orla for everyone to hear.

"That's great love" he said as he shook his father by the hand and hugged his mother. He was genuinely pleased to see them and it was first time that I could remember ever seeing him smile. "Mum, dad, this is Ken who works for me and this is Sam, she is one of my biggest owners" he said and I thought that must have hurt.

Sam struggled with the joviality and made her excuses and moved away from the small family group and Ken joined her back on the same step as before just in front of the bookmakers. She looked angry and whispered something in Ken's ear. Whatever it was it saw him depart back up towards the paddock at a brisk pace. I decided to join her again, much to her annoyance.

"Isn't that lovely, a whole family together? You will never break that you know, no matter how hard you try. That bond has an unbreakable seal and if you try and break it now you will only push him further away." I was goading her into a response.

She looked at me briefly; her eyes were full of tears.

"It will only get worse Sam, but what I don't understand is why Andy had to die, what did he do to end up at the bottom of a lake at Kempton Park racecourse? I know you were together and that you set up his exchange account for him. You forget I worked with the guy and he wasn't a gambler."

"Why don't you just fuck off? Where has that bloody idiot Ken gone?"

'The hare is on the move' announced the commentator.

I didn't need to watch the race, I just watched her reaction. I knew Rainbow Warrior would be slow away and with luck he would stay on strongly and fill either second or third place which would be good enough for him to reach the Final of the Golden Lead the following week. He finished third.

"Tommy will be pleased" I said and she looked at me in a rage I hadn't expected "he said no fecking woman would come into his house and tell him when he could back a dog. Nothing better than hitting them where it hurts most he said, in the pocket and I am guessing, actually I can almost guarantee, that you and your friends have lost a packet?"

"You have nothing on me Jackson; I will see you in hell before I tell you anything."

"Sam, as I said it's all over. I met with Lewis from your office on Monday and you are out of a job. I have seen the CCTV coverage of you dropping Andy's car off at the hotel in Holyhead" which was a lie "and we have images of Ken in Andy's car outside of Kempton Park the night he died and that Ben Henry is also a bit of a weasel so you are screwed either way. Blackmail, fraud and murder will see you behind bars for a long time."

I could see her clenching her fists, if she were a kettle I'd say she would be very close to boiling point. I was deliberately sniping and goading her. It didn't matter now whether she talked or not. Her reputation would be in tatters and she had no way of winning around her son, not whilst I was around. It wasn't just her that could ruin lives. I had the power now and the ammunition and I was destroying her.

The tears were now streaming and she tried to wipe them away with the sleeve of her jacket.

"I didn't kill him, it was an accident, it was his own bloody fault but you will never prove I had anything to do with him being dumped in the lake" she started to open up as Alice walked towards me, I indicated for her to stop and come no further. Sam was speaking loud enough for me to hear. There was no one else around as betting wouldn't begin on the next race for about five minutes when the throng would reassemble.

"Who did and how was it accident?"

"It was Andy's idea to manipulate the trials and I just put the money on when he told me which race had been carved up. The deal was that Richard wasn't to be told and there would be one or maybe two a week."

"What was in it for him if he didn't gamble?"

"Sex, drugs and a new flat in Towcester" she replied.

I hadn't expected drugs to be involved at all.

"I'd found out Andy had a drug habit, cocaine. I stayed behind after racing one night to have a quiet word and said I would expose his little secret unless he played ball and plotted a few of Richard's dogs up without him knowing. Richard is a useless punter and I couldn't see him just taking the money off me and the only thing his wife was good for was opening her legs. So I thought I'd try and get him an advantage with a few thrown in."

"Threatening to expose the cocaine habit didn't work so I offered him my body instead. I hadn't been with a man since my husband died and if I got what I wanted from it then it was worth the sacrifice. As it happens I quite enjoyed it. After about a month he puts this idea to me about cheating with the trial times and being able to guarantee having plenty of first time out winners. It bloody worked as well but he started to get itchy feet after a couple of months because of all those other gambles.

Andy was having a lot pressure put on him by Phil Clarke and he thought I'd been cutting him out of the deal as the dogs were trained by Richard. That's when I forked out for the new flat to keep him on side. Tommy said that he wasn't gambling it heavily but someone was."

I could really have stuck the knife in by saying Tommy was the brains behind them.

"Anyway, Andy gave me a call the day after the two dogs had won and said that he wants out as we were putting the track's future at risk and that Phil Clarke was investigating all of the winners Richard had been having. I told him I had that under control which I did. He told me to come down to the track so we could have it out. What he didn't know was I'd set up the exchange account in his name. I always had that as back up just in case he tried to drop me in it."

"So he had no idea he had the account? So who was the man at Kempton putting the money in his account and your account?" I asked.

"You mean Mark? I knew that Owen wouldn't ask too many questions and he just does what I tell him. I used to give him the odd dog tip as well but he was another useless punter. Mark was one of the guys who used to take my bets and that was him paying out and taking ten percent for himself."

"And the bookmakers at Stony Stratford, they did the same?"

"Pretty much, when we were gambling one they'd make the price as big as possible and back it with the big firms in lots of shops for small amounts so as not to set alarm bells ringing."

"So what happened when you went to see Andy?"

"Andy was in a right flap, I don't think he'd had his fix for a day or so as Phil Clarke had turned up unannounced the day before and he usually met his dealer on a Wednesday. He was frothing around the mouth and shouting that he was going to tell Phil everything and he had sent him a text earlier telling him where to look.

I told him not to be daft and showed him the three cheques that I had drawn out of his exchange account and if he said anything I would drop him in it. That just made things worse, his eyes were bulging and he was storming around the room and he went for me, grabbed me by the neck with both hands. That's when it happened."

"What happened?"

"I punched him in the bollocks. He staggered backwards but because of his bad leg he couldn't keep his balance and fell backwards and caught his head on that bloody marble based greyhound statue he had on the corner of his desk."

I knew the one she meant, I had used it as a doorstop during the summer months as the office had no air-conditioning.

"I checked for a pulse but he was dead, there was a hole in the back of his head and blood was seeping out. I put one of those presentation jackets under his head to soak up the blood and then called Ken. It took him about half an hour to get here. I told him Andy had tried to rape me and I had pushed him over and he banged his head. He was gullible enough to believe it. Ken took over from then on, carried the body down to Andy's car and put it in the boot."

I was surprised she was telling me so much and she seemed quite happy to do so. She showed no signs or remorse or guilt. The others had stuck to the plan and were keeping their distance. I could see Foxy over Sam's shoulder and he gave me the thumbs up.

It was time to dig a little further.

"So why are you telling me this now, you know I will tell the Police? There were also two guys in the car, who was the other one?" I asked.

"That would be me" said a voice I recognised as I felt something hard push into the side of my ribs that caused immediate pain "say another word and I will push a bit harder until your rib cracks, now you are coming with me. Don't make a fuss or your lady friend down there will be extremely disfigured if you ever see her again."

CHAPTER THIRTY EIGHT

I looked down towards Alice and she had two men around her, both were well over six foot and stoutly built. She looked scared. There was no sign of DC Tilbury whilst Alex and Phil were too far away to intervene.

I had underestimated the enemy, a huge mistake in any battle. I thought the element of surprise was mine but all Sam was doing by talking to me was using stalling tactics until reinforcements arrived. Ken had obviously been sent off to make the call, so where was he now?

"Now then, it would appear my friend here has some unfinished business to take care of Joe and I doubt I will be seeing you again" she said with a smug grin as she put her mobile phone to her ear "grab the boy and do it now." The only boy I could think of was Jamie.

I could see that Foxy was awake to the current predicament I was in. I struggled up the steps with the anonymous voice still poking something into my side. I was able to grab a quick glance over my right shoulder and could see Alice following, flanked on either side. The betting ring was the height of activity and nobody turned a hair as we made our way towards the exit and out into the poorly lit car park.

We were walking towards a dark coloured van. I was walking towards certain death; I was too young to die and so was Alice. Did they know she was a Policewoman?

I stopped walking; whatever was being pushed into my side was pushed a little deeper, "Keep going" said the anonymous voice.

"Give me a minute will you, you put me in this bloody condition remember so at least give me time to catch my breath?" I said turning to look at him for the first time; he was the other face from the image in the car. It had proved a good time to turn around as I saw DC Tilbury creeping between cars. "Did you know Alice here is a detective, I bet old Sam didn't tell you that? You can get rid of me all you like and nobody will give a toss in a couple of weeks but if you think the Police will let you get away with doing in one of their own, well think about it, you will never get away with it. They will hunt you down." It was my turn to use stalling tactics.

"Joe, shut up" shouted Alice.

"And then there is her father, ex-army, I'm sure he has contacts. Let her go and just take me and I will come willingly" I said as Ken arrived with one hand on the back of young Jamie's neck. He was shouting and kicking, full of fight. "Get your fecking hands of me you smelly bastard."

"Right, get these two in the van but leave the girl" said the anonymous voice. I heard Alice scream as she was thrown between cars on to the gravel. In the blink of an eye our mouths were taped shut and our hands tied behind our back. It took four of them to get us in the van and the door was slammed shut. Almost instantly we were on the move. No one would hear our muffled cries for help.

We left at speed and were thrown around in the back of the van like a single towel in a washing machine. I could have sworn the doctor said I should take it easy. I had no sooner got myself upright when we negotiated another roundabout at high speed, throwing me from one side of the van to the other. We were travelling at speed but I had no idea in what direction. I was scared. I could hear the muffled cries of Jamie from another part of the van. What had I got him into?

The van slowed and we took a sharp left. The terrain was rough; every pot hole sent a sharp pain through my side. We didn't go much further before the van came to an abrupt stop. I heard the driver's door open and footsteps.

The side-door was opened and the anonymous voice, with a torch pointing straight at me, gave instructions to the two heavies who had been by Alice's side for us to be removed. They weren't gentle.

There was no sign of Ken.

"You really are a pain in the arse. Why couldn't you just keep your little nose out of other people's business?"

I took in our surroundings; we were surrounded by tree's, tall trees. It was dark; it was off the beaten track and the ideal place to get rid of a body with the minimum of fuss.

"Put them over there by the bushes. Ken will be along in a minute with a couple of shovels. Make sure they are secure and their mouths are taped shut. Make sure your phone is on silent" he said in a tone that suggested he was used to having his orders carried out.

I looked at Jamie, he looked terrified. I was in no fit state to get away from our captors but he was. I needed to distract them and give him a small window of opportunity to make a run for it.

Richard's phone rang in his pocket.

"Where the bloody hell are you?" he shouted into the device as he walked away from his parents who were now seated in the warmth of the grandstand.

"That doesn't matter. Have you seen the woman that was with Joe at the Ball the other week?" asked Orla.

"Where are you?"

"Not now Richard, have you seen her or not. She was at the track earlier. Get her to call me ASAP please, it is really important. I will explain later but do it now" she whispered into the phone before ending the call.

Richard had seen the woman Joe had been with about two minutes ago. The track was swarming with Police and he'd seen her, Phil Clarke, Sam and another man heading in the direction of Paul Colley's office. He was annoyed that Orla hadn't told him more and he couldn't see Joe anywhere either. He made his way up the stairs towards Colley's office. The door was closed and he didn't bother to knock.

The group of four were in deep discussion, only Sam was seated. The one person who Richard didn't know tried to usher him out of the room but Richard was having none of it.

"My wife wants you to call her and she says it's urgent" shouted the irate trainer in the direction of Alice as he was finally manhandled out of the room.

Alice followed them out.

"Look here, I don't know what the hell is going on but my missus wants you to call her. She isn't at the track and she won't tell me where she is" he again shouted. "And where is that slimeball Jackson?"

Alice wished she knew. The blue van he had been dumped in with Jamie had taken off at some speed and so far no patrol car had seen it. A chopper had been summoned but was still some way off arriving. They were losing time and it was time they could ill afford to lose. Milton Keynes is a maze of roundabouts which would have slowed their exit slightly but not by much. It was now twenty minutes since they had left the track and no one knew in what direction they had gone. In twenty minutes they could be anywhere north, south, east or west.

She was worried.

"Dial her number for me" Alice said to Richard handing him her mobile. He did as asked and handed it back to her.

It was answered immediately.

"Orla, it's Alice, where are you and why do you want to talk to me?" she said with authority.

Alice could hardly hear her, "I followed the van from the track; they are parked up in amongst the trees just before you get to the entrance to Woburn Golf Club. I have no idea what the road is called but Woburn is on my right about 200 yards from the turn off which is on the left."

"Where are you now?" Alice asked.

"I am in amongst the trees about a hundred yards from the road and about fifty yards from the van. Joe and Jamie are still tied up. Gotta go, someone coming."

Alice knew the area well. If the golf course was on Orla's right then the van had probably headed towards the M1 before doubling back towards Woburn. She needed to find DCI Baker.

DCI Baker and Alice were studying a map on the bonnet of his car.

"According to Orla they are just down from the Golf Club entrance so if we park up on the driveway we can walk back to here" she said whilst marking a point on the map with a pen.

"Have you spoken to her since and is she sure it is them?" asked DCI Baker.

"Yes about five minutes ago, they are still parked up. They are probably waiting for replacement transport to come and pick them up. The van they were in had false plates on."

"Ok, let's go. Bring three cars in from the north and three from the south. The dog team have just arrived and the chopper is in the air awaiting guidance. Just before we go in call her and tell her to drop back to the road. There is only one road so we need to stop any traffic at either end until we have them. Make sure they turn off the blues and twos and no bloody sirens."

"Yes guv" said Alice before heading off to her car.

Orla was getting cold; she had just spoken to Alice again to tell her that nothing had changed. She didn't have much charge left on her mobile. Richard had called twice in the last five minutes and she terminated both calls without answering. She could visualise him getting angrier by the minute. She was fully focused on the men fifty yards in front of her. What was taking the Police so long to get here?

I could see that our captors were getting restless. The anonymous one had attempted three calls and none had been answered. He kicked the side of the van in frustration. I needed to get Jamie away from here. I was sure he was fit enough to out run the three heavies even with his hands tied behind his back. The full moon provided us with sufficient light to see what was going on. It was cold and would only get colder with a heavy frost having been predicted.

If I was going to die tonight I wasn't going to do so without putting up a struggle. I got to my feet and Jamie did likewise. The three men were in deep discussion, oblivious to the fact we had moved. I walk towards them, I did it slowly. Jamie meanwhile had made his way silently in amongst the undergrowth. I got to within three feet of them before they turned round.

"What the fuck" shouted the anonymous one before delivering a telling blow to my side with his right fist, quickly followed by another before I'd hit the ground. It was the distraction needed. The three heavies had failed to notice that Jamie had taken flight. One of the heavies went in pursuit, but it was in vain and he soon re-joined his partners in crime.

"Now what?" said the one who hadn't gone off in chase.

"We do nothing until she calls us" said the anonymous voice. "Put him back in the van and shut the door I will try and get hold of Ken. Knowing him he has probably got lost."

It only took Alice and her colleagues fifteen minutes to reach the Golf Course entrance. There were no flashing lights or sirens as instructed. She had noticed Orla's car parked up by the side of the road where she said it would be.

DCI Baker gave a short debrief to a team of officers and dog handlers whilst Alice went off to make the call to Orla asking her to drop back to the main road where she would meet them.

The screen on Orla's phone was flashing; she'd put it on silent so as not to attract attention. She ignored it as she witnessed Joe being punched by one of the three men from the van. She wanted to run and help him but knew she couldn't. She heard rustling in the bushes to her right and then a crack of a branch underfoot; whoever or whatever it was didn't mind being heard. The noise was getting louder and closer and was travelling at speed. She held her breath.

She caught a glimpse of the noise maker as it passed within a couple of feet of her, would it be friend of foe? It was friend. It was Jamie and he was running straight out towards the main road. She looked back towards the van and could see Joe being lifted back into the van, he looked limp. Her phone flashed again.

"Orla, you can drop back now as we are in position" said Alice.

"On my way and Jamie is running in your direction, he got away" Orla whispered before disconnecting.

Jamie hadn't seen Orla, he was concentrating on staying upright as he ran between the trees. He didn't know where he was going but he needed to get as far away as possible. He could make out building lights in front of him so headed that way. Only once had he stopped to listen out for any pursuer, he heard nothing.

Alice was the first to spot Jamie as he staggered out onto the road from the trees almost opposite where Orla had parked up. She ran towards him. He tried to change direction but with the lack of arm movement to control his balance, fell to the ground. He tried to return to his feet but Alice was soon upon him and with the assistance of a fellow officer they were able to bring him under control before he wriggled free.

Jamie didn't know Alice, why should he trust her and it was only the arrival of Orla that saw him relax, if relax was the right word under the circumstances.

Between them they removed the tape from his mouth and hands. He was shaking uncontrollably and Orla took him into her arms to reassure him, stroking the back of his neck and kissing his forehead as he sobbed into her shoulder. "It's okay Jamie, you're safe now" she said to him as a Policewoman brought over a jacket for him to wear.

"Orla, you stay here. DCI Baker is waiting to go in with armed officers and a couple of police dogs. Do you know if the guys who have Joe are armed?" asked Alice.

Orla shrugged her shoulders, "I don't know but they have put Joe back in the van. They gave him a going over after Jamie ran off. He looked out for the count."

I wasn't sure my ribs could take anymore punishment and I'd heard something crack with the second punch. It was some consolation knowing that Jamie had got away. How long before he could summon help was another matter altogether?

Who would get here first, Ken with his shovels or Alice and her colleagues? I lay on my good side, there was nothing I could do now but wait.

With no time to lose Alice ran back towards DCI Baker, they spoke briefly before he gave the instruction to move in.

In total there were a dozen officers including Alice and the element of surprise on this occasion had been theirs, moving in from three sides they had brought the situation to a swift conclusion and the abductors were now face down on the ground.

The darkness had been replaced by headlights and flashing blue lights. Orla and Alice reached the van at the same time; both were scared of what they may find inside.

I could hear shouting outside; I tried to sit up to hear more but failed abysmally and gave up at the third attempt. The shouting became louder and what was being said clearer.

It wasn't Ken with his shovels. The side door slid open, I don't know whether I cried due to relief or because of the pain I was in.

Alice and Orla soon removed the tape from my hands and face. This was becoming too much of a habit but at least I was conscious on this occasion. Yes my ribs hurt but I was breathing fine and I could walk under my own steam, albeit gingerly. In unison the pair insisted that I went to hospital once I had been given the once over. Orla brought Jamie over from the car, I was glad he was safe. I wasn't sure his grandfather would be too impressed when I told him the danger I'd put him in.

"That is the second time I thought I'd lost you" Alice said as she put her arms around me. "You must go to hospital Joe, you look dreadful."

I couldn't see Phil anywhere or DC Tilbury. Alex was on his phone as he idled up beside me. "Well that didn't go to plan did it Sherlock" he said with a wry smile on his face "but we got a result with a massive chunk of fortune?"

I smiled back at him. I knew he was right and I had underestimated the lengths Sam would go to remain in control. I had not only put myself in danger but also Alice and Jamie.

"What happened to DC Tilbury, I thought he was supposed to be staying alongside Alice?" I asked.

"His job was to follow Ken Kelly remember. When Kelly disappeared before the race he followed him to the paddock but the woman on the gate wouldn't let him in without the correct pass despite him showing her his warrant card. He didn't persist as the plan was to wait until the race was run. He stayed up there waiting for him to come out. When it all kicked off with you in the betting ring I radioed him to grab Kelly but when he eventually gained entry to the paddock he had gone out the back and had grabbed the boy.

Someone had already called the Police by the time I had called for back-up but we had no idea what direction you had gone."

Orla returned to join the group wearing a fluorescent Police jacket to protect her from the cold.

"Orla, I'm Detective Chief Inspector Baker, I'm heading up the investigation into Andy Whelan's murder. I was here tonight as part of Joe's master plan, which went wrong" he said and the pair shook hands.

"You have saved me an awful lot of work but I still have a lot of explaining to do" he said looking at me in a manner that suggested I was to blame for that. "If it hadn't been for this young lady Joe we may never have found you, especially this quickly."

Orla smiled.

"How do you mean?" I said.

"Tell him" Alice urged Orla.

"It was nothing really. Joe had told me to keep a close eye on Jamie after what had happened on Monday night. I met Jamie up in the paddock after Archie had run and helped clean him up. I was just putting the dog away in his kennel when Ken came running across, grabbed him and dragged him out of the back gate. I just followed him."

"It was dark but I could hear Jamie shouting so I knew what direction they were going in. I was crouched down by a van when a guy who said he was a Police Officer came up behind me. Frightened me senseless he did. Anyway the copper told me to stay put but I never do as I am told" she said "so I followed him."

"Then what?" asked Alice.

"Everything had come to a stop in front of me, Joe was talking and Jamie was still kicking and screaming so I took a chance and turned back on myself and came in from the top end of the car park and to the front of the van. I'd parked the car in the trainer's car park when I arrived with Richard's parents. I knew I didn't have much time. It was obvious where they were going to be putting them both. I got lucky that there was nothing parked in my way.

No one had seen me. I waited until they'd pulled away and just followed them. They weren't hanging around I can tell you. I thought I was going to lose them at one stage but I didn't want to get too close in case they saw me. When they pulled off the road I parked up and did the rest on foot. That's when I called Richard and asked him to find Alice."

We all looked at her. She was so calm and relaxed with the whole thing. I moved over to her and gave her a huge hug and kissed her on the forehead in thanks. "You can stop all that rubbish Joe; I'm a married woman you know!" We all burst out laughing as two Police cars pulled up beside us.

"So where is Ken?" I asked

"Foxy was waiting for him by his car. He hit him with a set of ignition cables by all accounts. He has already been taken into custody" replied Alice.

"So what about Sam, where is she, please tell me she didn't get away after all that?"

"She is in the General Managers office at the track with DC Tilbury and dad. She has no idea that her guys have been apprehended or that you are safe." said Alice. "She is screaming blue murder that the Police have no reason to hold her and that she will sue everyone."

"Right, well take me back there now. Where are we by the way?"

"Woburn Golf Course" replied Orla.

It didn't take us long to get back to the track. Alice came with me and Jamie returned with Orla. Richard was waiting for us as we pulled up and he was gunning for me. He was just about to have a go when I stopped him before he got started. "Richard, your wife has just saved my life and I will let her explain how but for what it is worth I am sorry for all the pain I caused you in the past. Neither of us thought of the consequences at the time but it is exactly that, in the past" I said offering him my hand in truce.

He was reluctant to take it but did eventually after gentle persuasion from Orla.

"Right" I said to Alice and Alex "let's go up to Colley's office and see what she has to say for herself."

"Hold on a minute" said Alex "we haven't exactly got a lot to hold her on apart from possible blackmail which we won't have confirmed until tomorrow at the earliest and if she turns up on the port CCTV footage."

"Alas Mr Watson young Sherlock here has one more surprise for you" I said teasing him as we walked through the packed restaurant as racing continued. Most of the diners were probably oblivious to what had gone on in the previous hour or so.

Foxy was waiting for me by the bar. I walked over to him. Neither of us said a word, I was indebted to him and always would be. We embraced as old friends do and he slipped the package into my pocket out of sight of my companions. I indicated that I needed to go and shook him by the hand.

Sam was sat in Paul Colley's chair, the same chair that he had sacked me from two years ago. How ironic it was that I would now be ending what she had started. I had no sympathy for her and would enjoy this last chapter. She stood up as I entered the room but DC Tilbury soon returned her to the seat. She looked shocked to see me and I said nothing.

"I fucking hate you, you little shit. My solicitor will tear you lot apart holding me here without good reason. With your history who do you think a jury will believe; a corrupt ex-racing manager or a woman of standing like me?" she said with such conviction that I honestly think she believed every word of it.

I looked across to Alex who was now stood beside Phil to my right. His facial expression suggested that what she had just said was right. I still said nothing. I put my hand in my pocket and pulled out the package Foxy had put there. It was a small tape recorder.

Unbeknown to Sam the whole of our exchange in the betting ring had been taped. Foxy had pinned a high powered micro-phone to my jacket when we had embraced when I first came on to the track.

I placed it on the desk in front of her and pressed play.

The conversation had been captured beautifully. I let it play all the way through, right up to the point where she gave instructions to Ken to grab Jamie. She was restless in the chair but with DC Tilbury behind her she had nowhere to go. I pressed stop, picked up the machine and handed it to DCI Baker with a smile. He smiled back.

I walked out the room and didn't look back. It was all over.

CHAPTER THIRTY NINE

One week later

The doctor had been right when he said the pain would ease in time, I almost felt back to normal until I sneezed or laughed. Life itself was returning to normal also. I had given the office shift a miss on Friday but commentated at Crayford on the Saturday night and returned to my flat after all the locks had been changed and the glass replaced. They had found my keys amongst Ken's possessions the day he had been arrested. I decided to change the locks just in case and it was time to upgrade the Mondeo to a newer model as well.

The CCTV from the port had shown Sam paying for a ticket and walking up the gangway. Alex had compared it to the images from the hotel in Holyhead and he was pretty certain they were one and the same.

It was on the Friday that Alex finally got the breakthrough he'd been searching for. The Police had Andy's body but still had no idea how it had been placed in the lake. The track's own CCTV coverage was extensive and no one had come in or out who shouldn't have; be it through one of the main entrances or where the horse boxes would enter the stabling yard.

Alex had released images of Ken and his partner in crime to the national media on the Thursday evening asking anyone for information that may help. It did the trick. Within hours they were following up a number of leads. The car had been spotted parked across the driveway of a man who was taking his dog out for a late night walk. It was crucial.

He had spotted two men coming out of a fenced off area at the furthest end of the track reserved for dog walkers. When he returned home the car was gone. The Police had sent in a search team and they found the presentation jacket that Sam had used on the back of Andy's head. They conducted a finger-tip search but still couldn't fathom how the pair could have got the body over the six foot fencing without being seen. They hadn't.

The fencing was of tubular design and four poles had been cut about a foot off the ground in the furthest corner by some bramble bushes. The Police had come across it by accident when an officer lost his footing close to where the bloodied jacket had been found and fell against the fence. To the naked eye you wouldn't have seen where the poles had been cut. The poles would have been pushed upwards and the Police were confident that this was where the pair, with Andy's body, had gained access to the track.

It would have taken them a while to carry the body over to the lake Alex had said from that point. There had been a sharp frost that evening he reminded me so visibility would have been good. The tractors had been working all night on the track as well to enable racing to go ahead the following day so even if they had been seen they would have looked like track workers. As long as they took their time they'd have no problem getting in and out and so it had proved.

Ken finally cracked on Friday. Whilst being interviewed he had been played the tape from the track on the Wednesday night, I was surprised it had taken them that long. He'd taken great exception to being called a buffoon and a useless one at that. He'd thought Sam had his back. He was wrong. The Forensic team had found his prints all over my bedroom so he didn't have a leg to stand on.

His accomplice had been named as Mitch Mardy and he was a man the Police had been interested in for some time but had never been able to pin anything on. In a nutshell he was a hired thug who'd been arrested previously for witness intimidation but never charged. He had a very good solicitor but even he would struggle with getting him off this.

Sam had lied about how Andy had died. Her story didn't tie up with the post mortem findings or the blood the forensic team found in his office. There was no blood at all on the statue she claimed he had banged his head on or on the floor where he had allegedly fallen. There was however plenty to be found on his desk chair and the surrounding floor. An attempt had been made to clean it up with bleach Alex advised but they'd left some behind. It was a common mistake.

Sam hadn't said anything to incriminate herself but she hadn't needed to. Ken was talking enough for the pair of them and although they didn't have the actual murder weapon in their possession as of yet the Police were happy to believe his version of events which tied in with the forensic evidence. Sam had told him she'd hit Andy over the back of the head with one of his golf clubs whilst he was sat in his chair threatening to confess all to Phil Clarke and she'd flown into a rage. Why she had kept Andy's phone remained a mystery. Ken had found it in the boot of the car after they'd dumped the body and given it to her the following morning he said when confessing all.

Unfortunately for the Police the golf club, which they had deduced to be a four-iron as it was the only one missing from Andy's golf bag that still remained in the racing office, was now in the lake at Kempton and was likely to remain there.

Alex was confident they had enough on Sam without it. The forensics on the blackmail picture Phil had received had come back with a finger print which matched to Sam. The thug who had pushed Alice to the ground had been driving the articulated lorry which had run into the back of her husband's car and killed him. It would appear Ben Henry had been right all along. It was a case the Police would need to re-open.

I'd rung Tommy from the track on Wednesday evening and filled him in on the night's events and told him Jamie was fine. I would wait another day before telling him the danger I had exposed him to. He took it upon himself to go around and see Father Sean and break it to him his sister had been arrested after having his grandson abducted. Sean blamed himself for the way his sister had turned out.

Deep down he knew searching for her son would only end his tears. They had spent a long time talking and Tommy admitted he actually felt sorry for his friend.

I hadn't seen or spoken to Orla since. She had milked the 'hero-status' she had been given by the media but that was already dying down.

Lewis had called Phil on Monday to inform him Sam had bet all of the money in Andy's account on Rainbow Warrior to win and a considerable amount from her own 'Sally-Ann' account as well. He had staff looking into it.

The three track bookmakers had been called in and warned about their future conduct. They would have been sacked normally but without them the track would have closed within the week. I didn't think it had much of a future anyway as the owners had a reputation for selling off tracks for housing. I was sure Stony Stratford would follow suit at some stage. The track bookmakers had lost a fair chunk of their own money when Rainbow Warrior had been beaten as well, much to the delight of the big firms who reported back to Phil they had made a considerable profit. His boss still wasn't happy and said he had taken an unnecessary risk. He soon piped down when Phil brought the Colombian nanny into the conversation.

All in all it had been a pretty hectic week.

I pulled into the track car park and the first person I saw as arranged was Foxy. It was the biggest night of the year at the track with the final of the Golden Lead being televised on a Satellite Sport Channel. Two big trucks with broadcasting equipment took up the bottom end of the car park, cable after cable snaking their way to different parts of the track where camera positions had been set up and extra lighting for the show's hosts. As a racing manager I used to love these nights, showcasing the track and the local talent who raced here on a regular basis.

I was again a paying guest who would have a prime position in the restaurant overlooking the winning line. My bets had already been placed; I had clocked over a hundred miles this afternoon, stopping at every betting shop I could find. I felt like I was one of Tommy's 'fellas' and mainly due to the racing being televised the restrictions being placed by bookmakers had been eased. The bets were all mine and Tommy wouldn't be getting his twenty per cent!

Alice and Phil were waiting for us when we arrived; Alex had been invited but sent his apologies as the death of Sam's husband needed to be investigated further. We had no sooner sat down and ordered a drink when Phil's phone rang. "You sort it out, it's your job and no you don't need to test him now as you will be testing him before the final anyway" he said with a fair degree of annoyance into the mouthpiece.

"Problem?" I asked.

"Stipendiary steward flapping again, she is bloody useless. Apparently one of Quinn's dogs has come in and they can't find the micro-chip anywhere on him. It's not the first time according to the trainer's wife so they are going to put another chip in after its race. She also wanted to know if she should sample Rainbow Warrior now the daft cow. It's a big final, all the dogs are sampled before they come out before the race; she should know that."

"So will Double Vision run then?" I said without thinking.

"How did you know it was Double Vision?" he quickly replied, giving me a look which suggested I knew more than I was letting on.

"Orla told me when she came to see me. I told you about it."

I hadn't but I wanted to change the subject. "I think he will run well tonight, I have already backed him, what about you Foxy?"

Phil seemed surprised. "You can't back that Joe; his two trial times have been poor. You said yourself you thought he was lame and he didn't go much faster last week either. You will get a good price though, I reckon he will be 10-1 at least" he said as the waitress arrived with our drinks.

"I got 12-1 and I think you will see a different dog tonight mate" I said and winked at Alice.

"It's a no bet race for me I'm afraid" said Foxy with a smile. He'd be backing it alright.

The crowd was the biggest of the year, with only a couple of days until Christmas the restaurant was full and the bars were doing a roaring trade. The owners would be pleased. Paul Colley popped down to see Phil just after the second race to ask if his complimentary meal was to his satisfaction. I didn't even bother to acknowledge him.

Double Vision's race was the third on the card and the second that would be shown on television. We had finished our starters and I politely asked the waitress to delay serving the main course until the third race had been run. I asked Phil if he wanted a bet placing as I was going outside to watch this one.

"No thanks, I think you are mad for backing the Quinn dog though, he has no chance on paper" he said as Foxy and I rose from our seats.

"Just as well they race on sand then isn't it?" I replied laughing.

"Have a tenner on for me Joey boy" said Alice handing me two five pound notes.

"So how confident are you then Joe? Phil is right; he has a lot to do to win this race."

"If he traps he wins, if he doesn't trap he just doesn't win by as far" I said replicating what he'd said when Sand Dancer had won a few weeks ago. We both laughed and made our way to the bookmakers which were already very busy and the dogs hadn't yet come out on parade.

'Six to four the favourite' shouted the bookmaker to our right. The three bookmakers had all priced Double Vision up as the total outsider at 8-1. We waited. The shouting bookmaker changed his price to 10-1 and the other two followed suit. We still waited, the greyhounds were now on parade and Jamie held the lead of Double Vision who was due to run from trap four. Double Vision priced moved again, there had been no takers at 8-1 or 10-1; the bookmakers were keen to drum up business for the one dog they had so far not taken a bet on.

'Fourteen to one the four dog' he shouted.

Like a team of synchronised swimmers six men, two for each bookmaker, moved forward down a step and with cash in hand and waved it in front of the bookmaker, 'three hundred on the four' said the first man and the bookmaker shouted to his clerk '£4,200 to £300 ticket eight six'. The same call was being made by the other two bookmakers to their assisting clerk.

There were eight bets struck that I saw all for the same amount. Should Double Vision win each would be collecting four and a half thousand pounds. The price had reduced to the original 8-1 as the greyhounds were taken behind the boxes. "Bollocks, I didn't back it for Alice" I said. "Don't worry, I have done it for her, all those guys were putting on for me" he said as we made our way to his lucky spot in front of the restaurant.

I spotted Orla and Richard together by the wall, his parents had come again. She waved up towards me and I smiled in return. She put her arm through Richard's and waited for the action to begin.

'The hare is on the move'

The traps opened and the six greyhounds came out level and headed at full pace towards the first bend.

'There are three in line as they go into opening corner' screamed the commentator as the action unfolded in front of us *'and two goes around in front from three as four is forced wide'*

"Oh shit" shouted Foxy as the greyhounds negotiated the second bend cleanly.

'They open up down the back straight and two leads with four in hot pursuit. They head towards the penultimate turn and two still leads but look at the pace of trap four who is flying.'

"Come on four" I shouted at the top of my voice and Foxy joined in.

'They are coming around the final bend, four is still finishing as two begins to tire, will he get there, he's getting there, he's going to get there, four wins with two back in second' he screamed and the tannoy fell silent.

We were jumping up and down and hugging each other. I was sure our screams would have been heard back in Leenane where Tommy, for the first time in seventeen years, had planned to go to the village pub to watch the racing on the television. It hadn't occurred to either of us that we were screaming home a dog that was owned by Sam Hampshire.

"Shall we go and collect?" I said to Foxy pointing in the direction of the bookmakers who looked like they'd all gone twelve rounds with a heavyweight boxer.

"Nah, they can pay me later" he said but handed me the one hundred and fifty pounds that Alice should have won. I tried to protest but given he was due to collect £36,000 later I didn't persist.

We made our way back into the restaurant to find Phil in deep conversation on his mobile, he looked far from happy. His glasses were now on the top of his head and he was pulling on the hairs of his left eyebrow with his right hand. Whoever he was speaking to wasn't improving his mood any. He brought the discussion to an abrupt end.

"Who was that?" I asked.

"The 'gigolo' of Holborn whinging his head off again" who I took to be his boss.

"What's wrong with him now?" I asked knowing full well what the answer would be.

"That last winner has been backed in doubles again all around the country with that Rainbow Warrior dog in the final. The big firm's liabilities are astronomical. He wants me pull it from the final so they only have to pay out on the single. I told him if he wants to do that he can get off his fat arse and do it himself. How would it look, a big final on television and we pull one out to appease the bookmakers?"

He stopped as the waitress arrived with our main course.

"It won't be happening on my watch that's for certain. I have just decided that after tonight I am going to retire gracefully. I can't put up with all his bollocks anymore especially when I know about him being blackmailed. The pompous Yorkshire ass can sort this crap out himself."

"So what do they stand to lose?" I asked knowing I stood to win just under forty thousand pounds if Rainbow Warrior won as I had taken a price of 5-2 in the final to go with the 12-1 for the dog who had just won.

"He reckons about one and a half million give or take a few thousand. The majority offered 12-1 about Double Vision and Rainbow Warrior was either 11-4 or 5-2; some firms were as high as 3-1. Because the meeting is on television they didn't put up any restriction warnings so they have been hammered everywhere" he advised and sat back in his seat.

"I suppose you two have doubled them up as well?" he said with a resigned look.

"I have, I told you it was a different dog, and it was" I said just before consuming my first piece of steak that had been grilled to perfection. I couldn't contain a smile, Phil knew I wasn't telling him everything and if he was resigning I might as well do it now. I could always threaten him with blackmail to stay silent!

"What aren't you telling me you crafty bugger?" he said as he ignored another phone call from his boss.

"Aren't you going to get that?" asked Alice.

"Sod the lot of them. I'm retired. Now explain yourself or I may have to reconsider whether you are suitable for my daughter" he said attempting and failing to knock the wide grin from my face. Alice said nothing but put her hand on my knee.

"It is quite simple really, the Double Vision that won tonight isn't the Double Vision that trialled last week but is the Double Vision that was part of the gamble the night before Andy disappeared. The Double Vision that trialled is currently sitting on young Jamie's bed back at the kennels."

"Which bit of that was simple?" asked Phil.

"God Phil you can be thick sometimes. There are two Double Vision's; one with a micro-chip and one without. The one that ran tonight had no micro-chip remember?" I said trying to remind him about his conversation with his less than useful stipendiary steward.

"That isn't possible. They would have checked the earmarks and the markings?"

"All the same" I replied.

"Don't be silly, we have too many checks in place. There has to be a mistake?"

"You had too many checks, had being the key word as you are

now retired remember. Trust me Phil; you have two identical dogs, even down to the colour of their toe nails but you aren't going to say a word as I promised Tommy when he helped us back in Ireland. This is the last time. If it hadn't been for the incompetence of your stipendiary steward and vet it would have been the last time when they landed the original double" I replied and it was true.

Phil put his knife and fork down; he had no interest in the fourth race runners who were now being placed into the traps. I had his full attention.

"Go on" he said.

"It is quite sad really with a happy ending unless you are a bookmaker" I said before divulging everything Tommy had told me just under a fortnight ago.

"There are three dogs in the litter, the two that have been named and a third one that never was. No one apart from Jamie could identify them by sight. On the day they were being earmarked by the Control Steward, a Bernard something, he was distracted by his wife calling him every couple of minutes about his daughters forthcoming wedding. He was also partial to the odd swig from a hip flask. On this particularly day he consumed the lot, he was all over the place.

He had hurried through the last of the three pups and rushed off to another kennel as he wanted to get home to resolve a family feud. He never reached it; he was involved in a fatal car accident ten miles down the road. Tommy was obviously devastated, the whole family were.

That evening Jamie brought Tommy down the paperwork for the pups who had been earmarked from the kennels; you know the ones I mean, the naming papers they send off to the Irish Coursing Club to register the dog with the ear markings stamped in the bottom corner in green?"

Phil nodded.

"Well, it turns out that Bernard was not only in a hurry but he wasn't concentrating either, he'd put the same earmarks on two dogs. Tommy was sure Bernard would have spotted it when he got home. Unfortunately, or in Tommy's case fortunately, Bernard's copies of the paperwork went up in flames with the car leaving Tommy with the only set. The new Control Steward paid him a visit a couple of weeks later but Tommy made sure there were only two dogs in the kennel. It was from that point the coup was planned.

He let the dogs mature over the winter and when he took them to the track for schooling, one of them, the dog that won tonight, proved to be considerably faster than the other with the same earmarks. The other in the litter just isn't much good, happens like that sometimes. So, there you have it, Tommy has waited almost two years for tonight and it has paid off."

"Not quite" replied Phil.

Had I misjudged our friendship and just landed Tommy right in it along with a nice pay out.

"How do you mean not quite, you said you were retired?" I said.

"I am, but the other one has to win first?" he said and emptied the contents of his glass.

"Trust in Jamie Phil. I have full trust in Jamie" I said before making an excuse to leave before I went to see him.

The Quinn kennel only had one more runner on the card and that was Archie in the big final. I made my way up towards the paddock and asked Maureen on the gate if young Jamie was around. "I will check for you Mr Jackson" she had replied, even after all this time she still didn't refer to me by my Christian name.

Jamie came out with Orla by his side. He nervously smiled and Orla leant forward for me to kiss her on the cheek. "Good evening you two; good win earlier Jamie?" to which Orla replied that it was a pleasant and welcome surprise.

"Orla, can I have quick word with Jamie, I have a message for him from his grandfather?" I said and she left us alone.

"Now if granddad wanted to talk to me do you not think he would have called me himself Joe? What can I be doing for you as I don't want to be too far away from Archie if I can help it?" he said looking back towards the paddock gate.

"Fair point Jamie; I will come straight out with it, how confident are you that Archie will win tonight?"

"Very" he said without a moment's hesitation.

"It's a hot race and what if he misses the start like he did last week?" I said probing.

"He won't" again it was said with complete confidence.

"Is that because you won't be telling him to 'sit'? I understand the dog sits down and gives you a paw on command, bit unusual for a racing greyhound you have to admit and it would explain why he would be slow away when he is beaten and never is when the money is down" I said hoping the bond we had developed over the attempted kidnap the previous week would get him to open up. The fact Tommy had told him I could be trusted also would work in my favour.

He laughed. "Yes he sits when asked, he does for anyone, but it isn't how it's done. I hadn't thought of that in fairness. I suppose it doesn't matter now, the last time I stopped him was last week and you knew about that but from now on he runs to his full potential and he needs to tonight as granddad has backed him."

"I know, so have I" I said showing him a variety of betting slips from my pocket. He looked through them and handed them back. "Nice few quid there Joe" he remarked.

"So are you going to tell me then or what, I'm not going to say a word but as an ex-racing manager I am totally intrigued? I have watched all his videos and seen him race live but can't spot anything unusual."

"The bloke who was killed did" he said much to my surprise. "I thought we had been rumbled and didn't know how to tell granddad as he'd put so much work into setting up the first big gamble when both dogs won. I thought the bookmakers would withhold payment if they knew what I'd done."

"What did he find out?" I asked, totally baffled.

"After Archie won to complete the double they went over him with a fine toothcomb. They took a urine test and some blood. They double checked his markings, his micro-chip, everything you could think of. Archie winning and Robin's, I mean Double Vision's missing micro-chip had Andy shouting and screaming that he wanted answers. I had never seen him like it and he had one of the paddock stewards in tears."

I wondered if Andy's lack of a drug fix that day had kicked in earlier than when Sam had thought.

"Everyone was trying to avoid him and then he called down from the steward's box to the paddock and said he wanted to see me in his office after the last race. So I went and that is when he really went mad. I walked in and he asked me to shut the door. He hobbled over from behind his desk and pinned me against the wall, his eyes were bulging. 'Tell me how you do it you little shit or I swear I will kill you' he said to me. I was scared. He then picked up that dog statue that was on his desk and threatened to hit me with it. He had one hand around my neck and the other up high with the statue in his hand."

It wasn't hard to imagine how scared Jamie must have been.

"So I told him. I told him how I did it" he said. "It was all to do with sugar. As a puppy Archie loved nothing more than to eat doughnuts and I love doughnuts" he said with a smile and I remembered what Orla had told me. "I'd give him a bit here and there and because he had the run of the kennels he'd pinch them off the plate in the feed room when mum brought up lunch. He was never supposed to race so it didn't matter if he was as fat as a house."

"Then it was agreed to put him in training, he took a while to get the hang of it but he was so fast and strong. One afternoon granddad asked me to help him and give the dog a quick school out of the traps as he was really flying and was due to go to Galway at the end of the week for his first trial. I was smartly dressed as we were going into Westport and didn't want to get dirty but granddad insisted. I was eating a doughnut as usual and my hands were covered in sugar. Normally I wiped off the excess on my jeans or overalls but this time I just wiped my hands down the Archie's shoulder as I put him in the trap.

I went around the front of the trap to make sure he was facing the right way. He was really restless and kept turning his head back towards where I had wiped my hands. I indicated to granddad to start the drag hare and Archie just walked out. He was more interested in getting to the sugar than chasing the hare. I wasn't sure if it was a one-off so I did it again for his first official trial at Galway and for his second as well. He was slow away on both occasions!"

"But surely the sugar would show up on the urine and blood sample as it is illegal to give a greyhound sugar? You would be bound to be found out" I said finding it hard to believe that it was as simple as that.

"Not if he never actually got to taste the sugar it wouldn't. I'd rub it in far enough back for him not to get it. I'd teased him with it as I'd put him in so he could smell it. Then when the race was over I would wipe away all the evidence as I walked back to the paddock" he said with a huge smile of satisfaction.

"So where would you keep the sugar, you couldn't exactly come out on track eating a doughnut, that would be a little bit obvious as food isn't allowed in the paddock area from what I can remember."

He again smiled, he was enjoying this and who could blame him. "I had an extra section sewn into the bottom of my parading jacket. When I bend down behind the traps to put the dog in I just dip a couple of fingers in without being noticed."

"And you told Andy all of this?" I asked. He nodded and I suddenly thought back to the text that Andy had sent Phil the day he had disappeared.

'Tings aren't always as they look at the start. Donut boy has deep pockets and the solution will b in touching dist.'

Andy had given a clue but it was one that a crack code breaking team from Bletchley in the Second World War would have struggled with. It made sense now.

Jamie looked relieved to have told someone. I wasn't going to say anything and I wouldn't even bother to tell Phil, there was no point. We were re-joined by Orla who indicated that it was time to get the dog out as he, along with all the other finalists were going to be routinely dope tested.

"Good luck and see you on the podium" I said.

"Yes you will and by the way Joe, do you like my new parading jacket, it has no pockets?" he shouted back with a huge smile.

We took up our usual position on the steps underneath the restaurant window. We'd had a brief look at the prices in the betting ring. Rainbow Warrior was even money favourite. The big firms had all dispatched a rep to the track to ensure the price was no bigger. It didn't matter from my perspective as I had secured 5-2 when my bets were placed. I would imagine Tommy's 'fella's' had done the same.

All we needed now was for Rainbow Warrior to win and he did.

I watched with excitement from my step as Jamie jumped up and down in the middle of the track, punching the air and screaming his baby home. He won like a champion, pulling further and further clear from his rivals down the back straight. The local crowd were in fine voice calling home a locally trained winner. Richard received pats on the back and Orla kisses and hugs in congratulation from well-wishers before they crossed the track for the trophy presentation. My eyes began to fill with tears as she hugged Jamie who was being interviewed by a roving reporter.

I smiled inwardly as I made my way back to the restaurant. I would ask Alice to help me to find a new car in the morning.

CHAPTER FORTY

Six months later

The sun was beating down in South West London for the biggest night of the greyhound year; anyone who was anyone in greyhounds would be at Wimbledon for the final of the Greyhound Derby. The restaurant had been sold out for months and the paper coverage had been extensive.

I was delighted to see Natalie-Jane and a team of volunteers on site wandering amongst the crowd with a retired greyhound in one hand and a collection bucket in the other. I pulled out my wallet and dropped in five twenty pound notes much to her delight. They worked so hard for every penny they raised and hopefully the large crowd tonight would bring in some much needed funds.

I walked into the track with Alice on my arm, she looked stunning in a long black dress and her hair tied up. She had bought a white rosette from Natalie-Jane to signify her support for trap three in the big final. It went well with her dress. Phil was running late so we made our way out to the front of the track to wait for him.

"Hello you two!" shouted Orla. I hadn't seen or spoken to her in months, there had been no need to. We had agreed to part as friends. She looked to have put on a bit of weight and the dress she was wearing exposed slightly more cleavage then she probably would have wanted. She could see where I was looking.

"Six months gone Joe, due in mid-September" she said as I averted my gaze. "Richard will be out in a minute, just meeting someone from Ireland, he wants to talk to you."

I wondered what it was that Richard could want to say to me.

"Here he comes now" said Orla looking over my shoulder so I turned around. He was with the last man I expected to see him with. This could be awkward.

"Good evening Joe" said Richard offering me his hand without hesitation. I was still looking at the man stood beside him and him in return. "I believe you have met Tomas Lowry" he said and I shook him by the hand.

"Yes I have" I said still puzzled and looked at Alice who also looked confused.

"I believe you recommended me to Tomas as an up and coming trainer and he has offered me a position at his kennels in Ireland. We can't make it pay over here and what with Orla being pregnant and the kids not yet school age we have decided to take him up on his offer" he said with a great deal of excitement.

"Yes Joe, I must thank you for that" said Tomas in a manner that urged me to play along.

"Not a problem, I wish you all luck" I said and meant it. Had Tomas told Richard he was his father?

Whether he had or he hadn't wasn't my concern. That was between them.

We made our way up to the restaurant where Tommy and Aoife were already seated. It was the first time Tommy had been back to England in over eighteen years. He looked extremely smart in his tuxedo and his hair recently cut. I was pleased to see he had left his flat cap at home. Phil joined us with Foxy and took up a seat opposite Alice. It was great to be surrounded by the people I admired and trusted most in the world.

"How is Jamie?" I asked.

"He is just grand, I am delighted to have him back home and he has already started to have extra kennels built" said Aoife. Tommy hadn't told me exactly how much he had won on the second big coup but Phil reckoned it would have been at least £250,000. He was officially retired now and had handed the training licence over to Jamie.

"I understand the court case starts next week for Sam? Sean

called me last week. He has retired as well now from the priesthood and is living back up in Dublin. I bought out his half in Rainbow Warrior and the GRB forced the sale of the other dogs in her name to settle an outstanding kennel bill to the trainer."

"She has also been charged over the murder of her husband" added Alice "she is looking at a life sentence."

"She really was a nasty piece of work" I said and settled back in my chair. Racing wasn't due to start for another hour.

Jamie looked as proud as punch as he walked his runner on parade for the Derby final. He had grown about six inches since I'd seen him last. He was no longer a boy but a man, a man with a trainer's licence who was leading out his own dog for the biggest race of the year. The six runners were paraded in front of the packed grandstands, their crisp white parading jackets reflecting off the overhead lights that stood on the inside perimeter of the running surface.

'Greyhounds are going behind'

The noise from the expectant crowd increased. Punters pushed and shoved as they tried to place a bet on their favoured selection and then return to any vantage point they could find.

'They are going in'

I watched as the last of the greyhounds was placed in the traps and their respective handler ran to the middle of the track to watch the race. In less than twenty nine seconds one of them would be collecting a Derby winner.

'The hare is on the move'

The famous Derby roar echoed around the ageing stadium as the mechanical hare made its journey from the back straight. The facilities weren't the best but the greyhounds just about to race certainly were.

'And they're off. Three gets a flier and leads from two four five one and six. They go into the first bend and Rainbow Warrior leads with Nezza's Yob in hot pursuit with two and four just behind. They head down the back straight now and Rainbow Warrior and Nezza's Boy are neck and neck but here comes trap four'

The crowd was roaring; the adrenalin was pumping; the excitement was immeasurable.

'They head towards the penultimate turn and the favourite in four is oh so close and the front three appear to have it between them as there is crowding in behind between one two and five.'

I could hardly hear myself think as those around me screamed.

'They turn for home and Rainbow Warrior is beginning to tie up in front as the favourite is now in overdrive. He looks like he is going to get up.'

The crowd noise had reached a new high; there was less than fifty metres to run. Race cards were being thrown in the air, arms were aloft and drinks were being spilt as the well-backed favourite began his customary surge for glory.

'The favourite is going to get up and he gets up to win the Derby.'

No one was listening, everyone was watching.

'What a fantastic result for rookie trainer Jamie Mulcahy as Double Vision wins the Derby with Nezza's Yob in second and Rainbow Warrior a close third.'

I looked towards the centre of the track and Jamie was jumping up and down, he was being hugged by Siobhan who had paraded the beautiful fawn dog. I was crying. I looked down towards the first bend where Tommy, Aoife and Double Vision's new owner Foxy were stood. They were all embracing. It was the perfect result in so many ways.

I made sure I turned off my commentary microphone before running down to join them.

So many lives had changed in the last seven months.

Where had it all gone right?

Printed in Great Britain
by Amazon.co.uk, Ltd.,
Marston Gate.